Probably the most famous, and certainly among the best of the many novels written about Atlantis, THE LOST CONTINENT has survived three-quarters of a century since first publication—and reads as though it were written yesterday. Vivid, rich, sweeping in scope, this is a magnificent tale of the ending of an era, indeed of a whole civilization. C. J. Cutliffe Hyne has managed to make the destruction and disappearance of a whole continent totally believable and has created unforgettable characters in Deucalion, the warrior-priest who fought a desperate battle to save his beloved Atlantis from the grasping, wholly courageous and monumentally selfish Queen Phorenice.

"One follows Deucalion through the rainbow of action and suspense, knowing the end was pre-ordained, vainly hoping that he would yet be rewarded with victory. I ended the story feeling that I had found a new friend."

Roscoe E. Wright

"*The* Atlantis classic—a tale of breathless interest!"

Tom Pace

For Ballantine Books,
Lin Carter has written:

Imaginary Worlds: The Art of Fantasy
Lovecraft: A Look Behind the "Cthulhu Mythos"
Tolkien: A Look Behind "The Lord of the Rings"

and has edited these
anthologies and collections:

At the Edge of the World / Beyond the Fields We Know /
Discoveries in Fantasy / The Doom That Came to Sarnath
/ Dragons, Elves, and Heroes / The Dream-Quest of Un-
known Kadath / Evenor / Golden Cities, Far / Great Short
Novels of Adult Fantasy I / Great Short Novels of Adult
Fantasy II / Hyperborea / New Worlds For Old / The
Spawn of Cthulhu / Xiccarph / The Young Magicians /
Zothique

THE LOST CONTINENT

C. J. Cutliffe Hyne

Introduction by Lin Carter

BALLANTINE BOOKS · NEW YORK

BALLANTINE BOOKS, INC.
201 East 50th Street, New York, N.Y. 10022

CONTENTS

The Last Queen of Atlantis

About 355 B.C. the Athenian philosopher Aristokles wrote two dialogues that were to have an immeasurable impact on fantasy fiction for the next twenty-three centuries.

This Aristokles is better known by his nickname, "Plato"—a reference to his broad shoulders—and the dialogues in question are the *Timaios* and its unfinished sequel, the *Kritias*. In them, Plato has one of the characters relate something of the history of a certain large, populous, wealthy and powerful island in the Atlantic Ocean called Atlantis. Plato tells of its mighty kings, its splendor and history, and of how the gods destroyed it in an earthquake and deluge many thousands of years before Plato's own day.

Today, Plato is credited with an influence on Western thought and civilization greater than that of any other Greek philosopher, and very many books have been written about his ideas. But, ironically, far *more* books have probably been written about his island empire of Atlantis. (Writing in 1954, L. Sprague de Camp estimated that "something like two thousand books and articles have been written about Atlantis and other supposed lost continents"; by now, we can suppose that number substantially increased.)

For all the studies that have been made of Plato,

no one has yet discovered exactly where he got the notion of this prehistoric lost civilization. Did he actually learn of it, as he claims, through the descendants of the great Athenian lawgiver, Solon, who reportedly heard the story from Egyptian priests? Did he invent the story out of whole cloth; or is it based on fragmentary information and rumor? Was there ever an actual Atlantis, or is it just a fairy tale? No one for more than two thousand years has discovered the answer to these questions.

Plato's contemporaries were divided in their reaction to the "Atlantean dialogues." Some thought the story pure fiction, others accepted it as history, while a few considered it some sort of allegory. One thing at least is certain: whether he invented Atlantis or not, Plato made a gigantic contribution to the writers of fantasy, ancient and modern.

The list of people who have written stories about Atlantis is a virtual *Who's Who* of modern fantasy. In *Tarzan and the Jewels of Opar* (1918), Edgar Rice Burroughs took his ape-man hero to a decaying African colony of Atlantis. In *L'Atlantide* (1920), Pierre Benoit brought a French officer to another Atlantean colony—this one far from decaying—in the Ahaggar Mountains of southern Algeria. In *The Maracot Deep* (1928), Sir Arthur Conan Doyle sent a party of scientists down in a bathysphere to find an Atlantean city roofed over and still flourishing on the ocean's floor. In *The Face in the Abyss* (1931), the great A. Merritt carried a Russian adventurer into the ancient colony of "Yu-Atlanchi," long hidden in the Peruvian Andes. And throughout the 1930's, in the pages of *Weird Tales,* cycles of Atlantis stories (variously penned by Robert E. Howard, Henry Kuttner, and Clark Ashton Smith), kept the Lost Continent alive. In *The Tritonian Ring* (1953), L. Sprague de Camp described an extant Atlantean civilization in a sort of "historical novel" laid in the Bronze Age on the island, a notion followed by the young English writer Jane Gaskell a decade later in her trilogy composed of *The Serpent, Atlan,* and *The City* (1963–66). In the 1970s the list will, of course, continue. My colleague Poul Anderson has written a novel called *The Dancer from Atlantis.* It is still unpublished at the time of this writing, as is my own novel, *The Black Star,* the first volume of a projected Atlantis trilogy.

The end, as the saying goes, is not yet in sight.

Of all these novels and stories penned (and I have mentioned only an armful out of several bookshelves!) my personal favorite was written before any of the above named: *The Lost Continent,* a novel written in 1899 by the British writer C. J. Cutcliffe Hyne.

Ever since my teens when I first read this splendidly colorful, imaginative, and gloriously entertaining story, it has seemed to me the best novel of Atlantis ever written. My colleagues are divided on this. I once asked Clark Ashton Smith which Atlantis novel was his favorite, and he named David M. Parry's *The Scarlet Empire* (1906), which seems to me a dreary and un-inspired anti-labor and anti-Socialist tract. L. Sprague de Camp, however, in his comprehensive study of "the Atlantis theme in history, science and literature," *Lost Continents* (1954; revised and reissued by Dover Books, 1970), has considerable praise for Cutcliffe Hyne's romance: "Despite the author's weakness for plesiosaurs and other anachronistic Mesozoic reptiles (who disappeared at least 60,000,000 years before the rise of man), the novel is a competent piece of story-telling: fast, well-constructed, colorful, with the leading characters well-drawn and occasional flashes of rather grim humor. Moreover, the story is not burdened with the sentimentality and didacticism that oppress so many novels of this group. . . . The author does not try to project our modern Western moral code on people of an ancient and supposedly different culture." Complet-ing his survey of the major Atlantean fictions, de Camp concludes: "When these tales are taken as a whole, I think the best entertainment is still provided by those which, like Hyne's *Lost Continent,* have no ideological axes to grind but simply tell a lively story in competent, professional style."*

C. J. Cutcliffe Hyne was a popular author of magazine fiction during the closing decades of the last century. His work appeared in magazines such as *Pall Mall* (together with stories by Rudyard Kipling, George Meredith, and the American writer Frank R. Stockton) and the great *Pearson's Magazine.* I suppose today no one remembers *Pearson's* (except for such connoisseurs as pulp era historian Sam Moskowitz), but it deserves a place with the immortals. It was the first magazine to publish such imaginative classics as H. Rider Haggard's *Lysbeth* and H. G. Wells's *The Invisible Man, The Sea Lady, The War of the Worlds,* and *The Food of the Gods.*†

Cutcliffe Hyne's *The Lost Continent* was serialized in the pages of *Pearson's* from July to December 1899. In his history of the early pulp magazine era, *Science Fiction by Gaslight* (World, 1968), Sam Moskowitz calls Cutcliffe's work *"Pearson's* really 'big' story for 1899," and he adds: "To the collector, *The Lost Continent* was the high point of J. [*sic*] Cutcliffe Hyne's career, and the book edition issued in 1900 by Harper's has become a highly desirable item. Fortunately it sold well enough to make copies far from rare."

Cutcliffe Hyne wrote many other books—among them *The Filibusters, The Trials of Commander McTurk, The Recipe for Diamonds, Honour of Thieves.*

---

* In almost exactly the same words I can recommend de Camp's *Lost Continents* to any reader interested in learning more about Atlantis. It is the best, the most thorough, the most entertaining, and the least biased of all the books ever written on this subject. It is a superb, even a brilliant, piece of work.

† Pearson's also published memorable nonfantasies, such as Rudyard Kipling's *Captains Courageous.*

He was quite well known in his day for his tales of the remarkable Captain Kettle, a tough, ruthless, Vandyke-bearded, and (in time, as the series went on) peg-legged little man whose bizarre exploits charmed readers on both sides of the Atlantic from his first adventure (which appeared in *Pearson's,* February 1897 issue) to *The Last Adventure of Captain Kettle* (in the issue of February 1903).

The Lost Continent, however, remains his classic—a splendid tale of fantastic adventure, an enduring story that is, simply, the best of its kind.

Cutcliffe Hyne opens with the discovery of a mysterious ancient manuscript in an island cave—always a delicious opening, from Stevenson's map in *Treasure Island* to Haggard's cryptic potsherd in *She*—but he moves swiftly into the story told by the manuscript itself. And a glorious and good story it is, with magic and mystery and mysticism, romance and adventure and thrills galore. As with the novels by de Camp and Gaskell, the author presents his yarn as "an historical novel laid in Atlantis." The reign of the superb and languorous Phorenice, last Queen of the doomed continent, is described with a wealth of imaginative detail and a vigor and freshness of style that belies the sober fact that the tale is now almost three-quarters of a century old.

It is hard to credit the fact of this novel's age—it reads as if it were written today—except, of course, that no one in the world writes quite this sort of forthright, robust, full-bodied fantastic romance these days, alas.

In December 1944, *The Lost Continent* appeared, severely abridged, in the great American reprint magazine, *Famous Fantastic Mysteries.* An enthusiastic fourteen-year-old reader named Lin Carter bought that issue at a newsstand and devoured the lead novel with relish and tingling excitement. I can still recall the staggeringly beautiful painting (by Lawrence) that adorned the cover: a formal portrait of the glorious Queen Phorenice, in close-up, staring out of the cover with unfathomable and mysterious green-gold eyes, her dark red hair enclosed in a glittering coronet of heavy gold, studded with pearls, cabochon emeralds, and flashing diamonds, a massive bracelet of what must have been carnelian plaques clasped about one slim wrist. Behind her, a moon-dim view of Atlantis, step-pyramids rising against a purple sky along the curving banks of a canal, down which floats an Atlantean galley. Ah, me! They don't paint covers like that any-more, either!

That was the last printing of *The Lost Continent* in any form—at least, the last known to me. Now, more than a quarter of a century later, it joins other great stories in the Ballantine Adult Fantasy Series. I wonder if there will be a few more enthusiastic fourteen-year-old readers in the audience, to catch fire from this edition?

— LIN CARTER
Editorial Consultant:
The Ballantine Adult Fantasy Series

Hollis, Long Island, New York

Prefatory:
The Legatees of Deucalion

We were both of us not a little stiff as the result of sleeping out in the open all that night, for even in Grand Canary the dew-fall and the comparative chill of darkness are not to be trifled with. For myself on these occasions I like a bit of a run as an early refresher. But here on this rough ground in the middle of the island there were not three yards of level to be found, and so as Coppinger proceeded to go through some sort of dumb-bell exercises with a couple of lumps of bristly lava, I followed his example. Coppinger has done a good deal of roughing it in his time, but being a doctor of medicine amongst other things—he takes out a new degree of some sort on an average every other year—he is great on health theories, and practises them like a religion.

There had been rain two days before, and as there was still a bit of stream trickling along at the bottom of the barranca, we went down there and had a wash, and brushed our teeth. Greatest luxury imaginable, a toothbrush, on this sort of expedition.

"Now," said Coppinger when we had emptied our pockets, "there's precious little grub left, and it's none the better for being carried in a local Spanish newspaper."

"Yours is mostly tobacco ashes."

1

"It'll get worse if we leave it. We've a lot more bad scrambling ahead of us."

That was obvious. So we sat down beside the stream there at the bottom of the barranca, and ate up all of what was left. It was a ten-mile tramp to the fonda at Santa Brigida, where we had set down our traps; and as Coppinger wanted to take a lot more photographs and measurements before we left this particular group of caves, it was likely we should be pretty sharp set before we got our next meal, and our next taste of the *patron's* splendid old country wine. My faith! If only they knew down in the English hotels in Las Palmas what magnificent wines one could get—with diplomacy —up in some of the mountain villages, the old vintage would become a thing of the past in a week.

Now to tell the truth, the two mummies he had gathered already quite satisfied my small ambition. The goatskins in which they were sewn up were as brittle as paper, and the poor old things themselves gave out dust like a puffball whenever they were touched. But you know what Coppinger is. He thought he'd come upon traces of an old Guanche university, or sacred college, or something of that kind, like the one there is on the other side of the island, and he wouldn't be satisfied till he'd ransacked every cave in the whole face of the cliff. He'd plenty of stuff left for the flashlight thing, and twenty-eight more films in his kodak, and said we might as well get through with the job then as make a return journey all on purpose. So he took the crowbar, and I shouldered the rope, and away we went up to the ridge of the cliff, where we had got such a baking from the sun the day before.

Of course these caves were not easy to come at, or else they would have been raided years before. Coppinger, who on principle makes out he knows all about these things, says that in the old Guanche days they had ladders of goatskin rope which they could pull up when they were at home, and so keep out undesirable callers; and as no other plan occurs to me, perhaps he may be right. Anyway the mouths of the caves were in a more or less level row thirty feet below the ridge of the cliff, and fifty feet above the bottom; and Spanish curiosity doesn't go in much where it cannot walk.

Now laddering such caves from below would have been cumbersome, but a light knotted rope is easily carried, and though it would have been hard to climb up this, our plan was to descend on each cave mouth from above, and then slip down to the foot of the cliffs, and start again *ab initio* for the next.

Coppinger is plucky enough, and he has a good head on a height, but there is no getting over the fact that he is portly and nearer fifty than forty-five. So you can see he must have been pretty keen. Of course I went first each time, and got into the cave mouth, and did what I could to help him in; but when you have to walk down a vertical cliff face fly-fashion, with only a thin bootlace of a rope for support, it is not much real help the man below can give, except offer you his best wishes.

I wanted to save him as much as I could, and as the first three caves I climbed to were small and empty, seeming to be merely store-places, I asked him to take them for granted, and save himself the rest. But he insisted on clambering down to each one in person, and as he decided that one of my granaries was a prison, and another a pot-making factory, and another a schoolroom for young priests, he naturally said he hadn't much reliance on my judgment, and would have to go through the whole lot himself. You know what these thorough-going archæologists are for imagination.

But as the day went on, and the sun rose higher, Coppinger began clearly to have had enough of it, though he was very game, and insisted on going on much longer than was safe. I must say I didn't like it. You see the drop was seldom less than eighty feet from the top of the cliffs. However, at last he was forced to give it up. I suggested marching off to Santa

Brigida forthwith, but he wouldn't do that. There were three more cave-openings to be looked into, and if I wouldn't do them for him, he would have to make another effort to get there himself. He tried to make out he was conferring a very great favour on me by offering to take a report solely from my untrained observation, but I flatly refused to look at it in that light. I was pretty tired also; I was soaked with perspiration from the heat; my head ached from the violence of the sun; and my hands were cut raw with the rope.

Coppinger might be tired, but he was still enthusiastic. He tried to make me enthusiastic also. "Look here," he said, "there's no knowing what you may find up there, and if you do lay hands on anything, remember it's your own. I shall have no claim whatever."

"Very kind of you, but I've got no use for any more mummies done up in goatskin bags."

"Bah! That's not a burial cave up there. Don't you know the difference yet in the openings? Now, be a good fellow. It doesn't follow that because we have drawn all the rest blank, you won't stumble across a good find for yourself up there."

"Oh, very well," I said, as he seemed so set on it; and away I stumbled over the fallen rocks, and along the ledge, and then scrambled up by that fissure in the cliff which saved us the two-mile round which we had had to take at first. I wrenched out the crowbar, and jammed it down in a new place, and then away I went over the side, with hands smarting worse at every new grip of the rope. It was an awkward job swinging into the cave mouth, because the rock above overhung, or else (what came to the same thing) it had broken away below; but I managed it somehow, although I landed with an awkward thump on my back, and at the same time I didn't let go the rope. It wouldn't do to have lost the rope then: Coppinger couldn't have flicked it into me from where he was below.

Now from the first glance I could see that this cave was of different structure to the others. They were for the most part mere dens, rounded out anyhow: this had been faced up with cutting tools, so that all the angles were clean, and the sides smooth and flat. The walls inclined inwards to the roof, reminding me of an architecture I had seen before but could not recollect where, and moreover there were several rooms connected up with passages. I was pleased to find that the other cave-openings which Coppinger wanted me to explore were merely the windows or the doorways of two of these other rooms.

Of inscriptions or markings on the walls there was not a trace, though I looked carefully, and except for bats the place was entirely bare. I lit a cigarette and smoked it through—Coppinger always thinks one is slurring over work if it is got through too quickly—and then I went to the entrance where the rope was, and leaned out, and shouted down my news.

He turned up a very anxious face. "Have you searched it thoroughly?" he bawled back.

"Of course I have. What do you think I've been doing all this time?"

"No, don't come down yet. Wait a minute. I say, old man, do wait a minute. I'm making fast the kodak and the flashlight apparatus on the end of the rope. Pull them up, and just make me half a dozen exposures, there's a good fellow."

"Oh, all right," I said, and hauled the things up, and got them inside. The photographs would be absolutely dull and uninteresting, but that wouldn't matter to Coppinger. He rather preferred them that way. One has to be careful about halation in photographing these dark interiors, but there was a sort of ledge like a seat by the side of each doorway, and so I lodged the camera on that to get a steady stand, and snapped off the flashlight from behind and above.

I got pictures of four of the chambers this way, and then came to one where the ledge was higher and wider. I put down the camera, wedged it level with scraps of stone, and then sat down myself to recharge the flashlight machine. But the moment my weight got on that ledge, there was a sharp crackle, and down I went half a dozen inches.

Of course I was up again pretty sharply, and snapped up the kodak just as it was going to slide off to the ground. I will confess, too, I was feeling pleased. Here at any rate was a Guanche cupboard of sorts, and as they had taken the trouble to hermetically seal it with cement, the odds were that it had something inside worth hiding. At first there was nothing to be seen but a lot of dust and rubble, so I lit a bit of candle and cleared this away. Presently, however, I began to find that I was shelling out something that was not cement. It chipped away, in regular layers, and when I took it to the daylight I found that each layer was made up of two parts. One side was shiny stuff that looked like talc, and on this was smeared a coating of dark toffee-coloured material, that might have been wax. The toffee-coloured surface was worked over with some kind of pattern.

Now I do not profess to any knowledge on these matters, and as a consequence took what Coppinger had told me about Guanche habits and acquirements as more or less true. For instance, he had repeatedly impressed upon me that this old people could not write, and having this in my memory, I did not guess that the patterns scribed through the wax were letters in some obsolete character, which, if left to myself, probably I should have done. But still at the same time I came to the conclusion that the stuff was worth looting, and so set to work quarrying it out with the heel of my boot and a pocket-knife.

The sheets were all more or less stuck together, and so I did not go in for separating them farther. They fitted exactly to the cavity in which they were stored, but by smashing down its front I was able to get at the foot of them, and then I hacked away through the bottom layers with the knife till I got the bulk out in one solid piece. It measured some twenty inches by fifteen, by fifteen, but it was not so heavy as it looked, and when I had taken the remaining photographs, I lowered it down to Coppinger on the end of the rope.

There was nothing more to do in the caves then, so I went down myself next. The lump of sheets was on the ground, and Coppinger was on all fours beside it. He was pretty nearly mad with excitement.

"What is it?" I asked him.

"I don't know yet. But it is the most valuable find ever made in the Canary Islands, and it's yours, you unappreciative beggar; at least what there is left of it. Oh, man, man, you've smashed up the beginning, and you've smashed up the end of some history that is probably priceless. It's my own fault. I ought to have known better than set an untrained man to do important exploring work."

"I should say it's your fault if anything's gone wrong. You said there was no such thing as writing known to these ancient Canarios, and I took your word for it. For anything I knew the stuff might have been something to eat."

"It isn't Guanche work at all," said he testily. "You ought to have known that from the talc. Great heavens, man, have you no eyes? Haven't you seen the general formation of the island? Don't you know there's no talc here?"

"I'm no geologist. Is this imported literature then?"

"Of course. It's Egyptian: that's obvious at a glance. Though how it's got here I can't tell yet. It isn't stuff you can read off like a newspaper. The character's a variant on any of those that have been discovered so far. And as for this waxy stuff spread over the talc, it's unique. It's some sort of a mineral, I think: perhaps asphalt. It doesn't scratch up like animal wax. I'll analyse that later. Why they once invented it, and then let such a splendid notion drop out of use, is just a marvel. I could stay gloating over this all day."

"Well," I said, "if it's all the same for you, I'd rather gloat over a meal. It's a good ten miles hard going to the fonda, and I'm as hungry as a hawk already. Look here, do you know it is four o'clock already? It takes longer than you think climbing down to each of these caves, and then getting up again for the next."

Coppinger spread his coat on the ground, and wrapped the lump of sheets with tender care, but would not allow it to be tied with a rope for fear of breaking more of the edges. He insisted on carrying it himself too, and did so for the larger part of the way to Santa Brigida, and it was only when he was within an ace of dropping himself with sheer tiredness that he condescended to let me take my turn. He was tolerably ungracious about it too. "I suppose you may as well carry the stuff," he snapped, "seeing that after all it's your own."

Personally, when we got to the fonda, I had as good a dinner as was procurable, and a bottle of that old Canary wine, and turned into bed after a final pipe. Coppinger dined also, but I have reason to believe he did not sleep much. At any rate I found him still poring over the find next morning, and looking very heavy-eyed, but brimming with enthusiasm.

"Do you know," he said, "that you've blundered upon the most valuable historical manuscript that the modern world has ever yet seen? Of course, with your clumsy way of getting it out, you've done an infinity of damage. For instance, those top sheets you shelled away and spoiled, contained probably an absolutely unique account of the ancient civilisation of Yucatan."

"Where's that, anyway?"

"In the middle of the Gulf of Mexico. It's all ruins to-day, but once it was a very prosperous colony of the Atlanteans."

"Never heard of them. Oh yes, I have though. They were the people Herodotus wrote about, didn't he? But I thought they were mythical."

"They were very real, and so was Atlantis, the continent where they lived, which lay just north of the Canaries here."

"What's that crocodile sort of thing with wings drawn in the margin?"

"Some sort of beast that lived in those bygone days. The pages are full of them. That's a cave-tiger. And that's some sort of colossal bat. Thank goodness he had the sense to illustrate fully, the man who wrote this, or we should never have been able to reconstruct the tale, or at any rate we could not have understood half of it. Whole species have died out since this was written, just as a whole continent has been swept away and three civilisations quenched. The worst of it is, it was written by a highly-educated man who somewhat naturally writes a very bad fist. I've hammered at it all the night through, and have only managed to make out a few sentences here and there"—he rubbed his hands appreciatively. "It will take me a year's hard work to translate this properly."

"Every man to his taste. I'm afraid my interest in the thing wouldn't last as long as that. But how did it get there? Did your ancient Egyptian come to Grand Canary for the good of his lungs, and write it because he felt dull up in that cave?"

"I made a mistake there. The author was not an Egyptian. It was the similarity of the inscribed character which misled me. The book was written by one Deucalion, who seems to have been a priest or general —or perhaps both—and he was an Atlantean. How it got there, I don't know yet. Probably that was told in the last few pages, which a certain vandal smashed up with his pocketknife, in getting them away from the place where they were stowed."

"That's right, abuse me. Deucalion you say? There was a Deucalion in the Greek mythology. He was one of the two who escaped from the Flood: their Noah, in fact."

"The swamping of the continent of Atlantis might very well correspond to the Flood."

"Is there a Pyrrha then? She was Deucalion's wife."

"I haven't come across her yet. But there's a Phorenice, who may be the same. She seems to have been the reigning Empress, as far as I can make out at present."

I looked with interest at illustrations in the margin. They were quite understandable, although the perspective was all wrong. "Weird beasts they seem to have had knocking about the country in those days. Whacking big size too, if one may judge. By Jove, that'll be a cave-tiger trying to pull down a mammoth. I shouldn't care to have lived in those days."

"Probably they had some way of fighting the creatures. However, that will show itself as I get along with the translation." He looked at his watch—"I suppose I ought to be ashamed of myself, but I haven't been to bed. Are you going out?"

"I shall drive back to Las Palmas. I promised a man to have a round at golf this afternoon."

"Very well, see you at dinner. I hope they've sent back my dress shirts from the wash. O, lord! I am sleepy."

I left him going up to bed, and went outside and ordered a carriage to take me down, and there I may say we parted for a considerable time. A cable was waiting for me in the hotel at Las Palmas to go home for business forthwith, and there was a Liverpool boat in the harbour which I just managed to catch as she was steaming out. It was a close thing, and the boatmen made a small fortune out of my hurry.

Now Coppinger was only an hotel acquaintance, and as I was up to the eyes in work when I got back to England, I'm afraid I didn't think very much more about him at the time. One doesn't with people one just meets casually abroad like that. And it must have been at least a year later that I saw by a paragraph in one of the papers, that he had given the lump of sheets to the British Museum, and that the estimated worth of them was ten thousand pounds at the lowest valuation.

Well, this was a bit of revelation, and as he had so repeatedly impressed on me that the things were mine by right of discovery, I wrote rather a pointed note to him mentioning that he seemed to have been making rather free with my property. Promptly came back a stilted letter beginning, "Doctor Coppinger regrets" and so on, and with it the English translation of the wax-upon-talc MSS. He "quite admitted" my claim, and "trusted that the profits of publication would be a sufficient reimbursement for any damage received."

Now I had no idea that he would take me unpleasantly like this, and wrote back a pretty warm reply to that effect; but the only answer I got to this was through a firm of solicitors, who stated that all further communications with Dr. Coppinger must be made through them.

I will say here publicly that I regret the line he has taken over the matter; but as the affair has gone so far, I am disposed to follow out his proposition. Accordingly the old history is here printed; the credit (and the responsibility) of the translation rests with Dr. Coppinger; and whatever revenue accrues from readers, goes to the finder of the original talc-upon-wax sheets, myself.

If there is a further alteration in this arrangement, it will be announced publicly at a later date. But at present this appears to be most unlikely.

1. *My Recall*

The public official reception was over. The sentence had been read, the name of Phorenice, the Empress, adored, and the new Viceroy installed with all that vast and ponderous ceremonial which had gained its pomp and majesty from the ages. Formally, I had delivered up the reins of my government; formally, Tatho had seated himself on the snake-throne, and had put over his neck the chain of gems which symbolised the supreme office; and then, whilst the drums and the trumpets made their proclamation of clamour, he had risen to his feet, for his first state progress round that gilded council chamber as Viceroy of the Province of Yucatan.

With folded arms and bended head, I followed him between the glittering lines of soldiers, and the brilliant throng of courtiers, and chiefs, and statesmen. The roof-beams quivered to the cries of "Long Live Tatho!" "Flourish the Empress!" which came forth as in duty bound, and the new ruler acknowledged the welcome with stately inclinations of the head. In turn he went to the three lesser thrones of the lesser governors—in the East, the North, and the South, and received homage from each as the ritual was; and I, the man whom his coming had deposed, followed with the prescribed meekness in his train.

It was a hard task, but we who hold the higher offices learn to carry before the people a passionless face. Once, twenty years before, these same fine obeisances had been made to me; now the Gods had seen fit to make fortune change. But as I walked bent and humbly on behind the heels of Tatho, though etiquette forbade noisy salutations to myself, it could not inhibit kindly glances, and these came from every soldier, every courtier, and every chief who stood there in that gilded hall, and they fell upon me very grate-fully. It is not often that the fallen meet such tender looks.

The form goes, handed down from immemorial custom, that on these great ceremonial days of changing a ruler, those of the people being present may bring forward petitions and requests; may make accusations against their retiring head with sure immunity from his vengeance; or may state their own private theories for the better government of the State in the future. I think it may be pardoned to my vanity if I record that not a voice was raised against me, or against any of the items of my twenty years of rule. Nor did any speak out for alterations in the future. Yes, even though we made the circuit for the three prescribed times, all present showed their approval in generous silence.

Then, one behind the other, the new Viceroy and the old, we marched with formal step over golden tiles of that council hall beneath the pyramid, and the great officers of state left their stations and joined in our train; and at the farther wall we came to the door of those private chambers which an hour ago had been mine own.

Ah, well! I had no home now in any of those wondrous cities of Yucatan, and I could not help feeling a bitterness, though in sooth I should have been thankful enough to return to the Continent of Atlantis with my head still in its proper station.

Tatho gave his formal summons of "Open ye to the Viceroy," which the ritual commands, and the slaves within sent the massive stone valves of the door gaping wide. Tatho entered, I at his heels; the others halted, sending valedictions from the threshold; and the valves of the door clanged on the lock behind us. We passed on to the chamber beyond, and then, when for the first time we were alone together, and the forced etiquette of courts was behind us, the new Viceroy turned with meekly folded arms, and bowed low before me.

"Deucalion," he said, "believe me that I have not sought this office. It was thrust upon me. Had I not accepted, my head would have paid forfeit, and another man—your enemy—would have been sent out as viceroy in your place. The Empress does not permit that her will shall ever be questioned."

"My friend," I made answer, "my brother in all but blood, there is no man living in all Atlantis or her territories to whom I had liefer hand over my government. For twenty years now have I ruled this country of Yucatan, and Mexico beyond, first under the old King, and then as minister to this new Empress. I know my colony like a book. I am intimate with all her wonderful cities, with their palaces, their pyramids, and their peoples. I have hunted the beasts and the savages in the forests. I have built roads, and made the rivers so that they will carry shipping. I have fostered the arts and crafts like a merchant; I have discoursed, three times each day, the cult of the Gods with mine own lips. Through evil years and through good have I ruled here, striving only for the prosperity of the land and the strengthening of Atlantis, and I have grown to love the peoples like a father. To you I bequeath them, Tatho, with tender supplications for their interest."

"It is not I that can carry on Deucalion's work with Deucalion's power, but rest content, my friend, that I shall do my humble best to follow exactly on in your footsteps. Believe me, I came out to this government with a thousand regrets, but I would have died sooner than take your place had I known how vigorously the supplanting would trouble you."

"We are alone here," I said, "away from the formalities of formal assemblies, and a man may give vent to his natural self without fear of tarnishing a ceremony. Your coming was something of the suddenest. Till an hour ago, when you demanded audience, I had thought to rule on longer; and even now I do not know for what cause I am deposed."

"The proclamation said: 'We relieve our well-beloved Deucalion of his present service, because we have great need of his powers at home in our kingdom of Atlantis.' "

"A mere formality."

Tatho looked uneasily round the hangings of the chamber, and drew me with him to its centre, and lowered his voice.

"I do not think so," he whispered. "I believe she has need of you. There are troublous times on hand, and Phorenice wants the ablest men in the kingdom ready to her call."

"You may speak openly," I said, "and without fear of eavesdroppers. We are in the heart of the pyramid here, built in every way by a man's length of solid stone. Myself, I oversaw the laying of every course. And besides, here in Yucatan, we have not the niceties of your old world diplomacy, and do not listen, because we count it shame to do so."

Tatho shrugged his shoulders. "I acted only according to mine education. At home, a loose tongue makes a loose head, and there are those whose trade it is to carry tales. Still, what I say is this: The throne shakes, and Phorenice sees the need of sturdy props. So she has sent this proclamation."

"But why come to me? It is twenty years since I sailed to this colony, and from that day I have not returned to Atlantis once. I know little of the old country's politics. What small parcel of news drifts out to us across the ocean, reads with slender interest here. Yucatan is another world, my dear Tatho, as you in the course of your government will learn, with new interests, new people, new everything. To us here, Atlantis is only a figment, a shadow, far away across the waters. It is for this new world of Yucatan that I have striven through all these years."

"If Deucalion has small time to spare from his government for brooding over his fatherland, Atlantis, at least, has found leisure to admire the deeds of her brilliant son. Why, sir, over yonder at home, your name carries magic with it. When you and I were lads together, it was the custom in the colleges to teach that the men of the past were the greatest this world has ever seen; but to-day this teaching is changed. It is Deucalion who is held up as the model and example. Mothers name their sons Deucalion, as the most valuable birth-gift they can make. Deucalion is a household word. Indeed, there is only one name that is near to it in familiarity."

"You trouble me," I said, frowning. "I have tried to do my duty for its own sake, and for the country's sake, not for the pattings and fondlings of the vulgar. And besides, if there are names to be in every one's mouth, they should be the names of the Gods."

Tatho shrugged his shoulders. "The Gods? They occupy us very little these latter years. With our modern science, we have grown past the tether of the older Gods, and no new one has appeared. No, my Lord Deucalion, if it were merely the Gods who were your competitors on men's lips, your name would be a thousand times the better known."

"Of mere human names," I said, "the name of this new Empress should come first in Atlantis, our lord the old King being now dead."

"She certainly would have it so," replied Tatho, and there was something in his tone which made me see that more was meant behind the words. I drew him to one of the marble seats, and bent myself familiarly towards him. "I am speaking," I said, "not to the new Viceroy of Yucatan, but to my old friend Tatho, a member of the Priests' Clan, like myself, with whom I worked side by side in a score of the smaller home governments, in hamlets, in villages, in smaller towns, in greater towns, as we gained experience in war and knowledge in the art of ruling people, and so tediously won our promotion. I am speaking in Tatho's private abode, that was mine own not two hours since, and I would have an answer with that plainness which we always then used to one another."

The new Viceroy sighed whimsically. "I almost forget how to speak in plain words now," he said. "We have grown so polished in these latter days, that mere bald truth would be hissed as indelicate. But for the memory of those early years, when we expended as much law and thought over the ownership of a haybyre as we should now over the fate of a rebellious city, I will try and speak plain to you even now, Deucalion. Tell me, old friend, what is it?"

"What of this new Empress?"

He frowned. "I might have guessed your subject," he said.

"Then speak upon it. Tell me of all the changes that have been made. What has this Phorenice done to make her throne unstable in Atlantis?"

Tatho frowned still. "If I did not know you to be as honest as our Lord the Sun, your questions would carry mischief with them. Phorenice has a short way with those who are daring enough to discuss her policies for other purpose than politely to praise them."

"You can leave me ignorant if you wish," I said with a touch of chill. This Tatho seemed to be different from the Tatho I had known at home, Tatho my workmate, Tatho who had read with me in the College of Priests, who had run with me in many a furious charge, who had laboured with me so heavily that the peoples under us might prosper. But he was quick enough to see my change of tone.

"You force me back to my old self," he said with a half smile, "though it is hard enough to forget the caution one has learned during the last twenty years, even when speaking with you. Still, whatever may have happened to the rest of us, it is clear to see that you at least have not changed, and, old friend, I am ready to trust you with my life if you ask it. In fact, you do ask me that very thing when you tell me to speak all I know of Phorenice."

I nodded. This was more like the old times, when there was full confidence between us. "The Gods will it now that I return to Atlantis," I said, "and what happens after that the Gods alone know. But it would be of service to me if I could land on her shores with some knowledge of this Phorenice, for at present I am as ignorant concerning her as some savage from Europe or mid-Africa."

"What would you have me tell?"

"Tell all. I know only that she, a woman, reigns, whereby the ancient law of the land, a man should rule; that she is not even of the Priestly Clan from which the law says all rulers must be drawn; and that, from what you say, she has caused the throne to totter. The throne was as firm as the everlasting hills in the old King's day, Tatho."

"History has moved with pace since then, and Phorenice has spurred it. You know her origin?"

"I know only the exact little I have told you."

"She was a swineherd's daughter from the mountains, though this is never even whispered now, as she has declared herself to be a daughter of the Gods, with a miraculous birth and upbringing. As she has decreed it a sacrilege to question this parentage, and has ordered to be burnt all those that seem to recollect her more earthly origin, the fable passes current for truth. You see the faith I put in you, Deucalion, by telling you what you wish to learn."

"There has always been trust between us."

"I know; but this habit of suspicion is hard to cast off, even with you. However, let me put your good faith between me and the torture further. Zaemon, you remember, was governor of the swineherd's province, and Zaemon's wife saw Phorenice and took her away to adopt and bring up as her own. It is said that the swineherd and his woman objected; perhaps they did; anyway, I know they died; and Phorenice was taught the arts and graces, and brought up as a daughter of the Priestly Clan."

"But still she was an adopted daughter only," I objected.

"The omission of the 'adopted' was her will at an early age," said Tatho dryly, "and she learnt early to have her wishes carried into fact. It was notorious that before she had grown to fifteen years she ruled not only the women of the household, but Zaemon also, and the province that was beyond Zaemon."

"Zaemon was learned," I said, "and a devout follower of the Gods, and searcher into the higher mysteries; but, as a ruler, he was always a flabby fellow."

"I do not say that opportunities have not come usefully in Phorenice's way, but she has genius as well. For her to have raised herself at all from what she was,

was remarkable. Not one woman out of a thousand, placed as she was, would have grown to be aught higher than a mere wife of some sturdy countryman, who was sufficiently simple to care nothing for pedigree. But look at Phorenice: it was her whim to take exercise as a man-at-arms and practise with all the utensils of war; and then, before any one quite knows how or why it happened, a rebellion had broken out in the province, and here was she, a slip of a girl, leading Zaemon's troops."

"Zaemon, when I knew him, was a mere derision in the field."

"Hear me on. Phorenice put down the rebellion in masterly fashion, and gave the conquered a choice between sword and service. They fell into her ranks at once, and were faithful to her from that moment. I tell you, Deucalion, there is a marvellous fascination about the woman."

"Her present historian seems to have felt it."

"Of course I have. Every one who sees her comes under her spell. And frankly, I am in love with her also, and look upon my coming here as detestable exile. Every one near to Phorenice, high and low, loves her just the same, even though they know it may be her whim to send them to execution next minute."

Perhaps I let my scorn of this appear.

"You feel contempt for our weakness? You were always a strong man, Deucalion."

"At any rate you see me still unmarried. I have found no time to palter with the fripperies of women."

"Ah, but these colonists here are crude and unfascinating. Wait till you see the ladies of the court, my ascetic."

"It comes to my mind," I said dryly, "that I lived in Atlantis before I came out here, and at that time I used to see as much of court life as most men. Yet then, also, I felt no inducement to marry."

Tatho chuckled. "Atlantis has changed so that you would hardly know the country to-day. A new era has come over everything, especially over the other sex. Well do I remember the women of the old King's time, how monstrous uncomely they were, how little they knew how to walk or carry themselves, how painfully barbaric was their notion of dress. I dare swear that your ladies here in Yucatan are not so provincial to-day as ours were then. But you should see them now at home. They are delicious. And above all in charm is the Empress. Oh, Deucalion, you shall see Phorenice in all her glorious beauty and her magnificence one of these fine days soon, and believe me you will go down on your knees and repent."

"I may see, and (because you say so) I may alter my life's ways. The Gods make all things possible. But for the present I remain as I am, celibate, and not wishful to be otherwise; and so in the meantime I would hear the continuance of your history."

"It is one long story of success. She deposed Zaemon from his government in name as well as in fact, and the news was spread, and the Priestly Clan rose in its wrath. The two neighbouring governors were bidden join forces, take her captive, and bring her for execution. Poor men! They tried to obey their orders; they attacked her surely enough, but in battle she could laugh at them. She killed both, and made some slaughter amongst their troops; and to those that remained alive and became her prisoners, she made her usual offer —the sword or service. Naturally they were not long over making their choice: to these common people one ruler is much the same as another: and so again her army was reinforced.

"Three times were bodies of soldiery sent against her, and three times was she victorious. The last was a final effort. Before, it had been customary to despise this adventuress who had sprung up so suddenly. But then the priests began to realise their peril; to see that the throne itself was in danger; and to know that if she were to be crushed, they would have to put forth their utmost. Every man who could carry arms was pressed into the service. Every known art of war was ordered to be put into employment. It was the largest army, and the best equipped army that Atlantis then had ever raised, and the Priestly Clan saw fit to put in supreme command their general, Tatho."

"You!" I cried.

"Even myself, Deucalion. And mark you, I fought my utmost. I was not her creature then; and when I set out (because they wanted to spur me to the uttermost) the High Council of the priests pointed out my prospects. The King we had known so long, was ailing and wearily old; he was so wrapped up in the study of the mysteries, and the joy of closely knowing them, that earthly matters had grown nauseous to him; and at any time he might decide to die. The Priestly Clan uses its own discretion in the election of a new king, but it takes note of popular sentiment; and a general who at the critical time could come home victorious from a great campaign, which moreover would release a harassed people from the constant application of arms, would be the idol of the moment. These things were pointed out to me solemnly and in the full council."

"What! They promised you the throne?"

"Even that. So you see I set out with a high stake before me. Phorenice I had never seen, and I swore to take her alive, and give her to be the sport of my soldiery. I had a fine confidence in my own strategy then, Deucalion. But the old Gods, in whom I trusted then, remained old, taught me no new thing. I drilled and exercised my army according to the forms you and I learnt together, old comrade, and in many a tough fight found to serve well; I armed them with the choicest weapons we knew of then, with sling and mace, with bow and spear, with axe and knife, with sword and the throwing fire; their bodies I covered with metal plates; even their bellies I cared for, with droves of cattle driven in the rear of the fighting troops.

"But when the encounter came, they might have been men of straw for all the harm they did. Out of her own

brain Phorenice had made fire-tubes that cast a dart
which would kill beyond two bowshots, and the fashion
in which she handled her troops dazzled me. They
threatened us on one flank, they harassed us on the
other. It was not war as we had been accustomed to.
It was a newer and more deadly game, and I had to
watch my splendid army eaten away as waves eat a
sandhill. Never once did I get a chance of forcing close
action. These new tactics that had come from Phorenice's invention, were beyond my art to meet or understand. We were eight to her one, and our close-packed
numbers only made us so much the more easy for
slaughter. A panic came, and those who could fled. Myself, I had no wish to go back and earn the axe that
waits for the unsuccessful general. I tried to die there
fighting where I stood. But death would not come. It
was a fine melée, Deucalion, that last one."

"And so she took you?"

"I stood with three others back to back, with a ring
of dead round us, and a ring of the enemy hemming us
in. We taunted them to come on. But at hand-to-hand
courtesies we had shown we could hold our own, and
so they were calling for fire-tubes with which they could
strike us down in safety from a distance. Then up came
Phorenice. 'What is this to-do?' says she. 'We seek to
kill Lord Tatho, who led against you,' say they. 'So
that is Tatho?' says she. 'A fine figure of a man
indeed, and a pretty fighter seemingly, after the old
manner. Doubtless he is one who would acquire the
newer method. See now Tatho,' says she, 'it is my custom to offer those I vanquish either the sword (which,
believe me, was never nearer your neck than now) or
service under my banner. Will you make a choice?'

" 'Woman,' I said, 'fairest that ever I saw, finest
general the world has ever borne, you tempt me sorely
by your qualities, but there is a tradition in our Clan,
that we should be true to the salt we eat. I am the
King's man still, and so I can take no service from you.'

" 'The King is dead,' says she. 'A runner has just

brought the tidings, meaning them to have fallen into your hands. And I am the Empress.'

" 'Who made you Empress?' I asked.

" 'The same most capable hand that has given me this battle,' says she. 'It is a capable hand, as you have seen: it can be a kind hand also, as you may learn if you choose. With the King dead, Tatho is a masterless man now. Is Tatho in want of a mistress?'

"Such a glorious mistress as you,' I said, 'yes.' And from that moment, Deucalion, I have been her slave. Oh, you may frown; you may get up from this seat and walk away if you will. But I ask you this: keep back your worst judgment of me, old friend, till after you have seen Phorenice herself in the warm and lovely flesh. Then your own ears and your own senses will be my advocates, to win me back your old esteem."

2. Back to Atlantis

The words of Tatho were no sleeping draught for me that night. I began to think that I had made somewhat a mistake in wrapping myself up so entirely in my government of Yucatan, and not contriving to keep more in touch with events that were passing at home in Atlantis. For many years past it had been easy to see that the mariner folk who did traffic across the seas spoke with restraint, and that only what news the Empress pleased was allowed to ooze out beyond her borders. But, as I say, I was fully occupied with my work in the colony, and had no curiosity to pull away a veil intentionally placed. Besides, it has always been against my principles to put to the torture men who had received orders for silence from their superiors, merely that they shall break these orders for my private convenience.

However, the iron discipline of our Priestly Clan left me no choice of procedure. As was customary, I had been deprived of my office at a moment's notice. From that time on, all papers and authority belonged to my successor, and, although by courtesy I might be permitted to remain as a guest in the pyramid that had so recently been mine, to see another sunrise, it was clearly enjoined that I must leave the territory then at the topmost of my speed and hasten to report in Atlantis.

Tatho, to give him credit, was anxious to further my interests to the utmost in his power. He was by my side again before the dawn, putting all his resources at my disposal.

I had little enough to ask him. "A ship to take me home," I said, "and I shall be your debtor."

The request seemed to surprise him. "That you may certainly have if you wish it. But my ships are foul with the long passage, and are in need of a careen. If you take them, you will make a slow voyage of it to Atlantis. Why do you not take your own navy? The ships are in harbour now, for I saw them there when we came in. Brave ships they are too."

"But not mine. That navy belongs to Yucatan."

"Well, Deucalion, you are Yucatan; or, rather, you were yesterday, and have been these twenty years."

I saw what he meant, and the idea did not please me. I answered stiffly enough that the ships were owned by private merchants, or belonged to the State, and I could not claim so much as a ten-slave galley.

Tatho shrugged his shoulders. "I suppose you know your own policies best," he said, "though to me it seems but risky for a man who has attained to a position like yours and mine not to have provided himself with a stout navy of his own. One never knows when a recall may be sent, and, through lack of these precautions, a life's earnings may very well be lost in a dozen hours."

"I have no fear for mine," I said coldly.

"Of course not, because you know me to be your friend. But had another man been appointed to this vice-royalty, you might have been sadly shorn, Deucalion. It is not many fellows who can resist a snug hoard ready and waiting in the very coffers they have come to line."

"My Lord Tatho," I said, "it is clear to me that you and I have grown to be of different tastes. All of the hoard that I have made for myself in this colony, few men would covet. I have the poor clothes you see me in this moment, and a box of drugs such as I have found useful to the stomach. I possess also three slaves, two of them scribes and the third a sturdy savage from Europe, who cooks my victual and fills for me the bath. For my maintenance during my years of service, here, I have bled the State of a soldier's ration and nothing beyond; and if in my name any man has mulcted a creature in Yucatan of so much as an ounce of bronze, I request you as a last service to have that man hanged for me as a liar and a thief."

Tatho looked at me curiously. "I do not know whether I admire you most or whether I pity. I do not know whether to be astonished or to despise. We had heard of much of your uprightness over yonder in Atlantis, of your sternness and your justice, but I swear by the old Gods that no soul guessed you carried your fancy so far as this. Why, man, money is power. With money and the resources money can buy, nothing could stop a fellow like you; whilst without it you may be tripped up and trodden down irrevocably at the first puny reverse."

"The Gods will choose my fate."

"Possibly; but for mine, I prefer to nourish it myself. I tell you with frankness that I have not come here to follow in the pattern you have made for a vice-royalty. I shall govern Yucatan wisely and well to the best of my ability; but I shall govern it also for the good of Tatho, the viceroy. I have brought with me here my navy of eight ships and a personal bodyguard. There is my wife also, and her women and her slaves. All these must be provided for. And why indeed should it be otherwise? If a people is to be governed, it should be their privilege to pay handsomely for their prince."

"We shall not agree on this. You have the power now, and can employ it as you choose. If I thought it would be of any use, I should like to supplicate you most humbly to deal with lenience when you come to tax these people who are under you. They have grown very dear to me."

"I have disgusted you with me, and I am grieved for it. But even to retain your good opinion, Deucalion— which I value more than that of any man living—I cannot do here as you have done. It would be impossible, even if I wished it. You must not judge all other men by your own strong standard: a Tatho is by no means a colossus like a Deucalion. And besides, I have a wife and children, and they must be provided for, even if I neglect myself."

"Ah, there," I said, "it does seem that I possess the advantage. I have no wife to clog me."

He caught up my word quickly. "It seems to me you have nothing that makes life worth living. You have neither wife, children, riches, cooks, retinue, dresses, nor anything else in proportion to your station. You will pardon my saying it, old comrade, but you are plaguey ignorant about some matters. For example, you do not know how to dine. During every day of a very weary voyage, I have promised myself when sitting before the meagre sea victual, that presently the abstinence would be more than repaid by Deucalion's welcoming feast. Oh, I tell you that feast was one of the vividest things that ever came before my eyes. And then when we get to the actuality, what was it? Why, a country farmer every day sits down to more delicate fare. You told me how it was prepared. Well, your savage from Europe may be lusty, and perchance is faithful, but he is a devil-possessed cook. Gods! I have lived better on a campaign.

"I know this is a colony here, without any of the home refinements; but if in the days to come, the deer of the forest, the fish of the stream, and the other resources of the place are not put to better use than heretofore, I shall see it my duty as ruler to fry some of the kitchen staff alive in grease so as to encourage better cookery. Gods! Deucalion, have you forgotten what it is to have a palate? And have you no esteem for your own dignity? Man, look at your clothes. You are garbed like a herdsman, and you have not a gaud or a jewel to brighten you."

"I eat," I said coldly, "when my hunger bids me, and I carry this one robe upon my person till it is worn out and needs replacement. The grossness of excessive banqueting, and the effeminacy of many clothes are attainments that never met my fancy. But I think we have talked here over long, and there seems little chance of our finding agreement. You have changed, Tatho, with the years, and perhaps I have changed also. These alterations creep imperceptibly into one's being as time advances. Let us part now, and, forgetting these present differences, remember only our friendship of twenty years agone. That for me, at any rate, has always had a pleasant savour when called up into the memory."

Tatho bowed his head. "So be it," he said.

"And I would still charge myself upon your bounty for that ship. Dawn cannot be far off now, and it is not decent that the man who has ruled here so long, should walk in daylight through the streets on the morning after his dismissal."

"So be it," said Tatho. "You shall have my poor navy. I could have wished that you had asked me something greater."

"Not the navy, Tatho; one small ship. Believe me, more is wasted."

"Now, there," said Tatho, "I shall act the tyrant.

I am viceroy here now, and will have my way in this. You may go naked of all possessions: that I cannot help. But depart for Atlantis unattended, that you shall not."

And so, in fine, as the choice was set beyond me, it was in the "Bear," Tatho's own private ship, with all the rest of his navy sailing in escort, that I did finally make my transit.

But the start was not immediate. The vessels lay moored against the stone quays of the inner harbour, gutted of their stores, and with crews exhausted, and it would have been suicide to have forced them out then and there to again take the seas.

So the courtesies were fulfilled by the craft whereon I abode hauling out into the entrance basin, and anchoring there in the swells of the fairway; and forthwith she and her consorts took in wood and water, cured meat and fish ashore, and refitted in all needful ways, with all speed attainable.

For myself there came then, as the first time during twenty busy years, a breathing space from work. I had no further connection with the country of my labours; indeed, officially, I had left it already. Into the working of the ship it was contrary to rule that I should make any inspection or interest, since all sea matters were the exclusive property of the Mariners' Guild, secured to them by royal patent, and most jealously guarded.

So there remained to me in my day, hours to gaze (if I would) upon the quays, the harbours, the palaces, and the pyramids of the splendid city before me which I had seen grow stone by stone from its foundations; or to roam my eye over the pastures and the grain lands beyond the walls, and to look longingly at the dense forests behind, from which field by field we had so tediously ripped our territory.

Would Tatho continue the work so healthily begun? I trusted so, even in spite of his selfish words. And at all hours, during the radiance of our Lord the Sun, or under the stars of night, I was free to pursue that study

of the higher mysteries, on which we of the Priests'
Clan are trained to set our minds, without aid of book
or instrument, of image or temple.

The refitting of the navy was gone about with speed.
Never, it is said, had ships been reprovisioned and
caulked, and remanned with greater speed for the over-
ocean voyage. Indeed, it was barely over a month from
the day that they brought up in the harbour, they put
out beyond the walls, and began their voyage eastward
over the hills and dale of the ocean.

Rowing-slaves from Europe for this long passage of
sea are not taken now, owing to the difficulty in pro-
visioning them, for modern humanity forbids the practice of letting them eat one another according to the
home custom of their continent; sails alone are but an
indifferent stand by; but modern science has shown how
to extract force from the Sun, when He is free from
cloud, and this (in a manner kept secret by mariners) is
made to draw sea-water at the forepart of the vessel,
and eject it with such force at the stern that she is
appreciably driven forward, even with the wind adverse.

In another matter also has navigation vastly im-
proved. It is not necessary now, as formerly, to trust
wholly to a starry night (when beyond sight of land) to
find direction. A little image has been made, and is
stood balanced in the forepart of every vessel, with an
arm outstretched, pointing constantly to the direction
where the Southern Cross lies in the Heavens. So, by
setting an angle, can a just course be correctly steered.
Other instruments have they also for finding a true position on the ocean wastes, for the newer mariner, when
he is at sea, puts little trust in the Gods, and confides
mightily in his own thews and wits.

Still, it is amusing to see these tarry fellows, even in
this modern day, take their last farewell of the harbour
town. The ship is stowed, and all ready for sea, and
they wash and put on all their bravery of attire. Ashore
they go, their faces long with piety, and seek some

obscure temple whose God has little flavour with shore folk, and here they make sacrifice with clamour and lavish outlay. And, finally, there follows a feast in honour of the God, and they arrive back on board, and put to sea for the most part drunken, and all heavy and evil-humoured with gluttony and their other excesses.

The voyage was very different to my previous sea-going. There was no creeping timorously along in touch with the coasts. We stood straight across the open gulf in the direction of home, came up with the band of the Carib Islands, and worked confidently through them, as though they had been signposts to mark the sea highway; and stopped only twice to replenish with wood, water, and fruit. These commodities, too, the savages brought us freely, so great was their subjection, and in neither place did we have even the semblance of a fight. It was a great certificate of the growing power of Atlantis and her finest over-sea colony.

Then boldly on we went across the vast ocean beyond, with never a sacrifice to implore the Gods that they should help our direction. One might feel censure towards these rugged mariners for their impiety, but one could not help an admiration for their lusty skill and confidence.

The dangers of the desolate sea are dealt out as the Gods will, and man can only take them as they come. Storms we encountered, and the mariners fought them with stubborn endurance; twice a blazing stone from Heaven hissed into the sea beside us, though without injuring any of our ships; and, as was unavoidable, the great beasts of the sea hunted us with their accustomed savagery. But only once did we suffer material loss from these last, and that was when three of the greater sea lizards attacked the "Bear," the ship whereon I travelled, at one and the same time.

The hour of their onset was during the blazing midday heat, and the Sun being at the full of His power, our machines were getting full force from Him. The vessel was travelling forward faster than a man on dry land could walk. But for the power escape she might as well have been standing still when the beasts sighted her. There were three of them, as I have said, and we saw them come up over the curve of the horizon, beating the sea into foam with their flappers, and waving their great necks like masts as they swam. Our navy was spread out in a long line of ships, and in olden days each of the beasts would have selected a separate prey, and proceeded for it; but, like man, these beasts have learned the necessities of warfare, and they hunt in pack now and do not separate their forces.

It was plain they were making for our ship, and Tob, the captain, would have had me go into the after-castle, and there be secure from their marauding. He was responsible to the Lord Tatho, he said, for my safe conduct; it was certain that the beasts would contrive to seize some of the ship's company before they were satiated; and if the hap came to the Lord Deucalion, he (the captain) would have to give himself voluntarily to the beasts then, to escape a very painful death at Tatho's hands later on.

However, my mind was set. A man can never have too much experience in fighting enemies, whether human or bestial, and the attack of these creatures was new to me, and I was fain to learn its method. So I gave the captain a letter to Tatho, saying how the matter lay (and for which, it may be mentioned, the rude fellow seemed little enough grateful), and stayed in my chair under the awning.

The beasts surged up to us with champing jaws, and all the shipmen stood armed on their defence. They came up alongside, two females (the smaller) on the flank of the ship, the giant male by himself on the other. Their great heads swooped about, as high as the yards that held the sails, and the reek from them gave one physical sickness.

The shipmen faced the monsters with a sturdy courage. Arrows were useless against the smooth, bull-like hides. Even the throwing fire could not so much as singe them; nothing but twenty axe blows delivered on an attacking head together could beat it back, and even these succeeded only through sheer weight of metal, and did not make so much as the scratch of a wound.

During all time beasts have disputed with man the mastery of the earth, and it is only in Atlantis and Egypt and Yucatan that man has dared to hold his own, and fight them with a mind made strong by many previous victories. In Europe and mid-Africa the greater beasts hold full dominion, and man admits his puny number and force, and lives in earth crannies and the higher tree-tops, as a fugitive confessed. And upon the great oceans, the beasts are lords, unchecked.

Still here, upon this desolate sea, although the giant lizards were new to me, it was a pleasure to pit my knowledge of war against their brute strength and courage. Ever since the first men did their business upon the great waters, they fulfilled their instincts in fighting the beasts with desperation. Hiding coward-like in a hold was useless, for if this enemy could not find men above decks to glut them, they would break a ship with their paddles, and so all would be slain. And so it was recognised that the fight should go forward as desperately as might be, and that it could only end when the beasts had got their prey and had gone away satisfied.

It was in a one-sided conflict after this fashion then, that I found myself, and felt the joy once more to have my thews in action. But after my axe had got in some dozen lusty blows, which, for all the harm they did, might have been delivered against some city wall, or, indeed, against the ark of the Mysteries itself, I sought about me till I found a lance, and with that made very different play.

The eyes of these lizards are small, and set deep in a bony socket, but I judged them to be vulnerable, and it was upon the eyes of the beast that I made my attack. The decks were slippery with the horrid slime of them. The crew surged about in their battling, and, moreover, constantly offered themselves as a rampart before me by reason of Tob, the captain's threats. But I gave a few shrewd progues with the lance to show that I did not choose my will to be overridden, and presently was given room for manœuvre.

Deliberately I placed myself in the sight of one of the lizards, and offered my body to its attack. The challenge was accepted. It swooped like a dropping stone, and I swerved and drove in the lance at its oozy eye.

I thanked the Gods then that I had been trained with the lance till certain aim was a matter of instinct with me. The blade went true to its mark and stuck there, and the shaft broke in my hand. The beast drew off, blinded and bellowing, and beating the sea with its paddles. In a great cataract of foam I saw it bend its great long neck, and rub its head (with the spear still fixed) against its back, thereby enduring new agonies, but without dislodging the weapon. And then presently, finding this of no avail, it set off for the place from which it came with extraordinary quickness, and rapidly grew smaller against the horizon.

The male and the other female lizard had also left us, but not in similar plight. Tob, the captain, seeing my resolve to take hazards, deliberately thrust a ship-man into the jaws of each of the others, so that they might be sated and get them gone. It was clear that Tob dreaded very much for his own skin if I came by harm, and I thought with a warming heart of the threats that Tatho must have used in his kind anxiety for my safety. It is pleasant when one's old friends do not omit to pay these little attentions.

3. A Rival Navy

Now, when we came up with the coasts of Atlantis, though Tob, with the aid of his modern instruments, had made his landfall with most marvellous skill and nearness, there still remained some ten days' more journey in which we had to retrace our course, till we came to that arm of the sea up which lies the great city of Atlantis, the capital.

The sight of the land, and the breath of earth and herbage which came off from it with the breezes, were, I believe, under the Gods, the means of saving the lives of all of us. For, as is necessary with long cross-ocean voyages, many of our ships' companies had died, and still more were sick with scurvy through the unnatural tossing, or (as some have it) through the salt, unnatural food inseparable from shipboard. But these last, the sight and the smells of land heartened up in extraordinary fashion, and from being helpless logs, unable to move even under blows of the scourge, they became active again, able to help in the shipwork, and lusty (when the time came) to fight for their lives and their vessels.

From the moment that I was deposed in Yucatan, despite Tatho's assurances, there had been doubts in my mind as to what nature would be my reception in Atlantis. But I had faced this event of the future without concern: it was in the hands of the Gods. The Empress Phorenice might be supreme on earth; she might cause my head to be lopped from its proper shoulders the moment I set foot ashore; but my Lord

the Sun was above Phorenice, and if my head fell, it
would be because He saw best that it should be so. On
which account, therefore, I had not troubled myself
about the matter during the voyage, but had followed
out my calm study of the higher mysteries with an un-
loaded mind.

But when our navy had retraced sufficiently the
course that had been overrun, and came up with the
two vast headlands which marked the entrance to the
inland waters, there, a bare two days from the Atlantis
capital, we met with another navy which was, beyond
doubt, waiting to give us a reception. The ships were
riding at anchor in a bay which lent them shelter, but
they had scouts on the high land above, who cried the
alarm of our approach, and when we rounded the headland, they were standing out to dispute our passage.

Of us there were now but five ships, the rest having
been lost in storms, or fallen behind because all their
crews were dead from the scurvy; and of the
strangers there were three fine ships, and three galleys
of many oars apiece. They were clean and bright and
black; our ships were storm-ragged and weather-worn,
and had bottoms that were foul with trailing ocean
weed. Our ships hung out the colours and signs of
Tatho and Deucalion openly and without shame, so that
all who looked might know their origin and errand; but
the other navy came on without banner or antient, as
though they were some low creatures feeling shame for
their birth.

Clear it seemed also that they would not let us pass
without a fight, and in this there was nothing un-
common; for no law carries out over the seas, and a
brother in one ship feels quite free to harry his brother
in another vessel if he meets him out of earshot of the
beach—more especially if that other brother be coming
home laden from foray or trading tour. So Tob, with
system and method, got our vessel into fighting trim,
and the other four captains did the like with theirs,
and drew close in to us to form a compact squadron.

They had no wish to smell slavery, now that the voyage had come so near to its end.

Our Lord the Sun shone brilliantly, giving full speed to the machines, as though He was fully willing for the affair to proceed, and the two navies approached one another with quickness, the three galleys holding back to stay in line with their consorts. But when some bare hundred ship-lengths separated us, the other navy halted, and one of the galleys, drawing ahead, flew green branches from her masts, seeking for a parley.

The course was unusual, but we, in our sea-battered state, were no navy to invite a fight unnecessarily. So in hoarse sea-bawls word was passed, and we too halted, and Tob hoisted a withered stick (which had to do duty for greenery), to show that we were ready for talk, and would respect the person of an ambassador.

The galley drew on, swung round, and backed till its stern rasped on our shield rail, and one of her people clambered up and jumped down upon our decks. He was a dandily rigged-out fellow, young and lusty, and all healthy from the land and land victual, and he looked round him with a sneer at our sea-tatteredness, and with a fine self-confidence. Then, seeing Tob, he nodded as one meets an acquaintance. "Old pot-mate," he said, "your woman waits for you up by the quay-side in Atlantis yonder, with four youngsters at her heels. I saw her not half a month ago."

"You didn't come out here to tell me home news," said Tob; "that I'll be sworn. I've drunk enough pots with you, Dason, to know your pleasantries thoroughly."

"I wanted to point out to you that your home is still there, with your wife and children ready to welcome you."

"I am not a man that ever forgets it," said Tob grimly; "and because I've got them always at the back of my mind, I've sailed this ship over the top of more than one pirate, when, if I'd been a single man, I might have been e'en content to take the hap of slavery."

"Oh, I know you're a desperate enough fellow," said Dason, "and I'm free to confess that if it does come to blows we are like to lose a few men before we get you and your cripples here, and your crazy ships comfortably sunk. Our navy has its orders to carry out, and the cause of my embassage is this: we wish to see if you will act the sensible part and give us what we want, and so be permitted to go on your way home, with a skin that is unslit and dry?"

"You have come to the wrong bird here for a plucking," said Tob with a heavy laugh. "We took no treasure or merchandise on board in Yucatan. We stayed in harbour long enough to cure our sea victual and fill with food and water, and no longer. We sail back as we sailed out, barren ships. You will not believe me, of course; I would not have believed you had our places been changed; but you may go into the holds and search if you choose. You will find there nothing but a few poor sailormen half in pieces with the scurvy. No, you can steal nothing here but blows, Dason, and we will give you those with but little asking."

"I am glad to see that you state your cargo at such slender value," said the envoy, "for it is the cargo I must take back with me on the galley, if you are to earn your safe conduct to home."

Tob knit his brows. "You had better speak more plain," he said. "I am a common sailor, and do not understand fancy talk."

"It is clear to see," said Dason, "that you have been set to bring Deucalion back to Atlantis as a prop for Phorenice. Well, we others find Phorenice hard enough to fight against without further reinforcements, and so we want Deucalion in our own custody to deal with after our own fashion."

"And if I do the miser, and deny you this piece of my freight?"

The spruce envoy looked round at the splintered ship, and the battered navy beside her. "Why, then, Tob, we shall send you all to the fishes in very short time, and instead of Deucalion standing before the Gods alone, he will go down with a fine ragged company limping at his heels."

"I doubt it," said Tob, "but we shall see. As for letting you have my Lord Deucalion, that is out of the question. For see here, pot-mate Dason; in the first place, if I went to Atlantis without Deucalion, my other lord, Tatho, would come back one of these days, and in his hands I should die by the slowest of slow inches; in the second, I have seen my Lord Deucalion kill a great sea lizard, and he showed himself such a proper man that day that I would not give him up against his will, even to Tatho himself; and in the third place, you owe me for your share in our last wine-bout ashore, and I'll see you with the nether Gods before I give you aught till you've settled that score."

"Well, Tob, I hope you'll drown easy. As for that wife of yours, I've always had a fancy for her myself, and I shall know how to find a use for the woman."

"I'll draw your neck for that, you son of a European," said Tob; "and if you do not clear off this deck I'll draw it here. Go," he cried, "you father of monkey children! Get away, and let me fight you fairly, or by my honour I'll stamp the inwards out of you, and make your silly crew wear them as necklaces."

Upon which Dason went to his galley.

Promptly Tob set going the machine on our own "Bear," and bawled his orders right and left to the other ships. The crew might be weak with scurvy, but they were quick to obey. Instantly the five vessels were all started, and because our Lord the Sun was shining brightly, got soon to the full of their pace. The whole of our small navy converged, singling out one ship of their opponents, and she, not being ready for so swift an attack, got flurried, and endeavoured to turn and run for room, instead of trying to meet us bows on. As a consequence, the whole of our five ships hit her together on the broadside, tearing her planking with their underwater beaks, and sinking her before we had backed clear from the engage.

But if we thus brought the enemy's number down to five, and so equal to our own, the advantage did not remain with us for long. The three nimble galleys formed into line: their boatswains' whips cracked as the slaves bent to their oars, and presently one of our own ships was gored and sunk, the men on her being killed in the water without hope of rescue.

And then commenced a tight-locked mêlée that would have warmed the heart of the greatest warrior alive. The ships and the galleys were forced together and lay savagely grinding one another upon the swells, as though they had been sentient animals. The men on board them shot their arrows, slashed with axes, thrust and hacked with swords, and hurled the throwing fire. But in every way the fight converged upon the "Bear." It was on her that the enemy spent the fiercest of their spite; it was to the "Bear," that the other crews of Tatho's navy rallied as their own vessels caught fire, or were sunk or taken.

Battle is an old acquaintance with us of the Priestly Clan, and for those of us who have had to carve out territories for the new colonies, it comes with enough frequency to cloy even the most chivalrous appetite. So I can speak here as a man of experience. Up till that time, for half a life-span, I had heard men shout "Deucalion" as a battlecry, and in my day had seen some lusty encounters. But this sea-fight surprised even me in its savage fierceness. The bleak, unstable element which surrounded us; the swaying decks on which we fought; the throwing fire, which burnt flesh and wood alike with its horrid flame; the great gluttonous man-eating birds that hovered in the sky overhead; the man-eating fish that swarmed up from the seas around, gnawing and quarrelling over those that fell into the waters, all went to make up a circumstance fit to daunt the bravest men-at-arms ever gathered for an army.

But these tarry shipmen faced it all with an indomitable courage, and never a cry of quailing. Life on the seas is so hard, and (from the beasts that haunt the great waters) so full of savage dangers, that Death has lost half his terrors to them through sheer familiarity. They were fellows who from pure lust for a fray would fight to a finish amongst themselves in the taverns ashore; and so here, in this desperate sea-battle, the passion for killing burned in them, as a fire stone from Heaven rages in a forest; and they took even their death-wounds laughing.

On our side the battle-cry was "Tob!" and the name of this obscure ship-captain seemed to carry a confidence with it for our own crews that many a well-known commander might have envied. The enemy had a dozen rallying cries, and these confused them. But as their other ship-commanders one by one were killed, and Dason remained, active with mischief, "Dason!" became the shout which was thrown back at us in response to our "Tob!"

However, I will not load my page with further long account of this obscure sea-fight, whose only glory was its ferocity. One by one all the ships of either side were sunk or lay with all their people killed, till finally only Dason's galley and our own "Bear" were left. For the moment we were being mastered. We had a score of men remaining out of all those that manned the navy when it sailed from Yucatan, and the enemy had boarded us and made the decks of the "Bear" the field of battle. But they had been over busy with the throwing fire, and presently, as we raged at one another, the smoke and the flame from the sturdy vessel herself let us very plainly know that she was past salvation.

But Tob was nothing daunted. "They may stay here and fry if they choose," he shouted with his great boisterous laugh, "but for ourselves the galley is good enough now. Keep a guard on Deucalion, and come with me, shipmates!"

"Tob!" our fellows shouted in their ecstasy of fighting madness, and I too could not forbear sending out a

"Tob!" for my battle-cry. It was a change for me not to be leader, but it was a luxury for once to fight in the wake of this Tob, despite his uncouthness of mien and plan. There was no stopping this new rush, though progress still was slow. Tob with his bloody axe cut the road in front, and we others, with the lust of battle filling us to the chin, raged like furies in his wake. Gods! but it was a fight.

Ten of us won to the galley, with the flames and the smoke from the poor "Bear" spurting at our heels. We turned and stabbed madly at all who tried to follow, and hacked through the grapples that held the vessels to their embrace. The sea-swells spurned the "Bear" away.

The slaves chained to the rowing-galley's benches had interest neither one way nor the other, and looked on the contest with dull concern, save when some stray missile found a billet amongst them. But a handful of the fighting men had scrambled desperately on board the galley after us, preferring any fate to a fiery death on the "Bear," and these had to be dealt with promptly. Three, with their fighting fury still red-hot in them, had most wastefully to be killed out of mischief's way; five, who had pitched their weapons into the sea, were chained to oar looms, in place of slaves who were dead; and there remained only Dason to have a fate apportioned.

The fight had cooled out of him, and he had thrown his arms to the sea, and stood sullenly ready for what might befall; and to him Tob went up with an exulting face.

"Ho, pot-mate Dason," cried he, "you made a lot of talk an hour ago about that woman of mine, who lives with her brats on the quay-side in Atlantis yonder. Now, I'll give you a pleasant choice; either I'll take you along home, and tell her what you said before the whole ship's company (that are for the most part dead now, poor souls!), and I'll leave her to perform on your carcase as she sees fit by way of payment; or, as the other choice, I'll deal with you here now myself."

"I thank you for the chance," said Dason, and knelt and offered his neck to the axe. So Tob cut off his head, sticking it on the galley's beak as an advertisement of what had been done. The body he threw over the side, and one of the great man-eating birds that hovered near, picked it up and flew away with it to its nest amongst the crags. And so we were free to get a meal of the fruits and the fresh meats which the galley offered, whilst the oar-slaves sent the galley rushing onwards towards the capital.

There was a wine-skin in the after-castle, and I filled a horn and poured some out at Tob's feet in salutation. "My man," I said, "you have shown me a fight."

"Thanks," said he, "and I know you are a judge. 'Twas pretty whilst it lasted; and, seeing that my lads were, for the most, scurvy-rotten, I will say they fought with credit. I have lost my Lord Tatho's navy, but I think Phorenice will see me righted there. If those that are against her took so much trouble to kill my Lord Deucalion before he could come to her aid, I can fancy she will not be niggard in her joy when I put Deucalion safe, if somewhat dented and blood-be-spattered, on the quay."

"The Gods know," I said, for it is never my custom to discuss policies with my inferiors, even though etiquette be for the moment loosened, as ours was then by the thrill of battle. "The Gods will decide what is best for you, Tob, even as they have decided that it is best that I should go on to Atlantis."

The sailor held a horn filled from the wine-skin in his hand, and I think was minded to pour a libation at my feet, even as I had done at his. But he changed his mind, and emptied it down his throat instead. "It is thirsty work, this fighting," he said, "and that drink comes very useful."

I put my hand on his blood-smeared arm. "Tob," I said, "whether I step into power again, or whether I go to the block to-morrow, is another matter which the Gods alone know, but hear me tell you now, that if a chance is given me of showing my gratitude, I shall not forget the way you have served me in this voyage, and the way you have fought this day."

Tob filled another brimming horn from the wine-skin and splashed it at my feet. "That's good enough surety for me," he said, "that my woman and brats never want from this day onward. The Lord Deucalion for the block, indeed!"

4. The Welcome of Phorenice

Now I can say it with all truth that, till the rival navy met us in the mouth of the gulf, I had thought little enough of my importance as a recruit for the Empress. But the laying in wait for us of those ships, and the wild ferocity with which they fought so that I might fall into their hands, were omens which the blindest could not fail to read. It was clear that I was expected to play a lusty part in the fortunes of the nation.

But if our coming had been watched for by enemies it seemed that Phorenice also had her scouts; and these saw us from the mountains, and carried news to the capital. The arm of the sea at the head of which the vast city of Atlantis stands, varies greatly in width. In places where the mountains have over-boiled, and sent their liquid contents down to form hard stone below, the channel has barely a river's wideness, and then beyond, for the next half-day's sail it will widen out into a lake, with the sides barely visible. Moreover, its course is winding, and so a runner who knows his way across the flats, and the swamps, and between the smoking hills which lie along the shore, and did not get overcome by fire-streams, or water, or wandering beasts, could carry news overland from seacoast to capital far speedier than even the most shrewdly whipped of galleys could ferry it along the water.

Of course there were heavy risks that a lone traveller would not make a safe passage by this land route, if he were bidden to sacrifice all precautions to speed. But Phorenice was no niggard with her couriers. She sent a corps of twenty to the headland that overlooks the sea-entrance to the straits; they started with the news, each on his own route; and it says much for their speed and cleverness, that no fewer than seven of these agile fellows came through scathless with their tidings, and of the others it was said that quite three were known to have survived.

Still, about this we had no means of knowing at the time, and pushed on in fancy that our coming was quite unheralded. The slaves on the galley's row-banks were for the most part savages from Europe, and the smell of them was so offensive that the voyage lost all its pleasures; and as, moreover, the wind carried with it an infinite abundance of small grit from some erupting fire mountain, we were anxious to linger as little as possible. Besides, if I may confess to such a thing without being unduly degraded, although by my priestly training I had been taught stoicism, and knew that all the future was in the hands of the Gods, I was frailly human still to have a very vast curiosity as to what would be the form of my own reception at Atlantis. I could imagine myself taken a formal prisoner on landing, and set on a formal trial to answer for my cure of the colony of Yucatan; I could imagine myself stepping ashore unknown and unnoticed, and after a due lapse, being sent for by the Empress to take up new duties; but the manner of my real welcome was a thing I did not even guess at.

We came in sight of the peak of the sacred mountain, with its glare of eternal fires which stand behind the city, one morning with the day's break, and the whips of the boatswains cracked more vehemently, so that those offensive slaves should give the galley a final spurt. The wind was adverse, and no sail could be spread, but under oars alone we made a pretty pace, and the sides of the sacred mountain grew longer, and presently the peaks of the pyramids in the city, the towers of the higher buildings, began to show themselves as though they floated upon the gleaming water. It was twenty years since I had seen Atlantis last, and my heart glowed with the thought of treading again upon her paving-stones.

The splendid city grew out of the sea as we approached, and to every throb of the oars, the shores leaped nearer. I saw the temple where I had been admitted first to manhood; I saw the pyramid in whose heart I had been initiated to the small mysteries; and then (as the lesser objects became discernible) I made out the house where a father and a mother had reared me, and my eyes became dim as the memories rose.

We drew up outside the white walls of the harbour, as the law was, and the slaves panted and sobbed in quietude over the oar-looms. For vessels thus stationed there is, generally, a sufficiency of waiting, for a port-captain is apt to be so uncertain of his own dignity, that he must e'en keep folks waiting to prove it to them. But here for us it might have been that the port-captain's boat was waiting. The signal was sounded from the two castles at the harbour's entrance, the chain which hung between them was dropped, and a ten-oared boat shot out from behind the walls as fast as oars could drive her. She raced up alongside and the questions were put:

"That should be Dason's galley?"

"It was," said Tob.

"Oh, I saw Dason's head on your beak," said the port-captain. "You were Tatho's captain?"

"And am still. Tatho's fleet was sent by Dason and

his friends to the sea-floor, and so we took this stinking galley to finish the voyage in, seeing that it was the only craft left afloat."

The port-captain was roving his eye over the group of us who stood on the after-deck. "I fear me, captain, that you'll have but a dangerous reception. I do not see my Lord Deucalion. Or does he come with some other navy? Gods, captain, if you have let him get killed whilst under your charge, the Empress will have the skin torn slowly off you living."

"What with Phorenice and Tatho both so curious for his welfare," said Tob, "my Lord Deucalion seems but a dangerous passenger. But I shall save my hide this voyage." He jerked at me with his thumb. "He's there to put in a word for me himself."

The port-captain stared for a moment, as if unbelieving, and then, as though satisfied, made obeisance like a fellow well used to ceremonial. "I trust my lord, in his infinite strength, will pardon my sin in not knowing him by his nobleness before. But truth to tell, I had looked to see my lord more suitably apparelled."

"Pish," I said; "if I choose to dress simply, I cannot object to being mistaken for a simple man. It is not my pleasure to advertise my quality by the gauds on my garb. If you think amends are due to me, I pray of your charity that this inquisition may end."

The fellow was all bows and obsequiousness. "I am the humblest of my lord's servants," he said. "It will be my exceeding honour to pilot my lord's galley into the berth appointed in harbour."

The boat shot ahead, and our galley-slaves swung into stroke again. Tob watched me with a dry smile as he stood directing the men at the helms.

"Well," I said, humouring his whim, "what is it?"

"I'm thinking," said Tob, "that my Lord Deucalion will remember me only as a very rude fellow when he steps ashore amongst all this fine gentility."

"You don't think," said I, "anything of the kind."

"Then I must prove my refinement," said Tob,

"and not contradict." He picked up my hand in his huge, hard fist, and pressed it. "By the Gods, Deucalion, you may be a great prince, but I've only known you as a man. You're the finest fighter of beasts and men that walks this world to-day, and I love you for it. That spear-stroke of yours on the lizard is a thing the singers in the taverns shall make chaunts about."

We drew rapidly into the harbour, the soldiers in the entrance castle blowing their trumpets in welcome as we passed between them. The captain of the port had run up my banner to the masthead of his boat, having been provided with one apparently for this purpose of announcement, and from the quays, across the vast basin of the harbour, there presently came to us the noises of musicians, and the pale glow of welcoming fires, dancing under the sunlight. I was almost awed to think that an Empress of Atlantis had come to such straits as to feel an interest like this in any mere returning subject.

It was clear that nothing was to be done by halves. The port-captain's boat led, and we had no choice but to follow. Our galley was run up alongside the royal quay and moored to its posts and rings of gold, all of which are sacred to the reigning house.

"If Dason could only have foreseen this honour," said Tob, with grisly jest, "I'm sure he'd have laid in a silken warp to make fast on the bollards instead of mere plebeian hemp. I'm sure there'd be a frown on Dason's head this minute, if the sun hadn't scorched it stiff. My Lord Deucalion, will you pick your way with niceness over this common ship and tread on the genteel carpet they've spread for you on the quay yonder?"

The port-captain heard Tob's rude banter and looked up with a face of horror, and I remembered, with a small sigh, that colonial freedom would have no place here in Atlantis. Once more I must prepare myself for all the dignity of rank, and make ready to tread the formalities of vast and gorgeous ceremonial.

But, be these things how they may, a self-respecting man must preserve his individuality also, and though I consented to enter a pavilion of crimson cloth, specially erected to shelter me till the Empress should deign to arrive, there my complaisance ended. Again the matter of clothes was harped upon. The three gorgeously caparisoned chamberlains, who had inducted me to the shelter, laid before me changes of raiment bedecked with every imaginable kind of frippery, and would have me transform myself into a popinjay in fashion like their own.

Curtly enough, I refused to alter my garb, and when one of them stammeringly referred to the Empress's tastes I asked him with plainness if he had got any definite commands on this paltry matter from her mightiness.

Of course, he had to confess that there were none.

Upon which I retorted that Phorenice had commanded Deucalion, the man, to attend before her, and had sent no word of her pleasure as to his outer casing.

"This dress," I said, "suits my temper well. It shields my poor body from the heat and the wind, and, moreover, it is clean. It seems to me, sirs," I added, "that your interfering savours somewhat of an impertinence."

With one accord the chamberlains drew their swords and pushed the hilts towards me.

"It would be a favour," said their spokesman, "if the great Lord Deucalion would take his vengeance now, instead of delivering us to the tormentors hereafter."

"Poof," I said, "the matter is forgotten. You make too much of a little."

Nevertheless, their action gave me some enlightenment. They were perfectly in earnest in offering me the swords, and I recognised that this was a different Atlantis that I had come home to, where a man had dread of the torture for a mere difference concerning the cut of a coat.

There was a bath in the pavilion, and in that I regaled myself gladly, though there was some paltry scent added to the water that took away half its refreshing power; and then I set myself to wait with all outward composure and placidity. The chamberlains were too well-bred to break into my calm, and I did not condescend to small talk. So there we remained, the four of us, I sitting, they standing, with our Lord the Sun smiting heavily on the scarlet roof of the pavilion, whilst the music blared, and the welcoming fires dispersed their odours from the great paved square without, which faced upon the quay.

It has been said that the great should always collect dignity by keeping those of lesser degree waiting their pleasure, though for myself I must say I have always thought the stratagem paltry and beneath me. Phorenice also seemed of this opinion, for (as she herself told me later) at the moment that Tob's galley was reported as having its flank against the marble of the royal quay, at that precise moment did she start out from the palace. The gorgeous procession was already marshalled, bedecked, and waiting only for its chiefest ornament, and as soon as she had mounted to her steed, trumpets gave the order, and the advance began.

Sitting in the doorway of the pavilion, I saw the soldiery who formed the head of this vast concourse emerge from the great broad street where it left the houses. They marched straight across to give me the salute, and then ranged themselves on the farther side of the square. Then came the Mariners' Guild, then more soldiers, all making obeisance in their turn, and passing on to make room for others. Following were the merchants, the tanners, the spear-makers and all the other acknowledged Guilds, deliberately attired (so it seemed to me) that they might make a pageant; and whilst most walked on foot, there were some who proudly rode on beasts which they had tamed into rendering them this menial service.

But presently came the two wonders of all that dazzling spectacle. From out of the eclipse of the houses there swung into the open no less a beast than a huge bull mammoth. The sight had sufficient surprise in it almost to make me start. Many a time during my life had I led hunts to kill the mammoth, when a herd of them had raided some village or cornland under my charge. I had seen the huge brutes in the wild ground, shaggy, horrid, monstrous; more fierce than even the cave-tiger or the cave-bear; most dangerous beast of all that fight with man for dominion of the earth, save only for a few of the greater lizards. And here was this creature, a giant even amongst mammoths, yet tame as any well-whipped slave, and bearing upon its back a great half-castle of gold, stamped with the outstretched hand, and bedecked with silver snakes. Its murderous tusks were gilded, its hairy neck was garlanded with flowers, and it trod on in the procession as though assisting at such pageantry was the beginning and end of its existence. Its tameness seemed a fitting symbol of the masterful strength of this new ruler of Atlantis.

Simultaneously with the mammoth, there came into sight that other and greater wonder, the mammoth's mistress, the Empress Phorenice. The beast took my eye at the first, from its very uncouth hugeness, from its show of savage power restrained; but the lady who sat in the golden half-castle on its lofty back quickly drew away my gaze, and held it immovable from then onwards with an infinite attraction.

I stood to my feet when the people first shouted at Phorenice's approach, and remained in the porchway of my scarlet pavilion till her vast steed had halted in the centre of the square, and then I advanced across the pavement towards her.

"On your knees, my lord," said one of the chamberlains behind me, in a scared whisper.

"At least with bent head," urged another.

But I had my own notions of what is due to one's own self-respect in these matters, and I marched across the bare open space with head erect, giving the Empress gaze for gaze. She was clearly summing me up. I was frankly doing the like by her. Gods! but those few short seconds made me see a woman such as I never imagined could have lived.

I know I have placed it on record earlier in this writing that, during all the days of a long official life, women have had no influence over me. But I have been quick to see that they often had a strong swaying power over the policies of others, and as a consequence I have made it my business to study them even as I have studied men. But this woman who sat under the sacred snakes in her golden half-castle on the mammoth's back, fairly baffled me. Of her thoughts I could read no single syllable. I coul' see a body slight, supple, and beautifully moulded; in figure rather small. Her face was a most perfect book of cleverness, yet she was fair, too, beyond belief, with hair of a lovely ruddiness, cut short in the new fashion, and bunching on her shoulders. And eyes! Gods! who could plumb the depths of Phorenice's eyes, or find in mere tint a trace of their heaven-made colour?

It was plain, also, that she in her turn was searching me down to my very soul, and it seemed that her scrutiny was not without its satisfaction. She moved her head in little nods as I drew near, and when I did the requisite obeisance permitted to my rank, she bade me in a voice loud and clear enough for all at hand to hear, never to put forehead on the ground again on her behalf so long as she ruled in Atlantis.

"For others," she said, "it is fitting that they should do so, once, twice, or several times, according to their rank and station, for I am Empress, and they are all so far beneath me; but you are Deucalion, my lord, and though till to-day I knew you only from pictures drawn with tongues, I have seen you now, and have judged for myself. And so I make this decree: Deucalion is above all other men in Atlantis, and if there is one who does not render him obedience, that man is enemy also of Phorenice, and shall feel her anger."

She made a sign, and a stair was brought, and then

she called to me, and I mounted and sat beside her in the golden half-castle under the canopy of royal snakes. The girl who stood behind in attendance fanned us both with perfumed feathers, and at a word from Phorenice the mammoth was turned, bearing us back towards the royal pyramid by the way through which it had come. At the same time also all the other machinery of splendour was put in motion. The soldiers and the gaudily bedecked civil traders fell into procession before and behind, and I noted that a body of troops, heavily armed, marched on each of the mammoth's flanks.

Phorenice turned to me with a smile. "You piqued me," she said, "at first."

"Your Majesty overwhelms me with so much notice."

"You looked at my steed before you looked at me. A woman finds it hard to forgive a slight like that."

"I envied you the greatest of your conquests, and do still. I have fought mammoths myself, and at times have killed, but I never dared even to think of taking one alive and bringing it into tameness."

"You speak boldly," she said, still smiling, "and yet you can turn a pretty compliment. Faugh! Deucalion, the way these people fawn on me gives me a nausea. I am not of the same clay as they are, I know; but just because I am the daughter of Gods they must needs feed me on the pap of insincerity."

So Tatho was right, and the swineherd was forgotten. Well, if she chose to keep up the fiction she had made, it was not my part to contradict her. Rightly or wrongly she was Empress, and without competitor, and anyway I was her servant.

"I have been pining this long enough for a stronger meat than they can give," she went on, "and at last I have sent for you. I have been at some pains to procure my tongue-pictures of you, Deucalion, and though you do not know me yet, I may say I knew you with all thoroughness even before we met. I can admire a man with a mind great enough to forego the silly gauds of clothes, or the excesses of feasts, or the pamperings of women." She looked down at her own silks and her glittering jewels. "We women like to carry colours upon our persons, but that is a different matter. And so I sent for you here to be my minister, and bear with me the burden of ruling."

"There should be better men in broad Atlantis."

"There are not, my lord, and I who know them all by heart tell you so. They are all enamoured of my poor person; they weary me with their empty phrases and their importunities; and, though they are always brimming with their cries of service, their own advancement and the filling of their own treasuries ever comes first with them. So I have sent for you, Deucalion, the one strong man in all the world. You at least will not sigh to be my lover?"

I saw her watching for my answer from the corner of her eyes. "The Empress," I said, "is my mistress, and I will be an honest minister to her. With Phorenice, the woman, it is likely that I shall have little enough to do. Besides, I am not the sort that sports with this toy they call love."

"And yet you are a personable man enough," she said rather thoughtfully. "But that still further proves your strength, Deucalion. You at least will not lose your head through weak infatuation for my poor looks and graces."—She turned to the girl who stood behind us. —"Ylga, fan not so violently."

Our talk broke off then for the moment, and I had time to look about me. We were passing through the chief street in the fairest, the most wonderful city this world has ever seen. I had left it a score of years before, and was curious to note its increase.

In public buildings the city had certainly made growth; there were new temples, new pyramids, new palaces, and statuary everywhere. Its greatness and magnificence impressed me more strongly even than usual, returning to it as I did from such a distance of time and space, for, though the many cities of Yucatan might each of them be princely, this great capital was a place not to be compared with any of them. It was imperial and gorgeous beyond descriptive words.

Yet most of all was I struck by the poverty and squalor which stood in such close touch with all this magnificence. In the throngs that lined the streets there were gaunt bodies and hungry faces everywhere. Here and there stood one, a man or a woman, as naked as a savage in Europe, and yet dull to shame. Even the trader, with trumpery gauds on his coat, apeing the prevailing fashion for display, had a scared, uneasy look to his face, as though he had forgotten the mere name of safety, and hid a frantic heart with his tawdry outward vauntings of prosperity.

Phorenice read the direction of my looks.

"The season," she said, "has been unhealthy of recent months. These lower people will not build fine houses to adorn my city, and because they choose to live on in their squalid, unsightly kennels, there have been calentures and other sicknesses amongst them, which make them disinclined for work. And then, too, for the moment, earning is not easy. Indeed, you may say trade is nearly stopped this last half-year, since the rebels have been hammering so lustily at my city gates."

I was fairly startled out of my decorum.

"Rebels!" I cried. "Who are hammering at the gates of Atlantis? Is the city in a state of siege?"

"Of their condescension," said Phorenice lightly, "they are giving us holiday to-day, and so, happily, my welcome to you comes undisturbed. If they were fighting, your ears would have told you of it. To give them their due, they are noisy enough in all their efforts. My spies say they are making ready new engines for use against the walls, which you may sally out to-morrow and break if it gives you amusement. But for to-day, Deucalion, I have you, and you have me, and there is peace round us, and some prettiness of display. If you ask for more I will give it you."

"I did not know of this rebellion," I said, "but as Your Majesty has made me your minister, it is well that I should know all about its scope at once. This is a matter we should be serious upon."

"And do you think I cannot take it seriously also?" she retorted. "Ylga," she said to the girl that stood behind, "set loose my dress at the shoulder."

And when the attendant had unlinked the jewelled clasp (as it seemed to me with a very ill grace), she herself stripped down the fabric, baring the pure skin beneath, and showing me just below the curve of the left breast a bandage of bloodstained linen.

"There is a guarantee of my seriousness yesterday, at any rate," she said, looking at me sidelong. "The arrow struck on a rib and that saved me. If it had struck between, Deucalion would have been standing beside my funeral pyre to-day instead of riding on this pretty steed of mine which he admires so much. Your eye seems to feast itself most on the mammoth, Deucalion. Ah, poor me. I am not one of your shaggy creatures, and so it seems I shall never be able to catch your regard. Ylga," she said to the girl behind, "you may link my dress up again with its clasp. My Lord Deucalion has seen wounds before, and there is nothing else here to interest him."

5. Zaemon's Curse

It appeared that for the present at any rate I was to have my residence in the royal pyramid. The glittering cavalcade drew up in the great paved square which lies before the building, and massed itself in groups.

The mammoth was halted before the doorway, and when a stair had been brought, the trumpets sounded, and we three who had ridden in the golden half-castle under the canopy of snakes, descended to the ground.

It was plain that we were going from beneath the open sky to the apartments which lay inside the vast stone mazes of the pyramid, and without thinking, the instinct of custom and reverence that had become part of my nature caused me to turn to where the towering rocks of the Sacred Mountain frowned above the city, and make the usual obeisance, and offer up in silence the prescribed prayer. I say I did this thing unthinking, and as a matter of common custom, but when I rose to my feet, I could have sworn I heard a titter of laughter from somewhere in that fancifully bedecked crowd of onlookers.

I glanced in the direction of the scoffers, frowningly enough, and then I turned to Phorenice to demand their prompt punishment for the disrespect. But here was a strange thing. I had looked to see her in the act and article of rising from an obeisance; but there she was, standing erect, and had clearly never touched her forehead to the ground. Moreover, she was regarding me with a queer look which I could not fathom.

But whatever was in her mind, she had no plan to bawl about it then before the people collected in the square. She said to me, "Come," and, turning to the doorway, cried for entrance, giving the secret word appointed for the day. The ponderous stone blocks, which barred the porch, swung back on their hinges, and with stately tread she passed out of the hot sunshine into the cool gloom beyond, with the fan-girl following decorously at her heels. With a heaviness beginning to grow at my heart, I too went inside the pyramid, and the stone doors, with a sullen thud, closed behind us.

We did not go far just then. Phorenice halted in the hall of waiting. How well I remembered the place, with the pictures of kings on its red walls, and the burning fountain of earth-breath which blazed from a jet of bronze in the middle of the flooring and gave it light. The old King that was gone had come this far of his complaisance when he bade me farewell as I set out twenty years before for my vice-royalty in Yucatan. But the air of the hall was different to what it had been in those old days. Then it was pure and sweet. Now it was heavy with some scent, and I found it languid and oppressive.

"My minister," said the Empress, "I acquit you of intentional insult; but I think the colonial air has made you a very simple man. Such an obeisance as you showed to that mountain not a minute since has not been made since I was sent to reign over this kingdom."

"Your Majesty," I said, "I am a member of the Priests' Clan and was brought up in their tenets. I have been taught, before entering a house, to thank the Gods, and more especially our Lord the Sun, for the good air that He and They have provided. It has been my fate more than once to be chased by streams of fire and stinking air amongst the mountains during one of their sudden boils, and so I can say the prescribed prayer upon this matter straight from my heart."

"Circumstances have changed since you left Atlantis," said Phorenice, "and when thanks are given now, they are not thrown at those old Gods."

I saw her meaning, and almost started at the impiety of it. If this was to be the new rule of things, I would have no hand in it. Fate might deal with me as it chose. To serve truly a reigning monarch, that I was prepared for; but to palter with sacrilege, and accept a swineherd's daughter as a God, who should receive prayers and obeisances, revolted my manhood. So I invited a crisis.

"Phorenice," I said, "I have been a priest from my childhood up, revering the Gods, and growing intimate with their mysteries. Till I find for myself that those old things are false, I must stand by that allegiance, and if there is a cost for this faithfulness I must pay it."

She looked at me with a slow smile. "You are a strong man, Deucalion," she said.

I bowed.

"I have heard others as stubborn," she said, "but they were converted." She shook out the ruddy bunches of her hair, and stood so that the light of the burning earth-breath might fall on the loveliness of her face and form. "I have found it as easy to convert the stubborn as to burn them. Indeed, there has been little talk of burning. They have all rushed to conversion, whether I would or no. But it seems that my poor looks and tongue are wanting in charm to-day."

"Phorenice is Empress," I said stolidly, "and I am her servant. To-morrow, if she gives me leave, I will clear away this rabble which clamours outside the walls. I must begin to prove my uses."

"I am told you are a pretty fighter," said she. "Well, I hold some small skill in arms myself, and have a conceit that I am something of a judge. To-morrow we will take a taste of battle together. But to-day I must carry through the honourable reception I have planned for you, Deucalion. The feast will be set ready soon, and you will wish to make ready for the feast. There are chambers here selected for your use, and stored with what is needful. Ylga will show you their places."

We waited, the fan-girl and I, till Phorenice had passed out of the glow of the light-jet, and had left the hall of waiting through a doorway amongst the shadows of its farther angle, and then (the girl taking a lamp and leading) we also threaded our way through the narrow mazes of the pyramid.

Everywhere the air was full of perfumes, and everywhere the passages turned and twisted and doubled through the solid stone of the pyramid, so that strangers might have spent hours—yes, or days—in search before they came to the chamber they desired. There was a fine cunningness about those forgotten builders who set up this royal pyramid. They had no mind that kings should fall by the hand of vulgar assassins who might come in suddenly from outside. And it is said also that the king of the time, to make doubly sure, killed all that had built the pyramid, or seen even the lay of its inner stones.

But the fan-girl led the way with the lamp swinging in her hand, as one accustomed to the mazes. Here she doubled, there she turned, and here she stopped in the middle of a blank wall to push a stone, which swung to let us pass. And once she pressed at the corner of a flagstone on the floor, which reared up to the thrust of her foot, and showed us a stair steep and narrow. That we descended, coming to the foot of an inclined way which led us upward again; and so by degrees we came unto the chamber which had been given for my use.

"There is raiment in all these chests which stand by the walls," said the girl, "and jewels and gauds in that bronze coffer. They are Phorenice's first presents, she bid me say, and but a small earnest of what is to come. My Lord Deucalion can drop his simplicity now, and fig himself out in finery to suit the fashion."

"Girl," I said sharply, "be more decorous with your tongue, and spare me such small advice."

"If my Lord Deucalion thinks this a rudeness, he can give a word to Phorenice, and I shall be whipped. If he asks it, I can be stripped and scourged before him. The Empress will do much for Deucalion just now."

"Girl," I said, "you are nearer to that whipping than you think for."

"I have got a name," she retorted, looking at me sullenly from under her black brows. "They call me Ylga. You might have heard that as we rode here on the mammoth, had you not been so wrapped up in Phorenice."

I gazed at her curiously. "You have never seen me before," I said, "and the first words you utter are those that might well bring trouble to yourself. There is some object in all this."

She went and pushed to the massive stone that swung

in the doorway of the chamber. Then she put her little jewelled fingers on my garment and drew me carefully away from the airshaft into the farther corner. "I am the daughter of Zaemon," she said. "whom you knew."

"You bring me some message from him?"

"How could I? He lives in the priests' dwellings on the Mountain you did obeisance to. I have not put eyes on him these two years. But when I saw you first step out from that red pavilion they had pitched at the harbour side, I—I felt a pity for you, Deucalion. I remembered you were my father's, Zaemon's, friend, and I knew what Phorenice had in store. She has been plotting it all these two months."

"I cannot hear words against the Empress."

"And yet——"

"What?"

She stamped her sandal upon the stone of the floor. "You must be a very blind man, Deucalion, or a very daring one. But I shall not interfere further; at least not now. Still, I shall watch, and if at any time you seem to want a friend I will try and serve you."

"I thank you for your friendship."

"You seem to take it lightly enough. Why, sir, even now I do not believe you know my power, any more than you guess my motive. You may be first man in this kingdom, but let me tell you I rank as second lady. And remember, women stand high in Atlantis now. Believe me, my friendship is a commodity that has been sought with frequence and industry."

"And as I say, I am grateful for it. You seem to think little enough of my gratitude, Ylga; but, credit me, I never have bestowed it on a woman before, and so you should treasure it for its rarity."

"Well," she said, "my lord, there is an education before you." She left me then, showing me how to call slaves when I wished for their help, and for a full minute I stood wondering at the words I had spoken to her. Who was this daughter of Zaemon that she should induce me to change the habit of a lifetime?

The slaves came at my bidding, and showed themselves anxious to deck me with a thousand foolishnesses
in the matter of robes and gauds, and (what seemed
to be the modern fashion of their class) holding out the
virtues of a score of perfumes and unguents. Their
manner irritated me. Clean I was already, and shaved;
my hair was trim, and my robe was unsoiled; and,
considering these pressing attentions of theirs something
of an impertinence, I set them to beat one another as a
punishment, promising that if they did not do it with
thoroughness, I would hand them on to the brander to
be marked with stripes which would endure. It is
strange, but a common menial can often surpass even a
rebellious general in power of ruffling one.

I had seen many strange sights that day, and under-
gone many new sensations; but of all the things which
came to my notice, Phorenice's manner of summoning
the guests to her feast surprised me most. Nay, it did
more; it shocked me profoundly; and I cannot say
whether amazement at her profanity, or wonder at her
power, was for the moment strongest in my breast. I sat
in my chamber awaiting the summons, when gradually,
growing out of nothing, a sound fell upon my ear which
increased in volume with infinitely small graduations,
till at last it became a clanging din which hurt the ear
with its fierceness; and then (I guessed what was
coming) the whole massive fabric of the pyramid
trembled and groaned and shook, as though it had been
merely a child's wooden toy brushed about by a strong
man's sandal.

It was the portent served out yearly by the chiefs of
the Priests' Clan on the Sacred Mountain, when they
bade all the world take count of their sins. It was the
sacred reminder that from roaring, raging fire, and from
the agony of monstrous earth-tremors, man had been
born, and that by these same agencies he would even-
tually be swallowed up—he and the sins within his
breast. And here the Empress was prostituting its

solemnities into a mere call to gluttony, and sign for ribald laughter and sensuous display.

But how had she acquired the authority to do this thing? Who was she that she should tamper with those dimly understood powers, the forces that dwell within the liquid heart of our mother earth? Had there been treachery? Had some member of the Priests' Clan forgotten his sacred vows, and babbled to this woman matters concerning the holy mysteries? Or had Phorenice discovered a key to these mysteries with her own agile brain?

If that last was the case, I could continue to serve her with silent conscience. Though she might be none of my making, at least she was Empress, and it was my duty to give her obedience. But if she had suborned some weaker member of the Clan on the Sacred Mount, that would be a different matter. For be it remembered that it was one of the elements of our constitution to preserve our secrets and mysteries inviolate, and to pursue with undying hatred both the man who had dared to betray them, and the unhappy recipient of his confidence.

It was with very undecided feelings, then, that I obeyed the summons of the earth-shaking, and bade the slaves lead me through the windings of the pyramid to the great banqueting-hall. The scene there was dazzling. The majestic chamber with its marvellous carvings was filled with a company decked out with all the gauds and colours that fancy could conceive. Little recked they of the solemn portent which had summoned them to the meal, of the death and misery that stalked openly through the city wards without, of the rebels which lay in leaguer beyond the walls, of the neglected Gods and their clan of priests on the Sacred Mountain. They were all gluttonous for the passions of the moment; it was their fashion and conceit to look at nothing beyond.

Flaming jets of earth-breath lit the great hall to the brightness of midday; and when I stepped out upon the pavement, trumpets blared, so that all might know of my coming. But there was no roar of welcome. "Deucalion," they lisped with mincing voices, bowing themselves ridiculously to the ground so that all their ornaments and silks might jangle and swish. Indeed, when Phorenice herself appeared, and all sent up their cries and made lawful obeisance, there was the same artificiality in the welcome. They meant well enough, it is true; but this was the new fashion. Heartiness had come to be accounted a barbarism by this new culture.

A pair of posturing, smirking chamberlains took me in charge, and ushered me with their flimsy golden wands to the daïs at the farther end. It appeared that I was to sit on Phorenice's divan, and eat my meat out of her dish.

"There is no stint to the honour the Empress puts upon me," I said, as I knelt down and took my seat.

She gave me one of her queer, sidelong looks. "Deucalion may have more beside, if he asks for it prettily. He may have what all the other men in the known world have sighed for, and what none of them will ever get. But I have given enough of my own accord; he must ask me warmly for those further favours."

"I ask," I said, "first, that I may sweep the boundaries clear of this rabble which is clamouring against the city walls."

"Pah," she said, and frowned. "Have you appetite only for the sterner pleasures of life? My good Deucalion, they must have been rustic folk in that colony of yours. Well, you shall give me news now of the toothsomeness of this feast."

Dishes and goblets were placed before us, and we began to eat, though I had little enough appetite for victual so broken and so highly spiced. But if this finicking cookery and these luscious wines did not appeal to me, the other diners in that gorgeous hall appreciated it all to the full. They sat about in groups on the pavement beneath the light-jets like a tangle of rainbows for colour, and according to the new custom they went into raptures and ecstasies over their enjoyment. Women and men both, they lingered over each titillation of the palate as though it were a caress of the Gods.

Phorenice, with her quick, bright eyes, looked on, and occasionally flung one or another a few words between her talk with me, and now and again called some favoured creature up to receive a scrap of viand from the royal dish. This the honoured one would eat with extravagant gesture, or (as happened twice) would put it away in the folds of his clothes as a treasure too dear to be profaned by human lips.

To me, this flattery appeared gross and disgustful, but Phorenice, through use, perhaps, seemed to take it as merely her due. There was, one had to suppose, a weakness in her somewhere, though truly to the outward seeing none was apparent. Her face was strong enough, and it was subtle also, and, moreover, it was wondrous comely. All the courtiers in the banqueting-hall raved about Phorenice's face and the other beauties of her body and limbs, and though not given to appreciation in these matters, I could not but see that here at least they had a groundwork for their admiration, for surely the Gods have never favoured mortal woman more highly. Yet lovely though she might be, for myself I preferred to look upon Ylga, the girl, who, because of her rank, was privileged to sit on the divan behind us as immediate attendant. There was an honesty in Ylga's face which Phorenice's lacked.

They did not eat to nutrify their bodies, these feasters in the banqueting-hall of the royal pyramid, but they all ate to cloy themselves, and they strutted forth new usages with every platter and bowl that the slaves brought. To me some of their manners were closely touching on disrespect. At the halfway of the meal, a gorgeous popinjay—he was a governor of an out-province driven into the capital by a rebellion in his own lands—this gorgeous fop, I say, walked up between the groups of feasters with flushed face and unsteady gait, and did obeisance before the divan. "Most astounding Empress," cried he, "fairest among the Goddesses, Queen regnant of my adoring heart, hail!"

Phorenice with a smile stretched him out her cup. I looked to see him pour respectful libation, but no such thing. He set the drink to his lips and drained it to the final drop. "May all your troubles," he cried, "pass from you as easily, and leave as pleasant a flavour."

The Empress turned to me with one of her quick looks. "You do not like this new habit?"

To which I replied bluntly enough that to pour out liquor at a person's feet had grown through custom to be a mark of respect, but that drinking it seemed to me mere self-indulgence, which might be practised anywhere.

"You still keep to the old austere teachings," she said. "Our newer code bids us enjoy life first, and order other things so as not to meddle with our more immediate pleasure."

And so the feast went on, the guests practising their gluttonies and their absurdities, and the guards standing to their arms round the circuit of the walls as motionless and as stern as the statues carven in the white stone beyond them. But a term was put to the orgy with something of suddenness. There was a stir at the farther doorway of the banqueting-hall, and a clash, as two of the guards joined their spears across the entrance. But the man they tried to stop—or perhaps it was to pin— passed them unharmed, and walked up over the pavement between the lights, and the groups of feasters. All looked round at him; a few threw him ribald words; but none ventured to stop his progress. A few, women chiefly, I could see, shuddered as he passed them by, as though a wintry chill had come over them; and in the end he walked up and stood in front of Phorenice's divan, and gazed fixedly on her, but without making obeisance.

He was a frail old man, with white hair tumbling on his shoulders, and ragged white beard. The mud of wayfaring hung in clots on his feet and legs. His wizened body was bare save for a single cloth wound about his shoulders and his loins, and he carried in his hand a wand with the symbol of our Lord the Sun glowing at its tip. That wand went to show his caste, but in no other way could I recognise him.

I took him for one of those ascetics of the Priests' Clan, who had forsworn the steady nurtured life of the Sacred Mountain, and who lived out in the dangerous lands amongst the burning hills, where there is daily peril from falling rocks, from fire streams, from evil vapours, from sudden fissuring of the ground, and from other movements of those unstable territories, and from the greater lizards and other monstrous beasts which haunt them. These keep constant in the memory the might of the Holy Gods, and the insecurity of this frail earth on which we have our resting-place, and so the sojourners there become chastened in the spirit, and gain power over mysteries which even the most studious and learned of other men can never hope to attain.

A silence filled the room when the old man came to his halt, and Phorenice was the first to break it. "Those two guards," she said, in her clear, carrying voice, "who held the door, are not equal to their work. I cannot have imperfect servants; remove them."

The soldiers next in the rank lifted their spears and drove them home, and the two fellows who had admitted the old man fell to the ground. One shrieked once, the other gave no sound: they were clever thrusts both.

The old man found his voice, thin, and high, and broken. "Another crime added to your tally, Phorenice. Not half your army could have hindered my entrance had I wished to come, and let me tell you that I am here to bring you your last warning. The Gods have shown you much favour; they gave you merit by which you could rise above your fellows, till at last only the throne stood above you. It was seen good by those on the Sacred Mountain to let you have this last ambition, and sit on this throne that has so long and honourably been filled by the ancient kings of Atlantis."

The Empress sat back on the divan smiling. "I seemed to get these things as I chose, and in spite of your friends' teeth. I may owe to you, old man, a small parcel of thanks, though that I offered to repay; but for my lords the priests, their permission was of small enough value when it came. I would have you remember that I was as firm on the throne of Atlantis as this pyramid stands upon its base when your worn-out priests came up to give their tottering benediction."

The old man waved aside her interruption. "Hear me out," he said. "I am here with no trivial message. There is nothing paltry about the threat I can throw at you, Phorenice. With your fire-tubes, your handling of troops, and your other fiendish clevernesses, you may not be easy to overthrow by mere human means, though, forsooth, these poor rebels who yap against your city walls have contrived to hold their ground for long enough now. It may be that you are becoming enervated; I do not know. It may be that you are too wrapped up in your feastings, your dressings, your pomps, and your debaucheries, to find leisure to turn to the art of war. It may be that the man's spirit has gone out from your arm and brain, and you are a woman once more—weak, and pleasure-loving; again I do not know.

"But this must happen: You must undo the evil you have done; you must give bread to the people who are starving, even if you take it from these gluttons in this hall; you must restore Atlantis to the state in which it was entrusted to you: or else you must be removed. It cannot be permitted that the country should sink back into the lawlessness and barbarism from which its ancient kings have digged it. You hear, Phorenice. Now give me true answer."

"Speak him fair. Oh! For the sake of your fortune, speak him fair," came Ylga's voice in a hurried whisper from behind us. But the Empress took no notice of it.

She leaned forward on the cushions of the divan with a knit brow.

"Do you dare to threaten me, old man, knowing what I am?"

"I know your origin," he said gravely, "as well as you know it yourself. As for my daring, that is a small matter. He need be but a timid man who dares to say words that the High Gods put on his lips."

"I shall rule this kingdom as I choose. I shall brook interference from no creature on this earth, or beneath it, or in the sky above. The Gods have chosen me to be Their regent in Atlantis, and They do not depose me through such creatures as you. Go away, old man, and play the fanatic in another court. It is well that I have an ancient kindliness for you, or you would not leave this place unharmed."

"Now, indeed, you are lost," I heard Ylga murmur from behind, and the old man in front of us did not move a step. Instead, he lifted up the Symbol of our Lord the Sun, and launched his curse. "Your blasphemy gives the reply I asked for. Hear me now make declaration of war on behalf of Those against whom you have thrown your insults. You shall be overthrown and sent to the nether Gods. At whatever cost the land shall be purged of you and yours, and all the evil that has been done to it whilst you have sullied the throne of its ancient kings. You will not amend, neither will you yield tamely. You vaunt that you sit as firm on your throne as this pyramid reposes on its base. See how little you know of what the future carries. I say to you that, whilst you are yet Empress, you shall see this royal pyramid which you have polluted with your debaucheries torn tier from tier, and stone from stone, and scattered as feathers spread before a wind."

"You may wreck the pyramid," said Phorenice contemptuously. "I myself have some knowledge of the earth forces, as I have shown this night. But though you crumble every stone above us now and grind it into grit and dust, I shall still be Empress. What force can you crazy priests bring against me that I cannot throw back and destroy?"

"We have a weapon that was forged in no mortal smithy," shrilled the old man, "whereof the key is now lodged in the Ark of the Mysteries. But that weapon can be used only as a last resource. The nature of it even is too awful to be told in words. Our other powers will be launched against you first, and for this poor country's sake I pray that they may cause you to wince. Yet rest assured, Phorenice, that we shall not step aside once we have put a hand to this matter. We shall carry it through, even though the cost be a universal burning and destruction. For know this, daughter of the swine-herd, it is agreed amongst the most High Gods that you are too full of sin to continue unchecked."

"Speak him fairly," Ylga urged from behind. "He has a power at which you cannot even guess."

The Empress made to rise, but Ylga clung to her skirt. "For the sake of your fame," she urged, "for the sake of your life, do not defy him." But Phorenice struck her fiercely aside, and faced the old man in a tumult of passion. "You dare call me a blasphemer, who blaspheme yourself? You dare cast slurs upon my birth, who am come direct from the most high Heaven? Old man, your craziness protects you in part, but not in all. You shall be whipped. Do you hear me? I say, whipped. The lean flesh shall be scourged from your scraggy bones, and you shall totter away from this place as a red and bleeding example for those who would dare traduce their Empress. Here, some of you, I say, take that man, and let him be whipped where he stands."

Her cry went out clearly enough. But not a soul amongst those glittering feasters stirred in his place. Not a soldier amongst the guards stepped from his rank. The place was hung in a terrible silence. It seemed as though no one within the hall dared so much as to draw a breath. All felt that the very air was big with fate.

Phorenice, with her head crouched forward, looked from one group to another. Her face was working. "Have I no true servants," she asked, "amongst all you pretty lip-servers?"

Still no one moved. They stood, or sat, or crouched like people fascinated. For myself, with the first words he had uttered, I had recognised the old man by his voice. It was Zaemon, the weak governor who had given the Empress her first step towards power; that earnest searcher into the mysteries, who knew more of their powers, and more about the hidden forces, than any other dweller on the Sacred Mountain, even at that time when I left for my colony. And now, during his strange hermit life, how much more might he not have learned? I was torn by warring duties. I owed much to the Priests' Clan, by reason of my oath and membership; it seemed I owed no less to Phorenice. And, again, was Zaemon the truly accredited envoy of the high council of the priests of the Sacred Mountain? And was the Empress of a truth deposed by the High Gods above, or was she still Empress, and still the commander of my duty? I could not tell, and so I sat in my seat awaiting what the event would show.

Phorenice's fury was growing. "Do I stand alone here?" she cried. "Have I pampered you creatures out of all touch with gratitude? It seems that at least I want a new chief to my guards. Ho! Who will be chief of the guards of the Empress?"

There was a shifting of eyes, a hesitation. Then a great burly form strode up from the farther end of the hall, and a perceptible shudder went up from all the others as they watched him.

"So, Tarca, you prefer to take the risks, and remain chief of the guard yourself?" she said with an angry scoff. "Truly there did not seem to be many thrusting forward to strip you of the office. I shall have a fine sorting up of places in payment for this night's work. But for the present, Tarca, do your duty."

The man came up, obviously timorous. He was a

solidly made fellow, but not altogether unmartial, and though but little of his cheek showed above his decorated beard, I could see that he paled as he came near to the priest. "My lord," he said quietly, "I must ask you to come with me."

"Stand aside," said the old man, thrusting out the Symbol in front of him. I could see his eyes gather on the soldier and his brows knit with a strain of will.

Tarca saw this too, and I thought he would have fallen, but with an effort he kept his manhood, and doggedly repeated his summons. "I must obey the command of my mistress, and I would have you remember, my lord, that I am but a servant. You must come with me to the whip."

"I warn you!" cried the old man. "Stand from out of my path, you!"

It must have been with the courage of desperation that the soldier dared to use force. But the hand he stretched out dropped limply back to his side the moment it touched the old man's bare shoulder, as though it had been struck by some shock. He seemed almost to have expected some such repulse; yet when he picked up that hand with the other, and looked at it, and saw its whiteness, he let out of him a yell like a wounded beast. "Oh, Gods!" he cried. "Not that. Spare me!"

But Zaemon was glowering at him still. A twitching seized the man's face, and he put up his sound hand to it and plucked at his beard, which was curled and plaited after the new fashion of the day. A woman standing near screamed as the half of the beard came off in his fingers. Beneath was silver whiteness over half his face. Zaemon had smitten him with a sudden leprosy that was past cure.

Yet the punishment was not ended even then. Other twitchings took him on other parts of the body, and he tore off his armour and his foppish clothes, and always where the bare flesh showed, there had the horrid plague written its white mark; and in the end, being able to endure no more, the man fell to the pavement and lay there writhing.

Zaemon said no further word. He lifted the Symbol before him, set his eyes on the farther door of the banqueting-hall and walked for it directly, all those in his path shrinking away from him with open shudders. And through the valves of the door he passed out of our sight, still wordless, still unchecked.

I glanced up at Phorenice. The loveliness of her face was drawn and haggard. It was the first great reverse, this, she had met with in all her life, and the shock of it, and the vision of what might follow after, dazed her. Alas, if she could only have guessed at a tenth of the terrors which the future had in its womb, Atlantis might have been saved even then.

6. *The Biters of the City Walls*

Here then was the manner of my reception back in the capital of Atlantis, and some first glimpse at her new policies. I freely confess to my own inaction and limpness; but it was all deliberate. The old ties of duty seemed lost, or at least merged in one another. Beforetime, to serve the king was to serve the Clan of the Priests, from which he had been chosen, and whose head he constituted. But Phorenice was self-made, and appeared to be a rule unto herself; if Zaemon was to be trusted, he was the mouthpiece of the Priests, and their Clan had set her at defiance; and how was a mere honest man to choose on the instant between the two?

But cold argument told me that governments were set up for the good of the country at large, and I said to myself that there would be my choice. I must find out which rule promised best for Atlantis, and do my poor best to prop it into full power. And here at once there opened up another path in the maze: I had heard some considerable talk of rebels; of another faction of Atlanteans who, whatever their faults might be, were at any rate strong enough to beleaguer the capital; and before coming to any final decision, it would be as well to take their claims in balance with the rest. So on the night of that very same day on which I had just re-planted my foot on the old country's shores, I set out to glean for myself tidings on the matter.

No one inside the royal pyramid gainsaid me. The banquet had ended abruptly with the terrible scene that I have set down above on these tablets, for with Tarca writhing on the floor, and thrusting out the gruesome scars of his leprosy, even the most gluttonous had little enough appetite for further gorging. Phorenice glowered on the feasters for a while longer in silent fury, but saying no further word; and then her eyes turned on me, though softened somewhat.

"You may be an honest man, Deucalion," she said, at length, "but you are a monstrous cold one. I wonder when you will thaw?" And here she smiled. "I think it will be soon. But for now I bid you farewell. In the morning we will take this country by the shoulders, and see it in some new order."

She left the banqueting-hall then, Ylga following; and taking precedence of my rank, I went out next, whilst all others stood and made salutation. But I halted by Tarca first, and put my hand on his unclean flesh. "You are an unfortunate man," I said, "but I can admire a brave soldier. If relief can be gained for your plague, I will use interest to procure it for you."

The man's thanks came in a mumble from his wrecked mouth, and some of those near shuddered in affected disgust. I turned on them with a black brow: "Your charity, my lords, seems of as small account as your courage. You affected a fine disbelief of Zaemon's sayings, and a simpering contempt for his priesthood, but when it comes to laying a hand on him, you show a discretion which, in the old days, we should have called by an ugly name. I had rather be Tarca, with all his uncleanness, than any of you now as you stand."

With which leave-taking I waited coldly till they gave me my due salutation, and then walked out of the banqueting-hall without offering a soul another glance. I took my way to the grand gate of the pyramid, called for the officer of the guard, and demanded exit. The man was obsequious enough, but he opened with some demur.

"My lord's attendants have not yet come up?"

"I have none."

"My lord knows the state of the streets?"

"I did twenty years back. I shall be able to pick my way."

"My lord must remember that the city is beleaguered," the fellow persisted. "The people are hungry. They prowl in bands after nightfall, and—I make no question that my lord would conquer in a fight against whatever odds, but——"

"Quite right. I covet no street scuffle to-night. Lend me, I pray you, a sufficiency of men. You will know best what are needed. For me, I am accustomed to a city with quiet streets."

A score of sturdy fellows were detailed off for my escort, and with them in a double file on either hand, I marched out from the close perfumed air of the pyramid into the cool moonlight of the city. It was my purpose to make a tour of the walls and to find out somewhat of the disposition of these rebels.

But the Gods saw fit to give me another education first. The city, as I saw it during that night walk, was no longer the old capital that I had known, the just accretion of the ages, the due admixture of comfort and splendour. The splendour was there, vastly increased. Whole wards had been swept away to make space for new palaces, and new pyramids of the wealthy, and I could not but have an admiration for the skill and the brain which made possible such splendid monuments.

And, indeed, gazing at them there under the silver of the moonlight, I could almost understand the emotions of the Europeans and other barbarous savages which cause them to worship all such great buildings as Gods, since they deem them too wonderful and majestic to be set up by human hands unaided.

Still, if it was easy to admire, it was simple also to see plain advertisement of the cost at which these great works had been reared. From each grant of ground, where one of these stately piles earned silver under the moon, a hundred families had been evicted and left to harbour as they pleased in the open; and, as a consequence, now every niche had its quota of sleepers, and every shadow its squad of fierce wild creatures, ready to rush out and rob or slay all wayfarers of less force than their own.

Myself, I am no pamperer of the common people. I say that, if a man be left to hunger and shiver, he will work to gain him food and raiment; and if not, why then he can die, and the State is well rid of a worthless fellow. But here beside us, as we marched through many wards, were marks of blind oppression; starved dead bodies, with the bones starting through the lean skin, sprawled in the gutter; and indeed it was plain that, save for the favoured few, the people of the great capital were under a most heavy oppression.

But at this, though I might regret it abominally, I could make no strong complaint. By the ancient law of the land all the people, great and small, were the servants of the king, to be put without question to what purposes he chose; and Phorenice stood in the place of the king. So I tried to think no treason, but with a sigh passed on, keeping my eyes above the miseries and the squalors of the roadway, and sending out my thoughts to the stars which hung in the purple night above, and to the High Gods which dwelt amongst them, seeking, if it might be, for guidance for my future policies. And so in time the windings of the streets brought us to the walls, and, coursing beside these and giving fitting answer to the sentries who beat their drums as we passed, we came in time to that great gate which was a charge to the captain of the garrison.

Here it was plain there was some special commotion. A noise of laughter went up into the still night air, and with it now and again the snarl and roar of a great beast, and now and again the shriek of a hurt man. But whatever might be afoot, it was not a scene to come upon suddenly. The entrance gates of our great capital were designed by their ancient builders to be no less strong than the walls themselves. Four pairs of valves were there, each a monstrous block of stone two man-heights square, and a man-height thick, and the wall was doubled to receive them, inclosing an open circus between its two parts. The four gates themselves were set one at the inner, one at the outer side of each of these walls, and a hidden machinery so connected them, that of each set one could not open till the other was closed; and as for forcing them without war engines, one might as foolishly try to push down the royal pyramid with the bare hand.

My escort made outcry with the horn which hung from the wall inviting such a summons, and a warder came to an arrow-slit, and did inspection of our persons and business. His survey was according to the ancient form of words, which is long, and this was made still more tedious by the noise from within, which ever and again drowned all speech between us entirely.

But at last the formalities had been duly complied with, and he shot back the massive bars and bolts of stone, and threw ajar one monstrous stone valve of the door. Into the chamber within—a chamber made from the thickness of the wall between the two doors—I and my fellows crowded, and then the warder with his machines pulled to the valve which had been opened, and came to me again through the press of my escort, bowing low to the ground.

"I have no vail to give you," I said abruptly. "Get on with your duty. Open me that other door."

"With respect, my lord, it would be better that I should first announce my lord's presence. There is a baiting going forward in the circus, and the tigers are as yet mere savages, and no respecters of persons."

"The what?"

"The tigers, if my lord will permit them the name. They are baiting a batch of prisoners with the two great beasts which the Empress (whose name be adored) has sent here to aid us keep the gate. But if my lord will, there are the ward rooms leading off this passage, and the galleries which run out from them commanding the circus, and from there my lord can see the sport undisturbed."

Now, the mere lust for killing excites only disgust in me, but I suspected the orders of the Empress in this matter, and had a curiosity to see her scheme. So I stepped into the warder's lodge, and on into the galleries which commanded the circus with their arrow-slits. The old builders of the place had intended these for a second line of defence, for, supposing the outer doors all forced, an enemy could be speedily shot down in the circus, without being able to give a blow in return, and so would only march into a death-trap. But as a gazing-place on a spectacle they were no less useful.

The circus was bright lit by the moonshine, and the air which came in to me from it was acrid with the reek of blood. There was no sport in what was going forward: as I said, it was mere killing, and the sight disgusted me. I am no prude about this matter. Give a prisoner his weapons, put him in a pit with beasts of reasonable strength, and let him fight to a finish if you choose, and I can look on there and applaud the strokes. The war prisoner, being a prisoner, has earned death by natural law, and prefers to get his last stroke in hot blood then to be knocked down by the headsman's axe. And it is any brave man's luxury either to help or watch a lusty fight. But this baiting in the circus between the gates was no fair battle like that.

To begin with, the beasts were no fair antagonists for single men. In fact, twenty men armed might well have fled from them. When the warder said tigers, I supposed he meant the great cats of the woods. But here, in the circus, I saw a pair of the most terrific of all the fur-bearing land beasts, the great tigers of the caves— huge monsters, of such ponderous strength that in hunger they will oftentimes drag down a mammoth, if they can find him away from his herd.

How they had been brought captive I could not tell. Hunter of beasts though I had been for all my days, I take no shame in saying that I always approached the slaying of a cave-tiger with stratagem and infinite caution. To entrap it alive and bring it to a city on a chain was beyond my most daring schemes, and I have been accredited with more new things than one. But here it was in fact, and I saw in these captive beasts a new certificate for Phorenice's genius.

The purpose of these two cave-tigers was plain: whilst they were in the circus, and loose, no living being could cross from one gate to the other. They were a new and sturdy addition to the defences of the capital. A collar of bronze was round the throat of each, and on the collar was a massive chain which led to the wall, where it could be payed out or hauled in by means of a windlass in one of the hidden galleries. So that at ordinary moments the two huge beasts could be tethered, one close to either end of the circus, as the litter of bones and other messes showed, leaving free passage-way between the two sets of doors.

But when I stood there by the arrow-slit, looking down into the moonlight of the circus, these chains were slackened (though men stood by the windlass of each), and the great striped brutes were prowling about the circus with the links clanking and chinking in their wake. Lying stark on the pavement were the bodies of some eight men, dead and uneaten; and though the cave-tigers stopped their prowlings now and again to nuzzle these, and beat them about with playful paw-blows, they made no pretence at commencing a meal. It was clear that this cruel sport had grown common to them, and they knew there were other victims yet to be added to the tally.

Presently, sure enough, as I watched, a valve of the farther gate swung back an arm's length, and a prisoner, furiously resisting, was thrust out into the circus. He fell on his face, and after one look around him he lay resolutely still, with eyes on the ground passively awaiting his fate. The ponderous stone of the gate clapped to in its place; the cave-tigers turned in their prowlings; and a chatter of wagers ran to and fro amongst the watchers behind the arrow-slits.

It seemed there were niceties of cruelty in this wretched game. There was a sharp clank as the wind-lasses were manned, and the tethering chains were drawn in by perhaps a score of links. One of the cave-tigers crouched, lashed its tail, and launched forth on a terrific spring. The chain tautened, the massive links sang to the strain, and the great beast gave a roar which shook the walls. It had missed the prone man by a hand's breadth, and the watchers behind the arrow-slits shrieked forth their delight. The other tiger sprang also and missed, and again there were shouts of pleasure, which mingled with the bellowing voices of the beasts. The man lay motionless in his form. One more cowardly, or one more brave, might have run from death, or faced it; but this poor prisoner chose the middle course—he permitted death to come to him, and had enough of doggedness to wait for it without stir.

The great cave-tigers were used, it appeared, to this disgusting sport. There were no more wild springs, no more stubbings at the end of the massive chains. They lay down on the pavement, and presently began to purr, rolling on to their sides and rubbing themselves luxuri-ously. The prisoner still lay motionless in his form.

By slow degrees the monstrous brutes each drew to the end of its chain and began to reach at the man with out-stretched forepaw. The male could not touch him; the female could just reach him with the far tip of a claw; and I saw a red scratch start up in the bare skin of his side at every stroke. But still the prisoner would not stir. It seemed to me that they must slack out more links of one of the tigers' chains, or let the vile play linger into mere tediousness.

But I had more to learn yet. The male tiger, either taught by his own devilishness, or by those brutes that were his keepers, had still another ruse in store. He rose to his feet and turned round, backing against the chain. A yell of applause from the hidden men behind the arrow-slits told that they knew what was in store; and then the monstrous beast, stretched to the utmost of its vast length, kicked sharply with one hind paw.

I heard the crunch of the prisoner's ribs as the pads struck him, and at that same moment the poor wretch's body was spurned away by the blow, as one might throw a fruit with the hand. But it did not travel far. It was clear that the she-tiger knew this manœuvre of her mate's. She caught the man on his bound, nuzzling over him for a minute, and then tossing him high into the air, and leaping up to the full of her splendid height after him.

Those other onlookers thought it magnificent; their gleeful shouts said as much. But for me, my gorge rose at the sight. Once the tigers had reached him, the man had been killed, it is true, without any unnecessary lingering. Even a light blow from those terrific paws would slay the strongest man living. But to see the two cave-tigers toying with the poor body was an insult to the pride of our race.

However, I was not there to preach the superiority of man to the beasts, and the indecency and degradation of permitting man to be unduly insulted. I had come to learn for myself the new balance of things in the kingdom of Atlantis, and so I stood at my place behind the arrow-slit with a still face. And presently another scene in this ghastly play was enacted.

The cave-tigers tired of their sport, and first one and then the other fell once more to prowling over the littered pavements, with the heavy chains scraping and chinking in their wake. They made no beginning to feast on the bodies provided for them. That would be for afterwards. In the present, the fascination of slaughter was big in them, and they had thought that it would be indulged further. It seemed that they knew their entertainers.

Again the windlass clanked, and the tethering chains drew the great beasts clear of the doorway; and again a valve of the farther door swung ajar, and another prisoner was thrust struggling into the circus. A sickness seized me when I saw that this was a woman, but still, in view of the object I had in hand, I made no interruption.

It was not that I had never seen women sent to death before. A general, who has done his fighting, must in his day have killed women equally with men; yes, and seen them earn their death-blow by lusty battling. Yet there seemed something so wanton in this cruel helpless sacrifice of a woman prisoner, that I had a struggle with myself to avoid interference. Still it is ever the case that the individual must be sacrificed to a policy, and so as I say, I watched on, outwardly cold and impassive.

I watched too (I confess it freely) with a quickening heart. Here was no sullen submissive victim like the last. She may have been more cowardly (as some women are), she may have been braver (as many women have shown themselves); but, at any rate, it was clear that she was going to make a struggle for her life, and to do vicious damage, it might be, before she yielded it up. The watchers behind the arrow-slits recognised this. Their wagers, and the hum of their appreciation, swept loudly round the ring of the circus.

They stripped their prisoners, before they thrust them out to this death, of all the clothes they might carry, for clothes have a value; and so the woman stood there bare-limbed in the moonlight.

She clapped her back to the great stone door by which she had entered, and faced fate with glowing eye. Gods! there have been times in early years when I could have plucked out sword and jumped down, and fought for her there for the sheer delight of such a battle. But now policy restrained me. The individual might want a helping hand, but it was becoming more and more clear that Atlantis wanted a minister also; and before these great needs, the lesser ones perforce must perish. Still, be it noted that, if I did not jump down, no other man there that night had sufficient manhood remaining to venture the opportunity.

My heart glowed as I watched her. She picked a bone from the litter on the pavement and beat off its head by blows against the wall. Then with her teeth she fashioned the point to still further sharpness. I could see her teeth glisten white in the moonrays as she bit with them.

The huge cave-tigers, which stood as high as her head as they walked, came nearer to her in their prowlings, yet obviously neglected her. This was part of their accustomed scheme of torment, and the woman knew it well. There was something intolerable in their noiseless, ceaseless paddings over the pavement. I could see the prisoner's breast heave as she watched them. A terror such as that would have made many a victim sick and helpless.

But this one was bolder than I had thought. She did not wait for a spring: she made the first attack herself. When the she-tiger made its stroll towards her, and was in the act of turning, she flung herself into a sudden leap, striking viciously at its eye with her sharpened bone. A roar from the onlookers acknowledged the stroke. The cave-tiger's eye remained undarkened, but the puny weapon had dealt it a smart flesh wound, and with a great bellow of surprise and pain it scampered away to gain space for a rush and a spring.

But the woman did not await its charge. With a shrill scream she sped forward, running at the full of her speed across the moonlight directly towards that shadowed part of the encircling wall within whose thickness I had my gazing place; and then, throwing every tendon of her body into the spring, made the greatest leap that surely any human being ever accomplished, even when spurred on by the utmost of terror and desperation. In an after day I measured it, and though of a certainty she must have added much to the tally by the sheer force of her run, which drove her clinging up the rough surface of the wall, it is a sure thing that in that splendid leap her feet must have dangled a man-height and a half above the pavement.

I say it was prodigious, but then the spur was more than the ordinary, and the woman herself was far out of the common both in thews and intelligence; and the end of the leap left her with five fingers lodged in the sill of the arrow-slit from which I watched. Even then she must have slipped back if she had been left to herself, for the sill sloped, and the stone was finely smooth; but I shot out my hand and gripped hers by the wrist, and instantly she clambered up with both knees on the sill, and her fingers twined round to grip my wrist in her turn.

And now you will suppose she gushed out prayers and promises, thinking only of safety and enlargement. There was nothing of this. With savage panting wordlessness she took fresh grip on the sharpened bone with her spare hand, and lunged with it desperately through the arrow-slit. With the hand that clutched mine she drew me towards her, so as to give the blows the surer chance, and so unprepared was I for such an attack, and with such fierce suddenness did she deliver it, that the first blow was near giving me my quietus. But I grappled with the poor frantic creature as gently as might be—the stone of the wall separating us always—and stripped her of her weapon, and held her firmly captive till she might calm herself.

"That was an ungrateful blow," I said. "But for my hand you'd have slipped and be the sport of a tiger's paw this minute."

"Oh, I must kill some one," she panted, "before I am killed myself."

"There will be time enough to think upon that some other day; but for now you are far enough off meeting further harm."

"You are lying to me. You will throw me to the beasts as soon as I loose my grip. I know your kind: you will not be robbed of your sport."

"I will go so far as to prove myself to you," said I, and called out for the warder who had tended the doors below. "Bid those tigers be tethered on a shorter chain," I ordered, "and then go yourself outside into the circus, and help this lady delicately to the ground."

The word was passed and these things were done; and I too came out into the circus and joined the woman, who stood waiting under the moonlight. But the others who had seen these doings were by no means suited at the change of plan. One of the great stone valves of the farther door opened hurriedly, and a man strode out, armed and flushed. "By all the Gods!" he shouted. "Who comes between me and my pastime?"

I stepped quietly to the advance. "I fear, sir," I said, "that you must launch your anger against me. By accident I gave that woman sanctuary, and I had not heart to toss her back to your beasts."

His fingers began to snap against his hilt.

"You have come to the wrong market here with your qualms. I am captain here, and my word carries, subject only to Phorenice's nod. Do you hear that? Do you know too that I can have you tossed to those striped gate-keepers of mine for meddling in here without an invitation?" He looked at me sharp enough, but saw plainly that I was a stranger. "But perhaps you carry a name, my man, which warrants your impertinence?"

"Deucalion is my poor name," I said, "but I cannot
expect you will know it. I am but newly landed here,
sir, and when I left Atlantis some score of years back,
a very different man to you held guard over these
gates." He had his forehead on my feet by this time. "I
had it from the Empress this night that she will tomorrow make a new sorting of this kingdom's dignities.
Perhaps there is some recommendation you would wish
me to lay before her in return for your courtesies?"

"My lord," said the man, "if you wish it, I can have
a turn with those cave-tigers myself now, and you can
look on from behind the walls and see them tear me."

"Why tell me what is no news?"

"I wish to remind my lord of his power; I wish to
beg of his clemency."

"You showed your power to these poor prisoners;
but from what remains here to be seen, few of them
have tasted much of your clemency."

"The orders were," said the captain of the gate, as
though he thought a word might be said here for his
defence, "the orders were, my lord, that the tigers
should be kept fierce and accustomed to killing."

"Then, if you have obeyed orders, let me be the last
to chide you. But it is my pleasure that this woman be
respited, and I wish now to question her."

The man got to his feet again with obvious relief,
though still bowing low.

"Then if my lord will honour me by sitting in my
room that overlooks the outer gate, the favour will
never be forgotten."

"Show the way," I said, and took the woman by the
fingers, leading her gently. At the two ends of the
circus the tigers prowled about on short chains, growling
and muttering.

We passed through the door into the thickness of
the outer wall, and the captain of the gate led us into
his private chamber, a snug enough box overlooking

the plain beyond the city. He lit a torch from his lamp and thrust it into a bracket on the wall, and bowing deeply and walking backwards, left us alone, closing the door in place behind him. He was an industrious fellow, this captain, to judge from the spoil with which his chamber was packed. There could have come very few traders in through that gate below without his levying a private tribute; and so, judging that most of his goods had been unlawfully come by, I had little qualm at making a selection. It was not decent that the woman, being an Atlantean, should go bereft of the dignity of clothes, as though she were a mere savage from Europe; and so I sought about amongst the captain's spoil for garments that would be befitting.

But, as I busied myself in this search for raiment, rummaging amongst the heaps and bales, with a hand and eye little skilled in such business, I heard a sound behind which caused me to turn my head, and there was the woman with a dagger she had picked from the floor, in the act of drawing it from the sheath.

She caught my eye and drew the weapon clear, but seeing that I made no advance towards her, or move to protect myself, waited where she was, and presently was took with a shuddering.

"Your designs seem somewhat of a riddle," I said. "At first you wished to kill me from motives which you explained, and which I quite understood. It lay in my power next to confer some small benefit upon you, in consequence of which you are here, and not—shall we say?—yonder in the circus. Why you should desire now to kill the only man here who can set you completely free, and beyond these walls, is a thing it would gratify me much to learn. I say nothing of the trifle of ingratitude. Gratitude and ingratitude are of little weight here. There is some far greater in your mind."

She pressed a hand hard against her breasts. "You are Deucalion," she gasped; "I heard you say it."

"I am Deucalion. So far, I have known no reason to feel shame for my name."

"And I come of those," she cried, with a rising voice, "who bite against this city, because they have found their fate too intolerable with the land as it is ordered now. We heard of your coming from Yucatan. It was we who sent the fleet to take you at the entrance to the Gulf."

"Your fleet gave us a pretty fight."

"Oh, I know, I know. We had our watchers on the high land who brought us the tidings. We had an omen even before that. Where we lay with our army before the walls here, we saw great birds carrying off the slain to the mountains. But where the fleet failed, I saw a chance where I, a woman, might——"

"Where you might succeed?" I sat me down on a pile of the captain's stuffs. It seemed as if here at last that I should find a solution for many things. "You carry a name?" I asked.

"They call me Naïs."

"Ah," I said, and signed to her to take the clothes that I had sought out. She was curiously like, so both my eyes and hearing said, to Ylga, the fan-girl of Phorenice, but as she had told me of no parentage I asked for none then. Still her talk alone let me know that she was bred of none of the common people, and I made up my mind towards definite understanding. "Naïs," I said, "you wish to kill me. At the same time I have no doubt you wish to live on yourself, if only to get credit from your people for what you have done. So here I will make a contract with you. Prove to me that my death is for Atlantis' good, and I swear by our Lord the Sun to go out with you beyond the walls, where you can stab me and then get you gone. Or else——"

"I will not be your slave."

"I do not ask you for service. Or else, I wished to say, I shall live so long as the High Gods wish, and do my poor best for this country. And for you—I shall set you free to do your best also. So how, I pray you, speak."

7. The Biters of the Walls
(further account)

"You will set me free," she said, regarding me from under her brows, "without any further exactions or treaty?"

"I will set you free exactly on those terms," I answered, "unless indeed we here decide that it is better for Atlantis that I should die, in which case the freedom will be of your own taking."

"My lord plays a bold game."

"Tut, tut," I said.

"But I shall not hesitate to take the full of my bond, unless my theories are most clearly disproved to me."

"Tut," I said, "you women, how you can play out the time needlessly. Show me sufficient cause, and you shall kill me where and how you please. Come, begin the accusation."

"You are a tyrant."

"At least I have not paraded my tyrannies in Atlantis these twenty years. Why, Naïs, I did but land yesterday."

"You will not deny you came back from Yucatan for a purpose."

"I came back because I was sent for. The Empress gives no reasons for her recalls. She states her will; and we who serve her obey without question."

"Pah, I know that old dogma."

"If you discredit my poor honesty at the outset like this, I fear we shall not get far with our unravelling."

"My lord must be indeed simple," said this strange woman scornfully, "if he is ignorant of what all Atlantis knows."

"Then simple you must write me down. Over yonder in Yucatan we were too well wrapped up in our own parochial needs and policies to have leisure to ponder much over the slim news which drifted out to us from Atlantis—and, in truth, little enough came. By example, Phorenice (whose office be adored) is a great personage here at home; but over there in the colony we barely knew so much as her name. Here, since I have been ashore, I have seen many new wonders; I have been carried by a riding mammoth; I have sat at a banquet; but in what new policies there are afoot, I have yet to be schooled."

"Then, if truly you do not know it, let me repeat to you the common tale. Phorenice has tired of her un-mated life——"

"Stay there. I will hear no word against the Empress."

"Pah, my lord, your scruples are most decorous. But I did no more than repeat what the Empress had made public by proclamation. She is minded to take to herself a husband, and nothing short of the best is good enough for Phorenice. One after another has been put up in turn as favourite—and been found wanting. Oh, I tell you, we here in Atlantis have watched her courtship with jumping hearts. First it was this one here, then it was that one there; now it was this general just returned from a victory, and a day later he had been packed back to his camp, to give place to some dashing governor who had squeezed increased revenues from his province. But every ship that came from the West said that there was a stronger man than any of these in Yucatan, and at last the Empress changed the wording of her vow. 'I'll have Deucalion for my husband,' said she, 'and then we will see who can stand against my wishes.'"

"The Empress (whose name be adored) can do as

she pleases in such matters," I said guardedly; "but that is beside the argument. I am here to know how it would be better for Atlantis that I should die?"

"You know you are the strongest man in the kingdom."

"It pleases you to say so."

"And Phorenice is the strongest woman."

"That is beyond doubt."

"Why, then, if the Empress takes you in marriage, we shall be under a double tyranny. And her rule alone is more cruelly heavy than we can bear already."

"I pass no criticism on Phorenice's rule. I have not seen it. But I crave your mercy, Naïs, on the new-comer into this kingdom. I am strong, say you, and therefore I am a tyrant, say you. Now to me this sequence is faulty."

"Who should a strong man use strength for, if not for himself? And if for himself, why that spells tyranny. You will get all your heart's desires, my lord, and you will forget that many a thousand of the common people will have to pay for them."

"And this is all your accusation?"

"It seems to be black enough. I am one that has a compassion for my fellow-men, my lord, and because of that compassion you see me what I am to-day. There was a time, not long passed, when I slept as soft and ate as dainty as any in Atlantis."

I smiled. "Your speech told me that much from the first."

"Then I would I had cast the speech off, too, if that is also a livery of the tyrant's class. But I tell you I saw all the oppression myself from the oppressor's side. I was high in Phorenice's favour then."

"That, too, is easy of credence. Ylga is the fan-girl to the Empress now, and second lady in the kingdom, and those who have seen Ylga could make an easy guess at the parentage of Naïs."

"We were the daughters of one birth; but I do not count with either Zaemon or Ylga now. Ylga is the creature of Phorenice, and Phorenice would have all the people of Atlantis slaves and in chains, so that she might crush them the easier. And as for Zaemon, he is no friend of Phorenice's; he fights with brain and soul to drag the old authority to those on the Sacred Mountain; and that, if it come down on us again, would only be the exchange of one form of slavery for another."

"It seems to me you bite at all authority."

"In fact," she said simply, "I do. I have seen too much of it."

"And so you think a rule of no-rule would be best for the country?"

"You have put it plainly in words for me. That is my creed to-day. That is the creed of all those yonder, who sit in the camp and besiege this city. And we number on our side, now, all in Atlantis save those in the city and a handful on the priests' Mountain."

I shook my head. "A creed of desperation, if you like, Naïs, but, believe me, a silly creed. Since man was born out of the quakings and the fevers of this earth, and picked his way amongst the cooler places, he has been dependent always on his fellow-men. And where two are congregated together, one must be chief, and order how matters are to be governed—at least, I speak of men who have a wish to be higher than the beasts. Have you ever set foot in Europe?"

"No."

"I have. Years back I sailed there, gathering slaves. What did I see? A country without rule or order. Tyrants they were, to be sure, but they were the beasts. The men and the women were the rudest savages, knowing nothing of the arts, dressing in skins and uncleanness, harbouring in caves and the tree-tops. The beasts roamed about where they would, and hunted them unchecked."

"Still, they fought you for their liberty?"

"Never once. They knew how disastrous was their masterless freedom. Even to their dull, savage brains it was a sure thing that no slavery could be worse; and to that state you, and your friends, and your theories, will reduce Atlantis, if you get the upper hand. But, then, to argue in a circle, you will never get it. For to conquer, you must set up leaders, and once you have set them up, you will never pull them down again."

"Aye," she said with a sigh, "there is truth in that last."

The torch had filled the captain's room with a resinous smoke, but the flame was growing pale. Dawn was coming in greyly through a slender arrow-slit, and with it ever and again the glow from some mountain out of sight, which was shooting forth spasmodic bursts of fire. With it also were mutterings of distant falling rocks, and sullen tremblings, which had endured all the night through, and I judged that earth was in one of her quaking moods, and would probably during the forthcoming day offer us some chastening discomforts.

On this account, perhaps, my senses were stilled to certain evidences which would otherwise have given me a suspicion; and also, there is no denying that my general wakefulness was sapped by another matter. This woman, Naïs, interested me vastly out of the common; the mere presence of her seemed to warm the organs of my interior; and whilst she was there, all my thoughts and senses were present in the room of the captain of the gate in which we sat.

But of a sudden the floor of the chamber rocked and fell away beneath me, and in a tumult of dust, and litter, and bales of the captain's plunder, I fell down (still seated on the flagstone) into a pit which had been digged beneath it. With the violence of the descent, and the flutter of all these articles about my head, I was in no condition for immediate action; and whilst I was still half-stunned by the shock, and long before I could get my eyes into service again, I had been seized, and bound, and half-strangled with a noose of hide. Voices were raised that I should be despatched at once out of the way; but one in authority cried out that, killing me at leisure, and as a prisoner, promised more genteel sport; and so I was thrust down on the floor, whilst a whole army of men trod in over me to the attack.

What had happened was clear to me now, though I was powerless to do anything in hindrance. The rebels with more craft than any one had credited to them, had driven a galley from their camp under the ground, intending so to make an entrance into the heart of the city. In their clumsy ignorance, and having no one of sufficient talent in mensuration, they had bungled sadly both in direction and length, and so had ended their burrow under this chamber of the captain of the gate. The great flagstone in its fall had, it appeared, crushed four of them to death, but these were little noticed or lamented. Life was to them a bauble of the slenderest price, and a horde of others pressed through the opening, lusting for the fight, and recking nothing of their risks and perils.

Half-choked by the foul air of the galley, and trodden on by this great procession of feet, it was little enough I could do to help my immediate self much less the more distant city. But when the chief mass of the attackers had passed through, and there came only here and there one eager to take his share at storming the gate, a couple of fellows plucked me up out of the mud on the floor, and began dragging me down through the stinking darkness of the galley towards the pit that gave it entrance.

Twenty times we were jostled by others hastening to the attack, either from hunger for fight, or from appetite for what they could steal. But we came to the open at last, and half-suffocated though I was, I contrived to do obeisance, and say aloud the prescribed prayer to the most High Gods in gratitude for the fresh, sweet air which They had provided.

Our Lord the Sun was on the verge of rising for His day, and all things were plainly shown. Before me were the monstrous walls of the capital, with the heads of its pyramids and higher buildings showing above them.

And on the walls, the sentries walked calmly their appointed paces, or took shelter against arrows in the casemates provided for them.

The din of fighting within the gate rose high into the air, and the heavy roaring of the cave-tigers told that they too were taking their share of the mêlée. But the massive stonework of the walls hid all the actual engagement from our view, and which party was getting the upper hand we could not even guess. But the sounds told how tight a fight was being hammered out in those narrow boundaries, and my veins tingled to be once more back at the old trade, and to be doing my share.

But there was no chivalry about the fellows who held me by my bonds. They thrust me into a small temple near by, which once had been a fane in much favour with travellers, who wished to show gratitude for the safe journey to the capital, but which now was robbed and ruined, and they swung to the stone entrance gate and barred it, leaving me to commune with myself. Presently, they told me, I should be put to death by torments. Well, this seemed to be the new custom of Atlantis, and I should have to endure it as best I could. The High Gods, it appeared, had no further use for my services in Atlantis, and I was not in the mood then to bite very much at their decision. What I had seen of the country since my return had not enamoured me very much with its new conditions.

The little temple in which I was gaoled had been robbed and despoiled of all its furnishments. But the light-slits, where at certain hours of the day the rays of our Lord the Sun had fallen upon the image of the God, before this had been taken away, gave me vantage places from which I could see over the camp of these rebel besiegers, and a dreary prospect it was. The people seemed to have shucked off the culture of centuries in as many months, and to have gone back for the most part to sheer brutishness. The majority harboured on the bare ground. Few owned shelter, and these were merely bowers of mud and branches.

They fought and quarrelled amongst themselves for food, eating their meat raw, and their grain (when they had it) unground. Many who passed my vision I saw were even gnawing the soft inside of tree bark.

The dead lay where they fell. The sick and the wounded found no hand to tend them. Great man-eating birds hovered about the camp or skulked about, heavy with gorging, amongst the hovels, and no one had public spirit enough to give them battle. The stink of the place rose up to heaven as a foul incense inviting a pestilence. There was no order, no trace of strong command anywhere. With three hundred well-disciplined troops it seemed to me that I could have sent those poor desperate hordes flying in panic to the forest.

However, there was no very lengthy space of time granted me for thinking out the policy of this matter to any great depth. The attack on the gate had been delivered with suddenness; the repulse was not slow. Of what desperate fighting took place in the galleries, and in the circus between the two sets of gates, the detail will never be told in full.

At the first alarm the great cave-tigers were set loose, and these raged impartially against keeper and foe. Of those that went in through the tunnel, not one in ten returned, and there were few of these but what carried a bloody wound. Some, with the ruling passion still strong in them, bore back plunder; one trailed along with him the head of the captain of the gate; and amongst them they dragged out two of the warders who were wounded, and whom revenge had urged them to take as prisoners.

Over these two last a hubbub now arose, that seemed likely to boil over into blows. Every voice shouted out for them what he thought the most repulsive fate. Some were for burning, some for skinning, some for impaling, some for other things: my flesh crept as I heard their ravenous yells. Those that had been to the trouble of making them captive were still breathless from the fight, and were readily thrust aside; and it seemed to me that the poor wretches would be hustled into death before any definite fate was agreed upon, which all would pass as sufficiently terrific. Never had I seen such a disorderly tumult, never such a leaderless mob. But, as always has happened, and always will, the stronger men by dint of louder voices and more vigorous shoulders got their plans agreed to at last, and the others perforce had to give way.

A band of them set off running, and presently returned at snails' pace, dragging with them (with many squeals from ungreased wheels) one of those huge war engines with which besiegers are wont to throw great stones and other missiles into the cities they sit down against. They ran it up just beyond bowshot of the walls, and clamped it firmly down with stakes and ropes to the earth. Then setting their lean arms to the windlasses, they drew back the great tree which formed the spring till its tethering place reached the ground, and in the cradle at its head they placed one of the prisoners, bound helplessly, so that he could not throw himself over the side.

Then the rude, savage, skin-clad mob stood back, and one who had appointed himself engineer knocked back the catch that held the great spring in place.

With a whirr and a twang the elastic wood flung upwards, and the bound man was shot away from its tip with the speed of a lightning flash. He sang through the air, spinning over and over with inconceivable rapidity, and the great crowd of rebels held their breath in silence as they watched. He passed high above the city wall, a tiny mannikin in the distance now, and then the trajectory of his flight began to lower. The spike of a new-built pyramid lay in the path of his terrific flight, and he struck it with a thud whose sound floated out to us afterwards, and then he toppled down out of our sight, leaving a red stain on the whiteness of the stone as he fell.

With a roar the crowd acknowledged the success of their device, and bellowed out insults to Phorenice, and insults to the Gods: a poor frantic crowd they showed themselves. And then with ravening shouts, they fell upon the other captive warder, binding him also into a compact helpless missile, and meanwhile getting the engine in gear again for another shot.

But for my part I saw nothing of this disgusting scene. I heard the bolt grate stealthily against the door of the little temple in which I was imprisoned, and was minded to give these brutish rebels somewhat of a surprise. I had rid myself of my bonds handily enough; I had rubbed my limbs to that perfect suppleness which is always desirable before a fight; and I had planned to rush out so soon as the door was swung, and kill those that came first with fist blows on the brow and chin.

They had not suspected my name, it was clear, for my stature and garb were nothing out of the ordinary; but if my bodily strength and fighting power had been sufficient to raise me to a vice-royalty like that of Yucatan, and let me endure alive in that government throughout twenty hard-battling years, why, it was likely that this rabble of savages would see something that was new and admirable in the practice of arms before the crude weight of their numbers could drag me down. Nay, I did not even despair of winning free altogether. I must find me a weapon from those that came up to battle, with which I could write worthy signatures, and I must attempt no standing fights. Gods! but what a glow the prospect did send through me as I stood there waiting.

A vainer man, writing history, might have said that always, before everything else, he held in mind the greater interests before the less. But for me—I prefer to be honest, and own myself human. In my glee at that forthcoming fight—which promised to be the greatest and most furious I had known in all a long life of battling—I will confess that Atlantis and her differing policies were clean forgot. I should go out an unknown man from that little cell of a temple, I should do my work, and then, whether I took freedom with me, or whether I came down at last myself on a pile of slain, these people would guess without being told the name, that here was Deucalion. Gods! what a fight we would have made!

But the door did not open wide to give me space for my first rush. It creaked gratingly outwards on its pivots, and a slim hand and a white arm slipped inside, beckoning me to quietude. Here was some woman. The door creaked wider, and she came inside.

"Naïs," I said.

"Silence, or they will hear you, and remember. At present those who brought you here are killed, and unless by chance some one blunders into this robbed shrine, you will not be found."

"Then, if that is so, let me go out and walk amongst these people as one of themselves."

She shook her head.

"But, Naïs, I am not known here. I am merely a man in very plain and mud-stained robe. I should be in no ways remarkable."

A smile twitched her face. "My lord," she said, "wears no beard; and his is the only clean chin in the camp."

I joined in her laugh. "A pest on my want of foppishness then. But I am forgetting somewhat. It comes to my mind that we still have unfinished that small discussion of ours concerning the length of my poor life. Have you decided to cut it off from risk of further mischief, or do you propose to give me further span?"

She turned to me with a look of sharp distress. "My lord," she said, "I would have you forget that silly talk of mine. This last two hours I thought you were dead in real truth."

"And you were not relieved?"

"I felt that the only man was gone out of the world —I mean, my lord, the only man who can save Atlantis."

"Your words give me a confidence. Then you would have me go back and become husband to Phorenice?"

"If there is no other way."

"I warn you I shall do that, if she still so desires it, and if it seems to me that that course will be best. This is no hour for private likings or dislikings."

"I know it," she said, "I feel it. I have no heart now, save only for Atlantis. I have schooled myself once more to that."

"And at present I am in this lone little box of a temple. A minute ago, before you came, I had promised myself a pretty enough fight to signalise my changing of abode."

"There must be nothing of that. I will not have these poor people slaughtered unnecessarily. Nor do I wish to see my lord exposed to a hopeless risk. This poor place, such as it is, has been given to me as an abode, and, if my lord can remain decorously till nightfall in a maiden's chamber, he may at least be sure of quietude. I am a person," she added simply, "that in this camp has some respect. When darkness comes, I will take my lord down to the sea and a boat, and so he may come with ease to the harbour and the watergate."

8. The Preacher from the Mountains

It was long enough since I had found leisure for a parcel of sleep, and so during the larger part of that day I am free to confess that I slumbered soundly, Naïs watching me. Night fell, and still we remained within the privacy of the temple. It was our plan that I should stay there till the camp slept, and so I should have more chance of reaching the sea without disturbance.

The night came down wet, with a drizzle of rain,

and through the slits in the temple walls we could see the many fires in the camp well cared for, the men and women in skins and rags toasting before them, with steam rising as the heat fought with their wetness. Folk seated in discomfort like this are proverbially alert and cruel in the temper, and Naïs frowned as she looked on the inclemency of the weather.

"A fine night," she said, "and I would have sent my lord back to the city without a soul here being the wiser; but in this chill, people sleep sourly. We must wait till the hour drugs them sounder."

And so we waited, sitting there together on that pavement so long unkissed by worshippers, and it was little enough we said aloud. But there can be good companionship without sentences of talk.

But as the hours drew on, the night began to grow less quiet. From the distance some one began to blow on a horn or a shell, sending forth a harsh raucous note incessantly. The sound came nearer, as we could tell from its growing loudness, and the voices of those by the fires made themselves heard, railing at the blower for his disturbance. And presently it became stationary, and standing up we could see through the slits in the walls the people of the camp rousing up from their uneasy rest, and clustering together round one who stood and talked to them from the pedestal of a war engine.

What he was declaiming upon we could not hear, and our curiosity on the matter was not keen. Given that all who did not sleep went to weary themselves with this fellow, as Naïs whispered, it would be simple for me to make an exit in the opposite direction.

But here we were reckoning without the inevitable busybody. A dozen pairs of feet splashing through the wet came up to the side of the little temple, and cried loudly that Naïs should join the audience. She had eloquence of tongue, it appeared, and they feared lest this speaker who had taken his stand on the war engine should make schisms amongst their ranks unless some skilled person stood up also to refute his arguments.

Here, then, it seemed to me that I must be elbowed into my skirmish by the most unexpected of chances, but Naïs was firmly minded that there should be no fight, if courage on her part could turn it. "Come out with me," she whispered, "and keep distant from the light of the fires."

"But how explain my being here?"

"There is no reason to explain anything," she said bitterly. "They will take you for my lover. There is nothing remarkable in that: it is the mode here. But oh, why did not the Gods make you wear a beard, and curl it, even as other men? Then you could have been gone and safe these two hours."

"A smooth chin pleases me better."

"So it does me," I heard her murmur as she leaned her weight on the stone which hung in the doorway, and pushed it ajar; "your chin." The ragged men outside—there were women with them also—did not wait to watch me very closely. A coarse jest or two flew (which I could have found good heart to have repaid with a sword-thrust) and they stepped off into the darkness, just turning from time to time to make sure we followed. On all sides others were pressing in the same direction—black shadows against the night; the rain spat noisily on the camp fires as we passed them; and from behind us came up others. There were no sleepers in the camp now; all were pressing on to hear this preacher who stood on the pedestal of the war engine; and if we had tried to swerve from the straight course, we should have been marked at once.

So we held on through the darkness, and presently came within earshot.

Still it was little enough of the preacher's words we could make out at first. "Who are your chiefs?" came the question at the end of a fervid harangue, and immediately all further rational talk was drowned in uproar. "We have no chiefs," the people shouted, "we are done with chiefs; we are all equal here. Take away your silly magic. You may kill us with magic if you choose, but rule us you shall not. Nor shall the other priests rule. Nor Phorenice. Nor anybody. We are done with rulers."

The press had brought us closer and closer to the man who stood on the war engine. We saw him to be old, with white hair that tumbled on his shoulders, and a long white beard, untrimmed and uncurled. Save for a wisp of rag about the loins, his body was unclothed, and glistened in the wet.

But in his hand he held that which marked his caste. With it he pointed his sentences, and at times he whirled it about, bathing his wet, naked body in a halo of light. It was a wand whose tip burned with an unconsuming fire, which glowed and twinkled and blazed like some star sent down by the Gods from their own place in the high heaven. It was the Symbol of our Lord the Sun, a credential no one could forge, and one on which no civilised man would cast a doubt.

Indeed, the ragged frantic crew did not question for one moment that he was a member of the Clan of Priests, the Clan which from time out of numbering had given rulers for the land, and even in their loudest clamours they freely acknowledged his powers. "You may kill us with your magic, if you choose," they screamed at him. But stubbornly they refused to come back to their old allegiance. "We have suffered too many things these later years," they cried. "We are done with rulers now for always."

But for myself I saw the old man with a different emotion. Here was Zaemon that was father to Naïs, Zaemon that had seen me yesterday seated on the divan at Phorenice's elbow, and who to-day could denounce me as Deucalion if so he chose. These rebels had expended a navy in their wish to kill me four days earlier, and if they knew of my nearness, even though Naïs were my advocate, her cold reasoning would have had little chance of an audience now. The High Gods who keep the tether of our lives hide Their secrets well, but I did not think it impious to be sure that mine was very near the cutting then.

The beautiful woman saw this too. She even went so far as to twine her fingers in mine and press them as a farewell, and I pressed hers in return, for I was sorry enough not to see her more. Still I could not help letting my thoughts travel with a grim gloating over the fine mound of dead I should build before these ragged, unskilled rebels pulled me down. And it was inevitable this should be so. For of all the emotions that can ferment in the human heart, the joy of strife is keenest, and none but an old fighter, face to face with what must necessarily be his final battle, can tell how deep this lust is embroidered into the very foundations of his being.

But for the time Zaemon did not see me, being too much wrapped in his outcry, and so I was free to listen to the burning words which he spread around him, and to determinate their effect on the hearers.

The theme he preached was no new one. He told that ever since the beginning of history, the Gods had set apart one Clan of the people to rule over the rest and be their Priests, and until the coming of Phorenice these had done their duties with exactitude and justice. They had fought invaders, carried war against the beasts, and studied earth-movements so that they were able to fore-tell earthquakes and eruptions, and could spread warn-ings that the people might be able to escape their de-vastations. They are no self-seekers; their aim was al-ways to further the interest of Atlantis, and so do honour to the kingdom on which the High Gods had set their special favour. Under the Priestly Clan, Atlantis had reached the pinnacle of human prosperity and happiness.

"But," cried the old man, waving the Symbol till his wet body glistened in a halo of light, "the people grew fat and careless with their easy life. They began to have a conceit that their good fortune was earned by their own puny brains and thews, and was no gift from the Gods above; and presently the cult of these Gods became neglected, and Their temples were barren of gifts and worshippers. Followed a punishment. The Gods in Their inscrutable way decreed that a wife of one of the Priests (that was a governor of no inconsiderable province) should see a woman child by the wayside, and take it for adoption. That child the Gods in their infinite wisdom fashioned into a scourge for Atlantis, and you who have felt the weight of Phorenice's hand, know with what completeness the High Gods can fashion their instruments.

"Yet, even as they set up, so can they throw down, and those that shall debase Phorenice are even now appointed. The old rule is to be re-established; but not till you who have sinned are sufficiently chastened to cry to it for relief." He waved the mysterious glowing Symbol before him. "See," he cried in his high old quavering voice, "you know the unspeakable Power of which that is the sign, and for which I am the mouthpiece. It is for you to make decision now. Are the Gods to throw down this woman who has scorned Them and so cruelly trodden on you? Or are you to be still further purged of your pride before you are ripe for deliverance?"

The old priest broke off with a gesture, and his ragged white beard sank on to his chest. Promptly a young man, skin clad and carrying his weapon, elbowed up through the press of listeners, and jumped on to the platform beside him. "Hear me, brethren!" he bellowed, in his strong young voice. "We are done with tyrants. Death may come, and we all of us here have shown how little we fear it. But own rulers again we will not, and that is our final say. My lord," he said, turning to the old man with a brave face, "I know it is in your power to kill me by magic if you choose, but I have said my say, and can stand the cost if needs be."

"I can kill you, but I will not," said Zaemon. "You

have said your silliness. Now go you to the ground again."

"We have free speech here. I will not go till I choose."

"Aye, but you will," said the old man, and turned on him with a sudden tightening of the brows. There was no blow passed; even the Symbol, which glowed like a star against the night, was not so much as lifted in warning; but the young man tried to retort, and, finding himself smitten with a sudden dumbness, turned with a spasm of fear, and jumped back whence he had come. The crowd of them thrilled expectantly, and when no further portent was given, they began to shout that a miracle should be shown them, and then perchance they would be persuaded back to the old allegiance.

The old man stooped and glowered at them in fury. "You dogs," he cried, "you empty-witted dogs! Do you ask that I should degrade the powers of the Higher Mysteries by dancing them out before you as though they were a mummers' show? Do you tickle yourselves that you are to be tempted back to your allegiance? It is for you to woo the Gods who are so offended. Come in humility, and I take it upon myself to declare that you will receive fitting pardon and relief. Remain stubborn, and the scourge, Phorenice, may torment you into annihilation before she in turn is made to answer for the evil she has put upon the land. There is the choice for you to pick at."

The turmoil of voices rose again into the wetness of the night, and weapons were upraised menacingly. It was clear that the party for independence had by far the greater weight, both in numbers and lustiness; and those who might, from sheer weariness of strife, have been willing for surrender, withheld their word through terror of the consequence. It was a fine comment on the freedom of speech, about which these unruly fools had made their boast, and, with a sly malice, I could not help whispering a word on this to Naïs as she stood at my elbow. But Naïs clutched at my hand, and implored me for caution. "Oh, be silent, my lord," she whispered back, "or they will tear you in pieces. They are on fire for mischief now."

"Yet a few hours back you were for killing me yourself," I could not help reminding her.

She turned on me with a hot look. "A woman can change her mind, my lord. But it becomes you little to remind her of her fickleness."

A man in the press beside me wrenched round with an effort, and stared at me searchingly through the darkness. "Oh!" he said. "A shaved chin. Who are you, friend, that you should cut a beard instead of curling it? I can see no wound on your face."

I answered him civilly enough that, with "freedom" for a watchword, the fashion of my chin was a matter of mere private concern. But as that did not satisfy him, and as he seemed to be one of those quarrelsome fellows that are the bane of every community, I took him suddenly by the throat and the shoulder, and bent his neck with the old, quick turn till I heard it crack, and had unhanded him before any of his neighbours had seen what had befallen. The fierce press of the crowd held him from slipping to the ground, and so he stood on there where he was, with his head nodded forward, as though he had fallen asleep through heaviness, or had fainted through the crushing of his fellows. I had no desire to begin that last fight of mine in a place like this, where there was no room to swing a weapon, nor chance to clear a battle ring.

But all this time the lean preacher from the mountains was sending forth his angry anathemas, and still holding the strained attention of the people. And next he set forth before them the cult of the Gods in the ancient form as is prescribed, and they (with old habit coming back to them) made response in the words and in the places where the old ritual enjoins. It was weird enough sight, that time-honoured service of adoration, forced upon these wild people after so long a period of irreligion.

They warmed to the old words as the high shrill voice of the priest cried them forth, and as they listened, and as they realised how intimate was the care of the Gods for the travails and sorrows of their daily lives, so much warmer grew their responses.

". . . *Who stilled the burning of the mountains, and made cool places on the earth for us to live!*—PRAISE TO THE MOST HIGH GODS.

"*Who took away the poisonous vapours, and gave us sweet air that we might breathe!*—PRAISE TO THE MOST HIGH GODS.

"*Who gave us mastery over the lesser beasts and skill of ten times to prevail!*—PRAISE TO THE MOST HIGH GODS. . . .*"

It thrilled one to hear their earnestness; it sorrowed one to know that they would yet be obdurate and not return to their old allegiance. For this is the way with these common people; they will work up an enthusiasm one minute, and an hour later it will have fled away and left them cold and empty.

But Zaemon made no further calls upon their loyalty. He finished the prescribed form of sentences, and stepped down off the platform of the war engine with the Symbol of our Lord the Sun thrust out resolutely before him. To all ordinary seeming the crowd had been packed so that no further compression was possible, but before the advance of the Symbol the people crushed back, leaving a wide lane for his passage.

And here came the turning point of my life. At first, like, I take it, every one else in that crowd, I imagined that the old man, having finished his mission, was making a way to return to the place from which he had come. But he held steadily to one direction, and as that was towards myself, it naturally came to my mind that, having dealt with greater things, he would now settle with the less; or, in plainer words, that having put his policy before the swarming people, he would now smite down the man he had seen but yesterday seated as Phorenice's minister. Well, I should lose that final fight I had promised myself, and that mound of slain for my funeral bed. It was clear that Zaemon was the mouthpiece of the Priests' Clan, duly appointed; and I also was a priest. If the word had been given on the Sacred Mountain to those who sat before the Ark of the Mysteries that Atlantis would prosper more with Deucalion sent to the Gods, I was ready to bow to the sentence with submissiveness. That I had regret for this mode of cutting off, I will not deny. No man who has practised the game of arms could abandon the promise of such a gorgeous final battle without a qualm of longing.

But I had been trained enough to show none of these emotions on my face, and when the old man came up to me, I stood my ground and gave him the salutation prescribed between our ranks, which he returned to me with circumstance and accuracy. The crowd fell back, being driven away by the ineffable force of the Sybmol, leaving us alone in the middle of a ring. Even Naïs, though she was a priest's daughter, was ignorant of the Mysteries, and could not withstand its force. And so we two men stood there alone together, with the glow of the Symbol bathing us, and lighting up the sea of ravenous faces that watched.

The people were quick to put their natural explanation on the scene. "A spy!" they began to roar out. "A spy! Zaemon salutes him as a Priest!"

Zaemon faced round on them with a queer look on his grim old face. "Aye," he said, "this is a Priest. If I give you his name, you might have further interest. This is the Lord Deucalion."

The word was picked up and yelled amongst them with a thousand emotions. But at least they were loyal to their policy; they had decided that Deucalion was their enemy; they had already expended a navy for his destruction; and now that he was ringed in by their masses, they lusted to tear him into rags with their fingers. But rave and rave though they might against me, the glare from the Symbol drove them shuddering back as though it had been a lava-stream; and Zaemon was not the man to hand me over to their fury until he had delivered formal sentence as the emissary of our Clan on the Sacred Mount. So the end was not to be yet.

The old man faced me and spoke in the sacred tongue, which the common people do not know. "My brother," he said, "which have you come to serve, Deucalion or Atlantis?"

"Words are a poor thing to answer a question like that. You will know all of my record. According to the Law of the Priests, each ship from Yucatan will have carried home its sworn report to lay at the feet of their council, and before I went to that vice-royalty, what I did was written plain here on the face of Atlantis."

"We know your doings in the past, brother, and they have found approval. You have governed well, and you have lived austerely. You set up Atlantis for a mistress, and served her well; but then, you have had no Phorenice to tempt you into change and fickleness."

"You can send me where I shall see her no more, if you think me frail."

"Yes, and lose your usefulness. No, brother, you are the last hope which this poor land has remaining. All other human means that have been tried against Phorenice have failed. You have returned from overseas for the final duel. You are the strongest man we have, and you are our final champion. If you fail, then only those terrible Powers which are locked within the Ark of the Mysteries remain to us, and though it is not lawful to speak even in this hidden tongue of their scope, you at least have full assurance of their potency."

I shrugged my shoulders. "It seems that you would save time and pains if you threw me to these wolves of rebels, and let them end me here and now."

The old man frowned on me angrily. "I am bidding

you do your duty. What reason have you for wishing to evade it?"

"I have in my memory the words you spoke in the pyramid, when you came in amongst the banqueters. 'Phorenice,' was your cry, 'whilst you are yet Empress, you shall see this royal pyramid, which you have polluted with your debaucheries, torn tier from tier, and stone from stone, and scattered as feathers before a wind.' It seems that you foresee my defeat."

The old man shuddered. "I cannot tell what she may force us to do. I spoke then only what it was revealed to me must happen. Perhaps when matters have reached that pass, she will repent and submit. But in the meanwhile, before we use the more desperate weapons of the Gods, it is fitting that we should expend all human power remaining to us. And so you must go, my brother, and play your part to the utmost."

"It is an order. So I obey."

"You shall be at Phorenice's side again by the next dawn. She has sent for you from Yucatan as a husband, and as one who (so she thinks, poor human conqueror) has the weight of arm necessary to prolong her tyrannies. You are a Priest, brother, and you are a man of convincing tongue. It will be your part to make her stubborn mind see the invincible power that can be loosed against her, to point out to her the utter hopelessness of prevailing against it."

"If it is ordered, I will do these things. But there is little enough chance of success. I have seen Phorenice, and can gauge her will. There will be no turning her once she has made a decision. Others have tried; you have tried yourself; all have failed."

"Words that were wasted on a maiden may go home to a wife. You have been brought here to be her husband. Well, take your place."

The order came to me with a pang. I had given little enough heed to women through all of a busy life, though when I landed, the taking of Phorenice to wife would not have been very repugnant to me if policy had demanded it. But the matters of the last two days had put things in a different shape. I had seen two other women who had strangely attracted me, and one of these had stirred within me a tumult such as I had never felt before amongst my economies.

To lead Phorenice in marriage would mean a severance from this other woman eternally, and I ached as I thought of it. But though these thoughts floated through my system and gave me harsh wrenches of pain, I did not thrust my puny likings before the command of the council of the Priests. I bowed before Zaemon, and put his hand to my forehead. "It is an order," I said. "If our Lord the Sun gives me life, I will obey."

"Then let us begone from this place," said Zaemon, and took me by the arm and waved a way for us with the Symbol. No further word did I have with Naïs, fearing to embroil her with these rebels who clustered round, but I caught one hot glance from her eyes, and that had to suffice for farewell. The dense ranks of the crowd opened, and we walked away between them scathless. Fiercely though they lusted for my life, brimming with hate though they made their cries, no man dared to rush in and raise a hand against me. Neither did they follow. When we reached the outskirts of the crowd, and the ranks thinned, they had a mind, many of them, to surge along in our wake; but Zaemon whirled the Symbol back before their faces with a blaze of lurid light, and they fell to their knees, grovelling, and pressed on us no more.

The rain still fell, and in the light of the camp fires as we passed them, the wet gleamed on the old man's wasted body. And far before us through the darkness loomed the vast bulk of the Sacred Mountain, with the ring of eternal fires encincturing its crest. I sighed as I thought of the old peaceful days I had spent in its temples and groves.

But there was to be no more of that studious leisure now. There was work to be done, work for Atlantis which did not brook delay. And so when we had progressed far out into the waste, and there was none near to view (save only the most High Gods), we found the place where the passage was, whose entrance is known only to the Seven amongst the Priests; and there we parted, Zaemon to his hermitage in the dangerous lands, and I by this secret way back into the capital.

9. Phorenice, Goddess

Now the passage, though its entrance had been cunningly hidden by man's artifice, was one of those veins in which the fiery blood of our mother, the Earth, had aforetime coursed. Long years had passed since it carried lava streams, but the air in it was still warm and sulphurous, and there was no inducement to linger in transit. I lit me a lamp which I found in an appointed niche, and walked briskly along my ways, coughing, and wishing heartily I had some of those simples which ease a throat that has a tendency to catarrh. But, alas! all that packet of drugs which were my sole spoil from the vice-royalty of Yucatan were lost in the sea-fight with Dason's navy, and since landing in Atlantis there had been little enough time to think for the refinements of medicine.

The network of earth-veins branched prodigiously, and if any but one of us Seven Priests had found a way into its recesses by chance, he would have perished hopelessly in the windings, or have fallen into one of those pits which lead to the boil below. But I carried the chart of the true course clearly in my head, remembering it from that old initiation of twenty years back, when, as an appointed viceroy, I was raised to the highest degree but one known to our Clan, and was given its secrets and working implements.

The way was long, the floor was monstrous uneven, and the air, as I have said, bad; and I knew that day would be far advanced before the signs told me that I had passed beneath the walls, and was well within the precincts of the city. And here the vow of the Seven hampered my progress; for it is ordained that under no circumstances, whatever the stress, shall egress be made from this passage before mortal eye. One branch after another did I try, but always found loiterers near the exits. I had hoped to make my emergence by that path which came inside the royal pyramid. But there was no chance of coming up unobserved here; the place was humming like a hive. And so, too, with each of the five next outlets that I visited. The city was agog with some strange excitement.

But I came at last to a temple of one of the lesser Gods, and stood behind the image for a while making observation. The place was empty; nay, from the dust which robed all the floors and the seats of the worshippers, it had been empty long enough; so I moved all that was needful, stepped out, and closed all entry behind me. A broom lay unnoticed on one of the pews, and with this I soon disguised all route of footmark, and took my way to the temple door. It was shut, and priest though I was, the secret of its opening was beyond me.

Here was a pretty pass. No one but the attendant priests of the temple could move the mechanism which closed and opened the massive stone which filled the doorway; and if all had gone out to attend this spectacle, whatever it might be, that was stirring the city, why there I should be no nearer enlargement than before.

There was no sound of life within the temple precincts; there were evidences of decay and disuse spread broadcast on every hand; but according to the ancient law there should be eternally one at least on watch in the priests' dwellings, so down the passages which led to them I made my way. It would have surprised me little to have found even these deserted. That the old order was changed I knew, but I was only then beginning to realise the ruthlessness with which it had been swept away, and how much it had given place to the new.

However, there can be some faithful men remaining even in an age of general apostasy, and on making my way to the door of the dwelling (which lay in the roof of the temple) I gave the call, and presently it was opened to me. The man who stood before me, peering dully through the gloom, had at least remained constant to his vows, and I made the salutation before him with a feeling of respect.

His name was Ro, and I remembered him well. We had passed through the sacred college together, and always he had been known as the dullard. He had capacity for learning little of the cult of the Gods, less of the arts of ruling, less still of the handling of arms; and he had been appointed to some lowly office in this obscure temple, and had risen to being its second priest and one of its two custodians merely through the desertion of all his colleagues. But it was not pleasant to think that a fool should remain true where cleverer men abandoned the old beliefs.

Ro did before me the greater obeisance. He wore his beard curled in the prevailing fashion, but it was badly done. His clothing was ill-fitting and unbrushed. He always had been a slovenly fellow. "The temple door is shut," he said, "and I only have the secret of its opening. My lord comes here, therefore, by the secret way, and as one of the Seven. I am my lord's servant."

"Then I ask this small service of you. Tell me, what stirs the city?"

"That impious Phorenice has declared herself Goddess, and declares that she will light the sacrifice

with her own divine fire. She will do it, too. She does
everything. But I wish the flames may burn her when
she calls them down. This new Empress is the bane of
our Clan, Deucalion, these latter days. The people
neglect us; they bring no offerings; and now, since these
rebels have been hammering at the walls, I might have
gone hungry if I had not some small store of my own.
Oh, I tell you, the cult of the true Gods is well-nigh
oozed quite out of the land."

"My brother, it comes to my mind that the Priests of
our Clan have been limp in their service to let these
things come to pass."

"I suppose we have done our best. At least, we did
as we were taught. But if the people will not come to
hear your exhortations, and neglect to adore the God,
what hold have you over their religion? But I tell you,
Deucalion, that the High Gods try our own faith hard.
Come into the dwelling here. Look there on my bed."

I saw the shape of a man, untidily swathed in
reddened bandages.

"This is all that is left of the poor priest that was my
immediate superior in this cure. It was his turn yesterday to celebrate the weekly sacrifice to our Lord the
Sun within the circle of His great stones. Faugh! Deucalion, you should have seen how he was mangled when
they brought him back to me here."

"Did the people rise on him? Has it come to that?"

"The people stayed passive," said Ro bitterly, "what
few of them had interest to attend; but our Lord the Sun
saw fit to try His minister somewhat harshly. The wood
was laid; the sacrifice was disposed upon it according
to the prescribed rites; the procession had been formed
round the altar, and the drums and the trumpets were
speaking forth, to let all men know that presently the
smoke of their prayer would be wafted up towards
Those that sit in the great places in the heavens. But
then, above the noise of the ceremonial, there came the
rushing sound of wings, and from out of the sky
there flew one of those great featherless man-eating

birds, of a bigness such as seldom before has been seen."

"An arrow shot in the eye, or a long-shafted spear receives them best."

"Oh, all men know what they were taught as children, Deucalion; but these priests were unarmed, according to the rubric, which ordains that they shall intrust themselves completely to the guardianship of the High Gods during the hours of sacrifice. The great bird swooped down, settling on the wood pyre, and attacked the sacrifice with beak and talon. My poor superior here, still strong in his faith, called loudly on our Lord the Sun to lend power to his arm, and sprang up on the altar with naught but his teeth and his bare arms for weapons. It may be that he expected a miracle—he has not spoke since, poor soul, in explanation—but all he met were blows from leathery wings, and rakings from talons which went near to disembowelling him. The bird brushed him away as easily as we could sweep aside a fly, and there he lay bleeding on the pavement beside the altar, whilst the sacrifice was torn and eaten in the presence of all the people. And then, when the bird was glutted, it flew away again to the mountains."

"And the people gave no help?"

"They cried out that the thing was a portent, that our Lord the Sun was a God no longer if He had not power or thought to guard His own sacrifice; and some cried that there was no God remaining now, and others would have it that there was a new God come to weigh on the country, which had chosen to take the form of a common man-eating bird. But a few began to shout that Phorenice stood for all the Gods now in Atlantis, and that cry was taken up till the stones of the great circle rang with it. Some may have made proclamations because they were convinced; many because the cry was new, and pleased them; but I am sure there were not a few who joined in because it was dangerous to leave such an outburst unwelcomed. The Empress can be hard enough to those who neglect to give her adulation."

"The Empress is Empress," I said formally, "and her name carries respect. It is not for us to question her doings."

"I am a priest," said Ro, "and I speak as I have been taught, and defend the Faith as I have been commanded. Whether there is a Faith any longer, I am beginning to doubt. But, anyway, it yields a poor enough livelihood nowadays. There have been no offerings at this temple this five months past, and if I had not a few jars of corn put by, I might have starved for anything the pious of this city cared. And I do not think that the affair of that sacrifice is likely to put new enthusiasm into our cold votaries."

"When did it happen?"

"Twenty hours ago. To-day Phorenice conducts the sacrifice herself. That has caused the stir you spoke about. The city is in the throes of getting ready one of her pageants."

"Then I must ask you to open the temple doors and give me passage. I must go and see this thing for myself."

"It is not for me to offer advice to one of the Seven," said Ro doubtfully.

"It is not."

"But they say that the Empress is not overpleased at your absence," he mumbled. "I should not like harm to come in your way, Deucalion," he said aloud.

"The future is in the hands of the most High Gods, Ro, and I at least believe that They will deal out our fates to each of us as They in Their infinite wisdom see best, though you seem to have lost your faith. And now I must be your debtor for a passage out through the doors. Plagues! man, it is no use your holding out your hand to me. I do not own a coin in all the world."

He mumbled something about "force of habit" as he led the way down towards the door, and I responded tartly enough about the unpleasantness of his begging customs. "If it were not for your sort and your customs, the Priests' Clan would not be facing this crisis to-day."

"One must live," he grumbled, as he pressed his levers, and the massive stone in the doorway swung ajar.

"If you had been a more capable man, I might have seen the necessity," said I, and passed into the open and left him. I could never bring myself to like Ro.

A motley crowd filled the street which ran past the front of this obscure temple, and all were hurrying one way. With what I had been told, it did not take much art to guess that the great stone circle of our Lord the Sun was their mark, and it grieved me to think of how many venerable centuries that great fane had up-reared before the weather and the earth tremors, with-out such profanation as it would witness to-day. And also the thought occurred to me, "Was our Great Lord above drawing this woman on to her destruction? Would He take some vast and final act of vengeance when she consummated her final sacrilege?"

But the crowd pressed on, thrilled and excited, and thinking little (as is a crowd's wont) on the deeper matters which lay beneath the bare spectacle. From one quarter of the city walls the din of an attack from the besiegers made itself clearly heard from over the house, and the temples and the palaces intervening, but no one heeded it. They had grown callous, these townsfolk, to the battering of rams, and the flight of fire-darts, and the other emotions of a bombardment. Their nerves, their hunger, their desperation, were strung to such a pitch that little short of an actual storm could stir them into new excitement over the siege.

All were weaponed. The naked carried arms in the hopes of meeting some one whom they could overcome and rob; those that had a possession walked ready to do a battle for its ownership. There was no security, no trust; the lesson of civilisation had dropped away from these common people as mud is washed from the feet by rain, and in their new habits and their thoughts they had gone back to the grade from which savages like those of Europe have never yet emerged. It was a grim commentary on the success of Phorenice's rule.

The crowd merged me into their ranks without question, and with them I pressed forward down the winding streets, once so clean and trim, now so foul and mud-strewn. Men and women had died of hunger in these streets these latter years, and rotted where they lay, and we trod their bones underfoot as we walked. Yet rising out of this squalor and this misery were great pyramids and palaces, the like of which for splendour and magnificence had never been seen before. It was a jarring admixture.

In time we came to the open space in the centre of the city, which even Phorenice had not dared to encroach upon wtih her ambitious building schemes, and stood on the secular ground which surrounds the most ancient, the most grand, and the breast of all this world's temples.

Since the beginning of time, when man first emerged amongst the beasts, our Lord the Sun has always been his chiefest God, and legend says that He raised this circle of stones Himself to be a place where votaries should offer Him worship. It is the fashion amongst us moderns not to take these old tales in a too literal sense, but for myself, this one satisfies me. By our wits we can lift blocks weighing six hundred men, and set them as the capstones of our pyramids. But to uprear the stones of that great circle would be beyond all our art, and much more would it be impossible to-day, to transport them from their distant quarries across the rugged mountains.

There were nine-and-forty of the stones, alternating with spaces, and set in an accurate circle, and across the tops of them other stones were set, equally huge. The stones were undressed and rugged; but the huge massiveness of them impressed the eye more than all the temples and daintily tooled pyramids of our wondrous city. And in the centre of the circle was that still greater stone which formed the altar, and round which was carved, in the rude chiselling of the ancients, the snake and the outstretched hand.

The crowd which bore me on came to a standstill before the circle of stones. To trespass beyond this is death for the common people; and for myself, although I had the right of entrance, I chose to stay where I was for the present, unnoticed amongst the mob, and wait upon events.

For long enough we stood there, our Lord the Sun burning high and fiercely from the clear blue sky above our heads. The din of the rebels' attack upon the walls came to us clearly, even above the gabble of the multitude, but no one gave attention to it. Excitement about what was to befall in the circle mastered every other emotion.

I learned afterwards that so pressing was the rebels' attack, and so destructive the battering of their new war engines, that Phorenice had gone off to the walls first to lend awhile her brilliant skill for its repulse, and to put heart into the defenders. But as it was, the day had burned out to its middle and scorched us intolerably, before the noise of the drums and horns gave advertisement that the pageant had formed in procession; and of those who waited in the crowd, many had fainted with exhaustion and the heat, and not a few had died. But life was cheap in the city of Atlantis now, and no one heeded the fallen.

Nearer and nearer drew the drums and the braying of the other music, and presently the head of a glittering procession began to arrive and dispose itself in the space which had been set apart. Many a thousand poor starving wretches sighed when they saw the wanton splendour of it. But these lords and these courtiers of this new Atlantis had no concern beyond their own bellies and their own backs, except for their one alien regard—their simpering affection for Phorenice.

I think, though, their loyalty for the Empress was

real enough, and it was not to be wondered at, since everything they had came from her lavish hands. Indeed, the woman had a charm that cannot be denied, for when she appeared, riding in the golden castle (where I also had ridden) on the back of her monstrous shaggy mammoth, the starved sullen faces of the crowd brightened as though a meal and sudden prosperity had been bestowed upon them; and without a word of command, without a trace of compulsion, they burst into spontaneous shouts of welcome.

She acknowledged it with a smile of thanks. Her cheeks were a little flushed, her movements quick, her manner high-strung, as all well might be, seeing the horrible sacrilege she had in mind. But she was undeniably lovely; yes, more adorably beautiful than ever with her present thrill of excitement; and when the stair was brought, and she walked down from the mammoth's back to the ground, those near fell to their knees and gave her worship, out of sheer fascination for her beauty and charm.

Ylga, the fan-girl, alone of all that vast multitude round the Sun temple contained herself within her formal paces and duties. She looked pained and troubled. It was plain to see, even from the distance where I stood, that she carried a heavy heart under the jewels of her robe. It was fitting, too, that this should be so. Though she had been long enough divorced from his care and fostered by the Empress, Ylga was a daughter of Zaemon, and he was the chiefest of our Lord the Sun's ministers here on earth. She could not forget her upbringing now at this supreme moment when the highest of the old Gods was to be formally defied. And perhaps also (having a kindness for Phorenice) she was not a little dreadful of the consequences.

But the Empress had no eye for one sad look amongst all that sea of glowing faces. Boldly and proudly she strode out into the circle, as though she had been the duly appointed priest for the sacrifice. And after her came a knot of men, dressed as priests, and bearing the victim. Some of these were creatures of her own, and it was easy to forgive mere ignorant laymen, won over by the glamour of Phorenice's presence. But some, to their shame, were men born in the Priests' Clan, and brought up in the groves and colleges of the Sacred Mountain, and for their apostasy there could be no palliation.

The wood had already been stacked on the altar-stone in the due form required by the ancient symbolism, and the Empress stood aside whilst those who followed did what was needful. As they opened out, I saw that the victim was one of the small, cloven-hoofed horses that roam the plains—a most acceptable sacrifice. They bound its feet with metal gyves, and put it on the pyre, where, for a while, it lay neighing. Then they stepped aside, and left it living. Here was an innovation.

The false priests went back to the farther side of the circle, and Phorenice stood alone before the altar. She lifted up her voice, sweet, tuneful, and carrying, and though the din of the siege still came from over the city, no ear there lost a word of what was spoken.

She raised her glance aloft, and all other eyes followed it. The heaven was clear as the deep sea, a gorgeous blue. But as the words came from her, so a small mist was born in the sky, wheeling and circling like a ball, although the day was windless, and rapidly growing darker and more compact. So dense had it become, that presently it threw a shadow on part of the sacred circle and soothed it into twilight, though all without where the people stood was still garish day. And in the ball of mist were little quick stabs and splashes of noiseless flame.

She spoke, not in the priests' sacred tongue—though such was her wicked cleverness, that she may very well have learned it—but in the common speech of the people, so that all who heard might understand; and she told of her wondrous birth (as she chose to name it), and of the direct aid of the most High Gods, which had enabled her to work so many marvels. And in the end she lifted both of her fair white arms towards the blackness above, and with her lovely face set with the strain of will, she uttered her final cry:

"O my high Father, the Sun, I pray You now to acknowledge me as Your very daughter. Give this people a sign that I am indeed a child of the Gods and no frail mortal. Here is sacrifice unlit, where mortal priests with their puny fires had weekly, since the foundation of this land, sent savoury smoke towards the sky. I pray You send down the heavenly fire to burn this beast here offered, in token that though You still rule on high, You have given me Atlantis to be my kingdom, and the people of the Earth to be my worshippers."

She broke off and strained towards the sky. Her face was contorted. Her limbs shook. "O mighty Father," she cried, "who hast made me a God and an equal, hear me! Hear me!"

Out of the black cloud overhead there came a blinding flash of light, which spat downwards on to the altar. The cloven-hoofed horse gave one shrill neigh, and one convulsion, and fell back dead. Flames crackled out from the wood pile, and the air became rich with the smell of burning flesh. And lo! in another moment the cloud above had melted into nothingness, and the flames burnt pale, and the smoke went up in a thin blue spiral towards the deeper blueness of the sky.

Phorenice, the Empress, stood there before the great stone, and before the snake and the outstretched hand of life which were inscribed upon it, flushed, exultant, and once more radiantly lovely; and the knot of priests within the circle, and the great mob of people without, fell to the ground adoring.

"Phorenice, Goddess!" they cried. "Phorenice, Goddess of all Atlantis!"

But for myself I did not kneel. I would have no part in this apostasy, so I stood there awaiting fate.

10. A Wooing

A murmur quickly sprang up round me, which grew into shouts. "Kneel," one whispered, "kneel, sir, or you will be seen." And another cried: "Kneel, you without beard, and to obeisance to the only Goddess, or by the old Gods I will make myself her priest and butcher you!" And so the shouts arose into a roar.

But presently the word "Deucalion" began to be bandied about, and there came a moderation in the zeal of these enthusiasts. Deucalion, the man who had left Atlantis twenty years before to rule Yucatan, they might know little enough about, but Deucalion, who rode not many days back beside the Empress in the golden castle beneath the canopy of snakes, was a person they remembered; and when they weighed up his possible ability for vengeance, the shouts died away from them limply.

So when the silence had grown again, and Phorenice turned and saw me standing alone amongst all the prostrate worshippers, I stepped out from the crowd and passed between two of the great stones, and went across the circle to where she stood beside the altar. I did not prostrate myself. At the prescribed distance I made the salutation which she herself had ordered when she made me her chief minister, and then hailed her with formal decorum as Empress.

"Deucalion, man of ice," she retorted.

"I still adhere to the old Gods!"

"I was not referring to that," said she, and looked at me with a sidelong smile.

But here Ylga came up to us with a face that was white, and a hand that shook, and made supplication for my life. "If he will not leave the old Gods yet," she pleaded, "surely you will pardon him? He is a strong man, and does not become a convert easily. You may change him later. But think, Phorenice, he is Deucalion; and if you slay him here for this one thing, there is no other man within all the marches of Atlantis who would so worthily serve——"

The Empress took the words from her. "You slut," she cried out. "I have you near me to appoint my wardrobe, and carry my fan, and do you dare to put a meddling finger on my policies? Back with you, outside this circle, or I'll have you whipped. Ay, and I'll do more. I'll serve you as Zaemon served my captain, Tarca. Shall I point a finger at you, and smite your pretty skin with a sudden leprosy?"

The girl bowed her shoulders, and went away cowed, and Phorenice turned to me. "My lord," she said. "I am like a young bird in the nest that has suddenly found its wings. Wings have so many uses that I am curious to try them all."

"May each new flight they take be for the good of Atlantis."

"Oh," she said, with an eye-flash, "I know what you have most at heart. But we will go back to the pyramid, and talk this out at more leisure. I pray you now, my lord, conduct me back to my riding beast."

It appeared then that I was to be condoned for not offering her worship, and so putting public question on her deification. It appeared also that Ylga's interference was looked upon as untimely, and, though I could not understand the exact reasons for either of these things, I accepted them as they were, seeing that they forwarded the scheme that Zaemon had bidden me carry out.

So when the Empress lent me her fingers—warm, delicate fingers they were, though so skilful to grasp the weapons of war—I took them gravely, and led her out of the great circle, which she had polluted with her trickeries. I had expected to see our Lord the Sun take vengeance on the profanation whilst it was still in act; but none had come: and I knew that He would choose his own good time for retribution, and appoint what instrument He thought best, without my raising a puny arm to guard His mighty honour.

So I led this lovely sinful woman back to the huge red mammoth which stood there tamely in waiting, and the smell of the sacrifice came after us as we walked. She mounted the stair to the golden castle on the shaggy beast's back, and bade me mount also and take seat beside her. But the place of the fan-girl behind was empty, and what we said as we rode back through the streets there was none to overhear.

She was eager to know what had befallen me after the attack on the gate, and I told her the tale, laying stress on the worthiness of Naïs, and uttering an opinion that with care the girl might be won back to allegiance again. Only the commands that Zaemon laid upon me when he and I spoke together in the sacred tongue, did I withhold, as it is not lawful to repeat these matters save only in the High Council of the Priests itself as they sit before the Ark of the Mysteries.

"You seem to have an unusual kindliness for this rebel Naïs," said Phorenice.

"She showed herself to me as more clever and thoughtful than the common herd."

"Ay," she answered, with a sigh that I think was real enough in its way, "an Empress loses much that meaner woman gets as her common due."

"In what particular?"

"She misses the honest wooing of her equals."

"If you set up for a Goddess——" I said.

"Pah! I wish to be no Goddess to you, Deucalion. That was for the common people; it gives me more power with them; it helps my schemes. All you Seven higher priests know that trick of calling down the fire, and it pleased me to filch it. Can you not be generous, and admit that a woman may be as clever in finding out these natural laws as your musty elder priests?"

"Remains that you are Empress."

"Nor Empress either. Just think that there is a woman seated beside you on this cushion, Deucalion, and look upon her, and say what words come first to your lips. Have done with ceremonies, and have done with statecraft. Do you wish to wait on as you are till all your manhood withers? It is well not to hurry unduly in these matters: I am with you there. Yet, who but a fool watches a fruit grow ripe, and then leaves it till it is past its prime?"

I looked on her glorious beauty, but as I live it left me cold. But I remembered the command that had been laid upon me, and forced a smile. "I may have been fastidious," I said, "but I do not regret waiting this long."

"Nor I. But I have played my life as a maid, time enough. I am a woman, ripe, and full-blooded, and the day has come when I should be more than what I have been."

I let my hand clench on hers. "Take me to husband then, and I will be a good man to you. But, as I am bidden speak to Phorenice the woman now, and not to the Empress, I offer fair warning that I will be no puppet."

She looked at me sidelong. "I have been master so long that I think it will come as enjoyment to be mastered sometimes. No, Deucalion, I promise that— you shall be no puppet. Indeed, it would take a lusty lung to do the piping if you were to dance against your will."

"Then, as man and wife we will live together in the royal pyramid, and we will rule this country with all the wit that it has pleased the High Gods to bestow on us. These miserable differences shall be swept aside; the rebels shall go back to their homes, and hunt, and fight the beasts in the provinces, and the Priests' Clan shall be pacified. Phorenice, you and I will throw ourselves brain and soul into the government, and we will make Atlantis rise as a nation that shall once more surpass all the world for peace and prosperity."

Petulantly she drew her hand away from mine. "Oh, your conditions, and your Atlantis! You carry a crudeness in these colonial manners of yours, Deucalion, that palls on one after the first blunt flavour has worn away. Am I to do all the wooing? Is there no thrill of love under all your ice?"

"In truth, I do not know what love may be. I have had little enough speech with women all these busy years."

"We were a pair, then, when you landed, though I have heard sighs and protestations from every man that carries a beard in all Atlantis. Some of then tickled my fancy for the day, but none of them have moved me deeper. No, I also have not learned what this love may be from my own personal feelings. But, sir, I think that you will teach me soon, if you go on with your coldness."

"From what I have seen, love is for the poor, and the weak, and for those of flighty emotions."

"Then I would that another woman were Empress, and that I were some ill-dressed creature of the gutter that a strong man could pick up by force, and carry away to his home for sheer passion. Ah! How I could revel in it! How I could respond if he caught my whim!" She laughed. "But I should lead him a sad life of it if my liking were not so strong as his."

"We are as we are made, and we cannot change our inwards which move us."

She looked at me with a sullen glance. "If I do not change yours, my Deucalion, there will be more trouble brewed for this poor Atlantis that you set such store upon. There will be ill doings in this coming household of ours if my love grows for you, and yours remains still unborn."

I believe she would have had me fondle her there in the golden castle on the mammoth's shabby back, before the city streets packed with curious people. She had little enough appetite for privacy at any time. But for the life of me I could not do it. The Gods know I was earnest enough about my task, and They know also how it repelled me. But I was a true priest that day, and I had put away all personal liking to carry out the commands which the Council had laid upon me. If I had known how to set about it, I would have fallen in with her mood. But where any of those shallow bedizened triflers about the court would have been glibly in his element, I stuck for lack of a dozen words.

There was no help for it but to leave all, save what I actually felt, unsaid. Diplomacy I was trained in, and on most matters I had a glib enough tongue. But to palter with women was a lightness I had always neglected, and if I had invented would-be pretty speeches out of my clumsy inexperience, Phorenice would have seen through the fraud on the instant. She had been nurtured during these years of her rule on a pap of these silly protestations, and could weigh their value with an expert's exactness.

Nor was it a case where honest confession would have served my purpose better. If I had put my position to her in plain words, it would have made relations worse. And so perforce I had to hold my tongue, and submit to be considered a clown.

"I had always heard," she said, "that you colonists in Yucatan were far ahead of those in Egypt in all the arts and graces. But you, sir, do small credit to your vice-royalty. Why, I have had gentry from the Nile come here, and you might almost think they had never left their native shores."

"They must have made great strides this last twenty years, then. When last I was sent to Egypt to report, the blacks were clearly masters of the land, and our people lived there only on sufferance. Their pyramids were puny, and their cities nothing more than forts."

"Oh," she said mockingly, "they are mere exiles still, but they remember their manners. My poor face seemed to please them, at least they all went into raptures over it. And for ten pleasant words, one of them cut off his own right hand. We made the bargain, my Egyptian gallant and I, and the hand lies dried on some shelf in my apartment to-day as a pleasant memento."

But here, by a lucky chance for me, an incident occurred which saved me from further baiting. The rebels outside the walls were conducting their day's attack with vigour and some intelligence. More than once during our procession the lighter missiles from their war engines had sang up through the air, and split against a building, and thrown splinters which wounded those who thronged the streets. Still there had been nothing to ruffle the nerves of any one at all used to the haps of warfare, or in any way to hinder our courtship. But presently, it seems, they stopped hurling stones from their war engines, and took to loading them with carcases of wood lined with the throwing fire.

Now, against stone buildings these did little harm, save only that they scorched horribly any poor wretch that was within splash of them when they burst; but when they fell upon the rude wooden booths and rush shelters of the poorer folk, they set them ablaze instantly. There was no putting out these fires.

These things also would have given to either Phorenice or myself little enough of concern, as they are the trivial and common incidents of every siege; but the mammoth on which we rode had not been so properly schooled. When the first blue whiff of smoke came to us down the windings of the street, the huge red beast hoisted its trunk, and began to sway its head uneasily. When the smoke drifts grew more dense, and here and there a tongue of flame showed pale beneath the sunshine, it stopped abruptly and began to trumpet.

The guards who led it, tugged manfully at the chains which hung from the jagged metal collar round its neck, so that the spikes ran deep into its flesh, and reminded it keenly of its bondage. But the beast's terror at the fire, which was native to its constitution, mastered all

its new-bought habits of obedience. From time unknown men have hunted the mammoth in the savage
ground, and the mammoth has hunted men; and the
men have always used fire as a shield, and mammoths
have learned to dread fire as the most dangerous of
all enemies.

Phorenice's brow began to darken as the great beast
grew more restive, and she shook her red curls viciously. "Some one shall lose a head for this blundering,"
said she. "I ordered to have this beast trained to stand
indifferent to drums, shouting, arrows, stones, and fire,
and the trainers assured me that all was done, and
brought examples."

I slipped my girdle. "Here," I said, "quick. Let me
lower you to the ground."

She turned on me with a gleam. "Are you afraid for
my neck, then, Deucalion?"

"I have no mind to be bereaved before I have
tasted my wedded life."

"Pish! There is little enough of danger. I will stay
and ride it out. I am not one of your nervous women,
sir. But go you, if you please."

"There is little enough chance of that now."

Blood flowed from the mammoth's neck where the
spikes of the collar tore it, and with each drop, so did
the tameness seem to ooze out from it also. With wild
squeals and trumpetings it turned and charged viciously down the way it had come, scattering like straws the
spearmen who tried to stop it, and mowing a great
swathe through the crowd with its monstrous progress.
Many must have been trodden under foot, many
killed by its murderous trunk, but only their cries came
to us. The golden castle, with its canopy of royal snakes,
was swayed and tossed, so that we two occupants had
much ado not to be shot off like stones from a catapult.
But I took a brace with my feet against the front, and
one arm around a pillar, and clapped the spare arm
round Phorenice, so as to offer myself to her as a cushion.

She lay there contentedly enough, with her lovely face just beneath my chin, and the faint scent of her hair coming in to me with every breath I took; and the mammoth charged madly on through the narrow streets. We had outstripped the taint of smoke, and the original cause of fear, but the beast seemed to have forgotten everything in its mad panic. It held furiously on with enormous strides, carrying its trunk aloft, and deafening us with its screams and trumpetings. We left behind us quickly all those who had trod in that glittering pageant, and we were carried helplessly on through the wards of the city.

The beast was utterly beyond all control. So great was its pace that there was no alternative but to try and cling on to the castle. Up there we were beyond its reach. To have leapt off, even if we had avoided having brains dashed out or limbs smashed by the fall, would have been to put ourselves at once at a frightful disadvantage. The mammoth would have scented us immediately, and turned (as is the custom of these beasts), and we should have been trampled into a pulp in a dozen seconds.

The thought came to me that here was the High God's answer to Phorenice's sacrilege. The mammoth was appointed to carry out Their vengeance by dashing her to pieces, and I, their priest, was to be human witness that justice had been done. But no direct revelation had been given me on this matter, and so I took no initiative, but hung on to the swaying castle, and held the Empress against bruises in my arms.

There was no guiding the brute: in its insanity of madness it doubled many times upon its course, the windings of the streets confusing it. But by degrees we left the large palaces and pyramids behind, and got amongst the quarters of artisans, where weavers and smiths gaped at us from their doors as we thundered past. And then we came upon the merchants' quarters where men live over their storehouses that do traffic with the people over seas, and then down an open space there glittered before us a mirror of water.

"Now here," thought I, "this mad beast will come to sudden stop, and as like as not will swerve round sharply and charge back again towards the heart of the city." And I braced myself to withstand the shock, and took fresh grip upon the woman who lay against my breast. But with louder screams and wilder trumpetings the mammoth held straight on, and presently came to the harbour's edge, and sent the spray sparkling in sheets amongst the sunshine as it went with its clumsy gait into the water.

But at this point the pace was very quickly slackened. The great sewers, which science devised for the health of the city in the old King's time, vomit their drainings into this part of the harbour, and the solid matter which they carry is quickly deposited as an impalpable sludge. Into this the huge beast began to sink deeper and deeper before it could halt in its rush, and when with frightened bellowings it had come to a stop, it was bogged irretrievably. Madly it struggled, wildly it screamed and trumpeted. The harbour-water and the slime were churned into one stinking compost, and the golden castle in which we clung lurched so wildly that we were torn from it and shot far away into the water.

Still there, of course, we were safe, and I was pleased enough to be rid of the bumpings.

Phorenice laughed as she swam. "You handle yourself like a sore man, Deucalion. I owe you something for lending me the cushion of your body. By my face! There's more of the gallant about you when it comes to the test than one would guess to hear you talk. How did you like the ride, sir? I warrant it came to you as a new experience."

"I'd liefer have walked."

"Pish, man! You'll never be a courtier. You should have sworn that with me in your arms you could have wished the bumping had gone on for ever. Ho, the boat there! Hold your arrows. Deucalion, hail me those fools in that boat. Tell them that, if they hurt so much as a hair of my mammoth, I'll kill them all by torture. He'll exhaust himself directly, and when his flurry's done we'll leave him where he is to consider his evil ways for a day or so, and then haul him out with windlasses, and tame him afresh. Pho! I could not feel myself to be Phorenice, if I had no fine, red, shaggy mammoth to take me out for my rides."

The boat was a ten-slave galley which was churning up from the farther side of the harbour as hard as well-plied whips could make oars drive her, but at the sound of my shouts the soldiers on her foredeck stopped their arrowshots, and the steersman swerved her off on a new course to pick us up. Till then we had been swimming leisurely across an angle of the harbour, so as to avoid landing where the sewers outpoured; but we stopped now, treading the water, and were helped over the side by most respectful hands.

The galley belonged to the captain of the port, a mincing figure of a mariner, whose highest appetite in life was to lick the feet of the great, and he began to fawn and prostrate himself at once, and to wish that his eyes had been blinded before he saw the Empress in such deadly peril.

"The peril may pass," said she. "It's nothing mortal that will ever kill me. But I have spoiled my pretty clothes, and shed a jewel or two, and that's annoying enough as you say, good man."

The silly fellow repeated a wish that he might be blinded before the Empress was ever put to such discomfort again.

But it seemed she could be cloyed with flattery. "If you are tired of your eyes," said she, "let me tell you that you have gone the way to have them plucked out from their sockets. Kill my mammoth, would you, because he has shown himself a trifle frolicsome? You and your sort want more education, my man. I shall have to teach you that port-captains and such small creatures are very easy to come by, and very small value when got, but that my mammoth is mine—mine, do you understand?—the property of Goddess Phorenice, and as such is sacred."

The port-captain abased himself before her. "I am an ignorant fellow," said he, "and heaven was robbed of its brightest ornament when Phorenice came down to Atlantis. But if reparation is permitted me, I have two prisoners in the cabin of the boat here who shall be sacrificed to the mammoth forthwith. Doubtless it would please him to make sport with them, and spill out the last lees of his rage upon their bodies."

"Prisoners you've got, have you? How taken?"

"Under cover of last night they were trying to pass in between the two forts which guard the harbour mouth. But their boat fouled the chain, and by the light of the torches the sentries spied them. They were caught with ropes, and put in a dungeon. There is an order not to abuse prisoners before they have been brought before a judgment?"

"It was my order. Did these prisoners offer to buy their lives with news?"

"The man has not spoken. Indeed, I think he got his death-wound in being taken. The woman fought like a cat also, so they said in the fort, but she was caught without hurt. She says she has got nothing that would be of use to tell. She says she has tired of living like a savage outside the city, and moreover that, inside, there is a man for whose nearness she craves most mightily."

"Tut!" said Phorenice. "Is this a romance we have swum to? You see what affectionate creatures we women are, Deucalion."—The galley was brought up against the royal quay and made fast to its golden rings. I handed the Empress ashore, but she turned again and faced the boat, her garments still yielding up a slender drip of water.—"Produce your woman prisoner, master captain, and let us see whether she is a runaway wife, or a lovesick girl mad after her sweetheart. Then I will deliver judgment on her, and as like as not will surprise you all with my clemency. I am in a mood for tender romance to-day."

The port-captain went into the little hutch of a cabin with a white face. It was plain that Phorenice's pleasantries scared him. "The man appears to be dead, Your Majesty. I see that his wounds—"

"Bring out the woman, you fool. I asked for her. Keep your carrion where it is."

I saw the fellow stoop for his knife to cut a lashing, and presently who should he bring out to the daylight but the girl I had saved from the cave-tigers in the circus, and who had so strangely drawn me to her during the hours that we had spent afterwards in companionship. It was clear, too, that the Empress recognised her also. Indeed, she made no secret about the matter, addressing her by name, and mockingly making inquiries about the ménage of the rebels, and the success of the prisoner's amours.

"This good port-captain tells me that you made a most valiant attempt to return, Naïs, and for an excuse you told that it was your love for some man in the city here which drew you. Come, now, we are willing to overlook much of your faults, if you will give us a reasonable chance. Point me out your man, and if he is a proper fellow, I will see that he weds you honestly. Yes, and I will do more for you, Naïs, since this day brings me to a husband. Seeing that all your estate is confiscate as a penalty for your late rebellion, I will charge myself with your dowry, and give it back to you. So come, name me the man."

The girl looked at her with a sullen brow. "I spoke a lie," she said; "there is no man."

I tried myself to give her advocacy. "The lady doubtless spoke what came to her lips. When a woman is in the grip of a rude soldiery, any excuse which can save her for the moment must serve. For myself, I should think it like enough that she would confess to having come back to her old allegiance, if she were asked."

"Sir," said the Empress, "keep your peace. Any in-

terest you may show in this matter will go far to offend
me. You have spoken of Naïs in your narrative before,
and although your tongue was shrewd and you did
not say much, I am a woman and I could read between
the lines. Now regard, my rebel, I have no wish to
be unduly hard upon you, though once you were my
fan-girl, and so your running away to these ill-kempt
malcontents, who beat their heads against my city walls,
is all the more naughty. But you must meet me halfway. You must give an excuse for leniency. Point me
out the man you would wed, and he shall be your
husband to-morrow."

"There is no man."

"Then name me one at random. Why, my pretty
Naïs, not ten months ago there were a score who would
have leaped at the chance of having you for a wife.
Drop your coyness, girl, and name me one of those. I
warrant you that I will be your ambassadress and will
put the matter to him with such delicacy that he will
not make you blush by refusal."

The prisoner moistened hir lips. "I am a maiden, and
I have a maiden's modesty. I will die as you choose,
but I will not do this indecency."

"Well, I am a maiden too, and though because I am
Empress also, questions of State have to stand before
questions of my private modesty, I can have a sympathy for yours—although in truth it did not obtrude
unduly when you were my fan-girl, Naïs. No, come
to think of it, you liked a tender glance and a pretty
phrase as well as any when you were fan-girl. You have
grown wild and shy, amongst these savage rebels, but
I will not punish you for that.

"Let me call your favourites to memory now. There
was Tarca, of course, but Tarca had a difference with
that ill-dressed father of yours, and wears a leprosy
on half his face instead of that beard he used to trim
so finely. And then there is Tatho, but Tatho is away
overseas. Eron, too, you liked once, but he lost an
arm in fighting t'other day, and I would not marry you

to less than a whole man. Ah, by my face! I have it, the dainty exquisite, Rota! He is the husband! How well I remember the way he used to dress in a change of garb each day to catch your proud fancy, girl. Well, you shall have Rota. He shall lead you to wife before this hour to-morrow."

Again the prisoner moistened her lips. "I will not have Rota, and spare me the others. I know why you mock me, Phorenice."

"Then there are three of us here who share one knowledge."—She turned her eyes upon me. Gods! who ever saw the like of Phorenice's eyes, and who ever saw them lit with such fire as burned within them then?—"My lord, you are marrying me for policy; I am marrying you for policy, and for another reason which has grown stronger of late, and which you may guess at. Do you wish still to carry out the match?"

I looked once at Naïs, and then I looked steadily back to Phorenice. The command given by the mouth of Zaemon from the High Council of the Sacred Mountain had to outweigh all else, and I answered that such was my desire.

"Then," said she, glowering at me with her eyes, "you shall build me up the pretty body of Naïs beneath a throne of granite as a wedding gift. And you shall do it too with your own proper hands, my Deucalion, whilst I watch your devotion."

And to Naïs she turned with a cruel smile. "You lied to me, my girl, and you spoke truth to the soldiers in the harbour forts. There is a man here in the city you came after, and he is the one man you may not have. Because you know me well, and my methods very thoroughly, your love for him must be very deep, or you would not have come. And so, being here, you shall be put beyond mischief's reach. I am not one of those who see luxury in fostering rivals.

"You came for attention at the hands of Deucalion. By my face! you shall have it. I will watch myself whilst he builds you up living."

11. An Affair with the Barbarous Fishers

So this mighty Empress chose to be jealous of a mere woman prisoner!

Now my mind had been trained to work with a soldierly quickness in these moments of stress, and I decided on my proper course on the instant the words had left her lips. I was sacrificing myself for Atlantis by order of the High Council of the Priests, and, if needful, Naïs must be sacrificed also, although in the same flash a scheme came to me for saving her.

So I bowed gravely before the Empress, and said I, "In this, and in all other things where a mere human hand is potent, I will carry out your wishes, Phorenice." And she on her part patted my arm, and fresh waves of feeling welled up from the depths of her wondrous eyes. Surely the Gods won for her half her schemes and half her battles when they gave Phorenice her shape, and her voice, and the matters which lay within the outlines of her face.

By this time the merchants, and the other dwellers adjacent to this part of the harbour, where the royal quay stands, had come down, offering changes of raiment, and houses to retire into. Phorenice was all graciousness, and though it was little enough I cared for mere wetness of my coat, still that part of the harbour into which we had been thrown by the mammoth was not over savoury, and I was glad enough to follow her example. For myself, I said no further word to Naïs, and refrained even from giving her a glance of farewell. But a small sop like this was no meal for

139

Phorenice, and she gave the port-captain strict orders for the guarding of his prisoner before she left him.

At the house into which I was ushered they gave me a bath, and I eased my host of the plainest garment in his store, and he was pleased enough at getting off so cheaply. But I had an hour to spend outside on the pavement listening to the distant din of bombardment before Phorenice came out to me again, and I could not help feeling some grim amusement at the face of the merchant who followed. The fellow was clearly ruined. He had a store of jewels and gauds of the most costly kind, which were only in fraction his own, seeing that he had bought them (as the custom is) in partnership with other merchants. These had pleased Phorenice's eye, and so she had taken all and disposed them on her person.

"Are they not pretty?" said she, showing them to me. "See how they flash under the sun. I am quite glad now, Deucalion, that the mammoth gave us that furious ride and that spill, since it has brought me such a bonny present. You may tell the fellow here that some day when he has earned some more, I will come and be his guest again. Ah! They have brought us litters, I see. Well, send one away and do you share mine with me, sir. We must play at being lovers to-day, even if love is a matter which will come to us both with more certainty to-morrow. No; do not order more bearers. My own slaves will carry us handily enough. I am glad you are not one of your gross, overfed men, Deucalion. I am small and slim myself, and I do not want to be husbanded by a man who will overshadow me."

"Back to the royal pyramid?" I asked.

"No, nor to the walls. I neither wish to fight nor to sit as Empress to-day, sir. As I have told you before, it is my whim to be Phorenice, the maiden, for a few hours, and if some one I wot of would woo me now, as other maidens are wooed, I should esteem it a luxury. Bid the slaves carry us round the harbour's rim, and give word to these starers that, if they follow,

I will call down fire upon them as I did upon the sacrifice."

Now, I had seen something of the unruliness of the streets myself, and I had gathered a hint also from the offcer at the gate of the royal pyramid that night of Phorenice's welcoming banquet. But as whatever there was in the matter must be common knowledge to the Empress, I did not bring it to her memory then. So I dismissed the guard which had come up, and drove away with a few sharp words the throng of gaping sightseers who always, silly creatures, must needs come to stare at their betters; and then I sat in the litter in the place where I was invited, and the bearers put their heads to the pole.

They swung away with us along the wide pavement which runs between the houses of the merchants and the mariner folk and the dimpling waters of the harbour, and I thought somewhat sadly of the few ships that floated on that splendid basin now, and of the few evidences of business that showed themselves on the quays. Time was when the ships were berthed so close that many had to wait in the estuary outside the walls, and memorials had been sent to the King that the port should be doubled in size to hold the glut of trade. And that, too, in the old days of oar and sail, when machines drawing power from our Lord the Sun were but rarely used to help a vessel speedily along her course.

The Egypt voyage and a return was a matter of a year then, as against a brace of months now, and of three ships that set out, one at least could be reckoned upon succumbing to the dangers of the wide waters and the terrible beasts that haunt them. But in those old days trade roared with lusty life, and was ever growing wider and more heavy. Your merchant then was a portly man and gave generously to the Gods. But now all the world seemed to be in arms, and moreover trade was vulgar. Your merchant, if he was a man of substance, forgot his merchandise, swore that chaffering was more indelicate than blasphemy and curled his beard after the new fashion, and became a courtier. Where his father had spent anxious days with cargo tally and ship-master, the son wasted hours in directing sewing men as they adorned a coat, and nights in vapouring at a banquet.

Of the smaller merchants who had no substance laid by, taxes and the constant bickerings of war had wellnigh ground them into starvation. Besides, with the country in constant uproar, there were few markets left for most merchandise, nor was there aught made now which could be carried abroad. If your weaver is pressed as a fire-tube man he does not make cloth, and if your farmer is playing at rebellion, he does not buy slaves to till his fields. Indeed, they told me that a month before my return, as fine a cargo of slaves had been brought into harbour as ever came out of Europe, and there was nothing for it but to set them ashore across the estuary, and leave them free to starve or live in the wild ground there as they chose. There was no man in all Atlantis who would hold so much as one more slave as a gift.

But though I was grieved at this falling away, all schemes for remedy would be for afterwards. It would only make ill worse to speak of it as we rode together in the litter. I was growing to know Phorenice's moods enough for that. Still, I think that she too had studied mine, and did her best to interest me between her bursts of trifling. We went out to where the westernmost harbour wall joins the land, and there the panting bearers set us down. She led me into a little house of stone which stood by itself, built out on a promontory where there is a constant run of tide, and when we had been given admittance, after much unbarring, she showed me her new gold collectors.

In the dry knowledge taught in the colleges and groves of the Sacred Mountain it had been a common fact to us that the metal gold was present in a dissolved state in all sea water, but of plans for dragging it forth into yellow hardness, none had ever been discussed. But here this field-reared upstart of an Empress had stumbled upon the trick as though it had been written in a book.

She patted my arm laughingly as I stared curiously round the place. "I tell all others in Atlantis that only the Gods have this secret," said she, "and that They gave it to me as one of themselves. But I am no Goddess to you, am I, Deucalion? And, by my face! I have no other explanation of how this plan was invented. We'll suppose I must have dreamed it. Look! The seawater sluices in through that culvert, and passes over these rough metal plates set in the floor, and then flows out again yonder in its natural course. You see the yellow metal caught in the ridges of the plates? That is gold. And my fellows here melt it with fire into bars, and take it to my smith's in the city. The tides vary constantly, as you priests know well, as the quiet moon draws them, and it does not take much figuring to know how much of the sea passes through these culverts in a month and how much gold to a grain should be caught in the plates. My fellows here at first thought to cheat me, but I towed two of them in the water once behind a galley till the cannibal fish ate them, and since then the others have given me credit for—for what do you think?"

"More divinity."

"I suppose it is that. But I am letting you see how it is done. Just have the head to work out a little sum, and see what an effect can be gained. You will be a God yet yourself, Deucalion, with these silly Atlanteans, if only you will use your wit and cleverness."

Was she laughing at me? Was she in earnest? I could not tell. Sometimes she pointed out that her success and triumphs were merely the reward of thought and brilliancy, and next moment she gave me some impossible explanation and left me to deduce that she must be more than mortal or the thing could never have been found. In good truth, this little woman with her supple mind and her supple body mystified me more and more the longer I stayed by her side; and more and more despairing did I grow that Atlantis could ever be restored by my agency to peace and the ancient Gods, even after I had carried out the commands of the High Council, and taken her to wife.

Only one plan seemed humanly possible, and that was to curb her further mischievousness by death and then leave the wretched country naturally to recover. It was just a dagger-stroke, and the thing was done. Yet the very idea of this revolted me, and when the desperate thought came to my mind (which it did ever and anon), I hugged to myself the answer that if it were fitting to do this thing, the High Gods in Their infinite wisdom would surely have put definite commands upon me for its carrying out.

Yet, such was the facination of Phorenice, that when presently we left her gold collectors, and stumbled into such peril, that a little withholding of my hand would have gained her a passage to the nether Gods, I found myself fighting when she called upon me, as seldom I have fought before. And though, of course, some blame for this must be laid upon that lust of battle which thrills even the coldest of us when blows begin to whistle and war-cries start to ring, there is no doubt also that the pleasure of protecting Phorenice, and the distaste for seeing her pulled down by those rude, uncouth fishers put special nerve and vehemence into my blows.

The cause of the matter was the unrest and the prevalency to street violence which I have spoken of above, and the desperate poverty of the common people, which led them to take any risk if it showed them a chance of winning the wherewithal to purchase a meal. We had once more mounted the litter, and once more the bearers, with their heads beneath the pole, bore us on at their accustomed swinging trot. Phorenice was telling me about her new supplies of gold. She had made fresh sumptuary laws, it appeared.

"In the old days," said she, "when yellow gold was tediously dredged up grain by grain from river gravels in the dangerous lands, a quill full would cost a rich man's savings, and so none but those whose high station fitted them to be so adorned could wear golden ornaments. But when the sea-water gave me gold here by the double handful a day, I found that the price of these river hoards decreased, and one day—could you credit it?—a common fellow, who was one of my smiths, came to me wearing a collar of yellow gold on his own common neck. Well, I had that neck divided, as payment for his presumption; and as I promised to repeat the division promptly on all other offenders, that special species of forwardness seems to be checked for the time. There are many exasperations, Deucalion, in governing these common people."

She had other things to say upon the matter, but at this point I saw two clumsy boats of fishers paddling to us from over the ripples, and at the same time amongst the narrow lanes which led between the houses on the other side of us, savage-faced men were beginning to run after the litter in threatening clusters.

"With permission," I said, "I will step out of the conveyance and scatter this rabble."

"Oh, the people always cluster round me. Poor ugly souls, they seem to take a strange delight in coming to stare at my pretty looks. But scatter them. I have said I did not wish to be followed. I am taking holiday now, Deucalion, am I not, whilst you learn to woo me?"

I stepped to the ground. The rough fishers in the boats were beginning to shout to those who dodged amongst the houses to see to it that we did not escape, and the numbers who hemmed us in on the shore side were increasing every moment. The prospect was unpleasant enough. We had come out beyond the merchants' quarters, and were level with those small huts of mud and grass which the fishing population deem sufficient for shelter, and which has always been a spot where turbulence might be expected. Indeed, even in those days of peace and good government in the old King's time, this part of the city had rarely been without its weekly riot.

The life of the fisherman is the most hard that any human toilers have to endure. Violence from the wind and waves, and pelting from firestones out of the sky are their daily portion; the great beasts that dwell in the seas hunt them with savage persistence, and it is a rare day when at least some one of the fishers' guild fails to come home to answer the tally.

Moreover, the manner which prevails of catching fish is not without its risks.

To each man there is a large sea-fowl taken as a nestling, and trained to the work. A ring of bronze is round its neck to prevent its swallowing the spoil for which it dives, and for each fish it takes and flies back with to the boat, the head and tail and inwards are given to it for a reward, the ring being removed whilst it makes the meal.

The birds are faithful, once they have got a training, and are seldom known to desert their owners; but, although the fishers treat them more kindly than they do their wives, or children of their own begetting, the life of the birds is precarious like that of their masters. The larger beasts and fish of the sea prey on them as they prey on the smaller fish, and so whatever care may be lavished upon them, they are most liable to sudden cutting off.

And here is another thing that makes the life of the fisher most precarious: if his fishing bird be slain, and the second which he has in training also come by ill fortune, he is left suddenly bereft of all utensils of livelihood, and (for aught his guild-fellows care) he may go starve. For these fishers hold that the Gods of the sea regulate their craft, and that if one is not pleasing to Them They rob him of his birds; after which it would be impious to have any truck or dealing with such a fellow; and accordingly he is left to starve or rob as he chooses.

All of which circumstances tend to make the fishers rude, desperate men, who have been forced into the trade because all other callings have rejected them. They are fellows, moreover, who will spend the gains of a month on a night's debauch, for fear that the morrow will rob them of life and the chance of spending; and, moreover, it is their one point of honour to be curbed in no desire by an ordinary fear of consequences. As will appear.

I went quickly towards the largest knot of these people, who were skulking behind the houses, leaving the litter halted in the path behind me, and I bade them sharply enough to disperse. "For an employment," I added, "put your houses in order, and clean the fish offal from the lanes between them. To-morrow I will come round here to inspect, and put this quarter into a better order. But for to-day the Empress (whose name be adored) wishes for a privacy, so cease your staring."

"Then give us money," said a shrill voice from amongst the huts.

"I will send you a torch in an hour's time," I said grimly. "and rig you a gallows, if you give me more annoyance. To your kennels, you!"

I think they would have obeyed the voice of authority if they had been left to themselves. There was a quick stir amongst them. Those that stood in the sunlight instinctively slipped into the shadow, and many dodged into the houses and cowered in dark corners out of sight. But the men in the two hide-covered fisher-boats that were paddling up, called them back with boisterous cries.

I signed to the litter-bearers to move on quickly along their road. There was need of discipline here, and I was minded to deal it out myself with a firm hand. I judged that I could prevent them following the Empress, but if she still remained as a glittering bait for them to rob, and I had to protect her also, it might be that my work would not be done so effectively.

But it seems I was presumptuous in giving an order which dealt with the person of Phorenice. She bade the bearers stand where they were, and stepped out, and drew her weapons from beneath the cushions. She came towards me strapping a sword on to her hip, and carrying a well-dinted target of gold on her left forearm. "An unfair trick," cried she, laughing. "If you will keep a fight to yourself now, Deucalion, where will your greediness carry you when I am your shrinking, wistful little wife? Are these fools truly going to stand up against us?"

I was not coveting a fight, but it seemed as if there would be no avoidance of it now. The robe and the glittering gauds of which Phorenice had recently despoiled the merchant, drew the eyes of these people with keen attraction. The fishers in the boats paddled into the surf which edged the beach, and leaped overside and left the frail basket-work structures to be spewed up sound or smashed, as chance ordered. And from the houses, and from the filthy lanes between them, poured out hordes of others, women mixed with the men, gathering round us threateningly.

"Have a care," shouted one on the outskirts of the crowd. "She called down fire for the sacrifice once to-day, and she can burn up others here if she chooses."

"So much the more for those that are left," retorted another. "She cannot burn all."

"Nay, I will not burn any," said Phorenice, "but you shall look upon my sword-play till you are tired."

I heard her say that with some malicious amusement, knowing (as one of the Seven) how she had called down the fires of the sky to burn that cloven-hoofed horse offered in sacrifice, and knowing too, full well, that she could bring down no fire here. But they gave us little enough time for wordy courtesies. Their Empress never went far unattended, and, for aught the wretches knew, an escort might be close behind. So what pilfering they did, it behoved them to get done quickly.

They closed in, jostling one another to be first, and the reek of their filthy bodies made us cough. A grimy hand launched out to seize some of the jewels which flashed on Phorenice's breast, and I lopped it off at the elbow, so that it fell at her feet, and a second later we were engaged.

"Your back to mine, comrade," cried she, with a laugh, and then drew and laid about her with fine dexterity. Bah! but it was mere slaughter, that first bout.

The crowd hustled inwards with such greediness to seize what they could, that none had space to draw back elbow for a thrust, and we two kept a circle round us by sheer whirling of steel. It is necessary to do one's work cleanly in these bouts, as wounded left on the ground unnoticed before one are as dangerous as so many snakes. But as we circled round in our battling I noted that all of Phorenice's quarry lay peaceful and still. By the Gods! but she could play a fine sword, this dainty Empress. She touched life with every thrust.

Yes, it was plain to see, now an example was given, that the throne of Atlantis had been won, not by a lovely face and a subtle tongue alone; and (as a fighter myself) I did not like Phorenice the less for the knowledge. I could but see her out of the corner of my eye, and that only now and again, for the fishers, despite their ill-knowledge of fence, and the clumsiness of their weapons, had heavy numbers, and most savage ferocity; and as they made so confident of being able to pull us down, it required more than a little hard battling to keep them from doing it. Ay, by the Gods! it was at times a fight my heart warmed to, and if I had not contrived to pluck a shield from one fool who came too vain-gloriously near me with one, I could not swear they would not have dragged me down by sheer ravening savageness.

And always above the burly uproar of the fight came very pleasantly to my ears Phorenice's cry of "Deucalion!" which she chose as her battle shout. I knew her, of course, to be a past-mistress of the art of compliment, and it was no new thing for me to hear the name roared out above a battle din, but it was given there under circumstances which were peculiar, and for the life of me I could not help being tickled by the flattery.

Condemn my weakness how you will, but I came very near then to liking the Empress of Atlantis in the way she wished. And as for that other woman who should have filled my mind, I will confess that the stress of the moment, and the fury of the engagement, had driven both her and her strait completely out beyond the marches of my memory. Of such frail stuff are we made, even those of us who esteem ourselves the strongest.

Now it is a temptation few men born to the sword can resist, to throw themselves heart and soul into a fight for a fight's sake, and it seems that women can be bitten with the same fierce infection. The attack slackened and halted. We stood in the middle of a ring of twisted dead, and the rest of the fishers and their women who hemmed us in shrank back out of reach of our weapons.

It was the moment for a truce, and the moment when a few strong words would have sent them back cowering to their huts, and given us free passage to go where we chose. But no, this Phorenice must needs sing a hymn to her sword and mine, gloating over our feats and invulnerability; and then she must needs ask payment for the bearers of her litter whom they had killed, and then speak balefully of the burnings, and the skinnings, and the sawings asunder with which this fishers' quarter would be treated in the near future, till they learned the virtues of deportment and genteel manners.

"It makes your backs creep, does it?" said Phorenice. "I do not wonder. This severity must have its unpleasant

side. But why do you not put it beyond my power
to give the order? Either you must think yourselves
Gods or me no Goddess, or you would not have gone
on so far. Come now, you nasty-smelling people, follow
out your theory, and if you make a good fight of it, I
swear by my face I will be lenient with those who do
not fall."

But there was no pressing up to meet our swords.
They still ringed us in, savage and sullen, beyond the
ring of their own dead, and would neither run back
to the houses, nor give us the game of further fight.
There was a certain stubborn bravery about them that
one could not but admire, and for myself I determined
that next time it became my duty to raise troops, I
would catch a handful of these men, and teach them
handiness with the utensils of war, and train them to
loyalty and faithfulness. But presently from behind
their ranks a stone flew, and though it whizzed between
the Empress and myself, and struck down a fisher, it
showed that they had brought a new method into their
attack, and it behoved us to take thought and meet it.

I looked round me up and down the beach. There
was no sign of a rescue. "Phorenice," I said in the
court tongue, which these barbarous fishers would
know little enough of, "I take it that a whiff of the
sea-breeze would come very pleasant after all this warm
play. As you can show such pretty sword work, will
you cut me a way down to the beach, and I will do
my poor best to keep these creatures from snapping at
our heels?"

"Oh!" cried she. "Then I am to have a courtier for
a husband after all. Why have you kept back your
flattering speeches till now? Is that your trick to make
me love you?"

"I will think out the reason for it another time."

"Ah, these stern, commanding husbands," said she,
"how they do press upon their little wives!" and with
that reaped over the ring of dead before her, and cut
and stabbed a way through those that stood between

her and the waters which creamed and crashed upon the beach. Gods! what a charge she made. It made me tingle with admiration as I followed sideways behind her, guarding the rear. And I am a man that has spent so many years in battlings, that it takes something far out of the common to move me to any enthusiasm in this matter.

There were two boats creaking and washing about in the edge of the surf, but in one, happily, the wicker-work which made its frame was crushed by the weight of the waves into a shapeless bundle of sticks, and would take half a day to replace. So that, let us but get the other craft afloat, and we should be free from further embroiling. But the fishers were quick to see the object of this new manœuvre. "Guard the boat," they shouted. "Smash her; slit her skin with your knives! Tear her with your fingers! Swim her out to sea! Oh, at least take the paddles!"

But, if these clumsy fishers could run, Phorenice was like a legged snake for speed. She was down beside the boat before any could reach it, laughing and shouting out that she could beat them at every point. Myself, I was slower of foot; and, besides, there was some that offered me a fight on the road, and I was not wishful to baulk them; and, moreover, the fewer we left clamouring behind, the fewer there would be to speed our going with their stones. Still I came to the beach in good order, and laid hands on the flimsy boat and tipped her dry.

"Fighting is no trade for me," I cried, "whilst you are here, Phorenice. Guard me my back and walk out into the water."

I took the boat, thrusting it afloat, and wading with it till two lines of the surf were past. The fishers swarmed round us, active as fish in their native element, and strove mightily to get hands on the boat and slit the hides which covered it with their eager fingers. But I had a spare hand, and a short stabbing-knife for such close-quarter work, and here, there, and everywhere was Phorenice the Empress, with her thirsty dripping sword. By the Gods! I laughed with sheer delight at seeing her art of fence.

But the swirl of a great fish into the shallows, and the squeal of a fisher as he was dragged down and borne away into the deep, made me mindful of foes that no skill can conquer, and no bravery avoid. Without taking time to give the Empress a word of warning, I stooped, and flung an arm round her, and threw her up out of the water into the boat, and then thrust on with all my might, driving the flimsy craft out to sea, whilst my legs crept under me for fear of the beasts which swam invisible beneath the muddied waters.

To the fishers, inured to these horrid perils by daily association, the seizing of one of their number meant little, and they pressed on, careless of their dull lives, eager only to snatch the jewels which still flaunted on Phorenice's breast. Of the vengeance that might come after they recked nothing; let them but get the wherewithal for one night's good debauch, and they would forget that such a thing as the morning of a morrow could have existence.

Two fellows I caught and killed that, diving down beneath, tried to slit the skin of the boat out of sight under the water; and Phorenice cared for all those that tried to put a hand on the gunwales. Yes, and she did more than that. A huge long-necked turtle that was stirred out of the mud by the turmoil, came up to daylight, and swung its great horn-lipped mouth to this side and that, seeking for a prey. The fishers near it dodged and dived. I, thrusting at the stern of the boat, could only hope it would pass me by and so offered an easy mark. It scurried towards me, champing its noisy lips, and beating the water into spray with its flippers.

But Phorenice was quick with a remedy and a rescue. She passed her sword through one of the fishers that pressed her, and then thrust the body towards the turtle. The great neck swooped towards it; the long slimy feelers which protruded from its head quivered and snuffled; and then the horny green jaws crunched on it, and drew it down out of sight.

The boat was in deep water now, and Phorenice called upon me to come in over the side, she the while balancing nicely so that the flimsy thing should not be overset. The fishers had given up their pursuit, finding that they earned nothing but lopped-off arms and split faces by coming within swing of this terrible sword of their Empress, and so contented themselves with volleying jagged stones in the hopes of stunning us or splitting the boat. However, Phorenice crouched in the stern, holding the two shields—her own golden target, and the rough hide buckler I had won—and so protected both of us whilst I paddled, and though many stones clattered against the shields, and hit the hide covering of the boat, so that it resounded like a drum, none of them did damage, and we drew quickly out of their range.

12. The Drug of Our Lady the Moon

Our Lord the Sun was riding towards the end of His day, and the smoke from a burning mountain fanned black and forbidding before His face. Phorenice wrung the water from her clothes and shivered. "Work hard with those paddles, Deucalion, and take me in through the water-gate and let me be restored to my comforts again. That merchant would rue if he saw how his pretty garments were spoiled, and I rue too, being a woman, and remembering that he at least has no others I can take in place of these." She looked at me sidelong, tossing back the short red hair from her eyes. "What think you of my wisdom in coming where we have come without an escort?"

"The Empress can do no wrong," I quoted the old formula with a smile.

"At least I have shown you that I can fight. I caught you looking your approval of me quite pleasantly once or twice. You were a difficult man to thaw, Deucalion, but you warm perceptibly as you keep on being near me. La, sir, we shall be a pair of rustic sweethearts yet, if this goes on. I am glad I thought of the device of going near those smelly fishers."

So she had taken me out in the litter unattended for the plain purpose of inviting a fight, and showing me her skill at arms, and perhaps, too, of seeing in person how I also carried myself in a moment of stress. Well, if we were to live on together as husband and wife, it was good that each should know to a nicety the other's powers; and also, I am too much of an old battler and too much enamoured with the glorious handling of arms to quarrel very deeply with any one who offers me a tough upstanding fight. Still for the life of me, I could not help comparing Phorenice with another woman. With a similar chance open before us, Naïs had robbed me of the struggle through a sheer pity for those squalid rebels who did not even call her chieftain; whilst here was this Empress frittering away two score of the hardiest of her subjects merely to gratify a whim.

Yet, loyal to my vow as a priest, and to the commands set upon me by the high council on the Sacred Mountain, I tried to put away these wayward thoughts and comparisons. As I rowed over the swingings of the waves towards the forts which guard the harbour's mouth, I sent prayers to the High Gods to give my tongue dexterity, and They through Their love for the country of Atlantis, and the harassed people, whom it was my deep wish to serve, granted me that power of speech which Phorenice loved. Her eyes glowed upon me as I talked.

This beach of the fishers where we had had our passage at arms is safe from ship attack from without, by reason of a chain of jagged rocks which spring up from the deep, and run from the harbour side to the end of the city wall. The fishers know the passes, and can oftentimes get through to the open water beyond without touching a stone; or if they do see a danger of hitting on the reef, leap out and carry their light boats in their hands till the water floats them again. But here I had neither the knowledge nor the dexterity, and, thought I, now the High Gods will show finally if They wish this woman who has defiled them to reign on in Atlantis, and if also They wish me to serve as her husband.

I cried these things in my heart, and waited to receive the omen. There was no half-answer. A great wave rose in the lagoon behind us, a wave such as could have only been caused by an earth tremor, and on its sleek back we were hurled forward and thrown clear of the reefs with their seaweeds licking round us, without so much as seeing a stone of the barrier. I bowed my head as I rowed on towards the harbour forts. It was plain that not yet would the High Gods take vengeance for the insults which this lovely woman had offered Them.

The sentries in the two forts beat drums at one another in their accustomed rotation, and in the growing dusk were going to pay little enough attention to the fishingboat which lay against the great chain clamouring to have it lowered. But luckily a pair of officers were taking the air of the evening in a stone-dropping turret of the roof of the nearer fort, and these recognised the tone of our shouts. They silenced the drums, torches were lowered to make sure of our faces, and then with a splash the great chain was dropped into the water to give us passage.

A galley lay inside, nuzzling the harbour wall, and

presently the ladder of ropes was let down from the
top of the nearest fort, and a crew came down to
man the oars. There were the customary changes of
raiment too, given as presents by the officers of the
fort, and these we put on in the cabin of the galley in
place of the sodden clothes we wore. There are fevers
to be gained by carrying wet clothes after sunset, and
though from personal experience I have learned that
these may be warded off with drugs, I noticed with
some grim amusement that the Empress had sufficiently
little of the Goddess about her to fear very much the
ailments which are due to frail humanity.

The galley rowed swiftly across the calm waters of
the harbour, and made fast to the rings of gold on
the royal quay, and whilst we were waiting for litters
to be brought, I watched a lantern lit in the boat
which stood guard over Phorenice's mammoth. The
huge red beast stood shoulder-deep in the harbour
water, with trunk up-turned. It was tamed now, and
the light of the boat's lantern fell on the little ripples
sent out by its tremblings. But I did not choose to
intercede or ask mercy for it. If the mammoth sank
deeper in the harbour mud, and was swallowed, I
could have borne the loss with equanimity.

To tell the truth, that ride on the great beast's
back had impressed me unfavourably. In fact, it
put into me a sense of helplessness that was wellnigh
intolerable. Perhaps circumstances have made me
unduly self-reliant: on that others must judge. But I
will own to having a preference for walking on my
own proper feet, as the Gods in fashioning our
shapes most certainly intended. On my own feet I
am able to guard my own head and neck, and have
done on four continents, throughout a long and active
life, and on many a thousand occasions. But on the
back of that detestable mammoth, pah! I grew as
nervous as a child or a dastard.

However, I had little enough leisure for personal
megrims just then. Whilst we waited, Phorenice asked

the port-captain (who must needs come up officiously to make his salutations) after the disposal of Naïs, and was told that she had been clapped into a dungeon beneath the royal pyramid, and the officer of the guard there had given his bond for her safe-keeping.

"It is to be hoped he understands his work," said the Empress. "That pretty Naïs knows the pyramid better than most, and it may be he will be sent to the tormentors for putting her in a cell which had a secret outlet. You would feel pleasure if the girl escaped, Deucalion?"

"Assuredly," said I, knowing how useless it would be to make a secret of the matter. "I have no enmity against Naïs."

"But I have," said she viciously, "and I am still minded to lock your faith to me by that wedding gift you know of."

"The thing shall be done," I said. "Before all, the Empress of Atlantis."

"Poof! Deucalion, you are too stiff and formal. You ought to be mightily honoured that I condescend to be jealous of your favours. Your hand, sir, please, to help me into the litter. And now come in beside me, and keep me warm against the night air. Ho! you guards there with the torches! Keep farther back against the street walls. The perfume you are burning stifles me."

Again there was a feast that night in the royal banqueting-hall; again I sat beside Phorenice on the raised daïs which stands beneath the symbols of the snake and the out-stretched hand. What had been taken for granted before about our forthcoming relationship was this time proclaimed openly; the Empress herself acknowledged me as her husband that was to be; and all that curled and jewelled throng of courtiers hailed me as greater than themselves, by reason of this woman's choice. There was method, too, in their salutation. Some rumour must have got about of my preference for the older and simpler habits, and there was no drinking wine to my health after the new and (as I considered) impertinent manner. Decorously, each lord and lady there came forward, and each in turn spilt a goblet at my feet; and when I called any up, whether man or woman, to receive tit-bits from my platter, it was eaten simply and thankfully, and not kissed or pocketed with any extravagant gesture.

The flaring jets of earth-breath showed me, too, so I thought, a plainer habit of dress, and a more sober mien amongst this thoughtless mob of banqueters. And, indeed, it must have been plain to notice, for Phorenice, leaning over till the ruddy curls on her shoulder brushed my face, chided me in a playful whisper as having usurped her high authority already.

"Oh, sir," she pleaded mockingly, "do not make your rule over us too ascetic. I have given no orders for this change, but to-night there are no perfumes in the air; the food is so plain and I have half a mind to burn the cook; and as for the clothes and gauds of these diners, by my face! they might have come straight from the old King's reign before I stepped in here to show how tasteful could be colours on a robe, or how pretty the glint of a jewel. It's done by no orders of mine, Deucalion. They have swung round to this change by sheer courtier instinct. Why, look at the beards of the men! There is not half the curl about many of them to-day that they showed with such exquisiteness yesterday. By my face! I believe they'd reap their chins to-morrow as smooth as yours, if you go on setting the fashions at this prodigious rate and I do not interfere."

"Why hinder them if they feel more cleanly shaven?"

"No, sir. There shall be only one clean chin where a beard can grow in all Atlantis, and that shall be carried by the man who is husband to the Empress. Why, my Deucalion, would you have no sumptuary laws? Would you have these good folk here and the common people outside imitate us in every cut of the hair and every fold of a garment which it pleases us to discover?

Come, sir, if you and I chose to say that our sovereignty was marked only by our superior strength of arm and wit, they would hate us at once for our arrogance; whereas, if we keep apart to ourselves a few mere personal decorations, these become just objects to admire and pleasantly envy."

"You show me that there is more in the office of a ruler than meets the eye."

"And yet they tell me, and indeed show me, that you have ruled with some success."

"I employed the older method. It requires a Phorenice to invent these nicer flights."

"Flatterer!" said she, and smote me playfully with the back of her little fingers on my arm. "You are becoming as great a courtier as any of them. You make me blush with your fine pleasantries, Deucalion, and there is no fan-girl here to-night to cool my cheek. I must choose me another fan-girl. But it shall not be Ylga. Ylga seems to have more of a kindness for you than I like, and if she is wise she will go live in her palace at the other side of the city, and there occupy herself with the ordering of her slaves, and the makings of embroideries. I shall not be hard on Ylga unless she forces me, but I will have no woman in this kingdom treat you with undue civility."

"And how am I to act," said I, falling in with her mood, "when I see and hear all the men of Atlantis making their protestations before you? By your own confession they all love you as ardently as they seem to have loved you hopelessly."

"Ah, now," she said, "you must not ask me to do impossibilities. I am powerful if you will. But I have no force which will govern the hearts of these poor fellows on matters such as that. But if you choose, you make proclamation that I am given now body and inwards to you, and if they continue to offend your pride in this matter, you may take your culprits, and give them over to the tormentors. Indeed, Deucalion, I think it would be a pretty attention to me if you did arrange some such ceremony. It seems to me a present," she added with a frown, "that the jealousy is too much on one side."

"You must not expect that a man who has been divorced from love for all of a busy life can learn all its niceties in an instant. Myself, I was feeling proud of my progress. With any other schoolmistress than you, Phorenice, I should not be near so forward. In fact (if one may judge by my past record), I should not have begun to learn at all."

"I suppose you think I should be satisfied with that? Well, I am not. I can be finely greedy over some matters."

The banquet this night did not extend to inordinate length. Phorenice had gone through much since last she slept, and though she had declared herself Goddess in the meantime, it seemed that her body remained mortal as heretofore. The black rings of weariness had grown under her wondrous eyes, and she lay back amongst the cushions of the divan with her limbs slackened and listless. When the dancers came and postured before us, she threw them a jewel and bade them begone before they had given a half of their performance, and the poet, a silly swelling fellow who came to sing the deeds of the day, she would not hear at all.

"To-morrow," she said wearily, "but for now grant me peace. My Lord Deucalion has given me much food for thought this day, and presently I go to my chamber to muse over the future policies of this State throughout the night. To-morrow come to me again, and if your poetry is good and short, I will pay you surprisingly. But see to it that you are not long-winded. If there are superflous words, I will pay you for those with the stick."

She rose to her feet then, and when the banqueters had made their salutation to us, I led her away from the banqueting-hall and down the passages with their secret doors which led to her private chambers. She clung on my arm, and once when we halted whilst a great stone block swung slowly ajar to let us pass, she drooped her head against my shoulder. Her breath came warm against my cheek, and the loveliness of her face so close at hand surpasses the description of words. I think it was in her mind that I should kiss the red lips which were held so near to mine, but willing though I was to play the part appointed, I could not bring myself to that. So when the stone block had swung, she drew away with a sigh, and we went on without further speech.

"May the High Gods treat you tenderly," I said, when we came to the door of her bed-chamber.

"I am my own God," said she, "in all things but one. By my face! you are a tardy wooer, Deucalion. Where do you go now?"

"To my own chamber."

"Oh, go then, go."

"Is there anything more I could do?"

"Nothing that your wit or your will would prompt you to. Yes, indeed, you are finely decorous, Deucalion, in your old-fashioned way, but you are a mighty poor wooer. Don't you know, my man, that a woman esteems some things the more highly if they are taken from her by rude force?"

"It seems I know little enough about women."

"You never said a truer word. Bah! And I believe your coldness brings you more benefit in a certain matter than any show of passion could earn. There, get you gone, if the atmosphere of a maiden's bed-chamber hurts your rustic modesty, and your Gods keep you, Deucalion, if that's the phrase, and if you think They can do it. Get you gone, man, and leave me solitary."

I had taken the plan of the pyramid out of the archives before the banquet and learned it thoroughly, and so was able to thread my way through its angular mazes without pause or blunder. I, too, was heavily wearied with what I had gone through since my last snatch of sleep, but I dare set apart no time for rest just then. Naïs must be sacrificed in part for the needs of Atlantis; but a plan had come to me by which it seemed that she need not be sacrificed wholly; and to carry this through there was need for quick thought and action.

Help came to me also from a quarter I did not expect. As I passed along the tortuous way between the ponderous stones of the pyramid, which led to the apartments that had been given me by Phorenice, a woman glided up out of the shadows of one of the side passages, and when I lifted my hand lamp, there was Ylga.

She regarded me half-sullenly. "I have lost my place," she said, "and it seems I need never have spoken. She intended to have you all along, and it was not a thing like that which could put her off. And you— you just think me officious, if, indeed, you have ever given me another thought till now."

"I never forget a kindness."

"Oh, you will learn that trick soon now. And you are going to marry her, you! The city is ringing with it. I thought at least you were honest, but when there is a high place to be got by merely taking a woman with it, you are like the rest. I thought, too, that you would be one of those men who have a distrust for ruddy hair. And, besides she is little."

"Ylga," I said, "you have taught me that these walls are full of crannies and ears. I will listen to no word against Phorenice. But I would have further converse with you soon. If you still have a kindness for me, go to the chamber that is mine and wait for me there. I will join you shortly."

She drooped her eyes. "What do you want of me, Deucalion?"

"I want to say something to you. You will learn who it concerns later."

"But is it—is it fitting for a maiden to come to a man's room at this hour?"

"I know little of your conventions here in this new Atlantis. I am Deucalion, girl, and if you still have qualms, remembering that, do not come."

She looked up at me with a sneer. "I was foolish," she said. "My lord's coldness has grown into a proverb, and I should have remembered it. Yes; I will come."

"Go now, then," said I, and waited till she had passed on ahead and was out of sight and hearing. With Ylga to help me, my tasks were somewhat lightened, and their sequence changed. In the first instance, now, I had got to make my way with as little delay and show as possible into a certain sanctuary which lay within the temple of our Lady the Moon. And here my knowledge as one of the Seven stood me in high favour.

All the temples of the city of Atlantis are in immediate and secret connection with the royal pyramid, but the passages are little used, seeing that they are known only to the Seven and to the Three above them, supposing that there are three men living at one time sufficiently learned in the highest of the highest mysteries to be installed in that sublime degree of the Three. And, even by these, the secret ways may only be used on occasions of the greatest stress, so that a generation well may pass without their being trodden by a human foot.

It was with some trouble, and after no little experiment that I groped my way into this secret alley; but once there, the rest was easy. I had never trodden it before certainly, but the plan of it had been taught me at my initiation as one of the Seven, and the course of the windings came back to me now with easy accuracy. I walked quickly, not only because the air on those deep crannies is always full of lurking evils, but also because the hours were fleeting, and much must be done before our Lord the Sun again rose to make another day.

I came to the spy-place which commands the temple, and found the holy place empty, and, alas! dust-covered, and showing little trace that worshippers ever frequented it these latter years. A vast stone of the wall swung outwards and gave me entrance, and presently (after the solemn prayer which is needful before attempting these matters), I took the metal stair from the place where it is kept, and climbed to the lap of the Goddess, and then, pulling the stair after me, climbed again upwards till my length lay against her calm mysterious face.

A shivering seized me as I thought of what was intended, for even a warrior hardened to horrid sights and deeds may well have qualms when he is called upon to juggle with life and death, and years and history, with the welfare of his country in one hand, and the future of a woman who is as life to him in the other. But again I told myself that the hours flew, and laid hold of the jewel which is studded into the forehead of the image with one hand, and then stretching out, thrust at a corner of the eyebrow with the other. With a faint creak the massive eyeball below, a stone that I could barely have covered with my back, swung inwards. I stepped off the stair, and climbed into the gap. Inside was the chamber which is hollowed from the head of the Goddess.

It was the first time I had seen this most secret place, but the aspect of it was familiar to me from my teaching, and I knew where to find the thing which would fill my need. Yet, occupied though I might be with the stress of what was to befall, I could not help having a wonder and an admiration for the cleverness with which it was hidden.

High as I was in the learning and mysteries of the Priestly Clan, the structure of what I had come to fetch was hidden from me. Beforetime I had known only of their power and effect; and now that I came to handle them, I saw only some roughly rounded balls, like nut kernels, grass green in colour, and in hardness like the wax of bees. There were three of these balls in the hidden place, and I took the one that was needful, concealing the others as I had found them. It may have been a drug, it may have been something more; what exactly it was I did not know; only of its power and effect I was sure, as that was set forth plainly in the teaching I had learned; and so I put it in a pouch of my garment, returning by the way I had come, and replacing all things in due order behind me.

One look I took at the image of the Goddess before I left the temple. The jet of earth-breath which burns eternally from the central altar lit her from head to toe, and threw sparkles from the great jewel in her forehead. Vast she was, and calm and peaceful beyond all human imaginings, a perfect symbolism of that rest and quietness which many sigh for so vainly on this rude earth, but which they will never attain unless by their piety they earn a place in the hereafter, where our Lady the Moon and the rest of the High Ones rein in Their eternal glorious majesty.

It was with tired dragging limbs that I made my way back again to the royal pyramid, and at last came to my own private chamber. Ylga awaited me there, though at first I did not see her. The suspicions of these modern days had taken a deep hold of the girl, and she must needs crouch in hiding till she made sure it was I who came to the chamber, and, moreover, that I came alone.

"Oh, frown at me if you choose," said she sullenly, "I am past caring now for your good opinion. I had heard so much of Deucalion, and I thought I read honesty in you when first you came ashore; but now I know that you are no better than the rest. Phorenice offers you a high place, and you marry her blithely to get it. And why, indeed, should you not marry her? People say she is pretty, and I know she can be warm. I have seen her warm and languishing to scores of men. She is clever, too, with her eyes, is our great Empress; I grant her that. And as for you, it tickles you to be courted."

"I think you are a very silly woman," I said.

"If you flatter yourself it matters a rap to me whom you marry, you are letting conceit run away with you."

"Listen," I said. "I did not ask you here to make foolish speeches which seem largely beyond my comprehension. I asked you to help me do a service to one of your own blood-kin."

She stared at me wonderingly. "I do not understand."

"It rests largely with you as to whether Naïs dies to-morrow, or whether she is thrown into a sleep from which she may waken on some later and more happy day."

"Nais!" she gasped. "My twin, Naïs? She is not here. She is out in the camp with those nasty rebels who bite against the city walls, if, indeed, still she lives."

"Naïs, your sister, is near us in the royal pyramid this minute, and under guard, though where I do not know." And with that I told her all that had passed since the girl was brought up a prisoner in the galley of that foolish, fawning captain of the port. "The Empress has decreed that Naïs shall be buried alive under a throne of granite which I am to build for her to-morrow, and buried she will assuredly be. Yet I have a kindness for Naïs, which you may guess at if you choose, and I am minded to send her into a sleep such as only we higher priests know of, from which at some future day she may possibly awaken."

"So it is Naïs; and not Phorenice, and not—not any other?"

"Yes; it is Naïs. I marry the Empress because Zaemon, who is mouthpiece to the High Council of the Priests, has ordered it, for the good of Atlantis. But my inwards remain still cold towards her."

"Almost I hate poor Naïs already."

"Your vengeance would be easy. Do not tell me where she is gaoled, and I shall not dare to ask. Even to give Naïs a further span of life I cannot risk making inquiries for her cell, when there is a chance that those who tell me might carry news to the Empress, and so cause more trouble for this poor Atlantis."

"And why should I not carry the news, and so bring myself into favour again? I tell you that being fangirl to Phorenice and second woman in the kingdom is a thing that not many would cast lightly aside."

I looked her between eyes and smiled. "I have no fear there. You will not betray me, Ylga. Neither will you sell Naïs."

"I seem to remember very small love for this same Naïs just now," she said bitterly. "But you are right about that other matter. I shall not buy myself back at your expense. Oh, I am a fool, I know, and you can give me no thanks that I care about, but there is no other way I can act."

"Then let us fritter no more time. Go you out now and find where Naïs is gaoled, and bring me news how I can say ten words to her, and press a certain matter into her clasp."

She bowed her head and left the chamber, and for long enough I was alone. I sat down on the couch, and rested wearily against the wall. My bones ached, my eyes ached, and most of all, my inwards ached. I had thought to myself that a man who makes his life sufficiently busy will find no leisure for these pains which assault frailer folk; but a philosophy like this, which carried one well in Yucatan, showed poorly enough when one tried it here at home. But that there was duty ahead, and the order of the High Council to be carried into effect, the bleakness of the prospect would have daunted me, and I would have prayed the Gods then to spare me further life, and take me unto Themselves.

Ylga came back at last, and I got up and went quickly after her as she led down a maze of passages and alleyways. "There has been no care spared over her guarding," she whispered, as we halted once to move a stone. "The officer of the guard is an old lover of mine, and I raised his hopes to the burning point again by a dozen words. But when I wanted to see his prisoner, there he was as firm as brass. I told him she was my sister, but that did not move him. I offered him —oh, Deucalion, it makes me blush to think of the things I did offer to that man, but there was no stirring him. He has watched the tormentors so many times, that there is no tempting him into touch of their instruments."

"If you have failed, why bring me out here?"

"Oh, I am not inveigling you into a lover's walk with myself, sir. You tickle yourself when you think your society is so pleasant as that."

"Come, girl, tell me then what it is. If my temper is short, credit it against my weariness."

"I have carried out my lord's commands in part. I know the cell where Naïs lives, and I have had speech with her, though not through the door. And moreover, I have not seen her or touched her hand."

"Your riddles are beyond me, Ylga, but if there is a chance, let us get on and have this business done."

"We are at the place now," said she, with a hard little laugh, "and if you kneel on the floor, you will find an airshaft, and Naïs will answer you from the lower end. For myself, I will leave you. I have a delicacy in hearing what you want to say to my sister, Deucalion."

"I thank you," I said. "I will not forget what you have done for me this night."

"You may keep your thanks," she said bitterly, and walked away into the shadows.

I knelt on the floor of the gallery, and found the air passage with my hand, and then, putting my lips to it, whispered for Naïs.

The answer came on the instant, muffled and quiet. "I knew my lord would come for a farewell."

"What the Empress said, has to be. You understand, my dear? It is for Atlantis."

"Have I reproached my lord, by word or glance?"

"I myself am bidden to place you in the hollow between the stones, and I must do it."

"Then my last sleep will be a sweet one. I could not ask to be touched by pleasanter hands."

"But it mayhap that a day will come when she whom you know of will be suffered by the High Gods to live on this land of Atlantis no longer."

"If my lord will cherish my poor memory when he is free again, I shall be grateful. He might, if he chose, write them on the stones: Here was buried a maid who died gladly for the good of Atlantis, even though she knew that the man she so dearly loved was husband to her murderess."

"You must not die," I whispered. "My breast is near broken at the very thought of it. And for respite, we must trust to the ancient knowledge, which in its day has been sent out from the Ark of the Mysteries."—I took the green waxy ball in my fingers, and stretched them down the crooked air-shaft to the full of my span.—"I have somewhat for you here. Reach up and try to catch it from me."

I heard the faint rustle of her arm as it swept against the masonry, and then the ball was taken over into her grasp. Gods! what a thrill went through me when the fingers of Naïs touched mine! I could not see her, because of the crookedness of the shaft, but that faint touch of her was exquisite.

"I have it," she whispered. "And what now, dear?"

"You will hide the thing in your garment, and when to-morrow the upper stone closes down upon you and the light is gone, then you will take it between your lips and let it dissolve as it will. Sleep will take you, my darling, then, and the High Gods will watch over you, even though centuries pass before you are roused."

"If Deucalion does not wake me, I shall pray never again to open an eye. And now go, my lord and my dear. They watch me here constantly, and I would not have you harmed by being brought to notice."

"Yes, I must go, my sweetheart. It will not do to have our scheme spoiled by a foolish loitering. May the most High Gods attend your rest, and if the sacrifice we make finds favour, may They grant us meeting here again on earth before we meet—as we must—when our time is done, and They take us up to Their own place."

"Amen," she whispered back, and then: "Kiss your fingers, dear, and thrust them down to me."

I did that, and for an instant felt her fondle them down the crook of the airshaft out of sight, and then heard her withdraw her little hand and kiss it fondly. Then again she kissed her own fingers and stretched them up, and I took up the virtue of that parting kiss on my finger-tips and pressed it sacredly to my lips.

"Living, sleeping, or dead, always my darling," she whispered. And then, before I could answer, she whispered again: "Go, they are coming for me." And so I went, knowing that I could do no more to help her then, and knowing that all our schemes would be spilt if any eye spied upon me as I lay there beside the air shaft. But my chest was like to have split with the dull, helpless anguish that was in it, as I made my way back to my chamber through the mazy alleys of the pyramid.

"Do not look upon mine eyes, dear, when the time comes," had been her last command, "or they will tell a tale which Phorenice, being a woman, would read. Remember, we make these small denials, not for our own likings, but for Atlantis, which is mother to us all."

13. The Burying Alive of Naïs

There is no denying that the wishes of Phorenice were carried into quick effect in the city of Atlantis. Her modern theory was that the country and all therein existed only for the good of the Empress, and when she had a desire, no cost could possibly be too great in its carrying out.

She had given forth her edict concerning the burying alive of Naïs, and though the words were that I was to build the throne of stone, it was an understood thing that the manual labour was to be done for me by others. Heralds made the proclamation in every ward of the city, and masons, labourers, stonecutters, sculptors, engineers, and architects took hands from whatever was occupying them for the moment, and hastened to the rendezvous. The architects chose a chief who gave directions, and the lesser architects and the engineers saw these carried into effect. Any material within the walls of the city on which they set their seal, was taken at once without payment or compensation; and as the blocks of stone they chose were the most monstrous that could be got, they were forced to demolish no few buildings to give them passage.

I have before spoken of the modern rage for erecting new palaces and pyramids, and even though at the moment an army of rebels was battering with war engines at the city walls, the building guilds were steadily at work, and their skill (with Phorenice's marvellous invention to aid them) was constantly on the increase. True, they could not move such massive blocks of stone as those which the early Gods planted for the sacred circle of our Lord the Sun, but they had got rams and trucks and cranes which could handle amazing bulks.

The throne was to be erected in the open square before the royal pyramid. Seven tiers of stone were there for a groundwork, each a knee-height deep, and each cut in the front with three steps. In the uppermost layer was a cavity made to hold the body of Naïs, and above this was poised the vast block which formed the seat of the throne itself.

Throughout the night, to the light of torches, relay after relay of the stonecutters, and the masons, and the sweating labourers had oiled over bringing up the stone and dressing it into fit shape, and laying it in due position; and the engineers had built machines for lifting, and the architects had proved that each stone lay in its just and perfect place. Whips cracked, and men fainted with the labour, but so soon as one was incapable another pressed forward into his place. No delay was brooked when Phorenice had said her wish.

And finally, as the square began to fill with people come to gape at the pageant of to-day, the chippings and the scaffolding were cleared away, and with it the bodies of some half-score of workmen who had died from accidents or their exertions during the building, and there stood the throne, splendid in its carvings, and all ready for completion. The lower part stood more than two man-heights above the ground, and no stone of its courses weighed less than twenty men; the upper part was double the weight of any of these, and was carved so that the royal snake encircled the chair, and the great hooded head overshadowed it. But at present the upper part was not on its bed, being held up high by lifting rams, for what purposes all men knew.

It was to face this scene, then, that I came out from the royal pyramid at the summons of the chamberlains in the cool of next morning. Each great man who had come there before me had banner-bearers and trumpeters to proclaim his presence; the middle classes were in all their bravery of apparel; and even poor squalid creatures, with ribs of hunger showing through their dusty skins, had turbans and wisps of colour wrapped about their heads to mark the gaiety of the day.

The trumpets proclaimed my coming, and the people shouted welcome, and with the gorgeous chamberlains walking backwards in advance, I went across to a scarlet awning that had been prepared, and took my seat upon the cushions beneath it.

And then came Phorenice, my bride that was to be that day, fresh from sleep, and glorious in her splendid beauty. She was borne out from the pyramid in an open litter of gold and ivory by fantastic savages from Europe, her own refinement of feature being thrown up into all the higher relief by contrast with their brutish ugliness. One could hear the people draw a deep breath of delight as their eyes first fell upon her; and it is easy to believe there was not a man in that crowd which thronged the square who did not envy me her choice, nor was there a soul present (unless Ylga was there somewhere veiled) who could by any stretch imagine that I was not overjoyed in winning so lovely a wife.

For myself, I summoned up all the iron of my training to guard the expression of my face. We were here on ceremonial to-day; a ghastly enough affair throughout all its acts, if you choose, but still ceremonial; and I was minded to show Phorenice a grand manner that would leave her nothing to cavil at. After all that had been gone through and endured, I did not intend a great scheme to be shattered by letting my agony and pain show themselves, in either a shaking hand or a twitching cheek. When it came to the point, I told myself, I would lay the living body of my love in the hollow beneath the stone as calmly, and with as little outward emotion, as though I had been a mere priest carrying out the burial of some dead stranger. And she, on her part, would not, I knew, betray our secret. With her, too, it was truly "Before all Atlantis."

I think it spared a pang to find that there was to be

no mockery or flippancy in what went forward. All was solemn and impressive; and, though a certain grandeur and sombreness which bit deep into my breast was lost to the vulgar crowd, I fancy that the outward shape of the double sacrifice they witnessed that day would not be forgotten by any of them, although the inner meaning of it all was completely hidden from their minds. When it suited her fancy, none could be more strict on the ritual of a ceremony than this many-mooded Empress, and it appeared that on this occasion she had given command that all things were to be carried out with the rigid exactness and pomp of the older manner.

So she was borne up by her Europeans to the scarlet awning, and I handed her to the ground. She seated herself on the cushions, and beckoned me to her side, entwining her fingers with mine as has always been the custom with rulers of Atlantis and their consorts. And there before us as we sat, a body of soldiery marched up, and opening out showed Naïs in their midst. She had a collar of metal round her neck, with chains depending from it firmly held by a brace of guards, so that she should not run in upon the spears of the escort, and thus get a quick and easy death, which is often the custom of those condemned to the more lingering punishments.

But it was pleasant to see that she still wore her clothing. Raiment, whether of fabric or skin, has its value, and custom has always given the garments of the condemned to the soldiers guarding them. So as Naïs was not stripped, I could not but see that some one had given moneys to the guards as a recompense, and in this I thought I saw the hand of Ylga, and felt a gratitude towards her.

The soldiers brought her forward to the edge of the pavilion's shade, and she was bidden prostrate herself before the Empress, and this she wisely did and so avoided rough handling and force. Her face was pale, but showed neither fear nor defiance, and her eyes were calm and natural. She was remembering what was due to Atlantis, and I was thrilled with love and pride as I watched her.

But outwardly I, too, was impassive as a man of stone, and though I knew that Phorenice's eye was on my face, there was never anything on it from first to last that I would not have had her see.

"Naïs," said the Empress, "you have eaten from my platter when you were fan-girl, and drunk from my cup, and what was yours I gave you. You should have had more than gratitude, you should have had knowledge also that the arm of the Empress was long and her hand consummately heavy. But it seems that you have neither of these things. And, moreover, you have tried to take a certain matter that the Empress has set apart for herself. You were offered pardon, on terms, and you rejected it. You were foolish. But it is a day now when I am inclined to clemency. Presently, seated on that carved throne of granite which he has built me yonder, I shall take my Lord Deucalion to husband. Give me a plain word that you are sorry, girl, and name a man whom you would choose, and I will remember the brightness of the occasion, you shall be pardoned and wed before we rise from these cushions."

"I will not wed," she said quietly.

"Think for the last time, Naïs, of what is the other choice. You will be taken, warm, and quick, and beautiful as you stand there this minute, and laid in the hollow place that is made beneath the throne-stone. Deucalion, that is to be my husband, will lay you in that awful bed, as a symbol that so shall perish all Phorenice's enemies, and then he will release the rams and lower the upper stone into place, and the world shall see your face no more. Look at the bright sky, Naïs, fill your chest with the sweet warm air, and then think of what this death will mean. Believe me, girl, I do not want to make you an example unless you force me."

"I will not wed," said the prisoner quietly.

The Empress loosed her fingers from my arm, and

lay back against the cushions. "If the girl presumes on our old familiarity, or thinks that I jest, show her now, Deucalion, that I do not."

"The Empress is far from jesting," I said. "I will do this thing because it is the wish of the Empress that it should be done, and because it is the command of the Empress that a symbol of it shall remain for ever as an example for others. Lead your prisoner to the place."

The soldiers wheeled, and the two guards with the chains of the collar which was on the neck of Naïs prepared to put out force to drag her up the steps. But she walked with them willingly, and with a colour unchanged, and I rose from my seat, and made obeisance to the Empress and followed them.

Before all those ten thousand eyes, we two made no display of emotion then, not only for Atlantis' sake, but also because both Naïs and I had a nicety and a pride in our natures. We were not as Phorenice to flaunt endearments before others.

Yet, when I had bidden the guards unhasp the collar which held the prisoner's neck, and clapped my arms round her, showing all the roughness of one who has no mind that his captive shall escape or even unduly struggle, a thrill gushed through me so potent that I was like to have fainted, and it was only by supreme strain of will that I held unbrokenly on with the ceremonial. I, who had never embraced a woman with aught but the arm of roughness before, now held pressed to me one whom I loved with an infinite tenderness, and the revelation of how love can come out and link with love was almost my undoing. Yet, outwardly, Naïs made so sign, but lay half-strangled in my arms, as any woman does that is being borne away by a spoiler.

I trod with her to the uppermost step, the vast throne-stone overhanging us, and then so that all of those who were gazing from the sides of the pyramids and the roofs of the buildings round might see, though we were beyond Phorenice's view, I used a force that was brutal in dragging her across the level, and putting her down into the hollow. And yet the girl resisted me with no one effort whatever.

So that the victim might not struggle out and be crushed, and so gain an easy death when the stone descended, there were brazen clamps to fit into grooves of the stones above the hollow where she lay, and these I fitted in place above her, and fastened one by one, doing this butcher's work with one hand, and still fiercely holding her down by the other. Gods! and the sweat of agony dripped from me on to the thirsty stone as I worked. I could not keep that in.

I clamped and locked the last two bars in place, and took my brute's hand away from her throat.

The hateful fingermarks showed as bloodless furrows in the whiteness of her skin. For the life of me, yes, even for the fate of Atlantis, I could not help dropping my glance upon her face. But she was stronger than I. She gave me no last look. She kept her eyes steadfastly fixed on the cruel stone above, and so I left her, knowing that it was best not to tarry longer.

I came out from under the stone, and gave the sign to the engineers who stood by the rams. The fires were taken away from their sides, and the metal in them began to contract, and slowly the vast bulk of the throne-stone began to creep down towards its bed.

But ah, so slowly! Gods! how my soul was torn as I watched and waited.

Yet I kept my face impassive, overlooking as any officer might a piece of work which others were carrying out under his direction, and on which his credit rested; and I stood gravely in my place till the rams had let the stone come down on its final resting place, and had been carried away by the engineers; and then I went round with the master architect with his plumbline and level, whilst he tested this last piece of the building and declared it perfect.

It was a useless form, this last, seeing that by calculation they knew exactly how the stone must rest;

but the guilds have their forms and customs, and on these occasions of high ceremonial, they are punctilious-ly carried out, because these middle-class people wish always to appear mysterious and impressive to the poor vulgar folk who are their inferiors. But perhaps I am hard there on them. A man who is needlessly taken round to plumb and duly level the tomb where his love lies buried living, may perhaps be excused by the assessors on high a little spirit of bitterness.

I had gone up the steps to do my hateful work a man full of grief, though outwardly unmoved. As I came down again I had a feeling of incompleteness; it seemed as though half my inwards had been left behind with Naïs in the hollow of the stone, and their place was taken by a void which ached wearily; but still I carried a passive face, and memory that before all these private matters stood the command of the High Council, which sat before the Ark of the Mysteries.

So I went and stood before Phorenice, and said the words which the ancient forms prescribed concerning the carrying out of her wish.

"Then, now," she said, "I will give myself to you as wife. We are not as others, you and I, Deucalion. There is a law and a form set down for the marrying of these other people, but that would be useless for our pur-poses. We will have neither priest nor scribe to join us and set down the union. I am the law here in Atlantis, and you soon will be part of me. We will not be de-meaned by profaner hands. We will make the ceremony for ourselves, and for witnesses, there are sufficient in waiting. Afterwards, the record shall be cut deep in the granite throne you have built for me, and the lettering filled in with gold, so that it shall endure and remain bright for always."

"The Empress can do no wrong," I said formally, and took the hand she offered me, and helped her to rise. We walked out from the scarlet awning into the glare of the sunshine, she leaning on me, flushed, and so radiantly lovely that the people began to hail her with rapturous shouts of "A Goddess; our Goddess Phorenice." But for me they had no welcoming word. I think the set grimness of my face both scared and repelled them.

We went up the steps which led to the throne, the people still shouting, and I sat her in the royal seat beneath the snake's outstretched head, and she drew me down to sit beside her.

She raised her jewelled hand, and a silence fell on that great throng, as though the breath had been suddenly cut short for all of them.

Then Phorenice made proclamation:

"Hear me, O my people, and hear me, O High Gods from whom I am come. I take this man Deucalion, to be my husband, to share with me the prosperity of Atlantis, and join me in guarding our great possession. May all our enemies perish as she is now perishing above whom we sit." And then she put her arms around my neck, and kissed me hotly on the mouth.

In turn I also spoke: "Hear me, O most High Gods, whose servant I am, and hear me also, O ye people. I take this Empress, Phorenice, to wife, to help with her the prosperity of Atlantis, and join with her in guarding the welfare of that great possession. May all the enemies of this country perish as they have perished in the past."

And then, I too, who had not been permitted by the fate to touch the lips of my love, bestowed the first kiss I had ever given woman to Phorenice, that was now being made my wife.

But we were not completely linked yet.

"A woman is one, and man is one," she proclaimed, following for the first time the old form of words, "but in marriage they merge, so that wife and husband are no more separate, but one conjointly. In token of this we will now make the symbolic joining together, so that all may see and remember." She took her dagger, and pricking the brawn on my forearm till a bead of blood appeared, set her red lips to it, and took it into herself.

"Ah," she said, with her eyes sparkling, "now you are part of me indeed, Deucalion, and I feel you have strengthened me already." She pulled down the neck of her robe. "Let me make you my return."

I pricked the rounded whiteness of her shoulder. Gods! when I remembered who was beneath us as we sat on that throne, I could have driven the blade through to her heart! And then I, too, put down my lips, and took the drop of her blood that was yielded to me.

My tongue was dry, my throat was parched, and my face suffused, and I thought I should have choked.

But the Empress, who was ordinarily so acute, was misled then. "It thrills you?" she cried. "It burns within you like living fire? I have just felt it. By my face! Deucalion, if I had known the pleasure it gives to be made a wife, I do not think I should have waited this long for you. Ah, yes; but with another man I should have had no thrill. I might have gone through the ceremony with another, but it would have left me cold. Well, they say this feeling comes to a woman but once in her time, and I would not change it for the glory of all my conquests and the whirl of all my power." She leaned in close to me so that the red curls of her hair swept my cheek, and her breath came hot against my mouth. "Tasted you ever any sweet so delicious as this knowledge that we are made one now, Deucalion, past all possible dissolving?"

I could not lie to her any more just then. The Gods know how honestly I had striven to play the part commanded me for Atlantis' good, but there is a limit to human endurance, and mine was reached. I was not all anger towards her. I had some pity for this passion of hers, which had grown of itself certainly, but which I had done nothing to check; and the indecent frankness with which it was displayed was only part of the livery of potentates who flaunt what meaner folk would coyly hide. But always before my eyes was a picture of the girl on whom her jealousy had taken such a bitter vengeance, and to invent spurious lover's talk then was a thing my tongue refused to do.

"Words are poor things," I said, "and I am a man unused to women, and have but a small stock of any phrases except the dryest. Remember, Phorenice, a week agone, I did not know what love was, and now that I have learned the lesson, somewhat of the suddenest, the language remains still to come to me. My inwards speak; indeed they are full of speech; but I cannot translate into bald cold words what they say."

And here, surely the High Gods took pity on my tied tongue and my misery, and made an opportunity for bringing the ceremony to an end. A man ran into the square shouting, and showing a wound that dripped, and presently all that vast crowd which stood on the pavements, and the sides of the pyramids, and the roofs of the temples, took up the cry, and began to feel for their weapons.

"The rebels are in!" "They have burrowed a path into the city!" "They have killed the cave-tigers and taken a gate!" "They are putting the whole place to the storm!" "They will presently leave no poor soul of us here alive!"

There then was a termination of our marriage cooings. With rebels merely biting at the walls, it was fine to put strong trust in the defences, and easy to affect contempt for the besiegers' powers, and to keep the business of pageants and state craft and marryings turning on easy wheels. But with rebel soldiers already inside the city (and hordes of others doubtless pressing on their heels), the affairs took a different light. It was no moment for further delay, and Phorenice was the first to admit it. The glow that had been in her eyes changed to the glare of the fighter, as the fellow who had run up squalled out his tidings.

I stood and stretched my chest. I seemed in need of air. "Here," I said, "is work that I can understand more clearly. I will go and sweep this rabble back to their burrows, Phorenice."

"But not alone, sir. I come too. It is my city still. Nay, sir, we are too newly wed to be parted yet."

"Have your will," I said, and together we went down the steps of the throne to the pavement below. Under my breath I said a farewell to Naïs.

Our armour-bearers met us with weapons, and we stepped into litters, and the slaves took us off hot foot. The wounded man who had first brought the news had fallen in a faint, and no more tidings was to be got from him, but the growing din of the fight gave us the general direction, and presently we began to meet knots of people who dwelt near the place of irruption, running away in wild panic, loaded down with their household goods.

It was useless to stop these, as fight they could not, and if they had stayed they would merely have been slaughtered like flies, and would in all likelihood have impeded our own soldiery. And so we let them run screaming on their blind way, but forced the litters through them with but very little regard for their coward convenience.

Now the advantage of the rebels, when it came to be looked upon by a soldier's eye, was a thing of little enough importance. They had driven a tunnel from behind a covering mound, beneath the walls, and had opened it cleverly enough through the floor of a middle-class house. They had come through into this, collecting their numbers under its shelter, and doubtless hoping that the marriage of the Empress (of which spies had given them information) would sap the watchfulness of the city guards. But it seems they were discovered and attacked before they were thoroughly ready to emerge, and, as a fine body of troops were barracked near the spot, their extermination would have been merely a matter of time, even if we had not come up.

It did not take a trained eye long to decide on this, and Phorenice, with a laugh, lay back on the cushions of the litter, and returned her weapons to the armour-bearer who came panting up to receive them. "We grow nervous with our married life, my Deucalion," she said. "We are fearful lest this new-found happiness be taken from us too suddenly."

But I was not to be robbed of my breathing-space in this wise. "Let me crave a wedding gift of you," I said

"It is yours before you name it."

"Then give me troops, and set me wide a city gate a mile away from here."

"You can gather five hundred as you go from here to the gate, taking two hundred of those that are here. If you want more, they must be fetched from other barracks along the walls. But where is your plan?"

"Why, my poor strategy teaches me this: these foolish rebels have set all their hopes on this mine, and all their excitement on its present success. If they are kept occupied here by a Phorenice, who will give them some dainty fighting without checking them unduly, they will press on to the attack and forget all else, and never so much as dream of a sortie. And meanwhile, a Deucalion with his troop will march out of the city well away from here, without tuck of drum or blare of trumpet, and fall most unpleasantly upon their rear. After which, a Phorenice will burn the house here at the mine's head, which is of wood, and straw thatched, to discourage further egress, and either go to the walls to watch the fight from there, or sally out also and spur on the rout as her fancy dictates."

"Your scheme is so pretty, I would I could rob you of it for my own credit's sake, and as it is, I must kiss you for your cleverness. But you got my word first, you naughty fellow, and you shall have the men and do as you ask. Eh, sir, this is a sad beginning of our wedded life, if you begin to rob your little wife of all the sweets of conquest from the outset."

She took back the weapons and target she had given to the armour-bearer, and stepped over the side of the litter to the ground. "But at least," she said, "if you are going to fight, you shall have troops that will do credit to my drill," and thereupon proceeded to tell off the companies of men-at-arms who were to accompany me. She left herself few enough to stem the influx of rebels who poured ceaselessly in through the tunnel; but as I had seen, with Phorenice, heavy odds added only to her enjoyment.

But for the Empress, I will own at the time to have given little enough of thought. My own proper griefs were raw within me, and I thirsted for that forgetfulness of all else which battle gives, so that for awhile I might have a rest from their gnawings.

It made my blood run freer to hear once more the tramp of practised troops behind me, and when all had been collected, we marched out through a gate of the city, and presently were charging through and through the straggling rear of the enemy. By the Gods! for the moment even Naïs was blotted from my wearied mind. Never had I loved more to let my fierceness run madly riot. Never have I gloated more abundantly over the terrible joy of battle.

Naïs must forgive my weakness in seeking to forget her even for a breathing-space. Had that opportunity been denied me, I believe the agony of remembering would have snapped my brain-strings for always.

14. *Again the Gods Make Change*

Now it would be tedious to tell how with a handful of highly trained fighting men, I charged and recharged, and finally broke up that horde of rebels which outnumbered us by fifteen times. It must be remembered that they grew suddenly panic-stricken in finding that of all those who went in under the city walls by the mine on which they had set such great store, none came back, and that the sounds of panic which had first broken out within the city soon gave way to cries of triumph and joy. And it must be carried in memory also that these wretched rebels were without training worthy of the name, were for the most part weaponed very vilely, and, seeing that their silly principles made each the equal of his neighbour, were practically without heads or leaders also.

So when the panic began, it spread like a malignant murrain through all their ragged ranks, and there were none to rally the flying, none to direct those of more desperate bravery who stayed and fought.

My scheme of attack was simple. I hunted them without a halt. I and my fellows never stopped to play the defensive. We turned one flank, and charged through a centre, and then we were harrying the other flank, and once more hacking our passage through the solid mass. And so by constantly keeping them on the run, and in ignorance of whence would come the next attack, panic began to grow amongst them and ferment, till presently those in the outer lines commenced to scurry away towards the forests and the spoiled corn-lands of the country, and those in the inner packs were only wishful of a chance to follow them.

It was no feat of arms this breaking up of the rebel leaguer, and no practised soldier would wish to claim it as such. It was simply taking advantage of the chances of the moment, and as such it was successful. Given an open battle on their own ground, these desperate rebels would have fought till none could stand, and by sheer ferocious numbers would have pulled down any trained troops that the city could have sent against them, whether they had advanced in phalanx or what formation you will. For it must be remembered they were far removed from cowards, being Atlantean all, just as were those within the city, and were, moreover, spurred to extraordinary savageness and desperation by the oppression under which they had groaned, and the wrongs they had been forced to endure.

Still, as I say, the poor creatures were scattered, and the siege was raised from that moment, and it was plain to see that the rebellion might be made to end, if no unreasonable harshness was used for its final suppression. Too great severity, though perhaps it may be justly their portion, only drives such malcontents to further desperations.

Now, following up these fugitives, to make sure that there was no halt in their retreat, and to send the lesson of panic thoroughly home to them, had led us a long distance from the city walls; and as we had fought all through the burning heat of the day and my men were heavily wearied, I decided to halt where we were for the night amongst some half-ruined houses which would make a temporary fortification. Fortunately, a drove of little cloven-hoofed horses which had been scared by some of the rebels in their flight happened to blunder into our lines, and as we killed five before they were clear again, there was a soldier's supper for us, and quickly the fires were lit and cooking it.

Sentries paced the outskirts and made their cries to one another, and the wounded sat by the fires and dressed their hurts, and with the officers I talked over the engagements of the day, and the methods of each charge, and the other details of the fighting. It is the special perquisite of soldiers to dally over these matters with gusto, though they are entirely without interest for laymen.

The hour drew on for sleep, and snores went up from every side. It was clear that all my officers were wearied out, and only continued the talk through deference to their commander. Yet I had a feverish dread of being left alone again with my thoughts, and pressed them on with conversation remorselessly. But in the end they were saved the rudeness of dropping off into unconsciousness during my talk. A sentry came up and saluted. "My lord," he reported, "there is a woman come up from the city whom we have caught trying to come into the bivouac."

"How is she named?"

"She will not say."

"Has she business?"

"She will say none. She demands only to see my lord."

"Bring her here to the fire," I ordered, and then on second thoughts remembering that the woman, whoever she might be, had news likely enough for my private ear (or otherwise she would not have come to so uncouth a rendezvous), I said to the sentry: "Stay," and got up from the ground beside the fire, and went with him to the outer line.

"Where is she?" I asked.

"My comrades are holding her. She might be a wench belonging to these rebels, with designs to put a knife into my lord's heart, and then we sentries would suffer. The Empress," he added simply, "seems to set good store upon my lord at present, and we know the cleverness of her tormentors."

"Your thoughtfulness is frank," I said, and then he showed me the woman. She was muffled up in hood and cloak, but one who loved Naïs as I loved could not mistake the form of Ylga, her twin sister, because of mere swathings. So I told the sentries to release her without asking her for speech, and then led her out from the bivouac beyond earshot of their lines.

"It is something of the most pressing that has brought you out here, Ylga?"

"You know mê, then? There must be something warmer than the ordinary between us two, Deucalion, if you could guess who walked beneath all these mufflings."

I let that pass. "But what's your errand, girl?"

"Aye," she said bitterly, "there's my reward. All your concern's for the message, none for the carrier.

Well, good my lord, you are husband to the dainty Phorenice no longer."

"This is news."

"And true enough, too. She will have no more of you, divorces you, spurns you, thrusts you from her, and, after the first splutter of wrath is done, then come pains and penalties."

"The Empress can do no wrong. I will have you speak respectful words of the Empress."

"Oh, be done with that old fable! It sickens me. The woman was mad for love of you, and now she's mad with jealousy. She knows that you gave Naïs some of your priest's magic, and that she sleeps till you choose to come and claim her, even though the day be a century from this. And if you wish to know the method of her enlightenment, it is simple. There is another airshaft next the one down which you did your cooing and billing, and that leads to another cell in which lay another prisoner. The wretch heard all that passed, and thought to buy enlargement by telling it.

"But his news came a trifle stale. It seems that with the pressure of the morning's ceremonies, they forgot to bring a ration, and when at last his gaoler did remember him, it was rather late, seeing that by then Phorenice had tied herself publicly to a husband, and poor Naïs had doubtless eaten her green drug. However, the fool must needs try and barter his tale for what it would fetch; and, as was natural, had such a silly head chopped off for his pains; and after that your Phorenice behaved as you may guess. And now you may thank me, sir, for coming to warn you not to go back to Atlantis."

"But I shall go back. And if the Empress chooses to cut my head also from its proper column, that is as the High Gods will."

"You are more sick of life than I thought. But I think, sir, our Phorenice judges your case very accurately. It was permitted me to hear the outbursting of this lady's rage. 'Shall I hew off his head?' said she. 'Pah! Shall I give him over to my tormentors, and stand by whilst they do their worst? He would not wrinkle his brow at their fiercest efforts. No; he must have a heavier punishment than any of these, and one also which will endure. I shall lop off his right hand and his left foot, so that he may be a fighting man no longer, and then I shall drive him forth crippled into the dangerous lands, where he may learn Fear. The beasts shall hunt him, the fires of the ground shall spoil his rest. He shall know hunger, and he shall breathe bad air. And all the while he shall remember that I have Naïs near me, living and locked in her coffin of stone, to play with as I choose, and to give over to what insults may come to my fancy.' That is what she said, Deucalion. Now I ask you again will you go back to meet her vengeance?"

"No," I said, "it is no part of my plan to be mutilated and left to live."

"So, being a woman of some sense, I judged. And, moreover, having some small kindness still left for you, I have taken it upon myself to make a plan for your further movement which may fall in with your whim. Does the name of Tob come back to your memory?"

"One who was Captain of Tatho's navy?"

"That same Tob. A gruff, rude fellow, and smelling vile of tar, but seeming to have a sturdy honesty of his own. Tob sails away this night for parts unknown, presumably to found a kingdom with Tob for king. It seems he can find little enough to earn at his craft in Atlantis these latter days, and has scruples at seeing his wife and young ones hungry. He told me this at the harbour side when I put my neck under the axe by saying I wanted carriage for you, sir, and so having me under his thumb, he was perhaps more loose-lipped than usual. You seem to have made a fine impression on Tob, Deucalion. He said—I repeat his hearty disrespect—you were just the recruit he wanted, but whether you joined him or not, he would go to the nether Gods to do you service."

"By the fellow's side, I gained some experience in fighting the greater sea beasts."

"Well, go and do it again. Believe me, sir, it is your only chance. It would grieve me much to hear the searing-iron hiss on your stumps. I bargained with Tob to get clear of the harbour forts before the chain was up for the night, and as he is a very daring fellow, with no fear of navigating under the darkness, he himself said he would come to a point of the shore which we agreed upon, and there await you. Come, Deucalion, let me lead you to the place."

"My girl," I said, "I see I owe you many thanks for what you have done on my poor behalf."

"Oh, your thanks!" she said. "You may keep them. I did not come out here in the dark and the dangers for mere thanks, though I knew well enough there would be little else offered."—She plucked at my sleeve. —"Now show me your walking pace, sir. They will begin to want your countenance in the camp directly, and we need hanker after no too narrow inquiries for what's along."

So thereon we set off, Ylga and I, leaving the lights of the bivouac behind us, and she showed the way, whilst I carried my weapons ready to ward off attacks whether from beasts or from men. Few words were passed between us, except those which had concern with the dangers natural to the way. Once only did we touch one another, and that was where a tree-trunk bridged a rivulet of scalding water which flowed from a boil-spring towards the sea.

"Are you sure of footing?" I asked, for the night was dark, and the heat of the water would peel the flesh from the bones if one slipped into it.

"No," she said, "I am not," and reached out and took my hand. I helped her over and then loosed my grip, and she sighed, and slowly slipped her hand away.

Then on again we went in silence, side by side, hour after hour, and league after league.

But at last we topped a rise, and below us through the trees I could see the gleam of the great estuary on which the city of Atlantis stands. The ground was soggy and wet beneath us, the trees were full of barbs and spines, the way was monstrous hard. Ylga's breath was beginning to come in laboured pants. But when I offered to take her arm, and help her, as some return against what she had done for me, she repulsed me rudely enough. "I am no poor weakling," said she, "if that is your only reason for wanting to touch me."

Presently, however, we came out through the trees, and the roughest part of our journey was done. We saw the ship riding to her anchors in shore a mile away, and a weird enough object she was under the faint starlight. We made our way to her along the level beaches.

Tob was keeping a keen watch. We were challenged the moment we came within stone or arrow shot, and bidden to halt and recite our business; but he was civil enough when he heard we were those whom he expected. He called a crew and slacked out his anchor-rope till his ship ground against the shingle, and then thrust out his two steering oars to help us clamber aboard.

I turned to Ylga with words of thanks and farewell. "I will never forget what you have done for me this night; and should the High Gods see fit to bring me back to Atlantis and power, you shall taste my gratitude."

"I do not want to return. I am sick of this old life here."

"But you have your palace in the city, and your servants, and your wealth, and Phorenice will not disturb you from their possession."

"Oh, as for that, I could go back and be fan-girl tomorrow. But I do not want to go back."

"Let me tell you it is no time for a gently nurtured

lady like yourself to go forward. I have been viceroy of Yucatan, Ylga, and know somewhat of making a foothold in these new countries. And that was nothing compared with what this will be. I tell you it entails hardships, and privations, and sufferings which you could not guess at. Few survive who go to colonise in the beginning, and those only of the hardiest, and they earn new scars and new batterings every day."

"I do not care, and, besides, I can share the work. I can cook, I can shoot a good arrow, and I can make garments, yes, though they were cut from the skins of beasts and had to be sewn with backbone sinews. Because you despise fine clothes, and because you have seen me only decked out as fan-girl, you think I am useless. Bah, Deucalion! Never let people prate to me about your perfection. You know less about a woman than a boy new from school."

"I have learned all I care to know about one woman, and because of the memory of her, I could not presume to ask her sister to come with me now."

"Aye," she said bitterly, "kick my pride. I knew well enough it was only second place to Naïs I could get all the time I was wanting to come. Yet no one but a boor would have reminded me of it. Gods! and to think that half the men in Atlantis have courted me, and now I am arrived at this!"

"I must go alone. It would have made me happier to take your esteem with me. But as it is, I suppose I shall carry only your hate."

"That is the most humiliating thing of all; I cannot bring myself to hate you. I ought to, I know, after the brutal way you have scorned me. But I do not, and there is the truth. I seem to grow the fonder of you, and if I thought there was a way of keeping you alive, and unmutilated, here in Atlantis, I do not think I should point out that Tob is tired of waiting, and will probably be off without you." She flung her arms suddenly about my neck, and kissed me hotly on the mouth. "There, that is for good-bye, dear. You see I am reckless. I care not what I do now, knowing that you cannot despise me more than you have done all along for my forwardness."

She ran back from me into the edge of the trees.

"But this is foolishness," I said. "I must take you through the dangers that lie between here and some gate of the city, and then come back to the ship."

"You need not fear for me. The unhappy are always safe. And, besides, I have a way. It is my solace to know that you will remember me now. You will never forget that kiss."

"Fare you well, Ylga," I cried. "May the High Gods keep you entirely in their holy care."

But no reply came back. She had gone off into the forest. And so I turned down to the beach, and splashed into the water, and climbed on board the ship up the steering oars. Tob gave the word to haul-to the anchor, and get her away from the beach.

"Greeting, my lord," said he, "but I'd have been pleased to see you earlier. We've small enough force and slow enough heels in this vessel, and it's my idea that the sooner we're away from here and beyond range of pursuit, the safer it will be for my woman and brats who are in that hutch of an after-castle. It's long enough since I sailed in such a small old-fashioned ship as this. She's no machines, and she's not even a steering mannikin. Look at the meanness of her furniture and (in your ear) I've suspicions that there's rottenness in her bottom. But she's the best I'd the means to buy, and if she reaches the place at the farther end I've got my eye on, we shall have to make a home there, or be content to die, for she'll never have strength to carry us farther or back. She's been a ship in the Egypt trade, and you know what that is for getting worm and rot in the wood."

"You'd enough hands for your scheme before I came?"

"Oh yes. I've fifty stout lads and eight women packed in the ship somehow, and trouble enough I've had to get them away from the city. That thief of a port-captain wellnigh skinned us clean before he could see it lawful that so many useful fighting men might go out of harbour. Times are not what they were, I tell you, and the sea trade's about done. All sailor men of any skill have taken a woman or two and gone out in companies to try their fortunes in other lands. Why, I'd trouble enough to get half a score to help me work this ship. All my balance are just landsmen raw and simple, and if I land half of them alive at the other end, we shall be doing well."

"Still with luck and a few good winds it should not take long to get across to Europe."

Tob slapped his leg. "No savage Europe for me, my lord. Now, see the advantage of being a mariner. I found once some islands to the north of Europe, separated from the main by a strait, which I called the Tin Islands, seeing that tin ore litters many of the beaches. I was driven there by storm, and said no word of the find when I got back, and here you see it comes in useful. There's no one in all Atlantis but me knows of those Tin Islands to-day, and we'll go and fight honestly for our ground, and build a town and a kingdom on it."

"With Tob for king?"

"Well, I have figured it out as such for many a day, but I know when I meet my better, and I'm content to serve under Deucalion. My lord would have done wiser to have brought a wife with him, though, and I thought it was understood by the good lady that spoke to me down at the harbour, or I'd have mentioned it earlier. The savages in my Tin Islands go naked and stain themselves blue with woad, and are very filthy and brutish to look upon. They are sturdy, and should make good slaves, but one would have to get blunted in the taste before one could wish to be father to their children."

"I am still husband to Phorenice."

Tob grinned. "The Gods give you joy of her. But it is part of a mariner's creed—and you will grow to be a mariner here—that wedlock does not hold across the seas. However, that matter may rest. But, coming to my Tin Islands again: they'll delight you. And I tell you, a kingdom will not be so hard to carve out as it was in Egypt, or as you found in Yucatan. There are beasts there, of course, and no one who can hunt need ever go hungry. But the greater beasts are few. There are cave-bears and cave-tigers in small numbers, to be sure, and some river-horses and great snakes. But the greater lizards seem to avoid the land; and as for birds, there is rarely seen one that can hurt a grown man. Oh, I tell you, it will be a most desirable kingdom."

"Tob seems to have imagined himself king of the Tin Islands with much reality."

He sighed a little. "In truth I did, and there is no denying it, and I tell you plain, there is not another man living that I would have broken this voyage for but Deucalion. But don't think I regret it, and don't think I want to push myself above my place. This breeze and the ebb are taking the old ship finely along her ways. See those fire baskets on the harbour forts? We're abreast of them now. We'll have dropped them and the city out of sight by daylight, and the flood will not begin to run up till then. But I fear unless the wind hardens down with the dawn we'll have to bring up to an anchor when the flood makes. Tides run very hard in these narrow seas. Aye, and there are some shrewdish tide-rips round my Tin Islands, as you shall see when we reach them."

There were many fearful glances backwards when day came and showed the waters, and the burning mountains that hemmed them in beyond the shores. All seemed to expect some navy of Phorenice to come surging up to take them back to servitude and starvation in the squalid wards of the city; and I confess ingenuously that I was with them in all truth when they swore they would fight the ship till she sank beneath them, before they would obey another of the commands of Phorenice. However, their brave heroics were displayed to no small purpose. For the full flow of the tide we hung in our place, barely moving past the land, but yet not seeing either oar or sail; and then, when the tide turned, away we went once more with speed, mightily comforted.

Tob's woman must needs bring drink on deck, and bid all pour libations to her as a future queen. But Tob cuffed her back into the after-castle, slamming to the hatch behind her heels, and bidding the crew send the liquor down their dusty throats. "We are done with that foolery," said he. "My Lord Deucalion will be king of this new kingdom we shall build in the Tin Islands, and a right proper king he'll make, as you untravelled ones would know, if you'd sailed the outer seas with him as I have done." Beneath which I read a regret, but said nothing, having made my plans from the moment of stepping on board, as will appear on a later sheet.

So on down the great estuary we made our way, and though it pleasured the others on board when they saw that the seas were desolate of sails, it saddened me when I recalled how once the waters had been whitened with the glut of shipping.

They had started off on their voyage with a bare two days' provision in their equipment, and so, of necessity even after leaving the great estuary, we were forced to voyage coastwise, putting into every likely river and sheltered beach to slay fish and meat for future victualling. "And when the winter comes," said Tob, "as its gales will be heavier than this old ship can stomach, I had determined to haul up and make a permanent camp ashore, and get a crop of grain grown and threshed before setting sail again. It is the usual custom in these voyages. And I shall do it still, subject to my lord's better opinion."

So here, having by this time completed a two months' leisurely journey from the city, I saw my opportunity to speak what I had always carried in my mind. "Tob," I said, "I am a poor, weak, defenceless man, and I am quite at your mercy, but what if I do not voyage all the way to the Tin Islands, and oust you of this kingship?"

He brightened perceptibly. "Aye," he grunted, "you are very weak, my lord, and mighty defenceless. We know all about that. But what's else? You must tell all your meaning plain. I'm a common mariner, and understand little of your fancy talk."

"Why, this. That it is not my wish to leave the continent of Atlantis. If you will put me down on any part of this side that faces Europe, I will commend you strongly to the Gods. I would I could give you money, or (better still) articles that would be useful to you in your colonising; but as it is, you see me destitute."

"As to that, you owe me nothing, having done vastly more than your share each time we have put in shore for the hunting. But it will not do, this plan of yours. I will shamedly confess that the sound of that kingship in my Tin Islands sounds sweet to me. But no, my lord, it will not do. You are no mariner yet, and understand little of geography, but I must tell you that the part of Atlantis there"—he jerked his thumb towards the line of trees, and the mountains which lay beyond the fringe of surf—"is called the Dangerous Lands, and a man must needs be a salamander and be learned in magic (so I am told) before he can live there."

I laughed. "We of the Priests' Clan have some education, Tob, though it may not be on the same lines as your own. In fact, I may say I was taught in the colleges concerning the boundaries and the contents of our continent with a nicety that would surprise you. And once ashore, my fate will still be under the control of the most High Gods."

He muttered something in his profane seaman's way about preferring to keep his own fate under control of his own most strong right arm, but saying that he would keep the matter in his thoughts, he excused himself hurriedly to go and see to somewhat concerning the working of the ship, and there left me.

But I think the sweets of kingly rule were a strong argument in favour of letting me have my way (which I should have had otherwise if it had not been given peacefully), and on the third day after our talk he put the ship inshore again for re-victualling. We lurched into a river-mouth, half swamped over a roaring bar, and ran up against the bank and made fast there to trees, but booming ourselves a safe distance off with oars and poles, so that no beast could leap on board out of the thicket.

Fish-spearing and meat-hunting were set about with promptitude, and on the second day we were happy enough to slay a yearling river-horse, which gave provisions in all sufficiency. A space was cleared on the bank, fires were lit, and the meat hung over the smoke in strips, and when as much was cured as the ship would carry, the shipmen made a final gorge on what remained, filled up a great stack of hollow reeds with drinking water, and were ready to continue the voyage.

With sturdy generosity did Tob again attempt to make me sail on with them as their future king, and as steadfastly did I make refusal; and at last stood alone on the bank amongst the gnawed bones of their feast, with my weapons to bear me company, and he, and his men, and the women stood in the little old ship, ready to drop down river with the current.

"At least," said Tob, "we'll carry your memory with us, and make it big in the Tin Islands for everlasting."

"Forget me," I said, "I am nothing. I am merely an incident that has come in your way. But if you want to carry some memory with you that shall endure, preserve the cult of the most High Gods as it was taught to you when you were children here in Atlantis. And afterwards, when your colony grows in power, and has come to sufficient magnificence, you may send to the old country for a priest."

"We want no priest, except one we shall make ourselves, and that will be me. And as for the old Gods—well, I have laid my ideas before the fellows here, and they agree to this: We are done with those old Gods for always. They seem worn out, if one may judge from Their present lack of usefulness in Atlantis, and, anyway, there will be no room for Them on the Tin Islands. —Let go those warps there aft, and shove her head out.—We are under weigh now, my lord, and beyond recall, and so I am free to tell you what we have decided upon for our religious exercises. We shall set up the memory of a living Hero on earth, and worship that. And when in years to come the picture of his face grows dim, we shall doubtless make an image of him, as accurate as our art permits, and build him a temple for shelter, and bring there our offerings and prayers. And as I say, my lord, I shall be priest, and when I am dead, the sons of my body shall be priests after me, and the eldest a king also."

"Let me plead with you," I said. "This must not be."

The ship was drifting rapidly away with the current, and they were hoisting sail. Tob had to shout to make himself heard. "Aye, but it shall be. For I, too, am a strong man after my kind, and I have ordered it so. And if you want the name of our Hero that some day shall be God, you wear it on yourself. Deucalion shall be God for our children."

"This is blasphemy," I cried. "Have a care, fool, or this impiety will sink you."

"We will risk it," he bawled back, "and consider the odds against us are small. Regard! Here is thy last horn of wine in the ship, and my woman has treasured it against this moment. Regard, all men, together with Those above and Those below! I pour this wine as a libation to Deucalion, great lord that is to-day, Hero that shall be to-morrow, God that will be in time to come!" And then all those on the ship joined in the acclaim till they were beyond the reach of my voice, and were battling their way out to sea through the roaring breakers of the bar.

Solitary I stood at the brink of the forest, looking after them and musing sadly. Tob, despite his lowly station, was a man I cared for more than many. Like all seamen, I knew that he paid his devotions to one of the obscurer Gods, but till then I had supposed him devout in his worship. His new avowal came to me as a desolating shock. If a man like Tob could forsake all the older Gods to set up on high some poor mortal who had momentarily caught his fancy, what could be expected from the mere thoughtless mob, when swayed by such a brilliant tongue as Phorenice's? It seemed I was to begin my exile with a new dreariness added to all the other adverse prospects of Atlantis.

But then behind me I heard the rustle of some great beast that had scented me, and was coming to attack through the thicket, and so I had other matters to think upon. I had to let Tob and his ship go out over the rim of the horizon unwatched.

15. *Zaemon's Summons*

Since the days when man was first created upon the earth by Gods who looked down and did their work from another place, there have always been areas of the land ill-adapted for his maintenance, but none more so than that part of Atlantis which lies over against the savage continents of Europe and Africa. The common people avoid it, because of a superstition which says that the spirits of the evil dead stalk about there in broad daylight, and slay all those that the more open dangers of the place might otherwise spare. And so it has happened often that the criminals who might have fled there from justice, have returned of their own free will, and voluntarily given themselves up to the tormentors, rather than face its fabulous terrors.

To the educated, many of these legends are known to be mythical; but withal there are enough disquietudes remaining to make life very arduous and stocked with peril. Everywhere the mountains keep their contents on the boil; earth tremors are every day's experience; gushes of unseen evil vapours steal upon one with such cunningness and speed, that it is often hard to flee in time before one is choked and killed; poisons well up into the rivers, yet leave their colour unchanged; great cracks split across the ground reaching down to the fires beneath, and the waters gush into these, and are shot forth again with davastating explosion; and always may be expected great outpourings of boiling mud or molten rock.

Yet with all this, there are great sombre forests in these lands, with trees whose age is unimaginable, and fires amongst the herbage are rare. All beneath the trees is water, and the air is full of warm steam and wetness. For a man to live in that constant hot damp is very mortifying to the strength. But strength is wanted, and cunning also beyond the ordinary, for these dangerous lands are the abode of the lizards, which of all beasts grow to the most enormous size and are the most fearsome to deal with.

There are countless families and species of these lizards, and with some of them a man can contend with prospect of success. But there are others whose hugeness no human force can battle against. One I saw, as it came up out of a lake after gaining its day's food, that made the wet land shake and pulse as it trod. It could have taken Phorenice's mammoth into its belly,* and even a mammoth in full charge could not have harmed it. Great horny plates covered its head and body, and on the ridge of its back and tail and limbs were spines that tore great slivers from the black trees as it passed amongst them.

Now and again these monsters would get caught in some vast fissuring of the ground, but not often. Their speed of foot was great, and their sagacity keen. They seemed to know when the worst boilings of the mountains might be expected, and then they found safety in the deeper lakes, or buried themselves in wallows of the mud. Moreover, they were more kindly constituted than man to withstand one great danger of these regions, in that the heat of the water did them no harm. Indeed, they will lie peacefully in pools where sudden stream-bursts are making the water leap into boiling fountains, and I have seen one run quickly across a flow of molten rock which threatened to cut it off, and not be so much as singed in the transit.

In the midst of such neighbours, then, was my new life thrown, and existence became perilous and hard to me from the outset. I came near to knowing what Fear was, and indeed only a fervent trust in the most High Gods, and a firm belief that my life was always under Their fostering care, prevented me from gaining that horrid knowledge. For long enough, till I learned somewhat of the ways of this steaming, sweltering land, I was in as miserable a case as even Phorenice could have wished to see me. My clothes rotted from my back with the constant wetness, till I went as naked as a savage from Europe; my limbs were racked with agues,

* *Translator's note:* Professor Reeder of the Wyoming State University has recently unearthed the skeleton of a Brontosaurus, 130 ft. in length, which would have weighed 50 tons when alive. It was 35 ft. in height at the hips, and 25 ft. at the shoulder, and 40 people could be seated with comfort within its ribs. Its thigh bone was 8 ft. long. The fossils of a whole series of these colossal lizards have been found.

and I could find no herbs to make drugs for their relief; for days together I could find no better food than tree-grubs and leaves; and often when I did kill beasts, knowing little of their qualities, I ate those that gave me pain and sickness.

But as man is born to make himself adaptable to his surroundings, so as the months dragged on did I learn the limitation of this new life of mine, and gather some knowledge of its resources. As example: I found a great black tree, with a hollow core, and a hole into its middle near the roots. Here I harboured, till one night some monstrous lizard, whose sheer weight made the tree rock like a sapling, endeavoured to suck me forth as a bird picks a worm from a hollow log. I escaped by the will of the Gods—I could as much have done harm to a mountain as injure that horny tongue with my weapons—but I gave myself warning that this chance must not happen again.

So I cut myself a ladder of footholes on the inside of the trunk till I had reached a point ten man-heights from the ground, and there cut other notches, and with tree branches made a floor on which I might rest. Later, for luxury, I carved me arrow-slit windows in the walls of my chamber, and even carried up sand for a hearth, so that I might cook my victual up there instead of lighting a fire in all the dangers of the open below.

By degrees, too, I began to find how the large-scaled fish of the rivers and the lesser turtles might be more readily captured, and so my ribs threatened less to start through their proper covering of skin as the days went on. But the lack of salads and gruels I could never overcome. All the green meat was tainted so powerfully with the taste of tars that never could I force my palate to accept it. And of course, too, there remained the peril of the greater lizards and the other dangers native to the place.

But as the months began to mount into years, and the brute part of my nature became more satisfied, there came other longings which it was less easy to provide for. From the ivory of a river horse's tooth I had endeavoured to carve me a representative of Naïs as last I had seen her. But, though my fingers might be loving, and my will good, my art was of the dullest, and the result—though I tried time and time again—was always clumsy and pitiful. Still, in my eyes it carried some suggestion of the original—a curve here, an outline there, and it made my old love glow anew within me as I sat and ate it with my eyes. Yet it did little to satisfy my longings for the woman I had lost; rather it whetted my cravings to be with her again, or at least to have some knowledge of her fate.

Other men of the Priests' Clan have come out and made an abode in these Dangerous Lands, and by mortifying the flesh, have gained an intimacy with the Higher Mysteries which has carried them far past what mere human learning and repetition could teach. Indeed, here and there one, who from some cause and another has returned to the abodes of men, has carried with him a knowledge that has brought him the reputation amongst the vulgar for the workings of magic and miracles, which—since all arts must be allowed which aid so holy a cause—have added very materially to the ardour with which these common people pursue the cult of the Gods. But for myself I could not free my mind to the necessary clearness for following these abstruse studies. During that voyage home from Yucatan I had communed with them with growing insight; but now my mind was not my own. Naïs had a lien upon it, and refused to be ousted; and, in truth, her sweet trespass was my chief solace.

But at last my longing could no further be denied. Through one of the arrow-slit windows of my treehouse I could see far away a great mountain top whitened with perpetual snow, which our Lord the Sun dyed with blood every night of His setting. Night after night I used to watch that ruddy light with wide straining eyes. Night after night I used to remember that in days agone when I was entering upon the priesthood, it had been my duty to adore our great Lord as He rose for His day behind the snows of that very mountain. And always the thought followed on these musings, that from that distant crest I could see across the continent to the Sacred Mount, which had the city below it where I had buried my love alive.

So at last I gave way and set out, and a perilous journey I made of it. In the heavy mists, which hung always on the lower ground, my way lay blind before me, and I was constantly losing it. Indeed, to say that I traversed three times the direct distance is setting a low estimate. Throughout all those swamps the great lizards hunted, and as the country was new to me I did not know places of harbour, and a hundred times was within an ace of being spied and devoured at a mouthful. But the High Gods still desired me for Their own purposes, and blinded the great beasts' eyes when I slunk to cover as they passed. Twice rivers of scalding water roared boiling across my path, and I had to delay till I could collect enough black timber from the forests to build rafts that would give me dry ferriage.

It will be seen then that my journey was in a way infinitely tedious, but to me, after all those years of waiting, the time passed on winged feet. I had been separated from my love till I could bear the strain no longer; let me but see from a distance the place where she lay, and feast my eyes upon it for a while, and then I could go back to my abode in the tree and there remain patiently awaiting the will of the Gods.

The air grew more chilly as I began to come out above the region of trees, on to that higher ground which glares down on the rest of the world, and I made buskins and a coat of woven grasses to protect my body from the cold, which began to blow upon me keenly. And later on, where the snow lay eternally, and was blown into gullies, and frozen into solid banks and bergs of ice, I had hard work to make any progress amongst its perilous mazes, and was moreover so numbed by the chill, that my natural strength was vastly weakened. Overhead, too, following me up with forbidding swoops, and occasionally coming so close that I had to threaten it with my weapons, was one of those huge man-eating birds which live by pulling down and carrying off any creature that their instincts tell them is weakly, and likely soon to die.

But the lure ahead of me was strong enough to make these difficulties seem small, and though the air of the mountain agreed with me ill, causing sickness and panting, I pressed on with what speed I could muster towards the elusive summit. Time after time I thought the next spurt would surely bring me out to the view for which my soul yearned, but always there seemed another bank of snow and ice yet to be climbed. But at last I reached the crest, and gave thanks to the most High Gods for Their protection and favour.

Far, far away I could see the Sacred Mountain with its ring of fires burning pale under the day, and although the splendid city which nestled at its foot could not be seen from where I stood, I knew its position and I knew its plan, and my soul went out to that throne of granite in the square before the royal pyramid, where once, years before, I had buried my love. Had Phorenice left the tomb unviolated?

I stood there leaning on my spear, filling my eye with the prospect, warming even to the smoke of mountains that I recognised as old acquaintances. Gods! how my love burned within me for this woman. My whole being seemed gone out to meet her, and to leave room for nothing beside. For long enough a voice seemed dimly to be calling me, but I gave it no regard. I had come out to that hoary mountain top for communion with Naïs alone, and I wanted none others to interrupt.

But at length the voice calling my name grew too loud to be neglected, and I pulled myself out of my sweet musing with a start to think that here, for the first time since parting with Tob and his company, I should see another human fellow-being. I gripped my weapon and asked who called. The reply came clearly from up the slopes of mountain, and I saw a man coming towards me over the snows. He was old and feeble. His body was bent, and his hair and beard were white as the ground on which he trod, and presently I recognised him as Zaemon. He was coming towards me with incredible speed for a man of his years and feebleness, but he carried in his hand the glowing Symbol of our Lord the Sun, and holy strength from this would add largely to his powers.

He came close to me and made the sign of the Seven, which I returned to him, with its completion, with due form and ceremony. And then he saluted me in the manner prescribed as messenger appointed by the High Council of the Priests seated before the Ark of the Mysteries, and I made humble obeisance before him.

"In all things I will obey the orders that you put before me," I said.

"Such is your duty, my brother. The command is, that you return immediately to the Sacred Mountain, so that if human means may still prevail, you, as the most skilful general Atlantis owns within her borders, may still save the country from final wreck and punishment. The woman Phorenice persists in her infamies. The poor land groans under her heel. And now she has laid siege to our Sacred Mountain itself, and swears that not one soul shall be left alive in all Atlantis who does not bend humbly to her will."

"It is a command and I obey it. But let me ask of another matter that is intimate to both of us. What of Naïs?"

"Naïs rests where you left her, untouched. Phorenice knows by her arts—she has stolen nearly all the ancient knowledge now—that still you live, and she keeps Naïs unharmed beneath the granite throne in the hopes that some time she may use her as a weapon against you. Little she knows the sternness of our Priests' creed, my brother. Why, even I, that am the girl's father, would sacrifice her blithely, if her death or ruin might do a tittle of good to Atlantis."

"You go beyond me with your devotion."

The old man leaned forward at me, with glowering brow. "What!"

"Or my old blind adherence to the ancient dogma has been sapped and weakened by events. You must buy my full obedience, Zaemon, if you want it. Promise me Naïs—and your arts I know can snatch her— and I will be true servant to the High Council of the Priest, and will die in the last ditch if need be for the carrying out of order. But let me see Naïs given over to the fury of that wanton woman, and I shall have no inwards left, except to take my vengeance, and to see Atlantis piled up in ruins as her funeral-stone."

Zaemon looked at me bitterly. "And you are the man the High Council thought to trust as they would trust one of themselves? Truly we are in an age of weak men and faithless now. But, my lord—nay, I must call you brother still: we cannot be too nice in our choosing to-day—you are the best there is, and we must have you. We little thought you would ask a price for your generalship, having once taken oath on the walls of the Ark of the Mysteries itself that always, come what might, you would be a servant of the High Council of the Clan without fee and without hope of advancement. But this is the age of broken vows, and you are going no more than trim with the fashion. Indeed, brothher, perhaps I should thank you for being no more greedy in your demands."

"You may spare me your taunts. You, by self-denial and profound search into the highest of the higher Mysteries, have made yourself something wiser than human; I have preserved my humanity, and with it its powers and frailties; and it seems that each of us has his proper uses, or you would not be come now here to me. Rather you would have done the generalling yourself."

"You make a warm defence, my brother. But I have no leisure now to stand before you with argument. Come to the Sacred Mountain, fight me this wanton, upstart Empress, and by my beard you shall have your Naïs as you left her as a reward."

"It is a command of the High Council which shall be obeyed. I will come with my brother now, as soon as he is rested."

"Nay," said the old man, "I have no tiredness, and as for coming with me, there you will not be able. But follow at what pace you may."

He turned and set off down the snowy slopes of the mountain and I followed; but gradually he distanced me; and so he kept on, with speed always increasing, till presently he passed out of my sight round the spur of an ice-cliff, and I found myself alone on the mountain side. Yes, truely alone. For his footmarks in the snow from being deep, grew shallower, and less noticeable, so that I had to stoop to see them. And presently they vanished entirely, and the great mountain's flank lay before me trackless, and untrodden by the foot of man since time began.

I was not shaken by any great amazement. Though it was beyond my poor art to compass this thing myself, having occupied my mind in exile more with memories of Naïs than in study of those uppermost recesses of the Higher Mysteries in which Zaemon was so prodigiously wise, still I had some inkling of his powers.

Zaemon I knew would be back again in his dwelling on the Sacred Mountain, shaken and breathless, even before I had found an end to his tracks in the snow, and it behoved me to join him there in the quickest possible time. I had his promise now for my reward, and I knew that he would carry it into effect. Beforetime I had made an error. I had valued Atlantis most, and Naïs, my private love, as only second. But now it was in my mind to be honest with others even as with myself. Though all the world were hanging on my choice, I could but love my Naïs most, and serve her first and foremost of all.

16. *Siege of the Sacred Mountain*

Now, my passage across the great continent of Atlantis, if tedious and haunted by many dangers, need not be recounted in detail here. Only one halt did I make of any duration, and that was unavoidable. I had killed a stag one day, bringing it down after a long chase in an open savannah. I scented the air carefully, to see if there was any other beast which could do me harm within reach, and thinking that the place was safe, set about cutting my meat, and making a sufficiency into a bundle for carriage.

But underfoot amongst the grasses there was a great legged worm, a monstrous green thing, very venomous in its bite; and presently as I moved I brushed it with my heel, and like the dart of light it swooped with its tiny head and struck me with its fangs in the lower thigh. With my knife I cut through its neck and it fell to writhing and struggling and twining its hundred legs into all manner of contortions; and then, cleaning my blade in the ground, I stabbed with it deep all round the wound, so that the blood might flow freely and wash the venom from its lodgement. And then with the blood trickling healthily down from my heel,

I shouldered the meat and strode off, thankful for being so well quit of what might have made itself a very ugly adventure.

As I walked, however, my leg began to be filled with a tightness and throbbing which increased every hour, and presently it began to swell also, till the skin was stretched like drawn parchment. I was taken, too, with a sickness, that racked me violently, and if one of the greater and more dangerous beasts had come upon me then, he would have eaten me without a fight. With the fall of darkness I managed to haul myself up into a tree, and there abode in the crutch of a limb, in wakefulness and pain throughout the night.

With the dawn, when the night beasts had gone to their lairs, I clambered down again, and leaning heavily on my spear, limped onwards through the sombre forests along my way. The moss which grows on the northern side of each tree was my guide, but gradually I began to note that I was seeing moss all round the trees, and, in fact, was growing light-headed with the pain and the swelling of the limb. But still I pressed onwards with my journey, my last instinct being to obey the command of the High Council, and so procure the enlargement of Naïs as had been promised.

My last memory was of being met by someone in the black forest who aided me, and there my waking senses took wings into forgetfulness.

But after an interval, wit returned, and I found myself on a bed of leaves in a cleft between two rocks, which was furnished with some poor skill, and fortified with stakes and buildings against the entrance of the larger marauding beasts. My wound was dressed with a poultice of herbs, and at the other side of the cavern there squatted a woman, cooking a mess of wood-grubs and honey over a fire of sticks.

"How came I here?" I asked.

"I brought you," said she.

"And who are you?"

"A nymph, they call me, and I practise as such,

collecting herbs and curing the diseases of those that come to me, telling fortunes, and making predictions. In return I receive what each can afford, and if they do not pay according to their means, I clap on a curse to make them wither. It's a lean enough living when wars and the pestilence have left so few poor folk to live in the land."

"Do you visit Atlantis?"

"Not I. Phorenice would have me boiled in brine, living, if she could lay easy hands on me. Our dainty Empress tolerates no magic but her own. They say she is for pulling down the Priests off their Mountain now."

"So you do get news of the city?"

"Assuredly. It is my trade to get good news, or otherwise how could I tell fortunes to the vulgar? You see, my lord, I detected your quality by your speech, and knowing you are not one of those that come to me for spells and potions, I have no fear in speaking to you plainly."

"Tell me then: Phorenice still reigns?"

"Most viley."

"As a maiden?"

"As the mother of twin sons. Tatho's her husband now, and has been these three years."

"Tatho! Who followed him as viceroy of Yucatan?"

"There is no Yucatan. A vast nation of little hairy men, so the tale goes, coming from the West overran the country. They had clubs of wood tipped with stone as their only arm, but numbers made their chief weapon. They had no desire for plunder, or the taking of slaves, or the conquering of cities. To eat the flesh of Atlanteans was their only lust, and they followed it prodigiously. Their numbers were like the bees in a swarm.

"They came to each of the cities of Yucatan in turn, and though the colonists slew them in thousands, the weight of numbers always prevailed. They ate clean each city they took, and left it to the beasts of the forest, and went on to the next. And so in time they reached the coast towns, and Tatho and the few that survived took ship, and sailed home. They even ate Tatho's wife for him. They must be curious persevering things, these little hairy men. The Gods send they do not get across the seas to Atlantis, or they would be worse plague to the poor country than Phorenice."

Now I had heard of these little hairy creatures before, and though indeed I had never seen them, I had gathered that they were a little less than human and a little more than bestial; a link so to speak between the two orders; and specially held in check by the Gods in certain forest solitudes. Also I had learned that on occasion, when punishment was needful, they could be set loose as a devastating army upon men, devouring all before them. But I said nothing of this to the nymph, she being but a vulgar woman, and indeed half silly, as is always the case with these self-styled sorceresses who gull the ignorant, common folk. But within myself I was bitterly grieved at the fate of that fine colony of Yucatan, in which I had expended such an infinity of pains to do my share of the building.

But it did not suit my purpose to have my name and quality blazoned abroad till the time was full, and so I said nothing to the nymph about Yucatan, but let the talk continue upon other matters. "What about Egypt?" I asked.

"In its accustomed darkness, so they say. Who cares for Egypt these latter years? Who cares for anyone or anything for that matter except for himself and his own proper estate? Time was when the country folk and the hunters hereabouts brought me offerings to this cave for sheer piety's sake. But now they never come near unless they see a way of getting good value in return for their gifts. And, by result, instead of living fat and hearty, I make lean meals off honey and grubs. It's a poor life, a nymph's, in these latter years I tell you, my lord. It's the fashion for all classes to believe in no kind of mystery now."

"What manner of pestilence is this you spoke of?"

"I have not seen it. Thank the Gods it has not come this way. But they do say that it has grown from the folk Phorenice has slain, and whose bodies remain unburied. She is always slaying, and so the bodies lie thicker than the birds and beasts can eat them. For which of our sins, I wonder, did the Gods let Phorenice come to reign? I wish that she and her twins were boiled alive in brine before they came between an honest nymph of the forest and her living.

"They say she has put an image of herself in all the temples of the city now, and has ordered prayers and sacrifices to be made night and morning. She has decreed all other Gods inferior to herself and forbidden their worship, and those of the people that are not sufficiently devout for her taste, have their hamstrings slit by their tormentors to aid them constantly into a devotional attitude.—Will you eat of my grubs and honey? There is nothing else. Your back was bloody with carrying meat when I met you, but you had lost your load. You must either taste this mess of mine now, or go without."

I harboured with that nymph in cave six days, she using her drugs and charms to cure my leg the while, and when I was recovered, I hunted the plains and killed her a fat cloven-hoofed horse as payment, and then went along my ways.

The country from there onwards had at one time carried a sturdy population which held its own firmly, and, as its numbers grew, took in more ground, and built more homesteads farther afield. The houses were perched in trees for the most part, as there they were out of reach of cave-bear and cave-tiger and the other more dangerous beasts. But others, and these were the better ones, were built on the ground, of logs so ponderous and so firmly clamped and dovetailed that the beasts could not pull them down, and once inside a house of this fashion its owners were safe, and could progue at any attackers through the interstices between the logs, and often wound, sometimes make a kill.

But not one in ten of these outlying settlers remained. The houses were silent when I reached them, the fire-hearth before the door weed-grown, and the patch of vegetables taken back by the greedy fingers of the forest into mere scrub and jungle. And farther on, when villages began to appear, strongly-walled as the custom is, to ward off the attacks of beasts, the logs which aforetime had barred the gateway lay strewn in a sprouting undergrowth, and naught but the kitchen middens remained to prove that once they had sheltered human tenants. Phorenice's influence seemed to have spread as though it were some horrid blight over the whole face of what was once a smiling and an easy-living land.

So far I had met with little enough interference from any men I had come across. Many had fled with their women into the depths of the forest at the bare sight of me; some stood their ground with a threatening face, but made no offer to attack, seeing that I did not offer them insult first; and a few, a very few, offered me shelter and provision. But as I neared the city, and began to come upon muddy beaten paths, I passed through governments that were more thickly populated, and here appeared strong chance of delay. The watcher in the tower which is set above each village would spy me and cry: "Here is a masterless man," and then the people that were within would rush out with intent to spoil me of my weapons, and afterwards to appoint me as a labourer.

I had no desire to slay these wretched folk, being filled with pity at the state to which they had fallen; and often words served me to make them stand aside from the path, and stare wonderingly at my fierceness, and let me go my ways. And when at other times words had no avail, I strove to strike as lightly as could be, my object being to get forward with my journey and leave no unnecessary dead behind me. Indeed, having found the modern way of these villages, it grew to be my custom to turn off into the forest, and make a circuit whenever I came within smell of their garbage.

Similarly, too, when I got farther on, and came amongst greater towns also, I kept beyond challenge of their walls, having no mind to risk delay from the whim of any new law which might chance to be set up by their governors. My progress might be slinking, but my pride did not upbraid me very loudly; indeed, the fever of haste burned within me so hot that I had little enough carrying space for other emotions.

But at last I found myself within a half-day's journey the city of Atlantis itself, with the Sacred Mountain and its ring of fires looming high beside it, and the call for caution became trebly accentuated. Everywhere evidences showed that the country had been drained of its fighting men. Everywhere women prayed that the battles might end with the rout of the Priests or the killing of Phorenice, so that the wretched land might have peace and time to lick its wounds.

An army was investing the sacred Mountain, and its one approach was most narrowly guarded. Even after having journeyed so far, it seemed as if I should have to sit hopelessly down without being able to carry out the orders which had been laid upon me by the High Council, and earn the reward which had been promised. Force would be useless here. I should have one good fight—a gorgeous fight—one man against an army, and my usefulness would be ended. . . . No; this was the occasion for guile, and I found covert in the outskirts of a wood, and lay there cudgelling my brain for a plan.

Across the plain before me lay the grim great walls of the city, with the heads of its temples, and its palaces, and its pyramids showing beyond. The step-sides of the royal pyramid held my eye. Phorenice had expended some of her new-found store of gold in overlaying their former whiteness with sheets of shining yellow metal. But it was not that change that moved me. I was remembering that, in the square before the pyramid, there stood a throne of granite carved with the snake and the outstretched hand, and in the hollow beneath the throne was Naïs, my love, asleep these eight years now because of the drug that had been given to her, but alive still, and waiting for me, if only I on my part could make a way to the place where Zaemon defied the Empress, and announce my coming.

In that covert of the woods I lay a day and a night raging with myself for not discovering some plan to get within the defences of the Sacred Mountain, but in the morning which followed, there came a man towards me running.

"You need not threaten me with your weapons," he cried. "I mean no harm. It seems that you are Deucalion; though I should not have known you myself in those rags and skins, and behind that tangle of hair and beard. You will give me your good word I know. Believe me, I have not loitered unduly."

He was a lower priest whom I knew, and held in little esteem; his name was Ro, a greedy fellow and not overworthy of trust. "From whom do you come?" I asked.

"Zaemon laid a command on me. He came to my house, though how he got there I cannot tell, seeing that Phorenice's army blocks all possible passage to and from the Mountain. I told him I wished to be mixed with none of his schemings. I am a peaceful man, Deucalion, and have taken a wife who requires nourishment. I still serve in the same temple, though we have swept out the old Gods by order of the Empress, and put her image in their place. The people are tidily pious nowadays, those that are left of them, and the living is consequently easy. Yes, I tell you there are far more offerings now than there were in the old days. And so I had no wish to be mixed with matters which might well make me be deprived of a snug post, and my head to boot."

"I can believe it all of you, Ro."

"But there was no denying Zaemon. He burst into one of his black furies, and while he spoke at me, I tell you I felt as good as dead. You know his powers?"

"I have seen some of them."

"Well, the Gods alone know which are the true Gods, and which are the others. I serve the one that gives me employment. But those that Zaemon serves give him power, and that's beyond denying. You see that right hand of mine? It is dead and paralysed from the wrist, and that is a gift of Zaemon. He bestowed it, he said, to make me collect my attention. Then he said more hard things concerning what he was pleased to term my apostasy, not letting me put up a word in my own defence of how the change was forced upon me. And finally, said he, I might either do his bidding on a certain matter to the letter, or take that punishment which my falling away from the old Gods had earned. 'I shall not kill you,' said he, 'but I will cover all your limbs with a paralysis, such as you have tasted already, and when at length death reaches you in some gutter, you will welcome it.' "

"If Zaemon said those words, he meant them. So you accepted the alternative?"

"Had I, with a wife depending on me, any other choice? I asked his pleasure. It was to find you when you came in here from some distant part of the land, and deliver to you his message.

" 'Then tell me where is the meeting place," said I, 'and when.'

" 'There is none appointed, nor is the day fixed,' said he. 'You must watch and search always for him. But when he comes, you will be guided to his place.' Well, Deucalion, I think I was guided, but how, I do not know. But now I have found you, and if there's such a thing as gratitude, I ask you to put in your word with Zaemon that this deadness be taken away from my hand. It's an awful thing for a man to be forced to go through life like this, for no real fault of his own. And Zaemon could cure it from where he sat, if he was so minded."

"You seem still to have a very full faith in some of the old Gods' priests," I said. "But so far, I do not see that your errand is done. I have had no message yet."

"Why, the message is so simple that I do not see why he could not have got some one else to carry it. You are to make a great blaze. You may fire the grasses of the plain in front of this wood if you choose. And on the night which follows, you are to go round to that flank of the Sacred Mountain away from the city where the rocks run down sheer, and there they will lower a rope and haul you up to their hands above."

"It seems easy, and I thank you for your pains. I will ask Zaemon that your hand may be restored to you."

"You shall have my prayers if it is. And look, Deucalion, it is a small matter, and it would be less likely to slip your memory if you saw to it at once on your landing. Later, you may be disturbed. Phorenice is bound to pull you down off your perch up there now she has made her mind to it. She never fails, once she has set her hand to a thing. Indeed, if she was no Goddess at birth, she is making herself into one very rapidly. She has got all the ancient learning of our Priests, and more besides. She has discovered the Secret of Life these recent months—"

"She has found that?" I cried, fairly startled. "How? Tell me how? Only the Three know that. It is beyond our knowledge even who are members of the Seven."

"I know nothing of her means. But she has the secret, and now she is as good an immortal (so she says) as any of them. Well, Deucalion, it is dangerous for me to be missing from my temple overlong, so I will go. You will carry that matter we spoke of in your mind? It means much to me."—His eye wandered over my ragged person—"And if you think my service is of value to you——"

"You see me poor, my man, and practically destitute."

"Some small coin," he murmured, "or even a link of bronze? I am at great expense just now buying nourishment for my wife. Well, if you have nothing, you cannot give. So I'll just bid you farewell."

He took himself off then, and I was not sorry. I had never liked Ro. But I wasted no more precious time then. The grass blazed up for a signal almost before his timorous heels were clear of it, and that night when the darkness gave me cover, I took the risk of what beasts might be prowling, and went to the place appointed. There was no rope dangling, but presently one came down the smooth cliff face like some slender snake. I made a loop, slipped it over a leg, and pulled hard as a signal. Those above began to haul, and so I went back to the Sacred Mountain after an absence of so many toilsome and warring years. There were none to disturb the ascent. Phorenice's troops had no thought to guard that gaunt, bare, seamless precipice.

The men who hauled me up were old, and panted heavily with their task, and, until I knew the reason, I wondered why a knot of younger priests had not been appointed for the duty. But I put no question. With us of the Priests' Clan on the Sacred Mountain, it is always taken as granted that when an order is given, it is given for the best. Besides, these priests did not offer themselves to question. They took me off at once to Zaemon, and that is what I could have wished.

The old man greeted me with the royal sign. "All hail to Deucalion," he cried, "King of Atlantis, duly called thereto by the High Council of the priests."

"Is Phorenice dead?" I asked

"It remains for you to slay her, and take your kingdom, if, indeed, when all is done, there remains a man or a rood of land to govern. The sentence has gone out that she is to die, and it shall be carried into effect, even though we have to set loose the most dreadful powers that are stored in the Ark of the Mysteries, and wreck this continent in our effort. We have borne with her infamies all these years by command sent down by the most High Gods; but now she has gone beyond endurance, and They it is who have given the word for her cutting off."

"You are one of the highest Three; I am only one of the Seven; you best know the cost."

"There can be no counting the cost now, my brother, and my king. It is an order."

"It is an order," I repeated formally, "so I obey."

"If it were not impious to do so, it would be easy to justify this decision of the Gods. The woman has usurped the throne; yet she was forgiven and bidden rule on wisely. She has tempered with our holy religion; yet she was forgiven. She has killed the peoples of Atlantis in greedy useless wars, and destroyed the country's trade; yet she ws forgiven. She has desecrated the old temples, and latterly has set up in them images of herself to be worshipped as a deity; yet she was forgiven. But at last her evil cleverness has discovered to her the remendous Secret of Life and Death, and there she overstepped the boundary of the High Gods' forbearance.

"I myself went to carry a final warning, and once more faced her in the great banqueting-hall. Solemnly I recited to her the edict, and she chose to take it as a challenge. She would live on eternally herself and she would share her knowledge with those that pleased her. Tatho that was her husband should also be immortal. Indeed, if she thought fit, she would cry the secret aloud so that even the common people might know it, and death from mere age would become a legend.

"She cared no wit how she might upset the laws of Nature. She was Phorenice, and was the highest law of all. And finally she defied me there in that banqueting-hall and defied also the High Gods that stood behind my mouth. 'My magic is as strong as yours, you pompous fool,' she cried, 'and presently you shall see the two stand side by side upon their trial.'

"She began to collect an army from that moment, and we on our part made our preparations. It was discovered by our arts that you still lived, and King of Atlantis you were made by solemn election. How you were summoned, you know as nearly as it is lawful that one of your degree should know; how you came, you understand best yourself; but here you are, my brother, and being King now, you must order all things as you see best for the preservation of your high estate, and we others live only to give you obedience."

"Then being King, I can speak without seeming to make use of a threat. I must have my Queen first, or I am not strong enough to give my whole mind to this ruling."

"She shall be brought here."

"So! Then I will be a General now, and see to the defences of this place, and view the men who are here to stand behind them."

I went out of the dwelling then, Zaemon giving place and following me. It was night still, but there is no darkness on the upper part of the Sacred Mountain. A ring of fires, fed eternally from the earth-breath which wells up from below, burns round one-half of the crest, lighting it always as bright as day, and in fact forming no small part of its fortification. Indeed, it is said that, in the early dawn of history, men first came to the Mountain as a stronghold because of the natural defence which the fires offered.

There is no bridging these flames or smothering them. On either side of their line for a hundred paces the ground glows with heat, and a man would be turned to ash who tried to cross it. Round full one-half the mountain slopes the fires make a rampart unbreakable, and on the other side the rock runs in one sheer precipice from the crest to the plain which spreads beyond its foot. But it is on this farther side that there is the only entrance way which gives passage to the crest of the Sacred Mountain from below. Running diagonally up the steep face of the cliff is a gigantic fissure, which succeeding ages (as man has grown more luxurious) have made more easy to climb.

Looking at the additions, in the ancient days, I can well imagine that none but the most daring could have made the ascent. But one generation has thrown a bridge over a bad gap here, and another has cut into the living stone and widened a ledge there, till in these latter years there is a path with cut steps and carved balustrade such as the feeblest or most giddy might traverse with little effort or exertion. But always when these improvers made smooth the obstacles, they were careful to weaken in no possible way the natural defences but rather to add to them.

Eight gates of stone there were cutting the pathway, each commanding a straight, steep piece of the ascent, and overhanging each gate was a gallery secure from arrow-shot, yet so contrived that great stones could be hurled through holes in the floor of it, in such a manner that they must irretrievably smash to a pulp any men advancing against it from below. And in caves dug out from the rock on either hand was a great hoard of these stones, so that no enemy through sheer expenditure of troops could hope to storm a gate by exhausting its ammunition.

But though there were eight of these granite gates in the series, we had the whole number to depend on no longer. The lowest gate was held by a garrison of Phorenice's troops, who had built a wall above them to protect their occupation. The gate had been gained by no brilliant feat of arms—it had been won by threats, bribery, and promises; or, in other words, it had been given up by the blackest treachery.

And here lay the keynote of the weakness in our defence. The most perfect ramparts that brain can invent are useless without men to line them, and it was men we lacked. Of students entering into the colleges of the

Sacred Mountain, there had been none now for many a year. The younger generation thought little of the older Gods. Of the men that had grown up amongst the sacred groves, and filled offices there, many had become lukewarm in their faith and remained on only through habit, and because an easy living stayed near them there; and these, when the siege began, quickly made their way over to the other side.

Phorenice was no fool to fight against unnecessary strength. Her heralds made proclamation that peace and a good subsistence would be given to those who chose to come out to her willingly; and as an alternative she would kill by torture and mutilation those she caught in the place when she took it by storm, as she most assuredly would do before she had finished with it. And so great was the prestige of her name, that quite one-half of these that remained on the mountain took themselves away from the defence.

There was no attempt to hold back these sorry priests, nor was there any punishing them as they went. Zaemon, indeed, was minded (so he told me with grim meaning himself) to give them some memento of their apostasy to carry away which would not wear out, but the others of the High Council made him stay his vengeful hand. And so when I came to the place the garrison numbered no more than eighty, counting even feeble old dotards who could barely walk; and of men not past their prime I could barely command a score.

Still, seeing the narrowness of the passages which led to each of the gates, up which in no place could more than two men advance together, we were by no means in desperate straits for the defence as yet; and if my new-given kingdom was so far small, consisting as it did in effect of the Sacred Mountain and no other part of Atlantis, at any rate there seemed little danger of its being further contracted.

Another of the wise precautions of the men of old stood us in good stead then. In the ancient times, when grain first was grown as food, it came to be looked upon as the acme of wealth. Tribute was always paid from the people to their Priests, and presently, so the old histories say, it was appointed that this should take the form of grain, as this was a medium both dignified and fitting. And those of the people who had it not, were forced to barter their other produce for grain before they could pay this tribute.

On the Sacred Mountain itself vast storehouses were dug in the rock, and here the grain was teemed in great yellow heaps, and each generation of those that were set over it, took a pride in adding to the accumulation.

In more modern days it had been a custom amongst the younger and more forward of the Priests to scoff at this ancient provision, and to hold that a treasure of gold, or weapons, or jewels would have more value and no less of dignity; and more than once it has been a close thing lest these innovators should not be out-voted. But as it was, the old constitution had happily been preserved, and now in these years of trial the Clan reaped the benefit. And so with these granaries, and a series of great tanks and cisterns which held the rainfall, there was no chance of Phorenice reducing our stronghold by mere close investment, even though she sat down stubbornly before it for a score of years.

But it was the paucity of men for the defence which oppressed me most. As I took my way about the head of the Mountain, inspecting all points, the emptiness of the place smote me like a succession of blows. The groves, once so trim, were now shaggy and unpruned. Wind had whirled the leaves in upon the temple floors, and they lay there unswept. The college of youths held no more now than a musty smell to bear witness that men had once been grown there. The homely palaces of the higher Priests, at one time so ardently sought after, lay many of them empty, because not even one candidate came forward now to canvass for election.

Evil thoughts surged up within me as I saw these

things, that were direct promptings from the nether Gods. "There must be something wanting," these tempters whispered, "in a religion from which so many of its Priests fled at the first pinch of persecution."

I did what I could to thrust these waverings resolutely behind me; but they refused to be altogether ousted from my brain; and so I made a compromise with myself: First, I would with the help that might be given me, destroy this wanton Phorenice, and regain the kingdom which had been given me to my own proper rule; and afterwards I would call a council of the Seven and council of the Three, and consider without prejudice if there was any matter in which our ancient ritual could be amended to suit the more modern requirements. But this should not be done till Phorenice was dead and I was firmly planted in her room. I would not be a party, even to myself, to any plan which smacked at all of surrender.

And there as I walked through the desolate groves and beside the cold altars, the High Gods were pleased to show their approval of my scheme, and to give me opportunity to bind myself to it with a solemn oath and vow. At that moment, from His distant resting-place in the East, our Lord the Sun leaped up to begin another day. For long enough from where I stood below the crest of the Mountain, He Himself would be invisible. But the great light of His glory spread far into the sky, and against it the Ark of the Mysteries loomed in black outline from the highest crag where it rested, lonely and terrible.

For anyone unauthorised to go nearer than a thousand paces to this storehouse of the Highest Mysteries meant instant death. On that day when I was initiated as one of the Seven, I had been permitted to go near and once press my lips against its ample curves; and the rank of my degree gave me the privilege to repeat that salute again once on each day when a new year was born. But what lay inside its great interior, and how it was entered, that was hidden from the Seven, even as it was from the other Priests and the common people in the city below. Only those who had been raised to the sublime elevation of the Three had a knowledge of the dreadful powers which were stored within it.

I went down on my knees where I was, and Zaemon knelt beside me, and together we recited the prayers which had been said by the Priests from the beginning of time, giving thanks to our great Lord that He has come to brighten another day. And then, with my eyes fixed on the black outline of the Ark of Mysteries I vowed that, come what might, I at least would be true servant of the High Gods to my life's end, and that my whole strength should be spent in restoring Their worship and glory.

17. Naïs the Regained

Now, from where we stood together just below the crest of the Sacred Mountain, we could see down into the city, which lay spread out below us like a map. The harbour and the great estuary gleamed at its farther side; and the fringe of hills beyond smoked and fumed in their accustomed fashion; the great stone circle of our Lord the Sun stood up grim and bare in the middle of the city; and nearer in reared up the great mass of the royal pyramid, the gold on its sides catching new gold from the Sun. There, too, in the square before the pyramid stood the throne of granite, dwarfed by the distance to the size of a mole's hill, in which these nine years my love had lain sleeping.

Old Zaemon followed my gaze. "Ay," he said with a sigh, "I know where your chief interest is. Deucalion when he landed here new from Yucatan was a strong man. The King whom we have chosen—and who is the best we have to choose—has his weakness."

"It can be turned into additional strength. Give me Naïs here, living and warm to fight for, and I am a stronger man by far than the cold viceroy and soldier that you speak about."

"I have passed my word to that already, and you shall have her, but at the cost of damaging somewhat this new kingdom of yours. Maybe too at the same time we may rid you of this Phorenice and her brood. But I do not think it likely. She is too wily, and once we begin our play, she is likely to guess whence it comes, and how it will end, and so will make an escape before harm can reach her. The High Gods, who have sent all these trials for our refinement, have seen fit to give her some knowledge of how these earth tremors may be set a-moving."

"I have seen her juggle with them. But may I hear your scheme?"

"It will be shown you in good time enough. But for the present I would bid you sleep. It will be your part to go into the city to-night, and take your woman (that is my daughter) when she is set free, and bring her here as best you can. And for that you will need all a strong man's strength."—He stepped back, and looked me up and down.—"There are not many folk that would take you for the tidy clean-chinned Deucalion now, my brother. Your appearance will be a fine armour for you down yonder in the city to-night when we wake it with our earth-shaking and terror. As you stand now, you are hairy enough, and shaggy enough, and naked enough, and dirty enough for some wild savage new landed out of Europe. Have a care that no fine citizen down younder takes a fancy to your thews, and seizes upon you as his servant."

"I somewhat pity him in his household if he does."

Old Zaemon laughed. "Why, come to think of it, so do I."

But quickly he got grave again. Laughter and Zaemon were very rare playmates. "Well, get you to bed, my King, and leave me to go into the Ark of Mysteries and prepare there with another of the Three the things that must be done. It is no light business to handle the tremendous powers which we must put into movement this night. And there is danger for us as there is for you. So if by chance we do not meet again till we stand up yonder behind the stars, giving account to the Gods, fare you well, Deucalion."

I slept that day as a soldier sleeps, taking full rest out of the hours, and letting no harassing thought disturb me. It is only the weak who permit their sleep to be broken on these occasions. And when the dark was well set, I roused and fetched those who should attend to the rope. Our Lady the Moon did not shine at that turn of the month: and the air was full of a great blackness. So I was out of sight all the while they lowered me.

I reached the tumbled rocks that lay at the deep foot of the cliff, and then commenced to use a nice caution, because Phorenice's soldiers squatted uneasily round their camp-fires, as though they had forebodings of the coming evil. I had no mind to further stir their wakefulness. So I crept swiftly along in the darkest of the shadows, and at last came to the spot where that passage ends which before I had used to get beneath the walls of the city.

The lamp was in place, and I made my way along the windings swiftly. The air, so it seemed to me, was even more noxious with vapours than it had been when I was down there before, and I judged that Zaemon had already begun to stir those internal activities which were shortly to convulse the city. But again I had difficulty in finding an exit, and this, not because there were people moving about at the places where I had to come out, but because the set of the masonry was entirely changed. In olden times the Priests' Clan oversaw all the architects' plans, and ruled out anything likely to clash with their secret passages and chambers. But in this modern day the Priests were of small account, and had no say in this matter, and the architects often through sheer blundering sealed up and made useless many of these outlets and hiding-places.

As it was then, I had to get out of the network of tunnels and galleries where I could, and not where I would, and in the event found myself at the farther side of the city, almost up to where the outer wall joins down to the harbour. I came out without being seen, careful even in this moment of extremity to preserve the ordinances, and closed all traces of exit behind me. The earth seemed to spring beneath my feet like the deck of a ship in smooth water; and though there was no actual movement as yet to disturb the people, and indeed these slept on in their houses and shelters without alarm, I could feel myself that the solid deadness of the ground was gone, and that any moment it might break out into devastating waves of movement.

Gods! Should I be too late to see the untombing of my love? Would she be laid there bare to the public gaze when presently the people swarmed out into the open spaces through fear at what the great earth tremor might cause to fall? I could see, in fancy, their rude, cruel hands thrust upon her as she lay there helpless, and my inwards dried up at the thought.

I ran madly down and down the narrow winding streets with the one thought of coming to the square which lay in front of the royal pyramid before these things came to pass. With exquisite cruelty I had been forced with my own hands to place her alive in her burying-place beneath the granite throne, and if thews and speed could do it, I would not miss my reward of taking her forth again with the same strong hands.

Few disturbed that furious hurry. At first here and there some wretch who harboured in the gutter cried: "A thief! Throw a share or I pursue." But if any of these followed, I do not know. At any rate, my speed them must have out-distanced anyone. Presently, too, as the swing of the earth underfoot became more keen, and the stonework of the buildings by the street side began to grate and groan and grit, and sent forth little showers of dust, people began to run with scared cries from out of their doors. But none of these had a mind to stop the ragged, shaggy, savage man who ran so swiftly past, and flung the mud from his naked feet.

And so in time I came to the great square, and was there none too soon. The place was filling with people who flocked away from the narrow streets, and it was full of darkness, and noise, and dust, and sickness. Beneath us the ground rippled in undulations like a sea, which with terrifying slowness grew more and more intense.

Ever and again a house crashed down unseen in the gloom, and added to the tumult. But the great pyramid had been planned by its old builders to stand rude shocks. It stones were dovetailed into one another with a marvellous cleverness, and were further clamped and joined by ponderous tongues of metal. It was a boast that one-half the foundations could be dug from beneath it, and still the pyramid would stand foursquare under heaven, more enduring than the hills.

Flickering torches showed that its great stone doors lay open, and ever and again I saw some frightened inmate scurry out and then be lost to sight in the gloom. But with the royal pyramid and its ultimate fate I had little concern; I did not even care then whether Phorenice was trapped, or whether she came out sound and fit for further mischief. I crouched by the granite throne which stood in the middle of that splendid square, and heard its stones grate together like the ends of a broken bone as it rocked to the earth-waves.

In that night of dust and darkness it was hard to see the outline of one's own hand, but I think that the Gods in some requital for the love which had ached so long within me, gave me special power of sight. As I watched, I saw the great carved rock which formed the capstone of the throne move slightly and then move again, and then again; a tiny jerk for each earth-pulse, but still there was an appreciable shifting; and, moreover, the stone moved always to one side.

There was method in Zaemon's desperate work, and this in my blind panic of love and haste, I had overlooked. So I went up the steps of the throne on the side from which the great capstone was moving, and clung there afire with expectation.

More and more violent did the earth-swing grow, though the graduations of its increase could not be perceived, and the din of falling houses and the shrieks and cries of hurt and frightened people went louder up into the night. Thicker grew the dust that filled the air, till one coughed and strangled in the breathing, and more black did the night become as the dust rose and blotted the rare stars from sight. I clung to an angle of the granite throne, crouching on the uppermost step but one below the capstone, and could scarcely keep my place against the violence of the earth tremors.

But still the huge capstone that was carved with the snake and the outstretched hand held my love fast locked in her living tomb, and I could have bit the cold granite at the impotence which barred me from her. The people who kept thronging into the square were mad with terror, but their very numbers made my case more desperate every moment. "Phorenice, Goddess, aid us now!" some cried, and when the prayer did not bring them instant relief, they fell to yammering out the old confessions of the faith which they had learned in childhood, turning in this hour of their dreadful need to those old Gods, which, through so many dishonourable years, they had spurned and deserted. It was a curious criticism on the balance of their real religion, if one had cared to make it.

Louder grew the crash of falling masonry; and from the royal pyramid itself, though indeed I could not even see its outline through the darkness, there came sounds of grinding stones and cracking bars of metal which told that even its superb majestic strength had a breaking strain. There came to my mind the threat that old Zaemon had thundered forth in that painted, perfumed banqueting-hall: "You shall see," he had cried to the Empress, "this royal pyramid which you have polluted with your debaucheries torn tier from tier, and stone from stone, and scattered as feathers spread before a wind!"

Still heavier grew the surging of the earth, and the pavement of the great square gaped and upheaved, and the people who thronged it screamed still more shrilly as their feet were crushed by the grinding blocks. And now too the great pyramid itself was commencing to split, and gape, and topple. The roofs of its splendid chambers gave way, and the ponderous masonry above shuttered down and filled them. In part, too, one could see the destruction now, and not guess at it merely from the fearful hearings of the darkness. Thunders had begun to roar through the black night above, and add their bellowings to this devil's orchestration of uproar, and vivid lightning splashes lit the flying dust-clouds.

It was perhaps natural that she should be there, but it came as a shock when a flare of the lightning showed me Phorenice safe out in the square, and indeed standing not far from myself.

She had taken her place in the middle of a great flagstone, and stood there swaying her supple body to the shocks. Her face was calm, and its loveliness was untouched by the years. From time to time she brushed away the dust as it settled on the short red hair which curled about her neck. There was no trace of fear written upon her face. There was some weariness, some contempt, and I think a tinge of amusement. Yes, it took more than the crumbling of her royal pyramid to impress Phorenice with the infinite powers of those she warred against.

Gods! How the sight of her cool indifference maddened me then. I had it in me to have strangled her with my hands if she had come within my reach. But as it was, she stood in her place, swaying easily to the earth-waves as a sailor sways on a ship's deck, and beside her, crouched on the same great flagstone, and overcome with nausea was Ylga, who again was raised to be her fan-girl. It came to my mind that Ylga was twin sister to Naïs, and that I owed her for an ancient kindness, but I had leisure to do nothing for her then, and indeed it was little enough I could have done. With each shock the great capstone of the throne to which I clung jarred farther and farther from its bed place, and my love was coming nearer to me. It was she who claimed all my service then.

Once in their blind panic a knot of the people in the square thought that the granite stone was too solid to be overturned, and saw in it an oasis of safety. They flocked towards it, many of them dragging themselves up the steep deep high steps on hands and knees because their feet had been injured by the billowing flagstones of the square.

But I was in no mood to have the place profaned by their silly tremblings and stares: I beat at them with my hands, tearing them away, and hurling them back down the steepness of the steps. They asked me what was my title to the place above their own, and I answered them with blows and gnashing teeth. I was careless as to what they thought me or who they thought me. Only I wished them gone. And so they went, wailing and crying that I was a devil of the night, for they had no spirit left to defend themselves.

Farther and farther the great stone that made the top of the throne slid out from its bed, but its slowness of movement maddened me. A life's education left me in that moment, and I had no trace of stately patience left. In my puny fury I thrust at the great block with my shoulder and head, and clawed at it with my hands till the muscles rose on me in great ropes and knots, and the High Gods must have laughed at my helplessness as They looked. All was being ordered by the Three who were Their trusted servants, in Their good time. The work of the Gods may be done slowly, but it is done exceeding sure.

But at last, when all the people of the city were numb with terror, and incapable of further emotion (save only for Phorenice who still had nerve enough to show no concern), what had been threatened came to pass. The capstone of the throne slid out till it reached the balance, and the next shock threw it with a roar and a clatter to the ground. And then a strange tremor seized me.

After all the scheming and effort, what I had so ardently prayed for had come about; but yet my inwards sank at the thought of mounting on the stone where I had mounted before, and taking my dear from the hollow where my hands had laid her. I knew Phorenice's vengefulness, and had a high value for her cleverness. Had she left Naïs to lie in peace, or had she stolen her away to suffer indignities elsewhere? Or had she ended her sleep with death, and (as a grisly jest) left the corpse for my finding? I could not tell; I dared not guess. Never during a whole hard-fighting life have my emotions been so wrenched as they were at that moment. And, for excuse, it must be owned that love for Naïs had sapped my hardihood over a matter in which she was so privately concerned.

It began to come to my mind, however, that the infernal uproar of the earth tremor was beginning to slacken somewhat, as though Zaemon knew he had done the work that he had promised, and was minded to give the wretched city a breathing space. So I took my fortitude in hand, and clambered up on to the flat of the stone. The lightning flashes had ceased and all was darkness again and stifling dust, but at any moment the sky might be lit once more, and if I were seen in that place, shaggy and changed though I might be,

Phorenice, if she were standing near, would not be slow to guess my name and errand.

So changed was I for the moment, that I will finely confess that the idea of a fight was loathsome to me then. I wanted to have my business done and get gone from the place.

With hands that shook, I fumbled over the face of the stone and found the clamps and bars of metal still in position where I had clenched them, and then reverently I let my fingers pass between these, and felt the curves of my love's body in its rest beneath. An exultation began to whirl within me. I did not know if she had been touched since I last left her; I did not know if the drug would have its due effect, and let her be awakened to warmth and sight again; but, dead or alive, I had her there, and she was mine, mine, mine, and I could have yelled aloud in my joy at her possession.

Still the earth shook beneath us, and masonry roared and crashed into ruin. I had to cling to my place with one hand, whilst I unhasped the clamps of metal that made the top of her prison with the other. But at last I swung the upper half of them clear, and those which pinned down her feet I let remain. I stooped and drew her soft body up on to the flat of the stone beside me, and pressed my lips a hundred times to the face I could not see.

Some mad thought took me, I believe, that the mere fierceness and heat of my kisses would bring her back again to life and wakefulness. Indeed I will own plainly, that I did but sorry credit to my training in calmness that night. But she lay in my arms cold and nerveless as a corpse, and by degrees my sober wits returned to me.

This was no place for either of us. Let the earth's tremors cease (as was plainly threatened), let daylight come, and let a few of these nerveless people round recover from their panic, and all the great cost that had been expended might be counted as waste. We should be seen, and it would not be long before some one put a name to Naïs; and then it would be an easy matter to guess at Deucalion under the beard and the shaggy hair and the browned nakedness of the savage who attended on her. Tell of fright? By the Gods! I was scared as the veriest trembler who blundered amongst the dust-clouds that night when the thought came to me.

With all that ruin spread around, it would be hopeless to think that any of those secret galleries which tunnelled under the ground would be left unbroken, and so it was useless to try a passage under the walls by the old means. But I had heard shouts from that frightened mob which came to me through the din and the darkness, that gave another idea for escape. "The city is accursed," they had cried: "if we stay here it will fall on us. Let us get outside the walls where there are no buildings to bury us."

If they went, I could not see. But one gate lay nearest to the royal pyramid, and I judged that in their panic they would not go farther than was needful. So I put the body of Naïs over my shoulder (to leave my right arm free) and blundered off as best I could through the stifling darkness.

It was hard to find a direction; it was hard to walk in that inky darkness over ground that was tossed and tumbled like a frozen sea: and as the earth still quaked and heaved, it was hard also to keep a footing. But if I did fall myself a score of times, my dear burden got no bruise, and presently I got to the skirts of the square, and found a street I knew. The most venomous part of the shaking was done, and no more buildings fell, but enough lay sprawled over the roadway to make walking into a climb, and the sweat rolled from me as I laboured along my way.

There was no difficulty about passing the gate. There was no gate. There was no wall. The Gods had driven their plough through it, and it lay flat, and proud Atlantis stood as defenceless as the open country. Though I knew the cause of this ruin, though, in fact,

I had myself in some measure incited it, I was almost sad at the ruthlessness with which it had been carried out. The royal pyramid might go, houses and palaces might be levelled, and for these I cared little enough; but when I saw those stately ramparts also filched away, there the soldier in me woke, and I grieved at this humbling of the mighty city that once had been my only mistress.

But this was only a passing regret, a mere touch of the fighting-man's pride. I had a different love now, that had wrapped herself round me far deeper and more tightly, and my duty was towards her first and foremost. The night would soon be past, and then dangers would increase. None had interfered with us so far, though many had jostled us as I clambered over the ruins; but this forbearance could not be reckoned upon for long. The earth tremors had almost died away, and after the panic and the storm, then comes the time for the spoiling.

All men who were poor would try to seize what lay nearest to their hands, and those of higher station, and any soldiers who could be collected and still remained true to command, would ruthlessly stop and strip any man they saw making off with plunder. I had no mind to clash with these guardians of law and property, and so I fled on swiftly through the night with my burden, using the unfrequented ways; and crying to the few folk who did meet me that the woman had the plague, and would they lend me the shelter of their house as ours had fallen. And so in time we came to the place where the rope dangled from the precipice, and after Naïs had been drawn up to the safety of the Sacred Mountain, I put my leg in the loop of the rope and followed her.

Now came what was the keenest anxiety of all. We took the girl and laid her on a bed in one of the houses, and there in the lit room for the first time I saw her clearly. Her beauty was drawn and pale. Her eyes were closed, but so thin and transparent had grown the lids that one could almost see the brown of the pupil beneath them. Her hair had grown to inordinate thickness and length, and lay as a cushion behind and beside her head.

There was no flicker of breath; there was none of that pulsing of the body which denotes life; but still she had not the appearance of ordinary death. The Naïs I had placed nine long years before to rest in the hollow of the stone, was a fine grown woman, full bosomed, and well boned. The Naïs that remained for me was half her weight. The old Naïs it would have puzzled me to carry for an hour: this was no burden to impede a grown man.

In other ways too she had altered. The nails of her fingers had grown to such a great length that they were twisted in spirals, and the fingers themselves and her hands were so waxy and transparent that the bony core upon which they were built showed itself beneath the flesh in plain dull outline. Her clay-cold lips were so white, that one sighed to remember the full beauty of their carmine. Her shoulders and neck had lost their comely curves, and made bony hollows now in which the dust of entombment lodged black and thickly.

Reverently I set about preparing those things which if all went well should restore her. I heated water and filled a bath, and tinctured it heavily with those essences of the life of beasts which the Priests extract and store against times of urgent need and sickness. I laid her chin-deep in this bath, and sat beside it to watch, maintaining that bath at a constant blood heat.

An hour I watched; two hours I watched; three hours—and yet she showed no flicker of life. The heat of her body given her by the bath, was the same as the heat of my own. But in the feel of her skin when I stroked it with my hand, there was something lacking still. Only when our Lord the Sun rose for His day did I break off my watching, whilst I said the necessary prayer which is prescribed, and quickly returned again to the gloom of the house.

I was torn with anxiety, and as the time went on and still no sign of life came back, the hope that had once been so high within me began to sicken and leave me downcast and despondent. From without, came the din of fighting. Already Phorenice had sent her troops to storm the passageway, and the Priests who defended it were shattering them with volleys of rocks. But these sounds of war woke no pulse within me. If Naïs did not wake, then the world for me was ended, and I had no spirit left to care who remained uppermost. The Gods in Their due time will doubtless smite me for this impiety. But I make a confession of it here on these sheets, having no mind to conceal any portion of this history for the small reason that it does me a personal discredit.

But as the hours went on, and still no flicker of life came to lessen the dumb agony that racked me, I grew more venturesome, and added more essences to the bath, and drugs also such as experience had shown might wake the disused tissues into life. I watched on with staring eyes, rubbing her wasted body now and again, and always keeping the heat of the bath at a constant. From the first I had barred the door against all who would have come near to help me. With my own hands I had laid my love to sleep, and I could not bear that others should rouse her, if indeed roused she should ever be. But after those first offers, no others came, and the snarl and din of fighting told of what occupied them.

It is hard to take note of small changes which occur with infinite slowness when one is all the while on the tense watch, and high strung though my senses were, I think there must have been some indication of returning life shown before I was keen enough to notice it. For of a sudden, as I gazed, I saw a faint rippling on the surface of the water of the bath. Gods! Would it come back again to my love at last—this life, this wakefulness? The ripple died out as if had come, and I stooped my head nearer to the bath to try if I could see some faint heaving of her bosom some small twitching of the limbs. No, she lay there still without even a flutter of movement. But as I watched, surely it seemed to my aching eyes that some tinge was beginning to warm that blank whiteness of skin?

How I filled myself with that sight. The colour was returning to her again beyond a doubt. Once more the dried blood was becoming fluid and beginning again to course in its old channels. Her hair floated out in the liquid of the bath like some brown tangle of the ocean weed, and ever and again it twitched and eddied to some impulse which in itself was too small for the eye to see.

She had slept for nine long years, and I knew that the wakening could be none of the suddenest. Indeed, it came by its own gradations and with infinite slowness, and I did not dare do more to hasten it. Further drugs might very well stop eternally what those which had been used already had begun. So I sat motionless where I was, and watched the colour come back, and the waxenness go, and even the fullness of her curves in some small measure return. And when growing strength gave her power to endure them, and she was racked with those pains which are inevitable to being born back again in this fashion to life, I too felt the reflex of her agony, and writhed in loving sympathy.

Still further, too, was I wrung by a torment of doubt as to whether life or these rackings would in the end be conqueror. After each paroxysm the colour ebbed back from her again, and for a while she would lie motionless. But strength and power seemed gradually to grow, and at last these prevailed, and drove death and sleep beneath them. Her eyelids struggled with their fastenings. Her lips parted, and her bosom heaved. With shivering gasps her breath began to pant between her reddening lips. At first it rattled dryly in her throat, but soon it softened and became more regular. And then with a last effort her eyes, her glorious loving eyes, slowly opened.

I leaned over and called her softly by name.

Her eyes met mine, and a glow arose from their depths that gave me the greatest joy I have met in all the world.

"Deucalion, my love," she whispered. "Oh, my dear, so you have come for me. How I have dreamed of you! How I have been racked! But it was worth it all for this."

18. Storm of the Sacred Mountain

It was Naïs herself who sent me to attend to my sterner duties. The din of the attack came to us in the house where I was tending her, and she asked its meaning. As pithily as might be, for she was in no condition for tedious listening, I gave her the history of her nine years' sleep.

The colour flushed more to her face. "My lord is the properest man in all the world to be King," she whispered.

"I refused to touch the trade till they had given me the Queen I desired, safe and alive, here upon the Mountain."

"How we poor women are made the chattels of you men! But, for myself, I seem to like the traffic well enough. You should not have let me stand in the way of Atlantis' good, Deucalion. Still, it is very sweet to know you were weak there for once, and that I was the cause of your weakness. What is that bath over yonder? Ah! I remember; my wits seem none of the clearest just now."

"You have made the beginning. Your strength will return to you by quick degrees. But it will not bear hurrying. You must have a patience."

"Your ear, sir, for one moment, and then I will rest in peace. My poor looks, are they all gone? You seem to have no mirror here. I had visions that I should wake up wrinkled and old."

"You are as you were, dear, that first night I saw you—the most beautiful woman in all the world."

"I am pleased you like me," she said, and took the cup of broth I offered her. "My hair seems to have grown; but it needs combing sadly. I had a fancy, dear, once, that you liked ruddy hair best, and not a plain brown." She closed her eyes then, lying back amongst the cushions where I had placed her, and dropped off into healthy sleep, with the smiles still playing upon her lips. I put the coverlet over her, and kissed her lightly, holding back my beard lest it should sweep her cheek. And then I went out of the chamber.

That beard had grown vastly disagreeable to me these last hours, and then I went into a room in the house, and found instruments, and shaved it down to the bare chin. A change of robe also I found there and took it instead of my squalid rags. If a man is in truth a king, he owes these things to the dignity of his office.

But, if the din of the fighting was any guide, mine was a narrowing kingdom. Every hour it seemed to grow fiercer and more near, and it was clear that some of the gates in the passage up the cleft in the cliff, impregnable though all men had thought them, had yielded to the vehemence of Phorenice's attack. And, indeed, it was scarcely to be marvelled at. With all her genius spurred on to fury by the blow that had been struck at her by wrecking so fair a part of the city, the Empress would be no light adversary even for a strong place to resist, and the Sacred Mountain was no longer strong.

Defences of stone, cunningly planned and mightily built, it still possessed, but these will not fight alone. They need men to line them, and, moreover, abundance of men. For always in a storm of this kind, some desperate fellows will spit at death and get to hand grips, or slingers and archers slip in their shot, or the throwing-fire gets home, or (as here) some new-fangled machine like Phorenice's fire-tubes, make one in a thousand of their wavering darts find the life; and so, though the general attacking loses his hundreds, the defenders also are not without their dead.

The slaughter, as it turned out, had been prodigious. As fast as the stormers came up, the Priests who held the lowest gate remaining to us rained down great rocks upon them till the narrow alley of the stair was paved with their writhing dead. But Phorenice stood on a spur of the rock below them urging on the charges, and with an insane valour company after company marched up to hurl themselves hopelessly against the defences. They had no machines to batter the massive gates, and their attack was as pathetically useless as that of a child who hammers against a wall with an orange; and meanwhile the terrible stones from above mowed them down remorselessly.

Company after company of the troops marched into this terrible death-trap, and not a man of all of them ever came back. Nor was it Phorenice's policy that they should do so. In her lust for this final conquest, she was minded to pour out troops till she had filled up the passes with the slain, so that at last she might march on to a level fight over the bridge of their poor bodies. It was no part of Phorenice's mood ever to count the cost. She set down the object which was to be gained, and it was her policy that the people of Atlantis were there to gain it for her.

Two gates then had she carried in this dreadful fashion, slaughtering those Priests that stood behind them who had not been already shot down. And here I came down from above to take my share in the fight.

There was no trumpet to announce my coming, no herald to proclaim my quality, but the Priests as a sheer custom picked up "Deucalion!" as a battle-cry; and some shouted that, with a King to lead, there would be no further ground lost.

It was clear that the name carried to the other side and bore weight with it. A company of poor, doomed wretches who were hurrying up stopped in their charge. The word "Deucalion!" was bandied round and handed back down the line. I thought with some grim satisfaction, that here was evidence I was not completely forgotten in the land.

There came shouts to them from behind to carry on their advance; but they did not budge; and presently a glittering officer panted up, and commenced to strike right and left amongst them with his sword. From where I stood on the high rampart above the gate, I could see him plainly, and recognised him at once.

"It matters not what they use for their battle-cry," he was shouting. "You have the orders of your divine Empress, and that is enough. You should be proud to die for her wish, you cowards. And if you do not obey, you will die afterwards under the instruments of the tormentors, very painfully. As for Deucalion, he is dead any time these nine years."

"There it seems you lie, my Lord Tatho," I shouted down to him.

He started, and looked up at me.

"So you are there in real truth, then? Well, old comrade, I am sorry. But it is too late to make a composition now. You are on the side of these mangy Priests, and the Empress has made an edict that they are to be rooted out, and I am her most obedient servant."

"You used to be skilful of fence," I said, and indeed there was little enough to choose between us. "If it please you to stop this pitiful killing, make yourself the champion of your side, and I will stand for mine, and we will fight out this quarrel in some fair place, and bind our parties to abide by the result."

"It would be a grand fight between us two, old friend, and it goes hard with me to balk you of it. But I cannot pleasure you. I am general here under Phorenice, and she has given me the strongest orders not to peril myself. And besides, though you are a great man, Deucalion, you are not chief. You are not even one of the Three."

"I am King."

Tatho laughed. "Few but yourself would say so, my lord."

"Few truly, but what there are, they are powerful. I was given the name for the first time yesterday, and as a first blow in the campaign there was some mischief done in the city. I was there myself, and saw how you took it."

"You were in Atlantis!"

"I went for Naïs. She is on the mountain now, and to-morrow will be my Queen. Tatho, as a priest to a priest, let me solemnly bring to your memory the infinite power you bite against on this Sacred Mountain. Your teaching has warned you of the weapons that are stored in the Ark of the Mysteries. If you persist in this attack, at the best you can merely lose; at the worst you can bring about a wreck over which even the High Gods will shudder as They order it."

"You cannot scare us back now by words," said Tatho doggedly. "And as for magic, it will be met by magic. Phorenice has found by her own cleverness as many powers as were ever stored up in the Ark of the Mysteries."

"Yet she looked on helplessly enough last night, when her royal pyramid was trundled into a rubbish heap. Zaemon had prophesied that this should be so, and for a witness, why I myself stood closer to her than we two stand now, and saw her."

"I will own you took her by surprise somewhat there. I do not understand these matters myself; I was never more than one of the Seven in the old days; and now, quite rightly, Phorenice keeps the knowledge of her magic to herself: but it seems time is needed when one magic is to be met by another."

"Well," I said, "I know little about the business either. I leave these matters now to those who are higher above me in the priesthood. Indeed, having a liking for Naïs, it seems I am debarred from ever being given understanding about the highest of the higher Mysteries. So I content myself with being a soldier, and when the appointed day comes, I shall fall and kiss my mother the Earth for the last time. You, so I am told, have ambition for longer life."

He nodded. "Phorenice has found the Great Secret, and I am to be the first that will share it with her. We shall be as Gods upon the earth, seeing that Death will be powerless to touch us. And the twin sons she has borne me, will be made immortal also."

"Phorenice is headstrong. No, my lord, there is no need to shake your head and try to deny it. I have had some acquaintance with her. But the order has been made, and her immortality will be snatched from her very rudely. Now, mark solemnly my words. I, Deucalion, have been appointed King of Atlantis by the High Council of the Priests who are the mouthpiece of the most High Gods, and if I do not have my reign, then there will be no Atlantis left to carry either King or Empress. You know me, Tatho, for a man that never lies."

He nodded.

"Then save yourself before it is too late. You shall have again your vice-royalty in Yucatan."

"But, man, there is no Yucatan. A great horde of little hairy creatures, that were something less than human and something more than beasts, swept down upon our cities and ate them out. Oh, you may sneer if you choose! Others sneered when I came home, till the Empress stopped them. But you know what a train of driver ants is, that you meet with in the forests? You may light fires across their path, and they will march into them in their blind bravery, and put them out with their bodies, and those that are left will march on in an unbroken column, and devour all that stands in their path. I tell you, my lord, those little hairy creatures were like the ants—aye, for numbers, and wooden bravery, as well as for appetite. As a result to-day, there is no Yucatan."

"You shall have Egypt, then."

He burst at me hotly. "I would not take seven Egypts and ten Yucatans. My lord, you think more poorly of me than is kind, when you ask me to become a traitor. In your place would you throw your Naïs away, if the doing it would save you from a danger?"

"That is different."

"In no degree. You have a kindness for her. I have all that and more for Phorenice, who is, besides, my wife and the mother of my children. If I have qualms —and I freely confess I know you are desperate men up there, and have dreadful powers at your command —my shiverings are for them and not for myself. But I think, my lord, this parley is leading to nothing, and though these common soldiers here will understand little enough of our talk, they may be picking up a word here and there, and I do not wish them to go on to their death (as you will see them do shortly) and carry evil reports about me to whatever Gods they chance to come before."

He saluted me with his sword and drew back, and once more the missiles began to fly, and the doomed wretches, who had been halting beside the steep rock walls of the pass began once more to press hopelessly foward. They had scaling-ladders certainly, but they had no chance of getting these planted. They could do naught but fill the narrow way with their bodies, and to that end they had been sent, and to that end they humbly died. Our Priests with crow and lever wrenched from their lodging-places the great rocks which had been made ready, and sent them crashing down, so that once more screams filled the pass, and the horrid butchery was renewed.

But ever and again, some arrow or some sling-stone, or some fire-tube's dart would find its way up from below and through the defences, and there we would be with a man the less to carry on the fight. It was well enough for Phorenice to be lavish with her troops; indeed, if she wished for success, there were no two ways for it; and when those she had levied were killed, she could readily press others into the service, seeing that she had the whole broad face of the country under her rule. But with us it was different. A man down on our side was a man whose arm would bitterly be missed, and one which could in no possible way be replaced.

I made calculation of the chances, and saw clearly that, if we continued the fight on the present plan, they would storm the gates one after another as they came to them, and that by the time the uppermost gate was reached, there would be no Priest alive to defend it. And so, not disdaining to fashion myself on Phorenice's newer plan, which held that a general should at times in preference plot coldly from a place of some safety, and not lead the thick of the fighting, I left those who stood to the gate with some rough soldier's words of cheer, and withdrew again up the narrow stair of the pass.

This one approach to the Sacred Mountain was, as I have said before, vastly more difficult and dangerous in the olden days when it stood as a mere bare cleft as the High Gods made it. But a chasm had been bridged here, a shelf cut through the solid rock there, and in many places the roadway was built up on piers from distant crags below so as to make all uniform and easy. It came to my mind now, that if I could destroy this path, we might gain a breathing space for further effort.

The idea seemed good, or at least no other occurred to me which would in any way relieve our desperate situation, and I looked around me for means to put it into execution. Up and down, from the mountain to the plains below, I had traversed that narrow stair of a pass some thousands of times, and so in a manner of speaking knew every stone, and every turn, and every cut of it by heart. But I had never looked upon it with an eye to shaving off all roadway to the Sacred Mountain, and so now, even in this moment of dreadful stress, I had to traverse it no less than three times afresh before I could decide upon the best site for demolition.

But once the point was fixed, there was little delay in getting the scheme in movement. Already I had sent men to the storehouses amongst the Priests' dwellings to fetch me rams, and crows, and acids, and hammers, and such other material as was needed, and these stood handy behind one of the upper gates. I put on every pair of hands that could be spared to the work, no matter what was their age and feebleness; yes, if Naïs could have walked so far I would have pressed her for the labour; and presently carved balustrade, and wayside statue, together with the lettered wall-stones and the foot-worn cobbles, roared down into the gulf below, and added their din to the shrieks and yells and crashes of the fighting. Gods! But it was a hateful task, smashing down that splendid handiwork of the men of the past. But it was better that it should crash down to ruin in the abyss below, than that Phorenice should profane it with her impious sandals.

At first I had feared that it would be needful to sacrifice the knot of brave men who were so valiantly defending the gate then being attacked. It is disgusting to be forced into a measure of this kind, but in hard warfare it is often needful to the carrying out of his schemes for a general to leave a part of his troops to fight to a finish, and without hope of rescue, as valiantly as they may; and all he can do for their reward is to recommend them earnestly to the care of the Gods. But when the work of destroying the pathway was nearly completed, I saw a chance of retrieving them.

We had not been content merely with breaking arches, and throwing down the piers. We had got our rams and levers under the living rock itself on which all the whole fabric stood; and fire stood ready to heat the rams for their work; and when the word was given, the whole could be sent crashing down the face of the cliffs beyond chance of repair.

All was, I say, finally prepared in this fashion, and then I gave the word to hold. A narrow ledge still remained undestroyed, and offered footway, and over this I crossed. The cut we had made was immediately below the uppermost gate of all, and below it there were three more massive gates still unviolated, besides the one then being so vehemently attacked. Already, the garrisons had been retired from these, and I passed through them all in turn, unchallenged and unchecked, and came to that busy rampart where the twelve Priests left alive worked, stripped to the waist, at heaving down the murderous rocks.

For awhile I busied myself at their side, stopping an occasional fire-tube dart or arrow on my shield and passing them the tidings. The attack was growing fiercer every minute now. The enemy had packed the pass below well-nigh full of their dead, and our battering stones had less distance to fall and so could do less execution. They pressed forward more eagerly than ever with their scaling ladders, and it was plain that soon they would inevitably put the place to the storm. Even during the short time I was there, their sling-stones and missiles took life from three more of the twelve who stood with me on the defence.

So I gave the word for one more furious avalanche of rock to be pelted down, and whilst the few living were crawling out from those killed by the discharge, and whilst the next band of reinforcements came scrambling up over the bodies, I sent my nine remaining men away at a run up the steep stairway of the path, and then followed them myself. Each of the gates in turn we passed, shutting them after us, and breaking the bars and levers with which they were moved, and not till we were through the last did the roar of shouts from below tell that the besiegers had found the gate they bit against was deserted.

One by one we balanced our way across the narrow ledge which was left where the path had been destroyed, and one poor Priest that carried a wound grew giddy, and lost his balance here, and toppled down to his death in the abyss below before a hand could be stretched out to steady him. And then, when we were all over, heat was put to the rams, and they expanded with their resistless force, and tore the remaining ledges from their hold in the rock. I think a pang went through us all then when we saw for ourselves the last connecting link cut away from between the poor remaining handful of our Sacred Clan on the Mountain, and the rest of our great nation, who had grown so bitterly estranged to us, below.

But here at any rate was a break in the fighting. There were no further preparations we could make for our defence, and high though I knew Phorenice's genius to be, I did not see how she could very well do other than accept the check and retire. So I set a guard on the ramparts of the uppermost gate to watch all possible movements, and gave the word to the others to go and find the rest which so much they needed.

For myself, dutifully I tried to find Zaemon first, going on the errand my proper self, for there was little enough of kingly state observed on the Sacred Mountain, although the name and title had been given me. But Zaemon was not to be come at. He was engaged inside the Ark of the Mysteries with another of the Three, and being myself only one of the Seven, I had not rank enough in the priesthood to break in upon their workings. And so I was free to turn where my likings would have led me first, and that was to the house which sheltered Naïs.

She waked as I came in over the threshold, and her eyes filled with a welcome for me. I went across and knelt where she lay, putting my face on the pillow beside her. She was full of tender talk and sweet endearments. Gods! What an infinity of delight I had missed by not knowing my Naïs earlier! But she had a will of her own through it all, and some quaint conceits which made her all the more adorable. She rallied me on the new cleanness of my chin, and on the robe which I had taken as a covering. She professed a pretty awe for my kingship, and vowed that had she known of my coming dignities she would never have dared to discover a love for me. But about my marriage with Phorenice she spoke with less lightness. She put out her thin white hand, and drew my face to her lips.

"It is weak of me to have a jealousy," she murmured, "knowing how completely my lord is mine alone; but I cannot help it. You have said you were her husband for awhile. It gives me a pang to think that I shall not be the first to lie in your arms, Deucalion."

"Then you may gaily throw your pang away," I whispered back. "I was husband to Phorenice in mere word for how long I do not precisely know. But in anything beyond, I was never her husband at all. She married me by a form she prescribed herself, ignoring all the old rites and ceremonies, and whether it would hold as legal or not, we need not trouble to inquire. She herself has most nicely and completely annulled that marriage as I have told you. Tatho is her husband now, and father to her children, and he seems to have a fondness for her which does him credit."

We said other things too in that chamber, those small repetitions of endearments which are so precious to lovers, and so beyond the comprehension of other folk, but they are not to be set down on these sheets. They are a mere private matter which can have no concern to any one beyond our two selves, and more weighty subjects are piling themselves up in deep index for the historian.

Phorenice, it seemed, had more rage against the Priests' Clan on the Mountain and more bright genius to help her to a vengeance than I had credited. Her troops stormed easily the gates we had left to them, and swarmed up till they stood where the pathway was broken down. In the fierceness of their rush, the foremost were thrust over the brink by those pressing up behind, before the advance could be halted, and these went screaming to a horrid death in the great gulf below. But it was no position here that a lavish spending of men could take, and presently all were drawn off, save for some half-score who stood as outpost sentries, and dodged out of arrow-shot behind angles of the rock.

It seems, too, that the Empress herself reconnoitered the place, using due caution and quickness, and so got for herself a full plan of its requirements without being obliged to trust the measuring of another eye. With extraordinary nimbleness she must have planned an engine such as was necessary to suit her purposes, and given orders for its making; for even with the vast force and resources at her disposal, the speed with which it was built was prodigious.

There was very little noise made to tell of what was afoot. All the woodwork and metalwork was cut, and tongued, and forged, and fitted first by skilled craftsmen below, in the plain at the foot of the cleft; and when each ponderous balk, and each crosspiece, and each plank was dragged up the steep pass through the conquered gates, it was ready instantly for fitting into its appointed place in the completed machine.

The cleft was straight where they set about their building, and there was no curve or spur of the cliff to hide their handiwork from those of the Priests who watched from the ramparts above our one remaining gate. But Phorenice had a coyness lest her engine should be seen before it was completed, and so to screen it she had a vast fire built at the uppermost point where the causeway was broken off, and fed diligently with wet sedge and green wood, so that a great smoke poured out, rising like a curtain that shut out all view. And so though the Priests on the rampart above the gate picked off now and again some of those who tended the fire, they could do the besiegers no further injury, and remained up to the last quite in ignorance of their tactics.

The passage up the cleft was in shadow during the night hours, for, though all the crest of the Sacred Mountain was always lit brightly by the eternal fires which made its defence on the farther side, their glow threw no gleam down that flank where the cliff ran sheer to the plains beneath. And so it was under cover of the darkness that Phorenice brought up her engine into position for attack.

Planking had been laid down for its wheels, and the wheels themselves well greased, and it may be that she hoped to march in upon us whilst all slept. But there was a certain creaking and groaning of timbers, and laboured panting of men, which gave advertisement that something was being attempted, and the alarm was spread quietly in the hope that if a surprise had been planned, the real surprise might be turned the other way.

A messenger came to me running, where I sat in the house at the side of my love, and she, like the soldier's wife she was made to be, kisesd me and bade me go quickly and care for my honour, and bring back my wounds for her to mend.

On the rampart above the gate all was silence, save for the faint rustle of armed men, and out of the black darkness ahead, and from the other side of the broken causeway, came the sounds of which the messenger had warned me.

The captain of the gate came to me and whispered: "We have made no light till the King came, not knowing the King's will in the matter. Is it wished I send some of the throwing-fire down yonder, on the chance that it does some harm, and at the same time lights up the place? Or is it willed that we wait for their surprise?"

"Send the fire," I said, "or we may find that Phorenice's brain has been one too many for us."

The captain of the gate took one of the balls in his hand, lit the fuse, and hurled it. The horrid thing burst amongst a mass of men who were labouring with a huge engine, spattering them with its deadly fire, and lighting their garments. The plan of the engine showed itself plainly. They had built them a vast great tower, resting on wheels at its base, so that it might be pushed forward from behind, and slanting at its foot to allow for the steepness of the path and leave it always upright.

It was storeyed inside, with ladders joining each floor, and through slits in the side which faced us bowmen could cover an attack. From its top a great bridge reared high above it, being carried vertically till the tower was brought near enough for its use. The bridge was hinged at the third storey of the tower, and fastened with ropes to its extreme top; but, once the ropes were cut, the bridge would fall, and light upon whatever came within its swing, and be held there by the spikes with which it was studded beneath.

I saw, and inwardly felt myself conquered. The cleverness of Phorenice had been too strong for my defence. No war-engine of which we had command could overset the tower. The whole of its massive timbers were hung with the wet new-stripped skins of beasts, so that even the throwing-fire could not destroy it. What puny means we had to impede those who pushed it forward would have little effect. Presently it would come to the place appointed, and the ropes would be cut, and the bridge would thunder down on the rampart above our last gate, and the stormers would pour out to their final success.

Well, life had loomed very pleasant for me these few days with a warm and loving Naïs once more in touch of my arms, but the High Gods in Their infinite wisdom knew best always, and I was no rebel to stay stiff-necked against their decision. But it is ever a soldier's privilege, come what may, to warm over a fight, and the most exquisitely fierce joy of all is that final fight of a man who knows that he must die, and who lusts only to make his bed of slain high enough to carry a due memory of his powers with those who afterwards come to gaze upon it. I gripped my axe, and the muscles of my arms stood out in knots at the thought of it. Would Tatho come to give me sport? I feared not. They would send only the common soldiers first to the storm, and I must be content to do my killing on those.

And Naïs, what of her? I had a quiet mind there. When any spoilers came to the house where she lay, she would know that Deucalion had been taken up to the Gods, and she would not be long in following him. She had her dagger. No, I had no fears of being parted long from Naïs now.

19. Destruction of Atlantis

A tottering old Priest came up and touched me on the shoulder.

"Well?" I said sharply, having small taste for interruption just now.

"News has been carried to the Three, my King, of what is threatened."

"Then they will know that I stand here now, brother, to enjoy the finest fight of all my life. When it is finished I shall go to the Gods, and be there standing behind the stars to welcome them when presently they also arrive. They have my regrets that they are too old and too feeble to die and look upon a fine killing themselves."

"I have commands from them, my King, to lay upon you, which I fear you will like but slenderly. You are forbidden to find your death here in the fighting. They have a further use for you yet."

I turned on the old man angrily enough. "I shall take no such order, my brother. I am not going to believe it was ever given. You must have misunderstood. If I am a man, if I am a Priest, if I am a soldier, if I am a King, then it stands to my honour that no enemy should pass this gate whilst yet I live. And you may go back and throw that message at their teeth."

The old man smiled enviously. He, too, had been a keen soldier in his day. "I told them you would not easily believe such a message, and asked them for a sign, and they bore with me, and gave me one. I was to give you this jewel, my King."

"How came they by that? It is a bracelet from the elbow of Naïs."

"They must have stripped her of it. I did not know it came from Naïs. The word I was to bring you said that the owner of the jewel was inside the Ark of the Mysteries, and waited you there. The use which the Three have for you further concerns her also."

Even when I heard that, I will freely confess that my obedience was sorely tried, and I have the less shame in setting it down on these sheets, because I know that all true soldiers will feel a sympathy for my plight. Indeed, the promise of the battle was very tempting. But in the end my love for Naïs prevailed, and I gave the salutation that was needful in token that I heard the order and obeyed it.

To the knot of Priests who were left for the defence, I turned and made my farewells. "You will have what I shall miss, my brothers," I said. "I envy you that fight. But, though I am King of Atlantis, still I am only one of the Seven, and so am the servant of the

Three and must obey their order. They speak in words the will of the most High Gods, and we must do as they command. You will stand behind the stars before I come, and I ask of you that you will commend me to Those you meet there. It is not my own will that I shall not appear there by your side."

They heard my words with smiles, and very courteously saluted me with their weapons, and there we parted. I did not see the fight, but I know it was good, from the time which passed before Phorenice's hordes broke out on to the crest of the Mountain. They died hard, that last remnant of the lesser Priests of Atlantis.

With a sour enough feeling I went up to the head of the pass, and then through the groves, and between the temples and colleges and houses which stood on the upper slopes of the Sacred Mountain, till I reached that boundary, beyond which in milder days it was death for any but the privileged few to pass. But the time, it appeared to me, was past for conventions, and, moreover, my own temper was hot; and it is likely that I should have strode on with little scruple if I had not been interrupted. But in the temple which marked the boundary, there was old Zaemon waiting; and he, with due solemnity of words, and with the whole of some ancient ritual ordained for that purpose, sought dispensation from the High Gods for my trespass, and would not give me way till he was through with his ceremony.

Already Phorenice's tower and bridge were in position, for the clash and yelling of a fight told that the small handful of Priests on the rampart of the last gate were bartering their lives for the highest return in dead that they could earn. They were trained fighting men all, but old and feeble, and the odds against them were too enormous to be stemmed for over long. In a very short time the place would be put to the storm, and the roof of the Sacred Mountain would be at the open mercy of the invader. If there was any further thing to be done, it was well that it should be set about quickly whilst peace remained. It seemed to me that the moment for prompt action, and the time for lengthy pompous ceremonial was done for good.

But Zaemon was minded otherwise. He led me up to the Ark of the Mysteries, and chided my impatience, and waited till I had given it my reverential kiss, and then he called aloud, and another old man came out of the opening which is in the top of the Ark, and climbed painfully down by the battens which are fixed on its sides. He was a man I had never seen before, hoary, frail, and emaciated, and he and Zaemon were then the only two remaining Priests who had been raised to the highest degree known to our Clan, and who alone had knowledge of the highest secrets and powers and mysteries.

"Look!" cried Zaemon, in his shrill old voice, and swept a trembling finger over the shattered city, and the great spread of sea and country which lay in view of us below. I followed his pointing and looked, and a chill began to crawl through me. All was plainly shown. Our Lord the Sun burned high overhead in a sky of cloudless blue, and day shimmered in His heat. All below seemed from that distance peaceful and warm and still, save only that the mountains smoked more than ordinary, and some spouted fires, and that the sea boiled with some strange disorder.

But it was the significance of the sea that troubled me most. Far out on the distant coast it surged against the rocks in enormous rolls of surf; and up the great estuary, at the head of which the city of Atlantis stands, it gushed in successive waves of enormous height which never returned. Already the lower lands on either side were blotted out beneath tumultuous waters, the harbour walls were drowned out of sight, and the flood was creeping up into the lower wards of the great city itself.

"You have seen?" asked Zaemon.

"I have seen."

"You understand?"

"In part."

"Then let me tell you all. This is the beginning, and the end will follow swiftly. The most High Gods, that sit behind the stars, have a limit to even Their sublime patience; and that has been passed. The city of Atlantis, the great continent that is beyond, and all that are in them are doomed to unutterable destruction. Of old it was foreseen that this great wiping-out would happen through the sins of men, and to this end the Ark of the Mysteries was built under the direction of the Gods. No mortal implements can so much as scratch its surface, no waves or rocks wreck it. Inside is stored on sheets of the ancient writing all that is known in the world of learning that is not shared by the common people, also there is grain in a store, and sweet water in tanks sufficient for two persons for the space of four years, together with seeds, weapons, and all such other matters as were deemed fit.

"Out of all this vast country it has been decreed by the High Gods that two shall not perish. Two shall be chosen, a man and a woman, who are fit and proper persons to carry away with them the ancient learning to dispose of it as they see best, and afterwards to rear up a race who shall in time build another kingdom and do honour to our Lord the Sun and the other Gods in another place. The woman is within the Ark already, and seated in the place appointed for her, and though she is a daughter of mine, the burden of her choosing is with you. For the man, the choice has fallen upon yourself."

I was half numb with the shock of what was befalling. "I do not know that I care to be a survivor."

"You are not asked for your wishes," said the old man. "You are given an order from the High Gods, who know you to be Their faithful servant."

Habit rode strong upon me. I made salutation in the required form, and said that I heard and would obey.

"Then it remains to raise you to the sublime degree

of the Three, and if your learning is so small that you will not understand the keys to many of the Powers, and the highest of the Mysteries, when they are handed to you, that fault cannot be remedied now."

Certainly the time remaining was short enough. The fight still raged down at the gate in the pass, though it was a wonder how the handful of Priests had held their ground so long. But the ocean rolled in upon the land in an ever-increasing flood, and the mountains smoked and belched forth more volleys of rock as the weight increased on their lower parts, and presently those that besieged the Mountain could not fail to see the fate that threatened them. Then there would be no withholding their rush. In their mad fury and panic they would sweep all obstruction resistlessly before them, and those who stood in their path might look to themselves.

But there was no hurrying Zaemon and his fellow sage. They were without temple for the ceremony, without sacrifice or incense to decorate it. They had but the sky for a roof to make their echoes, and the Gods themselves for witnesses. But they went through the work of raising me to their own degree, with all the grand and majestic form which has gathered dignity from the ages, and by no one sentence did they curtail it. A burning mountain burst with a bellowing roar as the incoming waters met its fires, but gravely they went on, in turn reciting their sentences. Phorenice's troops broke down the last resistance, and poured in a frenzied stream amongst the groves and temples, but still they quavered never in the ritual.

It had been said that this ceremony is the grandest and the most impressive of all those connected with our holy religion; and certainly I found it so; and I speak as one intimate with all the others. Even the tremendous circumstances which hemmed them in could do nothing to make these frail old men forget the deference which was due to the highest order of the Clan.

For myself, I will freely own I was less rapt. I stood

there bareheaded in the heat, a man trying to concentrate himself, and yet torn the while by a thousand foreign emotions. The awful thing that was happening all around compelled some of my attention. A continent was in the very act and article of meeting with complete destruction, and if Zaemon and the other Priest were strong enough to give their minds wholly up to a matter parochial to the priesthood, I was not so stoical. And moreover, I was filled with other anxieties and thoughts concerning Naïs. Yet I managed to preserve a decent show of attention to the ceremony; making all those responses which were required of me; and trying as well as might be to preserve in my mind those sentences which were the keys to power and learning, and not mere phrasings of grandeur and devotion.

But it became clear that if the ceremony of my raising did not soon arrive at its natural end, it would be cut short presently with something of suddenness. Phorenice's conquering legions swarmed out on to the crest of the Mountain, and now carried full knowledge of the dreadful thing that was come upon the country. They were out of all control, and ran about like men distracted; but knowing full well that the Priests would have brought this terrible wreck to pass by virtue of the powers which were stored within the Ark of the Mysteries, it would be their natural impulse to pour out a final vengeance upon any of these same Priests they could come across before it was too late.

It began to come to my mind that if the ceremony did not very shortly terminate, the further part of the plan would stand very small chance of completion, and I should come by my death after all by fighting to a finish, as I had pictured to myself before. My flickering attention saw the soldiers coming always nearer in their frantic wanderings, and saw also the sea below rolling deeper and deeper in upon the land.

The fires, too, which ringed in half the mountain, spurted up to double their old height, and burned with an unceasing roar. But for all distraction these things gave to the two old Priests who were raising me, we might have been in the quietness of some ancient temple, with not so much as a fly to buzz an interruption.

But at last an end came to the ceremony. "Kneel," cried Zaemon, "and make obeisance to your mother the Earth, and swear by the High Gods that you will never make improper use of the powers over Her which this day you have been granted."

When I had done that, he bade me rise as a fully installed and duly initiated member of the Three. "You will have no opportunity to practise the workings of this degree with either of us, my brother," said he, "for presently our other brother and I go to stand before the Gods to deliver to Them an account of our trust, and of how we have carried it out. But what items you remember here and there may turn of use to you hereafter. And now we two give you our farewells, and promise to commend you highly to the Gods when soon we meet Them in Their place behind the stars. Climb now into the Ark, and be ready to shut the door which guards it, if there is any attempt by these raging people to invade that also. Remember, my brother, it is the Gods' direct will that you and the woman Naïs go from this place living and sound, and you are expressly forbidden to accept challenge or provocation to fight on any pretext whatever. But as long as may be done in safety, you may look out upon Atlantis in her death-throes. It is very fitting that one of the only two who are sent hence alive, should carry the full tale of what has befallen."

I went to the top of the Ark of Mysteries then, climbing there by the battens which are fastened to the sides, and then descended by the stair which is inside and found Naïs in a little chamber waiting for me.

"I was bidden stay here by Zaemon," she said, "who forced me to this place by threats and also by promises that my lord would follow. He is very ungentle, that father of mine, but I think he has a kindness for us both, and any way he is my father and I cannot help loving him. Is there no chance to save him from what is going to happen?"

"He will not come into this Ark, for I asked him. It has been ordained from the ancient time when first the Ark was built, that when the day for its purpose came, one woman and one man should be its only tenants, and they are here already. Zaemon's will in the matter is not to be twisted by you or by me. He has a message to be delivered to the Gods, and (if I know him at all), he grudges every minute that is lost in carrying it to them."

I left her then, and went out again up the stair, and stood once more on the roof of the Ark. On the Mountain top men still ran about distracted, but gradually they were coming to where the Ark rested on the highest point. For the moment, however, I passed them lightly. The drowning of the great continent that had been spread out below filled the eye. Ocean roared in upon it with still more furious waves. The plains and the level lands were foaming lakes. The great city of Atlantis had vanished eternally. The mountains alone kept their heads above the flood, and spewed out rocks, and steam, and boiling stone, or burst when the waters reached them, and created great whirlpools of surging sea, and twisted trees, and bubbling mud.

In the space of a few breaths every living creature that dwelt in the lower grounds had been smothered by the waters, save for a few who huddled in a pair of galleys that were driven oarless inland, over what had once been black forest and hunting land for the beasts. And even as I watched, these also were swallowed up by the horrid turmoil of sea, and nothing but the sea beasts, and those of the greater lizards which can live in such outrageous waters, could have survived even that state of the destruction. Indeed, none but those men who had now found standing-ground on the upper slopes of the Sacred Mountain survived, and it was plain that their span was short, for the great mass of the continent sank deeper and more deep every minute before our aching eyes, beneath the boiling inrush of the seas.

But though the great mass of the soldiery were dazed and maddened at the prospect of the overwhelming which threatened them, there were some with a strength of mind too valiant to give any outward show of discomposure. Presently a compact little body of people came from out the houses and the temples, and headed directly across the open ground towards the Ark. On the outside marched Phorenice's personal guards with their weapons new blooded. They had been forced to fight a way through their own fellow soldiers. The poor demented creatures had thought it was every one for himself now, till these guards (by their mistress's order) proved to them that Phorenice still came first.

And in the middle of them, borne in a litter of gold and ivory by her grotesque Europoean slaves, rode the Empress, still calm, still lovely, and seemingly divided in her sentiments between contempt and amusement. Her two children lay in the litter at her feet. On her right hand marched Tatho gorgeously apparelled, and with a beard curled and plaited into a thousand ringlets. On the other side, plying her industry with unruffled defence, walked Ylga, once again fangirl, and so still second lady in this dwindling kingdom.

The party of them halted half a score of paces from the Ark by Phorenice's order. "Do not go nearer to those unclean old men. They carry a rank odour with them, and for the moment we are short of essences to sweeten the air of their neighbourhood." She lifted her eyebrows and looked up at me. "Truly a quiet little gathering of old acquaintants. Why, there is Deucalion, that once I took the flavour of and threw aside when he cloyed me."

"I have Naïs here," I said, "and presently we two will be all that are left alive of this nation."

"Naïs is quite welcome to my leavings," she laughed. "I will look down upon your country cooings when presently I go back to the Place behind the stars from which I came. You are a very rustic person, Deucalion. They tell me too that three or four of these smelling old men up here have named you King. Did you swell much with dignity? Or did you remember that there was a pretty Empress left that would still be Empress so long as there was an Atlantis to govern? Come, sir, find your tongue. By my face! you must have hungered for me very madly these years we have been parted, if new-grown ruggedness of feature is an evidence."

"Have your gibe. I do not gibe back at a woman who presently will die."

"Bah! Deucalion, you live behind the times. Have they not told you that I know the Great Secret and am indeed a Goddess now? My arts can make life run on eternally."

"Then the waters will presently test them hard," I said, but there the talk was taken into other lips. Zaemon went forward to the front of the litter with the Symbol of our Lord the Sun glowing in his hand, and burst into a flow of cursing. It was hard for me to hear his words. The roar of the waters which poured up over the land, and beat in vast waves against the Sacred Mountain itself, grew nearer and more loud. But the old man had his say.

Phorenice gave orders to her guards for his killing; yes, tried even to rise from the litter and do the work herself; but Zaemon held the Symbol to his front, and its power in that supreme moment mastered all the arts that could be brought against it. The majesty of the most High Gods was vindicated, and that splendid Empress knew it and lay back sullenly amongst the cushions of her litter, a beaten woman.

Only one person in that rigid knot of people found power to leave the rest, and that was Ylga. She came out to the side of the Ark, and leaned up, and cried me a farewell through the gathering roar of the flood.

"I would I might save you and take you with us," I said.

"As for that," she said, with a gesture, "I would not come if you asked me. I am not a woman that will take anything less than all. But I shall meet what comes presently with the memory that you will have me always somewhere in your recollection. I know somewhat of men, even men of your stamp, Deucalion, and you will never forget that you came very near to loving me once."

I think, too, she said something further, concerning Naïs, but the bellowing rush of the waters drowned all other words. A great mist made from the stream sent up by the swamped burning mountains stopped all accurate view, though the blaze from the fires lit it like gold. But I had a last sight of a horde of soldiery rushing up the slopes of the Mountain, with a scum of surge billowing at their heels, and licking many of them back in its clutch. And then my eye fell on old Zaemon waving to me with the Symbol to shut down the door in the roof of the Ark.

I obeyed his last command, and went down the stair, and closed all ingress behind me. There were bolts placed ready, and I shot these into their sockets, and there were Naïs and I alone, and cut off from all the rest of our world that remained.

I went to the place where she lay, and put my arms tightly around her. Without, we heard men beating desperately on the Ark with their weapons, and some even climbed by the battens to the top and wrenched to try and move the door from its fastenings. The end was coming very nearly to them now, and the great crowd of them were mad with terror.

I would have given much to have know how Phorenice fared in that final tumult, and how she faced it. I could see her, with her lovely face, and her wondrous eyes, and her ruddy hair curling about her neck, and by all the Gods! I thought more of her at that last moment than of the poor land she had conquered, and misgoverned, and brought to this horrid destruction. There is no denying the fascination which Phorenice carried with her.

But the end did not dally long with its coming. There was a little surge that lifted the Ark a hand's breadth or so in its cardle, and set it back again with a jar and a quiver. The blows from axes and weapons ceased on its lower part, but redoubled into frenzied batterings on its rounded roof. There were some screams and cries also which came to us but dully through the thickness of its ponderous sheathing, though likely enough they were sent forth at the full pitch of human lungs outside. And then another surge came, roaring and thundering, which picked up the great vessel as though it had been a feather, and spun it giddily; and after that we touched earth or rock no more.

We tossed about on the crest and troughs of delirious seas, a sport for the greedy Gods of the ocean. The lamp had fallen, and we crouched there in darkness, dully weighed with the burden of knowledge that we alone were saved out of what was yesterday a mighty nation.

20. On the Bosom of the Deep

The Ark was rudderless, oarless, and machineless, and could travel only where the High Gods chose. The inside was dark, and full of an ancient smell, and crowded with groanings and noise. I could not find the fire-box to relight the fallen lamp, and so we had to endure blindly what was dealt out to us. The waves tossed us in merciless sport, and I clung on by the side of Naïs, holding her to the bed. We did not speak much, but there was full companionship in our bereavement and our silence.

When Atlantis sank to form new ocean bed, she left great whirlpools and spoutings from her drowned fires as a fleeting legacy to the Gods of the Sea. And then, I think (though in the black belly of the Ark we could not see these things), a vast hurricane of wind must have come on next so as to leave no piece of the desolation imcomplete. For seven nights and seven days did this dreadful turmoil continue, as counted for us afterwards by the reckoner of hours which hung within the Ark, and then the howling of the wind departed, and only the roll of a long still swell remained. It was regular and it was oily, as I could tell by the difference of the motion, and then for the first time I dared to go up the stair, and open the door which stood in the roof of the Ark.

The sweet air came gushing down to freshen the foulness within, and as the Ark rode dryly over the seas, I went below and brought up Naïs to gain refreshment from the curing rays of our Lord the Sun. Duly the pair of us adored Him, and gave thanks for His great mercy in coming to light another day, and then we laid ourselves down where we were to doze, and take that easy rest which we so urgently needed.

Yet, though I was tired beyond words, for long enough sleep would not visit me. Wearily I stared out over the oily sunlit waters. No blur of land met the eye. The ring of ocean was unbroken on every side, and overhead the vault of heaven remained unchanged. The bosom of the deep was littered with the poor wreckage of Atlantis, to remind one, if there had been a need, that what had come about was fact, and not some horrid dream. Trees, squared timber, a smashed and upturned boat of hides, and here and there the rounded corpse of a man or beast shouldered over the swells, and kept convoy with our Ark as she drifted on in charge of the Gods and the current.

But sleep came to me at last, and I dropped off into unconsciousness, holding the hand of Naïs in mine, and when next I woke, I found her open-eyed also and watching me tenderly. We were finely rested, both of us, and rest and strength bring one complacency. We were more ready now to accept the station which the High Gods had made for us without repining, and so we went below again into the belly of the Ark to eat and drink and maintain strength for the new life which lay before us.

A wonderful vessel was this Ark, now we were able to see it at leisure and intimately. Although for the first time now in all its centuries of life it swam upon the waters, it showed no leak or suncrack. Inside, even its floors was bone dry. That it was built from some wood, one could see by the grainings, but nowhere could one find suture or joint. The living timbers had been put in place and then grown together by an art which we have lost to-day, but which the Ancients knew with much perfection; and afterwards some treatment, which is also a secret of those forgotten builders, had made the wood as hard as metal and impervious to all attacks of the weather.

In the gloomy cave of its belly were stored many matters. At one end, in great tanks on either side of a central alley, was a prodigious store of grain. Sweet water was in other tanks at the other end. In another place were drugs and simples, and essences of the life of beasts; all these things being for use whilst the Ark roamed under the guidance of the Gods on the bosom of the deep. On all the walls of the Ark, and on all the partitions of the tanks and the other woodwork, there were carved in the rude art of bygone time representations of all the beasts which lived in Atlantis; and on these I looked with a hunter's interest, as some of them were strange to me, and had died out with the men who had perpetuated them in these sculptures. There was a

good store of weapons too and the tools for handi-
crafts.

Now, for many weeks, our life endured in this Ark
as the Gods drove it about here and there across the
face of the waters. We had no government over direction; we could not by so much as a hair's breadth a
day increase her speed. The High Gods that had
chosen the two of us to be the only ones saved out of
all Atlantis, had sole control of our fate, and into Their
hands we cheerfully resigned our future direction.

Of that land which we reached in due time, and
where we made our abiding place, and where our
children were born, I shall tell of in its place; but since
this chronicle has proceeded so far in an exact order
of the events as they came to pass, it is necessary
first to narrate how we came by the sheets on which
it is written.

In a great coffer, in the centre of the Ark's floor,
the whole of the Mysteries learned during the study of
ages were set down in accurate writing. I read through
some of them during the days which passed, and the
awfulness of the Powers over which they gave control
appalled me. I had seen some of these Powers set loose
in Atlantis, and was a witness of her destruction. But
here were Powers far higher than those; here was the
great Secret of Life and Death which Phorenice also
had found, and for which she had been destroyed; and
there were other things also of which I cannot even
bring my stylo to scribe.

The thought of being custodian of these writings
was more than I could endure, and the more the matter
rested in my mind, the more intolerable became the
burden. And at last I took hot irons, and with them
seared the wax on the sheets till every letter of the
old writings was obliterated. If I did wrong, the High
Gods in Their infinite justice will give me punishment;
if it is well that these great secrets should endure on
earth, They in their infinite power will dictate them
afresh to some fitting scribes; but I destroyed them

there as the Ark swayed with us over the waves; and later, when we came to land, I rewrote upon the sheets the matters which led to great Atlantis being dragged to her death-throes.

Naïs, that I love so tenderly——

[*Translator's Note:* The remaining sheets are too broken to be legible.]

CLASSIC
ADULT FANTASY
FROM
BALLANTINE BOOKS

THE WORM OUROBOROS	*E. R. Eddison*
THE SONG OF RHIANNON	*Evangeline Walton*
THE WELL AT THE WORLD'S END Volume I	*William Morris*
THE WELL AT THE WORLD'S END Volume II	*William Morris*
THE KING OF ELFLAND'S DAUGHTER	*Lord Dunsany*
A VOYAGE TO ARCTURUS	*David Lindsay*
THE LAST UNICORN	*Peter Beagle*
* TITUS GROAN	*Mervyn Peake*
* GORMENGHAST	*Mervyn Peake*
* TITUS ALONE	*Mervyn Peake*
THE BROKEN SWORD	*Poul Anderson*
THE DREAM QUEST OF UNKNOWN KADATH	*H. P. Lovecraft*
LILITH	*George MacDonald*
THE LOST CONTINENT	*C. J. Cutliffe Hyne*
THE CHARWOMAN'S SHADOW	*Lord Dunsany*

* The Gormenghast Trilogy

To order by mail, send $1.25 per book plus 25¢
per order for handling to Ballantine Cash Sales,
P.O. Box 505, Westminster, Maryland 21157.
Please allow three weeks for delivery

The World's Best Adult Fantasy

Ballantine Books

1973

To order by mail, send $1.25 per book plus 25¢
per order for handling to Ballantine Cash Sales,
P.O. Box 505, Westminster, Maryland 21157.
Please allow three weeks for delivery.